THE
FOREST
GRIMM

ALSO BY
KATHRYN PURDIE

THE BONE GRACE DUOLOGY

Bone Crier's Moon
Bone Crier's Dawn

THE BURNING GLASS SERIES

Burning Glass
Crystal Blade
Frozen Reign

THE
FOREST
GRIMM

A NOVEL

KATHRYN PURDIE

WEDNESDAY BOOKS
NEW YORK

First published in the United States by Wednesday Books, an imprint of St. Martin's Publishing Group

THE FOREST GRIMM. Copyright © 2023 by Kathryn Purdie. All rights reserved. Printed in the United States of America. For information, address St. Martin's Publishing Group, 120 Broadway, New York, NY 10271.

www.wednesdaybooks.com

Designed by Devan Norman

Case stamp wolf illustration © Nadiiiya / Shutterstock.com

The Library of Congress cataloging-in-publication data is available upon request.

ISBN 978-1-250-87300-2 (hardcover)
ISBN 978-1-250-32444-3 (international, sold outside the U.S., subject to rights availability)
ISBN 978-1-250-87301-9 (ebook)

Our books may be purchased in bulk for promotional, educational, or business use. Please contact your local bookseller or the Macmillan Corporate and Premium Sales Department at 1-800-221-7945, extension 5442, or by email at MacmillanSpecialMarkets@macmillan.com.

First Edition: 2023

10 9 8 7 6 5 4 3 2 1

For Isabelle and Ivy,
who represent everything fierce
and enchanting

THE
FOREST
GRIMM

PROLOGUE

BEFORE THE CURSE

"Tell me again, Grandmère, the story of how I die."

The girl had waited until twilight to approach her grandmother, when the work of the day was done and the old woman sat close to the warmth of the hearth, her violet eyes half-closed and the valerian tincture bottle propped on the small table beside her, its cork removed.

The girl stepped closer. Clara was a rarity in Grimm's Hollow to dwell on death instead of life, and all that life could become for her. The other children in the village dreamed of the happiness that awaited them when they came of age at sixteen. But with a fortune such as Clara's, she doubted she would even live another seven years.

A deep wrinkle puckered the skin between Grandmère's slender brows. "*Ma petite chérie,*" she said in a language no one else spoke in their village, not even Clara's grandfather, though he had long since passed away. "I do not like that story."

Clara slid the tincture bottle to the edge of the table to make room for a deck of painted fortune-telling cards that she held behind her back. She squared her thin shoulders and stood as tall as her nine-year-old frame would stretch. "Then tell me a new story," she said, and presented the cards.

Grandmère's gaze fell to the deck. Embers snapped in the

fireplace, reflecting in the old woman's pupils like startled fireflies. She was the only person Clara knew who had a little magic of her own, though it wasn't the strongest magic known to Grimm's Hollow. While the villagers respected Grandmère's gift to read the future, what they truly revered was a separate magic entirely unrelated—the magic of the Forest Grimm. It held the power to grant wishes and make dreams come true.

That power was bound up in a book, a remarkable gift from the forest, which was said to have appeared in the village over one hundred years ago. In a bordering meadow, the volume arrived fully formed on a bed of red-spotted mushrooms and four-leaf clovers. Wood from the trees formed the paper, leaves dyed the ink, and fine roots threaded the binding. *Sortes Fortunae* was engraved on the cover, which in the common tongue meant "Book of Fortunes."

The book's magic could be called upon only once in a person's lifetime, so long as they had come of age. Grandmère had come of age decades ago, but she didn't live in Grimm's Hollow when she was sixteen. She came here in her twenty-third year, and two years afterward she claimed her moment. Although she had the ability to foretell the future, that didn't prevent her from wanting what the book could also offer, as it did for each villager. Grandmère made a wish to change her fate.

Clara never discovered what that wish was. The old woman would never speak of it. Like every wise villager before her, Grandmère kept her wish sacred and secret. If she revealed it, the spell would be reversed.

"*Non.*" Grandmère shook her head, denying Clara's request for a card reading. "We have played this game before, and I cannot give you false hope again."

It wasn't like her grandmother to call fortune-telling a game, but Clara had wearied her with dozens of requests over the past few months. The five times Grandmère had relented, the reading—or the "story" as she called it—had failed to present Clara with a future that didn't spell an ill-timed death.

The little girl sucked her lower lip between her teeth. "But what if—?"

"My cards never lie, child." With a heavy exhale, Grandmère tucked an errant lock of hair back into Clara's crown braid and patted her cheek. "I am sorry, but fate does not change its mind."

Until yesterday, Clara might have believed such words. But last night a farmer's wife had come to their cottage for a reading, and that evening had proved exceptional.

It wasn't the visit itself that was novel. Villagers often implored Grandmère to reveal their fates. Most had already made their one wish on the Book of Fortunes, and they still yearned to find ways to influence new seasons of their lives—or at the very least, prepare for success or failure in the future.

Would their crops grow or die? Would romantic love flourish or fade? Would a wound heal or fester? Grandmère's cards revealed the clues.

Last night, the farmer's wife had come to find out if the babe in her womb would thrive or wither, and, nervous to learn the answer, she delayed Grandmère's reading by asking about each of her thirty-six cards.

"This is the Red Card," Grandmère had replied when the clock cuckooed an hour past Clara's bedtime.

From where she overheard their conversation, out of sight in the narrow hallway, Clara pictured that card. The other fortune-telling cards in the deck bore intricate and mysterious images, but the Red Card was simply painted crimson, and none of its edges were worn.

"Such an ordinary name," the farmer's wife remarked. "Such an ordinary card."

"And yet it is extraordinary," Grandmère replied. "Its true name is 'Changer of Fate,' you see, and I have never drawn it before in a reading."

Clara didn't hear any more after that. Her ears started to buzz, and she placed a hand on the wood-paneled wall to steady herself. She'd never known what the Red Card had meant until that moment, and now she understood it was the one card that could save her.

Although the Red Card couldn't tell her *how* to change her fate, like the Book of Fortunes did in magic ink when a person made a wish, it did something even more reassuring: it *foretold* that she *would* change fate.

If Grandmère drew the Red Card for Clara, could Clara's story finally end differently?

That night Clara dreamed in red, and when she tended to her chores the next day, all she saw was red. The wattle under the rooster's neck. The whortleberries in the thicket past the sheep pasture. The ladybugs climbing the fennel in the herb garden.

Now standing by the hearth at twilight, Clara set her small hand on top of her grandmother's and whispered, "*S'il te plaît.*" She only knew a few words in Grandmère's native tongue, and these were the ones that meant "please."

Perhaps it was hearing the language of her faraway home beyond the forested mountain range that moved Grandmère. Perhaps it was gazing into her granddaughter's large and earnest emerald eyes. Perhaps it was a shared secret wish that one more reading might indeed change Clara's terrible fate. Whatever the reason, Grandmère nodded and fanned the deck of cards face-down on the table.

In haste, Clara retrieved the fortune-telling veil, and when the old woman drew it over her eyes, Clara rested her hand over hers once more. With painstaking care, Grandmère blindly drew the cards.

Clara had witnessed readings that revealed as many as seven cards for a person, although three was much more common. Clara's readings, however, had always been stunted to two cards. With any luck, this time would be different.

Grandmère turned over the first card: the Midnight Forest. It represented that which was forbidden.

She drew the second card: the Fanged Creature.

Clara's heart sank. The Fanged Creature was the worst and most dreaded card, the card that foretold an untimely death.

It was hopeless. Her story had remained unchanged. A forbidden choice would cut her life short. Unless . . .

Grandmère's hand stilled over the only card on the table with crisp, unworn edges. Clara's breath caught deep in her chest. Ever so gently, she nudged her grandmother's weathered fingers toward that hiding red paint.

But Grandmère never turned the Red Card over. Indeed, she never touched it. She unveiled her face, looked down at the two cards drawn, and hung her head low. "That is all," she said. "Your blood has stopped singing to me."

Clara blinked back tears and managed a fleeting smile. "That's all right. Don't feel bad, *Mémère*." She called Grandmère by the name she had used when she was a much smaller child. "It isn't your fault."

The front door swung open. In walked a full-grown copy of Clara with near-black hair, a milky complexion, and radiant green eyes. The woman set down a pail of well water and placed her hand on her hip. "What's all this?" she asked, taking in the two somber faces of her mother and daughter, and though her question was pointed, it wasn't sharp. Rosamund Thurn was a frank woman, but rarely enraged.

Neither Grandmère nor Clara answered, for the answer was as plain as a sheep in need of shearing. All Rosamund had to do was glance at the two upturned cards.

She lifted a brow, removed her apron, and hung it on a peg by the door. Walking to a high shelf in the corner, she removed something from a canister and slipped it into her dress pocket. Turning to her daughter, the only child she had ever been able to conceive, she extended a hand. "Come with me. I want to show you something."

Without question, Clara laced her fingers through her mother's, and they walked outside past the garden, the sheep pasture, the fence woven with twigs and reeds, and finally the stream that divided their farmland from the Forest Grimm.

"Did you know I once had my cards read by Grandmère?" her mother said as they approached a large oak tree. The moon brightened and chased away the twilight, limning the scalloped leaves with shimmering silver.

"Truly?" Clara stared up at her. Her mother had never seemed interested in Grandmère's fortune-telling, though that didn't mean she wasn't curious about her own fate. Clara knew as much since her mother had already used her one wish on *Sortes Fortunae* to make her secret desire come true. Clara's father had done the same.

"I was a year younger than you are now."

Clara tried to guess which cards Grandmère had drawn for her mother. The Lady with the Lily for untarnished beauty. The Stone Castle for a long life. The Nine-Strand Knot for an unbreakable family bond. "What story did the cards tell you?" she asked as they walked beneath the tree.

Under the dark of the oak, her mother's face and form dimmed and blurred, looking more shadowy than solid. "I was told *your* story."

Clara didn't understand. "Did Grandmère draw the Dappled Fawn for you?" That card foretold birth and children.

"No." Her mother's voice hitched like she either held back a laugh or stifled a sob. Perhaps she did both. "You and I share the same story. We were given the same reading. Grandmère also drew the Midnight Forest and the Fanged Creature for me."

Clara shifted backward, unnerved by her mother's newly ghostly appearance. "But . . . you're still alive."

"Yes." Her mother walked around the trunk of the tree and traced its girth with her hand. "Oh, how I begged Mother to read the cards for me, but once she did, I cried for days. Father finally consoled me by helping me plant this oak. It was just a sapling back then, and look at it now. This is no short-lived tree."

Clara tipped her head back and gazed at the branches above her. The highest ones had to be even taller than the pitched roof of their cottage. "Can't oaks live hundreds of years?"

"That's exactly my meaning," her mother replied. "They're almost eternal."

But Clara had thought of a different meaning: this oak, as large as it was, had only lived a tiny measure of the years it still deserved.

A flood of hot emotions swelled within her, and she flung her arms around her mother's waist. She no longer had a care for her own life. She only worried for her mother's. She couldn't bear the thought of her dying before her time.

Startled, her mother fell silent. With the backs of her fingers, she combed the loose hair at Clara's nape, which had fallen from her crown braid. "Do not fret, dear heart." Her voice was soft as lambswool. "Look in my pocket. I've brought something special."

Clara unfurled herself from her mother and did as she bid her, withdrawing a small, round object. She couldn't see it in the darkness, but her thumb brushed its smooth shell and rough cup hat. An acorn.

"I collected it last autumn," her mother said. "Did you know Grimm oaks take twenty years to produce acorns? This is the first one I found growing on this tree." Pressing a kiss to Clara's brow, she added, "I want you to have it."

"Why?" Clara frowned. She didn't want to own something that represented her mother's life. What if she mishandled it or lost it? "Shouldn't you keep it?"

"Whatever for?" Her mother gave a gentle laugh. "This autumn I'll have barrels full."

But how many autumns after that?

As soon as Clara had the thought, another struck her, jarring her mind like a wagon wheel against a stone.

I don't need to fear for my mother. I can save her.

She didn't need the Red Card to change her fate. All she needed was a wish.

A wish Clara could claim from the Book of Fortunes when she came of age at sixteen.

She squeezed the acorn tightly. She would live another seven years to see her mother's story changed. After that, it didn't matter how Clara's own story ended. She would gladly die so her mother could live.

"Thank you, Mama." She tucked herself into her mother's warm embrace. "I'll keep it."

CHAPTER 1

SEVEN YEARS LATER

I am haunted by my mother. I hear her voice ringing on the wind that chases the ravens from our sheep pasture, her stifled cries in the creaking of the pulley over our dry well. Her laughter glances off jagged flickers of dry lightning. Her rage gathers in low peals of rolling thunder.

The storms are only mockery. Their rainfall scarcely touches the earth anymore, and when it does, all I hear in its patter are my mother's footsteps treading away from me, beckoning me to follow.

I am haunted by my mother . . . if hauntings weren't a mystery of the dead, but rather an echo of the living. And she must be living. I will her to be. She isn't dead, only missing—lost within the Forest Grimm. Three years have passed since she embarked on a journey there, soon after the magic of the forest had turned on our village, and she never returned.

Strips of fabric and ribbon in every color dangle from a large hazel at the edge of the forest. The Tree of the Lost. Mother wasn't the only villager to go missing. Sixty-six others—the Lost Ones, as we call them—were also never seen nor heard from again after venturing into the forest. Each had their own reasons for wandering away since the onset of the curse, though most of those motives remain a mystery. The only known link between them is the state of despair they were in before leaving Grimm's Hollow.

As for Mother, she should have known she wouldn't return home. The Midnight Forest card had warned her long ago not to make a forbidden choice. But she left in search of Father, and she didn't know he wasn't Lost, not in that way. She entered the Forest Grimm soon after his disappearance, and she became the first Lost One.

The tokens on the hazel quiver in the summer breeze, stirring the ends of my sable hair. Mother's hair is the same warm shade of darkest brown, but her cloth strip has been dyed rose red. Grandmère chose that color because it's Mother's favorite, and I spun the yarn myself from our flock's finest wool.

I lift my hand to touch it, squinting against the morning sunlight that pierces the tight weave. Three years have passed since I first knotted it to this tree, and in that time the elements have frayed its edges and worn the cloth threadbare.

What if Mother is also this ragged and bone-thin?

I will come for you, I promise. *Soon.*

And by soon I mean today.

"Ten minutes until the lottery!" the village clockmaker calls.

My heart lurches like a cuckoo bird springing on the hour. I hitch my skirt to my calves and dart through the gathering crowd in the meadow. Monthly Devotion Day always draws out villagers like myself who haven't given up hope that our Lost Ones are still alive. It also attracts those who enjoy the spectacle of the lottery and the danger that follows it. The focus of Devotion Day has always been the lottery and its culmination.

I reach the lottery table, where two glass-blown goblets perch side by side, one amber and the other moss green. Each holds scraps of folded paper with names of villagers scrawled upon them.

Today is the day I'll be chosen—finally permitted—to enter the forest to search for the Lost Ones. *Again.* Again, because my name is in the moss-green goblet, discarded with others that were already chosen this year, plucked from the amber goblet on previous Devotion Days. My turn came several months ago, when I was finally old enough to take part in the lottery after coming of age at sixteen.

Claiming my chance to enter the forest through the sanction of the lottery was all I could do to save Mother from her foretold early death. It still remains my only hope. Despite the resolution I made seven years ago to make a wish on the Book of Fortunes, that choice has been taken from me.

Two years before I turned sixteen, the Forest Grimm cursed the village, and the book went missing. And soon we discovered why: someone had committed murder, and to complicate matters, they'd used their one wish on *Sortes Fortunae* to make it happen.

The murderer's identity still remains unknown. All we can be sure of is that on the day the victim's body was discovered, the Book of Fortunes vanished.

Just as mysteriously as it had first appeared in Grimm's Hollow, the book disappeared from the pavilion where the villagers kept it in this very meadow. Many believe that a large willow uprooted itself and stole the book away with weeping branches. However it happened, the willow also went missing, and a trail of root-like footprints remained, leading to and from the pavilion.

Without the book—without a wish that so many others were able to obtain before me—I hoped the forest would compensate with kindness when my name was drawn in the lottery. But it didn't grant me any favors. To be fair, it never welcomes anyone chosen from the amber goblet. None of us make it more than a few yards inside the forest before we're spit back out again. I certainly didn't.

So far this ritual is just as cursed as our village.

But today will be different. Today I'm determined to succeed. I've made a detailed map of the forest, gleaned from the knowledge of what the villagers remember from days before the curse when they could come and go freely. And I won't wait another month for the lottery year to end, when the names will be reshuffled, to test my luck with it.

All I have to do is be chosen again. And for that I have a strategy.

I'm alone at the table, but I glance over my shoulder to make sure no villagers are watching. Those who are missing Lost Ones like I am are busy presenting gifts at the carved altar, just shy of the trailhead. One foot beyond it is the stark line of ashes that marks the forest border, and no one so much as lets a bootlace slip past it.

The forest doesn't allow anyone to enter anymore, not unless they're destined to become Lost—and no one willfully chooses that. Our offerings are given in hopes to pacify the forest to yield to our attempt on every Devotion Day.

Ingrid Struppin, who lost her husband, drags her patched skirt away from the line and sets a bowl of porridge on the altar. Gretchen Ottel, who lost her brother, bends her willowy frame to rest a bouquet of wildflowers beside it, then sneezes. She claps a hand over her mouth and stares ahead wide-eyed. That sneeze surely crossed the line, but thankfully the forest doesn't stir.

"Gesundheit," Hans Muller tells her, steadying a cup of ale by Gretchen's wildflowers—weak ale if it's anything like the jug I bartered a skein of yarn for five days ago. Once the cup is placed, he scampers back from the line of ashes. As he removes his straw hat and bows his head, he murmurs something. I think it's the name of his Lost mother, Rilla.

The villagers' offerings are more meager than they once were, but they're the best anyone can afford nowadays. The curse that fell upon us three years ago takes a harder toll with every passing month. This meadow is proof. No flowers bloom here anymore.

The parched wild grass is too choked by thorny drought-tolerant weeds.

As futile as Devotion Day always is, our desperation to save the Lost Ones drives us to play out this ritual month after month. No one, including me, knows what else to do to regain the forest's good graces, cross its border, and be permitted to make the dangerous journey to recover the Lost.

And finding the Lost is only half the task. The lottery winner is also expected to obtain the Book of Fortunes, wherever it's hidden in the Forest Grimm. If the woods allow it to be retrieved, we believe the curse will be lifted. The land will be healed, and the Lost will find their way back home.

This much we've learned from a riddle that the book left behind. Not all of *Sortes Fortunae* went missing. A single page remained in the pavilion on a pedestal, and on that page were the following green-inked, magicked words:

A murderous wish
An end of peace
The curse is wrought
My blessings cease.

Falling water
Lost words found
A selfless wish
The curse unbound.

The first half of the riddle explained what set the curse in motion—a wish on the book that resulted in murder—and the last half revealed how to break the curse. The riddle also gave the only clue to how to find the book: near "falling water." A waterfall seems the obvious conclusion, but if it were that simple, the

Lost Ones would have already found the book and returned home. None have.

No matter the difficulty, I vow to find *Sortes Fortunae*. It feels just as much my destiny as the one Grandmère foretold for me. The Fanged Creature card may have spelled my untimely death, but I won't let it happen before I save my mother from *her* death. Ending the curse and saving her—they're both intertwined. I need the book to make a wish to rescue her from the forest, as well as her fate.

When I'm sure no one has eyes on me, I refocus on my task. Quick as a falcon, I pluck a handful of folded papers from my apron pocket, cast them into the amber goblet, and rush away.

Seconds later, a youthful baritone voice calls from a few yards behind me, "Where are you running off to, Clara?" I know he's smiling from the teasing lilt of his tone. "I can't remember a time you missed the lottery, even when you weren't old enough to enter."

I fight an eye roll as I slowly spin to face Axel. Of course he had to rub in our age difference, as if the two years between us mean he's gleaned that much more experience in the lottery. He's only ever had his name drawn once, same as me.

Every year more than thirty villagers place their names in the amber goblet, of their own free will, but only one name is drawn monthly, when the dark of the moon has passed and then waxed to a crescent. A sign of good luck for travelers. The people of Grimm's Hollow cling to any superstition that might help bring back the Lost Ones and break the curse on our village.

I haven't answered Axel yet. I'm still scavenging my brain for an excuse as he walks toward me with that easy swagger of his, confident yet unaffected. Like everything else about him, it exudes a natural charm he's oblivious to, which makes the village girls bat their lashes in such a flutter you'd think they'd developed tics.

They'd need to bat him over the head with a cudgel to get him to notice. He's only ever had eyes for one girl, and she's Lost just like my mother.

"Well?" He leans his weight on one leg, hands stuffed in his homespun trouser pockets. His casual air carries over to the rest of his appearance. The sleeves of his shirt are rolled back to reveal corded tawny arms, and his spruce-blue vest is unbuttoned, flapping in the breeze like bed linens on a clothesline. He chews on the end of a long piece of straw that glints as golden as his perfectly imperfect tousled hair. "What's the rush?"

I fold my arms at his smirk. "I forgot my hat. If I'm chosen today, I'll need it."

"You never wear a hat. Not here, not anywhere." His riverblue eyes lower to my nose. "All those freckles say the same."

I shrug. "Today they begged for shade."

Silent laughter ripples across his broad shoulders. "C'mon, Clara. I saw you throw something into the amber goblet just now."

Heat surges into my cheeks. "It was only clover for good luck."

"Clover isn't white."

"It is when it's in bloom."

His smile deepens, and he nods, humoring me. He pulls the straw from his mouth, dips his head nearer, and whispers conspiratorially, "How many papers were in your hand, hmm? How many times did you enter your name?"

I whirl to bolt, but he catches my arm and turns me back around. He's a full head taller than I am, and standing this close, I have to tilt up my face to meet his gaze. I do so begrudgingly.

"Do you really think I'll snitch on you?" He gives my arm a playful rattle. "You know me better than that."

I suppose I do. When my father was alive, Axel used to help him during the lambing season. I helped Father too, as often as Mother and Grandmère could spare me.

One night, when I was thirteen and Axel was fifteen, two ewes went into labor. Father assisted the first one, and Axel and I worked together to deliver twins from the second—a nerve-racking endeavor. Neither of us had ever helped a ewe give birth without Father at our side.

Matters grew precarious when the second lamb was born and not breathing. Axel and I did our best to rouse him. We shook him by his hind legs and rubbed his body down with straw. When the lamb's tiny lungs finally released a strong bleat, I burst into tears. Axel pulled me close and let me sob against his shoulder.

"How many papers were in your hand?" he prods again.

I stand taller and lock my knees. "Seven."

"Seven!" He buckles with laughter. I smack his arm and bite down on a smile of my own. When he laughs, he wheezes, and it's infuriatingly infectious.

I peek at the villagers. Several of them, including Herr Oswald, chairman of the village's governing council, stare at us with eyebrows so angled they rival the slanted tufts of great horned owls. Eventually the villagers lose interest, and once they look away, Axel nudges me with his elbow.

"Hurry. If we're quick, we can fix this."

"Fix what?"

"All those extra names. They have to come out of the goblet."

I dig my heels into the dead wild grass. "No."

"People will realize you've fiddled with the order of things. Your name has already been drawn this year."

"Who's counting back as far as eleven months? I'm seventeen now and—"

"Clara—"

"The hour has come!" the village clockmaker calls. His voice rings loudly, but holds the weight of a death knell. "Gather round for the lottery."

Any chatter on the air hushes in an instant. The only sound now is the whisper of the grass as the villagers pad through it, silent like mourners at a funeral. For many, hope that this month's ritual will produce a favorable result hangs upon a thread spun thinner than spider silk.

Axel's easygoing manner falters. He rubs the back of his neck and bends close to my ear. "You could still talk to Herr Oswald," he says quietly. "It isn't too late to tell him what you've done."

I pull away and cross my arms. Why doesn't Axel want me to be chosen? "Do you doubt my capability?" I keep my voice as low as his.

"It isn't that."

"You've seen my map. I'm more prepared than anyone."

"I believe you, but the forest . . ." His eyes slide to the towering trees past the meadow, and his shoulders twitch. "You shouldn't tempt fate."

I cock a brow. "Isn't it about time someone did?" I chance a smile. Hopefully it will spark one of his own. I'd rather be teased than worried over.

He shakes his head and finally cracks a small grin. "Fair enough."

Satisfaction flits through me, but then my chest tightens. I got the smile I wanted, but I see past it to the ache Axel's so good at hiding behind his mask of effortless charm.

He peeks around us at the other villagers. We're still out of earshot, if that's what he's worried about. "If you're chosen—"

"I'll find her for you. I promise."

His throat contracts with a hard swallow. "Then you'll be the first lottery winner to be welcomed by the forest."

"I will be." I lift my chin. I've already placed my offering on the altar, the acorn Mother gave me seven years ago. If the Forest Grimm doesn't accept it as the most precious thing I can sacrifice to gain its good graces, I don't know what it ever will.

Axel searches my face for a long moment, like he's going to say something more, but he doesn't. He only nods, turns away abruptly, and meanders over to the parents of Ella, the girl he Lost last summer.

Her mother clasps Axel's hand, and her father squeezes his shoulder. The Dantzers have taken him in like the son they never had but always wanted.

Herr Oswald steps up to the lottery table and clears his throat, slicking back his thinning hair with spindly fingers. He meets the eyes of everyone present, maybe thirty people, and when his gaze settles on me, I school my features, trying not to rouse any suspicion. I can't appear overconfident at my odds.

"Never was a people more blessed by magic than we simple folk of Grimm's Hollow," he says, addressing the crowd as I slip in at the back of them. "Never was magic of this kind ever heard of among the forested mountain lands, or indeed anywhere that traveling merchants could bring tale of. But our ancestors sensed it. It's what drew them to this place and helped them thrive here, favored with bountiful crops and healing well water."

I know this story by heart. It's the same one Herr Oswald shares every Devotion Day. If only I could be the one to tell it. His tone is reverent, but it's lost all its fervor and hope.

"Our people respected the forest and lived in harmony among each other, ever generous, gentle, and kind. The Forest Grimm loved us in return—a love so strong that its magic culminated over a century ago to create *Sortes Fortunae*."

I remember seeing the Book of Fortunes from a distance. The pedestal it was kept on still remains in this meadow, as well as the small pavilion that sheltered it. I wasn't allowed to touch the book. No one was, not unless they had decided to use their one wish.

"When the villagers whispered their deepest desires to *Sortes Fortunae,* the book revealed how to obtain them," Herr Oswald continues. "Each villager was given that chance when they came of age, and one chance was all. The book never answered a second wish."

Sortes Fortunae doesn't reward greedy hearts. Over the years, the people of Grimm's Hollow came to realize that. Not only did the Book of Fortunes never grant anyone an additional wish, it also reversed the wishes of those who revealed them.

Gilly Himmel wished for beauty, but when she boasted of how *Sortes Fortunae* taught her how to achieve the most flawless skin in the mountain regions, she caught a pox that scarred her face with deep gouges.

Friedrich Brandt wished for wealth. But when the Book of Fortunes instructed him to mine his farmland and he struck a vein of silver, he celebrated with one too many cups of tavern ale. Tongue loosened, he spilled the secret of how he came by his riches. The next day, the tunnel with the silver vein collapsed, and every tunnel he dug afterward also caved in.

In time, the villagers came to appreciate the limitations of the Book of Fortunes, which helped keep *Sortes Fortunae* a secret unto itself. After all, if knowledge of its existence ever became widespread, people from all corners of the world would flock here, overrun this place, and abuse its resources. Grimm's Hollow would no longer be the small haven that it is. Or once was.

"All was well for a time," Herr Oswald continues, bringing my thoughts back to life before the curse, "until someone used *Sortes Fortunae* for an evil purpose—to kill another person."

Shifty gazes turn on each other in the crowd. No one knows

who it was that murdered Bren Zimmer, and if they did, what good would it do now? The blacksmith would still be in his grave. Even the magic of the forest doesn't have the power to bring the dead back to life. If it did, the villagers would have tested it. They would have used their wishes to resurrect loved ones.

"Afterward, the Forest Grimm took the book away," Herr Oswald says. "The well water turned rancid, and our crops died from disease."

The villagers bow their heads. *Sortes Fortunae* vanished the day Bren Zimmer's body was discovered, lying facedown in a stream with a kitchen knife stuck in his back.

"Many of us have tried to make amends with the forest to restore the book to our village, but every time someone crossed its border to find it, they never returned."

That was back before monthly Devotion Days were held, back when people could still enter the forest without immediately being rejected. Over time, the forest started to cast out anyone who made an attempt. Devotion Days remain our last hope to regain the forest's good will. If these woods can sense how much we still hold them in honor, even in the depths of our humbled circumstances, will they finally let us enter, find the book, break the curse, and bring back our Lost Ones?

I glance at the Tree of the Lost and the fluttering strip of rose-red wool. My chest pinches in the center of my rib cage, a spot that never loosens.

Mother was the first villager to venture into the forest after *Sortes Fortunae* was taken. Father had been missing for four days, and she was wrought with worry. I tried to placate her. Father had to be searching for a lost lamb, I had said. He'd been absent this long before. But she had insisted this time was different.

It was only when Grandmère explained on the fourth night that I finally understood why. Relaxed by her valerian tincture, she confessed that Father had asked her to read his fortune a few days prior, and she'd drawn for him three cards: the Moonless Night, Love Lost, and Water Wild.

The Moonless Night represented the night of the new moon—which was when Father disappeared.

Love Lost foretold lovers parted by a tragedy—anything from a heated argument to a grievous death. Mother feared death, as no harsh words had come between them.

And Water Wild symbolized an eventful circumstance in or around a moving body of water, such as a stormy sea or a turbulent river. As Grimm's Hollow was a month's travel from the sea, Mother feared Water Wild meant an occurrence in one of the raging rivers in the Forest Grimm.

On the morning of the fifth day, she refused to wait any longer for Father's return. She set off after him, heading for the stream that divides our sheep farm from the forest.

"Don't go!" I'd cried, clutching her sleeve. I couldn't lose two parents. Father may have had a formidable card reading, but Mother's fortune was more direct, more bleak. The Fanged Creature meant her untimely death, and the Midnight Forest her forbidden choice. I knew deep in my bones that she was making that choice right then. The choice that would ultimately kill her. "Grandmère needs you! *I* need you!"

She tugged her arm away, which only made me sob harder, but then she stooped to cup my chin with her hand. "Never doubt your own strength, Clara. You were made to weather fiercer trials than this."

"But you promised me you would live a long life." I let my tears fall unchecked. "You said you were like the Grimm oak. You gave me its acorn so I'd never forget."

"Oh, dear heart." She smiled sadly at me. "I promised you nothing. The acorn was about *your* life, not mine."

Before I could argue, she swiftly kissed my brow, her eyes wet, and crossed the stream. I might have followed her—the forest didn't cast people out then—but my legs wilted like reeds. I collapsed, my heart in my throat, my chest overflowing with anguish.

Grandmère found me then—she'd raced after me after I'd bolted after Mother—and she knelt beside me in the grass. She didn't say anything. She just rested a heavy hand on my back.

I already believed in fate by then. I'd lived fourteen years watching the comings and goings of villagers whose card readings had proven to be true. But in that minute after my mother left, I stopped believing in fate. What I felt was stronger. I *knew* it to be true. And so did Mother, despite always pretending otherwise. If she didn't, she wouldn't have feared so deeply for Father. She would have promised me she'd return. She would have said the acorn represented *all* of our lives.

"We have never given up on making peace," Herr Oswald says, and I tear my gaze from the Tree of the Lost and Mother's rose-red strip of wool, though I can't blink away my last memory with her so easily. "And so we return to this place every month and present our offerings. We try once more to see if the forest will yield to us." He raises his voice a notch louder. "Who will finally be the victor? Shall we see who will be given the chance?"

Three years ago, the villagers would have roared with enthusiasm. Two years ago, they would have at least produced a few shouts. This year, their embers burn low. All they can summon is a smattering of small nods and weak claps. I'm the anomaly. Inside, I've channeled my heartache into hope. I'm ignited, blazing, ready to burst.

All my desires hinge on being chosen in the lottery—the only way I can enter the forest. Until I do, I won't be able to find the Book of Fortunes and accomplish the one thing that can reverse Mother's terrible fate—make my one wish to save her.

Herr Oswald's bony hand reaches into the amber goblet. My heart stampedes. Axel catches my eye and winks.

The chairman stirs the papers three times. Digs his fingers into the bowl. Retrieves a folded slip.

Feign genuine surprise, I instruct myself. *Remember what you've rehearsed.* When he reads "Clara Thurn," I'm going to place a hand on my chest and gasp. I'll take a steeling breath and square my shoulders. I'll show everyone I'm ready to cross the line of ashes.

Herr Oswald unfolds the paper. The corner of his mouth lifts. Approval? I stand taller. My nerves tingle from head to foot.

He holds the paper aloft for the crowd to see. I can't make out the words. I shift two steps closer, squinting. He calls in a resounding voice, "Axel Furst!"

CHAPTER 2

I stumble. Blood rushes to my head. My hand flies to my heart. I gasp, head spinning. Unwittingly, I've done what I rehearsed. Only it's wrong. Because the name is wrong. It has to be, with such odds in my favor.

"No!" I blurt, heaving all my pent-up breath.

Heads turn. People shuffle backward. I stand exposed. My temples throb. The paper Herr Oswald holds pulses in each flash of my vision.

"No?" he repeats, his face elongating as he frowns.

I trip forward two more steps. I finally make out the words on the paper. They truly read "Axel Furst."

I turn a sharp glance on my friend. What trick has he been playing?

His eyes are wide, clapped on mine. His tawny skin has turned bone pale. He gives a small shake of his head. He hasn't played any trick. Of course not. He would never deceive me in anything. Besides, his name hasn't been drawn this year. It was in the amber goblet, just like it had every right to be. He won, and he won fairly.

The stares of the villagers tunnel in on me. My cheeks burn, and I wrap my arms across my stomach. I meet Herr Oswald's appalled eyes and clear my throat. "What I meant to say is . . ." My voice thins, and I swallow. "No, Axel can't enter the forest without my map." I pull the folded parchment from my pocket. "It will give him the best chance to succeed."

Herr Oswald raises a brow, but he nods, accepting my answer. "Congratulations, Axel," he declares. "Save our village. Save our Lost."

"Save our village. Save our Lost," I repeat with everyone, the mantra we tell every lottery winner.

Several people walk to Axel and shake his hand. Others wander closer to the forest border, taking up positions to watch his attempt. A few drift away from the meadow, their eyes dull and their shoulders drooping.

I trudge to the altar and pocket my acorn. No, it should stay. I place it back on the carved wooden bench. Axel will do his best to find Mother for me, just like I promised him I'd find Ella if my name had been drawn.

Herr Oswald is shaking Axel's hand now. The color has returned to my friend's face. He's excited, and he should be. He has the opportunity to save the person he loves.

My chest aches. I squirm to nudge away the sensation. I can't pretend my grief is worse than anyone else's in Grimm's Hollow, even if it's hard to imagine them missing someone more than I miss my mother.

Ella's father stands beside Axel and beams. Ella's mother dabs her wet eyes with a handkerchief. They take turns embracing him and share a few words. When they part ways, Axel meanders back to me—I've aimlessly drifted off to the middle of the meadow—and he blows out a breath, tugging at his collar. "Clara, I didn't mean to—"

"I really do want you to have this." I press my map into his hand. "I meant what I said. It's your best chance to succeed."

He lowers his head, his fingers reverently trailing the edge of the folded parchment. He's asked me about my map before, and I've shown it to him on more than one occasion. I've spent most of the last year sketching out everything I know about the Forest

Grimm. Villagers have stories of better days when they were able to venture within the forest, and I've pieced together what they've told me on this map.

Axel slides it into his trouser pocket. "I'll give it back if I can't—"

"You're not going to fail." *Do I really believe that?* "Just promise to—"

"I'll find her for you," he says, echoing my words from earlier.

My eyes sting. I give him a hug, wobbling on my tiptoes to reach his height. His head dips, and his nose presses into the crook of my neck.

When we delivered the twin lambs, Axel's arms had trembled with joy and relief. They don't quiver now, but I still feel his strong emotions in the tightness of his hold around me. Maybe he's afraid. He could meet his death when he enters the forest.

In the first year of the curse, three lottery winners were killed when they crossed the line of ashes. Last year, two died the same way, although they made it a little farther within. This year, no one has been killed. Not yet, anyway. The villagers have learned to be more cautious with their luck.

As for me, I've accepted that my untimely death will come at the hands of the forest. I haven't forgotten the two-card fate I share with my mother. If Axel doesn't save her, I vow that I will. Somehow I'll get the book back, and with it the wish I'll be able to claim.

I pull away from his arms and meet his eyes. "Take my luck," I whisper, something the villagers of Grimm's Hollow have come to say since the curse fell upon us. It feels more hopeful than saying "good luck," even if only by a sliver.

"Thank you." He grins crookedly in his unaffected and charming way. His gaze cuts to Ella's parents, and he draws a shaky breath. They're counting on him to bring their daughter safely back.

As Axel goes to meet Herr Oswald near the trailhead, I move to stand behind a group of girls near my age who are waiting to watch his attempt. Half of them weren't here a few minutes ago. Word has spread quickly that he won the lottery.

"Isn't he terribly romantic?" Frieda Kraus whispers to Lotte Dittmar.

Lotte nods, toying with the end of her long braid. "What if Ella is still wearing her wedding veil when he finds her?"

I picture beautiful Ella in her white dress and red veil. Before the curse, villagers didn't marry so young, but life feels shorter now. No one wants to waste any time they've been given. For Ella and Axel, that time was stolen. She became Lost last summer, only hours before they were to wed.

Ella's sister, my best friend Henni, woke up in the night to find her missing from the bedroom they shared. Henni looked out the window, and under the light of the full moon, she found Ella wandering toward the Forest Grimm.

Ella wasn't acting like herself, Henni said. She didn't turn when her sister called her name, not even when Henni started crying. Ella was wearing her veil and white wedding dress, but the gown was streaked with black—cinders, the family later realized, because the soot in the kitchen fireplace had been disturbed. Villagers later called Ella "Cinderella," the tragic Lost bride of the Forest Grimm.

Axel takes a traveling pack from Herr Oswald and slings it over his shoulder. He's oblivious to the girls' conversation about him. His jaw is squared, his brows pulled low, and his gaze fixed on the forest.

Axel was staying at the Dantzers' farm on the eve of his

wedding day. By the time Henni woke up her parents and the three of them raced outside to stop Ella, they found Axel well ahead of them. He was bolting after his fiancée, shouting her name as she neared the Forest Grimm.

He was too late.

The trees spread their branches open like welcoming arms, and once Ella stepped past their border, they closed against Axel. Roots shot up from the ground and tangled into a barrier of branches. He slammed against it, tried to climb it, yank it apart, but it wouldn't yield. The barrier shoved him away, its roots and branches lashing like whips.

He doesn't speak of that night, but Henni told me he wept and raged and finally fell to his knees. Ella's family caught up to him, sobbing as they wrapped their arms around each other.

Together, they watched Ella wander deeper into the forest. Through a small window in the branches, they saw her pass under a shaft of moonlight. The train of her dress dragged along the ground, clawing at the stones and roots, and her red veil billowed, iridescent like blood.

She never looked back.

Axel takes his first step toward the forest, and my heart lurches. He's still a yard from the line of ashes, but I'm already holding my breath. The other villagers freeze, also watching.

He presses forward until he reaches the line. He pauses and closes his eyes. Mouths something imperceptible. Stands taller. Lifts his right foot.

A bead of sweat rolls down my neck.

He sets his foot down across the line of ashes. Exhales slowly. Opens his eyes. Brings his left foot across the line. Inhales through his nose. Takes two more steps. Nods to himself.

I nod too. *Keep going.*

He continues onward, cautious but determined. The first two trees of the Forest Grimm loom a few feet ahead, a pair of towering guardians.

Most lottery winners don't make it past the Twins, as we call them. The path cuts between their trunks and arching branches—and those branches are deadly. They whip and shove, stab and strangle.

One lottery winner, Franz Hagen, abandoned the path, trying to avoid the Twins, but he found out the hard way that their roots stretch far. They sprang from the earth and yanked him underground. As the dirt closed over his head, the villagers watched, breath bated, for him to surface. He never did. That ground became his grave.

Axel is under the shadow of the Twins now. His pace doesn't slow, but his fists clench, and his shoulders go rigid.

This is the second time he's won the lottery. The first time he also made it to the Twins, but the moment he stepped between them, their branches swooped down and hurled him back fifteen feet. He landed on a boulder and broke his left arm.

When I won the lottery eleven months ago, I made it just as far—and not a step farther. The earth rose up like a great wave and pushed me back in one rolling motion until I fell behind the line of ashes again. An insult at my attempt to enter. I didn't even get a bruise.

Axel takes another step. He's standing in that pivotal spot between the Twins. My hands press together over my nose and mouth. He looks at the trees like he's pleading with them.

"Let him through," I whisper on a strangled breath.

One step. Two. Three, four, five. My breath hitches. I release a frenzied laugh. He's past the Twins. He just might succeed.

He keeps walking. Hope builds in the crowd. A few cheers

ring out. People call his name, urging him on. Frieda and Lotte bounce on their toes and squeal. I skirt around them for a better view.

"Stay calm," I say to Axel, even though he can't hear me. "Don't run." It's always the temptation. The rare lottery winners who make it this far will impulsively rush forward, racing deeper into the forest as if they'll find more safety. They never do.

Axel advances three more steps. A low groan rumbles behind him. It's coming from the Twins. They rock and sway, unsettled on their roots.

I curse. He stiffens. Bends his knees in a lunge. He's an arrow in a bowstring, ready to launch.

"Don't do it," I plead under my breath.

A loud *crack* shudders the air. A thick branch snaps off the left Twin. Axel dodges it just in time. It slams to the ground, a hair from crushing him. He stares at it, wide-eyed, and scrambles farther away—toward the forest. His legs don't slow. They build momentum.

No, no, no.

He's running. Barreling. I've never seen him move so fast.

Panic floods me. I watch in horror as the overreaching branches of the Twins claw out for him. Their limbs grow at an impossible rate.

He isn't running fast enough. Once the forest rejects you, you can't change its mind.

Branches snake around Axel's waist. He's lifted high into the air, hovering above the Twins. My nerves fire. *Don't drop him.* He won't survive that fall.

"Axel!" I plunge across the line of ashes. I don't know what I'm thinking. I can't catch him or help him. He's too far up. But I can't stop running.

"Clara!" Herr Oswald shouts. I've done the forbidden.

Crossed the line without the sanction of the lottery. I don't turn back. I sprint onward. Rush closer to my friend.

"Don't hurt him!" I yell at the Twins. "He isn't your enemy!" My mother wasn't either. No villagers were except for the unknown murderer, but the forest holds us all to blame. "Put him down!"

The wild grass wraps around my ankles. I fall forward on my hands and knees. I'm near the Twins. Their roots snap up from the ground and writhe, ready to strike. The full stupidity of what I've done crashes down on me like a tower of bricks. If I die now, I'll never save my mother.

I scoot back a few inches, but I can't budge any more. The wild grass tethers my ankles. "Please!" I call to the Twins, a prayer for Axel and me and my mother. A supplication for every hope I have in my tangled fate with the Forest Grimm.

Axel arcs over the Twins in the grip of their branches. He wheels down toward the meadow. Twelve feet from the ground, the trees release him. He falls in a heap beside me and gasps for breath, rolling onto his back as he gapes at the sky.

"Are you all right?" I ask. An absurd question. Of course he isn't all right. But at least he's alive.

His head turns to me, his brows tilted upward. His eyes rove over my face. "Why are you—? You shouldn't have—"

The Twins groan again. Axel curses. "Hurry."

I try to stand, but my ankles are still bound. I rip at the wild grass. The Twins' roots reach for me. Axel digs into his pack. Miraculously he's kept hold of it. He pulls out a small knife and hacks at the grass. The sharpened edge nicks my skin, but I don't feel the pain, not even when blood trickles down my leg.

A large root slaps Axel in the back. He lurches forward and drops the knife. When he reaches for it, the root shoves him toward the meadow.

I take up the knife. Cut the last blades of grass. Clamber after Axel. Not fast enough. Roots whip my backside. I push to my feet. Axel darts back for me. He grabs my hand. We race for the line of ashes, dodging holes of freshly opened earth and snares of weeds.

The line is a yard away. We squeeze each other's hands and leap.

We clear the line and tumble to the ground. My head lands hard on Axel's stomach. He grunts, some of the air knocked out of him.

Dizzily, I pull myself into a sitting position. He does the same. As one, we gaze back at the forest. The landscape settles. The holes fill with earth, the weeds shrink, and the roots of the Twins burrow back underground. Their towering branches retract and steady, and the Twins resume their posts as statuesque guardians again. All that moves now is what the natural breeze can rustle, only the fluttering leaves and rolling wild grass.

Once more, the deadly Forest Grimm has fallen back asleep. For now.

CHAPTER 3

I hobble beside Axel on the path that skirts the village and follows the ash-lined border. My back aches from tumbling to the ground after our leap from the forest. He offers me a steadying arm, but I quicken my pace and pretend not to see it.

I should have never catapulted into the forest after him. I only put him in more danger—and myself into the throng of gossip. Once Axel and I reached safety, the villagers couldn't stop speculating about what had provoked me to such stupidity. I tried to ignore them, but their whispers were loud enough to wake the dead.

Just as passionate as her mother.

Just as headstrong.

But it wasn't those words that troubled me. I lifted my chin to be compared to my mother. It was what I heard next that set my ears ablaze.

Perhaps her heart has gone soft for the Furst boy.

Foolish girl. No one could ever break his devotion to Ella.

My teeth clenched, and they've been grinding ever since. It's the villagers who have gone soft—soft in the head. I acted on impulse because Axel is a longtime friend, nothing more. Not every bold deed requires romance as its reason.

Axel and I reach the Dantzer farm, where he lives with Ella's family. I blurt a goodbye and rush off to search for Henni.

I poke around the dairy stalls—Henni loves to be alone with the cows—but she isn't there. She isn't in the house either, so she could be anywhere. If her chores are done for the day, she often wanders off to do whatever small things please her, and she always returns home by sundown.

Henni's absences never trouble her parents, which is a wonder after what happened with Ella. But Ella still remains their constant worry. They're so heartbroken over her that they never think to fear for their second daughter. Though, truth be told, Ella always captured their attention, even before she became Lost.

Eventually I give up my search for Henni and travel homeward. A half mile beyond the Dantzer farm, I pass an abandoned cottage, the place where the Tragers used to live before they became Lost. And when I curve around the path to the other side, I spy my best friend.

Henni is on her knees with a basket at her elbow, foraging wild lingonberries from a bush near the line of ashes. Everything grows better when it's closest to the forest. Past the forest side of the border, the landscape is lush and green, but on the village side, the green withers to a yellowish and rotten shade. Scarcely any birds, squirrels, or other wild animals frequent Grimm's Hollow anymore. Unlike the villagers, animals can cross the line of ashes freely, and they would rather live where the food is plentiful.

"If those are for jam," I say to Henni, "promise to let me taste it."

She looks over her shoulder and grins. The apples of her cheeks glow rosy in the summer heat, and for a moment she looks as robust as she once was.

In the last year, ever since Ella went Lost, Henni's round face has thinned, and her full figure has sharpened at the edges. She looks more like Ella now that she's getting older. Both girls share the same petite nose, large doe eyes, and shiny light chestnut hair. But in most ways, they're opposites. Ella is tall and lithe, and Henni is short and larger boned. Ella walks with long and graceful strides, but Henni takes small and timid steps. Ella's beauty is striking and intimidating, but Henni's loveliness is simple and welcoming.

She laughs at me. "If you know someone with sugar, I'll gladly make jam."

My mouth waters. How I wish someone had sugar. "Are those for your paints, then?" Lingonberries aren't pleasant to eat on their own, though I know many who have resorted to doing so. But not Henni. She'd rather use them for her artwork. She's always experimenting with new ways to make colors.

"I was hoping for a darker red," she says, "but this is the best shade I can find." She frowns as she peers into her basket. "Though I doubt I'll be able to make much paint."

I limp a step closer, my hand on my throbbing lower back. Her basket isn't even a quarter full, and this bush is nearly picked clean. "I'll help you find some more then."

"Thank you." Her smile wavers as she eyes the crooked way I'm standing. "But you should fix your wedge-lift first."

It's only then that I notice the little wedge in my left shoe isn't in its proper spot beneath my heel. I sit on the ground, untie my laces, and slide it back into place.

My back has an S-shaped curve that makes my hips uneven. The wedge-lift I wear straightens them and alleviates most of my back pain, though I'm sure it will keep smarting today just to remind me of my foolishness.

Henni's gaze lowers to the grass stains and dirt smudges on my skirt. "Who won the lottery?"

She has never attended Devotion Day, even though she turns sixteen soon. She can't stomach the idea of watching someone get hurt—or suffering a worse fate—when the forest rejects them.

I pinch my lips together and take my time tightening my laces.

Henni tilts her head. "You weren't chosen, were you?" Her tone, always kind, has a scratch in it. "You couldn't have been."

I never told her about my plan—she might have talked me out of it—and I don't feel much like confiding now. Besides, all the evidence is gone. Before I left the meadow, I snuck every scrap of paper with my name on it back out of the amber goblet. The scraps are in my apron pocket now, along with the acorn my mother gave me. Most people leave their offerings. I'd done so at first, hoping the forest would be kind to Axel. But after we were both attacked, I wasn't in the mood, and I snatched the acorn back.

"Clara," Henni prods.

"I wasn't chosen." I leave it at that as I finish tying my laces. "Oh, I think I see more berries." I stand abruptly and walk to a patch of nearby brambles, making a show of rummaging through the leaves.

I don't know what's the matter with me. I sought out Henni, and now all I want to do is be alone with my map. Except I don't have it. I let Axel borrow it to make a copy. It was my way of apologizing. I tempted the fates today. I'm sure that's why he was chosen and everything went wrong.

I bend over, my back twinging as I gaze deeper into the bush. It's clearly barren. Henni must know that. Thankfully, my friend lets me be.

A flash of red beyond the brambles catches my eye. A cluster of tiny flowers—a darker shade of red than Henni's lingonberries. The color she was wanting.

I weave through the brambles and approach the flowers. Each long stem holds several of them. They tip downward like bells and have five pointed petals that form little stars.

Something about these tiny star flowers pricks the corners of my mind. They're familiar, though I can't put my finger on why.

I pluck a stem, and it comes up by the root, which is also dark red. It looks like a small carrot or parsnip. Perfect. Henni can use the root for her paint too.

I take a few more steps and gather more star flowers. I can't wait to show her. Henni deserves all the small kindnesses this life can offer, which are hard to come by since the curse fell on Grimm's Hollow. I give what I can, though it's usually just my friendship. I don't have her talent for making beautiful things.

Once she gave me a small painting of my cottage—how it looked before my mother's rosebushes withered. In return, I embroidered her a pillowcase. A maddening endeavor. I kept pricking my finger on the needle and tangling the thread. But she insisted on receiving the gift, no matter how clumsily made. Mortified, I presented her with a pillowcase that looked like a butcher's apron. She didn't even laugh. She just hugged me and said she'd treasure it forever.

Grinning at the star flowers, I open my mouth to call her name, but she calls mine first. My heart stops at the sound of her voice. It's choked, only a thin gasp of air.

I whirl around. All the rosiness has leached from Henni's cheeks, and her eyes are terror-stricken.

"What's wrong?" My mind races. "The berries . . ." What if they weren't lingonberries, but something poisonous? "Did you eat any?"

She shakes her head. Her body rattles. She looks at me as though she's seeing a ghost. She mouths something, but I can't understand the words. She's lost her voice fully now. I'm frozen in place, unsure what to do.

She raises a quivering hand. Beckons me with her fingers. Mouths something again. I finally make it out: *Come back!*

Icy dread stabs my veins. My heart thuds, each beat like the painful strike of a hammer. I'm keenly aware of where I'm standing now. My eyes flicker to the line of ashes. I've gone five feet past it.

Henni finds enough of her voice to scrape out one word: "Hurry!"

I stumble forward, my legs water, my vision blurry.

The quickest path to safety lies through the brambles. They grow over the ash line. That's why I didn't see it.

I squirm through them, wincing. Will they grab me? Strangle me? I've already tested the forest's patience once today.

I cross the line. My shoes meet safe ground again. Henni barrels into me. She hugs me in a death grip like I'm Ella no longer Lost. "Are you hurt?" she cries. "What were you thinking, Clara?"

I pull back and stare at the crushed flowers between us. My mind is in a haze. "A darker red . . . for your paints."

"My paints don't matter!" She shakes me. "Promise to never do that again."

"I didn't mean to . . ." I look past the brambles to the star flowers. None of them wrapped around my legs like the wild grass did when I chased after Axel. The earth didn't rise up and shove me away either.

I shift around the brambles to get a clearer view of the line of ashes. My nerves prickle with hope.

"What are you doing?" Henni squeaks. "Don't!"

I step over the line, the flowers clutched tight in my fist.

She grabs for my arm.

I swerve out of reach.

"Have you lost your mind, Clara?"

No. I'm not Lost. Not in any way.

The forest isn't harming me, and I'm grounded, nothing like the way Henni said that Ella had acted when she wandered into the Forest Grimm last summer.

Henni breaks out into a sweat. She paces back and forth rapidly. For her sake, I cross back over the line. The flowers I'm holding will wilt in a few hours anyway. I'll need longer than that to save my mother.

My friend inhales, red-faced, like she's going to berate me again. I don't give her the chance.

"We have to go to my cottage!" I grasp her hand. Frenzied energy flashes through my veins and pebbles my skin.

I know where I've seen these star flowers before.

CHAPTER 4

I kneel at the foot of a large chest carved with evergreens and woodland animals. It rests beneath the window overlooking the north sheep pasture, and beyond it, the hedgerow that divides our land from the Forest Grimm.

"I've used flowers like these for my paints before." Henni sits at the table that Grandmère and I use for cooking and eating and everything else besides card readings. "Except they were purple. The roots too. I've never seen red ones until today."

I dig past knitted blankets, a gray fur, spare linens, and a small collection of books written in Grandmère's native tongue. One is a volume of children's stories she used to translate for me, frightening tales that made me shiver long into the night. I loved them anyway. No matter how gruesome they were, they always had happy endings. And happy endings were magical for someone like me with a two-card fate.

I lift higher on my knees and peek above the windowsill. No sign of Grandmère. She's probably gone fetching water from the spring a mile east of our cottage. A never-ending chore since our well ran dry two years ago.

"Keep searching." Henni stands, moving closer to the window. "I'll let you know if I see her."

"Thanks." I keep rummaging through the chest.

"What does she care about what you do with a cape, anyway?" Henni asks, no scorn in her voice, only genuine curiosity.

I think back to three years ago, a month after my mother became Lost. I'd drifted into her room, the first time I'd let myself enter that space to mourn her. When I sat down on her bed, the straw-filled mattress didn't cave in the middle like it once did. I turned it over and found a seam had been cut open and stitched back together again with black thread. I picked it apart and discovered something hidden inside: a hooded red cape.

Grandmère had burst into the bedroom, a fire in her eyes I'd never seen before. She yanked the cape from my hands and rushed into the sitting room, open to our kitchen.

I feared she would thrust the cape into the fire below the hearth's kettle, but instead she opened the carved chest and stuffed the cape inside. "Leave this be," she warned me. "We have already lost too much."

I never promised her, never said the words. If she really wanted me to stay away, she should have made me swear an oath.

I meet Henni's eyes. "All I know is that the cape belonged to my mother, and any reminder of her causes Grandmère pain."

Why Mother hid the cape in the mattress, I cannot fathom. She'd sewn it in plain sight, planning to wear it on the journey to find Father. But she never took it.

I never realized that until I found it left behind.

My heart twinges. Mother should have never gone after Father. He wasn't Lost in the forest. Four days after she set off after him, his body washed up from Mondfluss, the river that cuts through Grimm's Hollow. A fishing accident, the villagers told us. Father's body was found tangled up in his net.

I swallow and dig deeper in the chest. What if Grandmère eventually destroyed the cape? My best chance at saving Mother will be gone, just when I've discovered it.

I've almost reached the bottom when, at last, my fingers brush the cape's unforgettably soft fabric. I break into a wide grin and pull it out.

"You found it!" Henni sits on the floor beside me. She strokes the cape along the grain of its smooth weave. "It's beautiful. Thurn sheep always make the best wool."

Pride in my family's trade swells inside me. The wool is by far the cape's best feature. It's otherwise simple with a roomy hood and a long length meant to fall at the knee. The cape isn't even lined. Mother could have sewn in a fur lining, I suppose, but Father went missing in the warm months, so it makes sense that she didn't.

"Where is it embroidered?" Henni leans closer. On the way here, I told her what I was looking for, the places on the cape where I'd seen the star flowers.

I turn it over and locate the strings that tie the cape together at the base of the hood. There, on both sides of the front panels, little clusters of star flowers glisten in shining threads, embroidered in the same dark red shade as the wool.

"Mother must have dyed the cape with the root of the star flowers," I say. "Somehow she figured out they would offer her protection."

Henni's eyes slowly round. "Will you wear it on the next Devotion Day, then?"

Another month is too far away. "I can't wait that long for only the chance to be chosen." My hand closes around a fistful of the cape's fine wool. "Mother made this for me," I whisper, not daring to voice that wish any louder. Could it really be true? Could she have been counting on me all this time to save her? Did she realize she might not return?

It can't be coincidence that we share the same fate.

Fate . . .

Grandmère's singing floats on the air through the open shutters. Henni startles. "She's back!"

I stuff the cape in the chest, snap the lid shut, and take both of Henni's hands, my pulse tripping in staccato. "Will you do something for me?"

Her palms go sweaty. "What did you have in mind?"

"Can you ask Grandmère to read your fortune?"

"Oh, Clara. No." She blanches. "I don't want to know my fate."

Grandmère's singing grows louder, accompanied by the creak of the handcart she uses to lug back pails of water.

"Don't worry," I say. "It won't be your fate. It will be mine."

"That doesn't make any sense."

I stand, pulling her up with me. "Do you trust me?"

"Yes, but—"

Grandmère walks through the front door, idly glancing at us. "Hello, girls."

"Hello, Grandmère," we recite together, our backs stiff.

She arches a gray brow, and her violet eyes narrow, already suspicious of us. She removes the kerchief from her hair. "How is your dairy farm, Henrietta?" she asks my friend, forgoing any questions she might have posed to me about Devotion Day. Like Henni, she never attends. Her lack of curiosity makes sense, at least for today. She thinks my name wasn't in the amber goblet. "Are your cows still producing milk? We'd be happy to trade some sheep cheese for a pail."

"That would be—" Henni squirms. "I'm sure we could arrange—"

I nudge her.

"Can you read my fortune?" she blurts.

Grandmère freezes. "Pardon?"

"I'd like it read, please."

"Right now?"

Henni nods, clutching the sides of her apron. A nervous habit. "I, um, promised Father I'd be home soon."

Grandmère's keen eyes slide between us. "But you've never had an interest in my cards, *ma chère*."

"That isn't true. I've always loved how you've painted them. I just wasn't ready to know my fate until today."

Poor Henni. Her face is scarlet, and her voice keeps squeaking. She wouldn't be so flustered if I'd had more time to explain my plan.

"You are sure you're truly ready?" Grandmère blots her brow with her kerchief. Her perspiration must be from the summer heat. As slender and old as she is, she's stronger and in better health than most villagers. "Surely Clara has told you that fate isn't always a comfort."

"I w-want to know." Henni forces an exhale. "Please."

Grandmère catches my eye, and I nod. Henni will be all right. Her fortune won't really be read, but mine will be. I'm going to trick Grandmère into thinking I'm my best friend. A necessary deception. She would never willingly read cards for me again.

My stomach flips and flutters like a fish in a net. Somehow I'll survive the next few minutes. I haven't had my fortune read since the night my mother gave me the acorn. Until now I never believed my fate could change.

"Very well." Grandmère draws herself taller, which is tall indeed, though not overly tall for a woman. Sadly, I don't take after her in height, like Mother. I'd like to think I have some of Grandmère's beauty, though. It never diminishes, no matter how gray her hair grows or how deep her wrinkles slice into her face. "Clara, help prepare the room."

Obediently, I walk to the windows and close the shutters for privacy. From a box on the corner shelf, I retrieve Grandmère's fortune-telling veil and cards and bring them to the small round table she uses for readings. Her favorite chair is already tucked up beside it and draped in sheepskin.

I draw up a simple kitchen chair for Henni, who gives me a pleading look as she takes her seat. I squeeze her arm. The worst is almost over—for her anyway.

Grandmère sits across from her and starts shuffling the cards, splitting the deck, fanning it faceup and facedown, her customary routine to ensure the cards are in random order.

Henni's knee bounces. Her hands wring in her lap. "Such pretty cards. Yes, yes, so pretty," she babbles. "I love the contrasting shapes and colors. I don't see this style of painting in the mountain regions. Is it common in your homeland?"

If anyone else, including me, had asked about Grandmère's past, her eyes would have shuttered while her jaw clamped closed. But because Henni is guileless and the sweetest person in existence, Grandmère answers, "Not in my homeland, but among the family I had there. They taught me how to paint the cards and then to read them."

A shadow of a smile flickers across Grandmère's mouth. I wish she would share more about what she remembers, but all too soon, her eyes grow heavy and her almost-smile ghosts away. I know from experience she won't say more.

What I've gleaned of the life she led before coming to Grimm's Hollow, I learned from Grandfather while he was still alive.

Marlène Danior, who became Marlène Thurn, had a wanderer's heart, he told me. It drove her to this place from a far-off land, hundreds of miles beyond our mountain ranges, though she stopped her wandering after she discovered our haven. But I suspect the true reason Grandmère drifted to our village was because her heart was sore and lonely, and falling in love here with Grandfather had eased some of that pain.

She was the sole survivor of her family. The Daniors were brutally killed in their native country. If Grandfather ever learned how or why, he never shared it with me. And when I dared to ask

Grandmère once myself, she only answered, "My gift lies with the future, *ma petite chérie*. I never had any talent for divining the past. Let it be buried where it burned to ash."

Part of me feels buried with it—the bloodline I'll never know, the connections we might share—but I'm living my life half in the grave anyway, tiptoeing around my fated death as long as possible. The only thing that emboldens me is my vow to save Mother before my time runs out.

"If only I could find such vivid colors for my paints." Henni prattles even faster now that Grandmère's shuffling is near an end. "Nothing vibrant grows here anymore unless it's near the forest border. I've had the most difficult time searching for the right shade of red. Thankfully Clara came along today and—"

"We made do with lingonberries." I talk over her before she can reveal anything about how I crossed the line of ashes.

Oblivious to my concern, Henni asks, "What did you use to make paint for *that* card?" She points to the Red Card. Grandmère has just exposed it in cutting the deck.

A sudden hitch mars Grandmère's fluid movements. She clears her throat. "The root of a flower called red rampion," she answers. "It only blooms on rare occasions. Sometimes years pass before I can find it again." She slips the card back into the deck and out of sight.

Her words ring in my ears along with the whooshing of my heartbeat. I can't believe it. The same root that dyed the cape red was also used to paint the Red Card. It's another sign that the time is ripe to save my mother. But I need a *real* sign. I need that card—Changer of Fate—to be drawn for me.

"Rampion! Yes, of course," Henni says. "I forgot the name. Until today, the purple ones were all I—"

"Ready to begin?" I ask before she can divulge anything more.

I press the veil into Grandmère's hands, and she frowns at me, one eye squinted.

"Patience, Clara. Do you need to wait in your room?"

"No." I retreat a step. "You won't know I'm here, I promise."

She grumbles and slips the veil over her head. It's silky black and covers her face entirely, the hem hitting just below her shoulders. She fans the deck of cards facedown one last time. I poke Henni's arm and hold my finger to my lips.

What do I do? she mouths.

I motion for her to move out of the chair. She does so with a rare silent grace that would have made Ella proud.

Just as quietly, I slide into her vacated spot, but tug on her skirt to keep her beside me. Catching on, she crouches so our heads are level.

"Set your hand on top of mine," Grandmère instructs.

I do as she says, my fingers trembling. *You shouldn't tempt fate,* I recall Axel saying this morning.

"Relax, child. I must feel your blood sing."

I blow out slowly through my mouth and try to clear my mind. I push out the image of Axel's earnest blue eyes and struggle to make room for the hope I once had as a little girl that my fate could indeed change.

"Good." Grandmère's hand hovers across the fanned cards, gliding back and forth, searching for the right one. It isn't long before her fingers stop abruptly above a card with a torn corner.

Cold flashes through my body. I know that card before she turns it over. Once she does, its silhouetted trees, painted black, stare up at me. A yellow crescent moon winks behind them.

The Midnight Forest, always the first card drawn of my two-card fate.

It's fine, I reassure myself. The Midnight Forest means anything forbidden, and for me it must mean the literal Forest Grimm—a forbidden place. Of course my fate lies there. That's where I need to go to save Mother. That's why she made me the cape.

Grandmère's hand moves again, only momentarily, and then stills a second time. My breath snags. It's too soon. I've never seen her draw a second card so quickly.

She flips it over. I curse inwardly, glaring at the animal on the card, indeterminate in breed, but with sharp canine teeth. The Fanged Creature. It foretells an untimely death—*my* untimely death.

Henni's large brown eyes pin me with sympathy. I squeeze my own eyes closed, vainly trying to shut out the burn of my unchanged fortune. I just wanted a blessing for once, a good omen rather than a bad one.

It doesn't matter. I don't need a sign. I'll try my luck in the forest, anyway. I'll throw the red cape over my shoulders and bring back my mother and the Book of Fortunes.

"Your blood is dancing, Henni." Awe trickles through Grandmère's voice. "It isn't finished singing to me yet."

My pulse leaps. I exchange startled glances with Henni. Her expression mirrors my cautious hope.

Grandmère leans closer, her veiled face tilting. Her hand below mine moves over the deck, suspending in the air over the only card in the spread with crisp edges. The Red Card. Changer of Fate. The card Grandmère has never drawn before in a reading.

Her hand doesn't still above the card. It swings left and right, like the pendulum of a cuckoo clock.

My heart is in my throat. *Stop, stop, stop,* I command Grandmère's hand, but it keeps rocking, undecided. Maybe I've confused her. She thinks I'm Henni. *I'm Clara!* I want to shout. *You painted the Red Card for me.*

Please let it be true.

Her pointer finger lowers, touching the overlap where two cards meet, the crisp-edged card and another one. "Interesting," she murmurs. "Which card is yours?"

The Red Card, unturned, is on the left. It takes all my restraint not to press her hand toward it.

Grandmère seems to feel my inward push.

Her finger slides left.

She turns the Red Card over.

My mouth drops open. Light-headedness rushes through me. Laughter bubbles up my throat. I swallow to trap it in, but my shoulders tremble and my cheeks ache from smiling. My whole life locks into place, a puzzle piece that never fit before.

My fate is my own now. Because I can *change* fate. That's what this card means: Changer of Fate. Which also means I can change my mother's fate. The red rampion, the red cape, the Red Card. They must all add up to this.

Grandmère's hand shifts right. "This is also your fate, child. This is where your blood stops singing."

My mind grinds to a halt. She reaches for the last card, the one the Red Card overlapped.

What's happening? I don't want another card.

She turns it over anyway, and I gasp.

CHAPTER 5

Goose bumps prickle down my arms. My gaze drops to the most beautiful card in Grandmère's deck. Two white swans with curved necks touch beak-to-beak, their joined shapes forming a heart. Within that heart, two arrows cross, piercing the swans' breasts.

The Pierced Swans.

The card with dueling meanings.

It either foretells truest love or star-crossed lovers, a happy fate or a miserable one. The other cards drawn determine the outcome—the story, as Grandmère calls it. But I don't know how to weave those meanings together. That's her gift, not mine.

She pulls her hand away and reaches for her veil. She hasn't seen the upturned cards yet. Her readings are always blind until this moment.

I jerk to my feet. The table tips sideways. The cards slide off and flutter to the floor. I hop back and shoot Henni a pointed look. She doesn't follow. I wildly gesture for her to take my place.

Grandmère's veil is lifting. Henni stumbles forward.

The veil is off. Grandmère looks in dismay from Henni's flushed face to the toppled cards. "Are you well, *ma chère*?"

"Yes—I mean no! I f-feel faint."

"Sit back down then." Grandmère motions me toward the kitchen window. "Clara, open the shutters and let in the breeze."

I rush to do her bidding.

"I warned you, child." Grandmère *tsk*s at Henni. "I asked if you were truly ready to know your fate."

"I thought I was. Sorry."

"Which four cards did I draw?" Grandmère asks her.

My hand freezes on the shutter latch.

"I-I don't remember," Henni says.

"It's better to tell me, dear. The meanings might not be as grim as you think."

I peek over my shoulder. Poor Henni looks like a deer caught in the aim of an arrow. "It's all right," I tell her. "You can go home. Your father is waiting."

She doesn't need to be told twice. She springs away and darts out the door.

My gut needles. Somehow I'll make this up to her. I'll make her jars and jars of lingonberry jam. I'll raid every house in the village for sugar. Someone must have a hidden crock.

"You're too protective of your friend, *ma petite chérie*." Grandmère's head shakes side to side. "You should have made her stay. I could have comforted her."

I avert my gaze. "She'll come back when she's ready to know what the cards mean," I say casually. I flip the latch, push open the shutters, and fill my lungs with a deep breath of summer air. It's not as stifling anymore, not as tainted by the curse of Grimm's Hollow.

I'm the Changer of Fate. I pinch myself like a child would to see if they're awake and not dreaming. The Red Card, never drawn before, was finally drawn—and for me. None of the other cards matter anymore.

Or do they?

I squint past the hedgerow to the Forest Grimm beyond. How much of my fate has been predetermined in those dark woods?

"What cards did I draw for Henni?" Grandmère asks again, her chair squeaking as she rises.

I open my mouth to say, *I didn't see the cards. The room was too dim.* But I can't spin that yarn convincingly. I was always the child to sneak in on Grandmère's readings and spy the cards she drew, even by the light of the dying hearth fire. And she was always the woman who pretended not to notice.

I think through the meanings of the four cards drawn. . . .

The Midnight Forest: a forbidden choice.

The Fanged Creature: an untimely death.

The Red Card: Changer of Fate.

The Pierced Swans: either truest love or star-crossed lovers.

"The Pierced Swans and the Midnight Forest," I answer, beginning with two truths. "What do you make of those cards paired together?" I fiddle with my sleeve cuff. "Do they mean forbidden love? The Pierced Swans would represent star-crossed lovers then, right?"

"*Oui.*" Grandmère kneels to gather the cards. "Unless a more powerful card changed their meaning."

I drift closer. "Are there any cards more powerful than the Midnight Forest?"

She points to two faceup cards on the floor. "The Fanged Creature and the Red Card." Throwing me a sharp glance, she adds, "Please tell me I didn't draw those for Henni."

I shake my head, forcing a smile while my stomach churns. "You drew the Ice-Capped Mountain and the Woodsman's Hatchet," I lie.

"Hmm. I wonder what card upset the poor dear then."

I shrug and crouch to help clean up the mess. "Must have been the Midnight Forest."

"Perhaps."

The breeze whistles through the empty spaces of our cottage, the nooks and crannies and dusty corners—places Mother's presence would have somehow filled and buffered the silence.

I suck in a tight breath. "What if you *had* drawn the Fanged Creature and the Red Card?" I labor to keep my voice steady. "The Fanged Creature wouldn't matter then, right? None of the cards would. The Red Card would cancel them out. It would change fate."

Grandmère laughs and scoops up the remainder of the deck. "The Red Card does not change the meaning of the other cards, Clara."

"Why not?"

In the shadow of the card table, Grandmère's violet irises shrink, eclipsed by her pupils. "Let us say that the cards I drew for Henni had indeed been the Fanged Creature and the Red Card, as well as the Midnight Forest and the Pierced Swans. If Henni had a fate to change, it would be something different from what the other cards foretold—her untimely death, that which is forbidden, and her truest or star-crossed love. Those fates are still required. The Red Card cannot alter them. In fact it needs them. It is like a spider in that sense."

"A spider?" My eyes fall to the gathered cards in my hand, and their painted images swirl together, a labyrinth that runs deeper the longer I keep staring. "I don't understand."

"Fate is a web, you see," Grandmère continues, "and every card drawn is one of its silken threads."

"Except for the Red Card?"

"That is right, *ma chère*." She shifts closer, and one of her violet eyes comes out of shadow. "And a spider needs a web to catch its prey."

A bitter and coppery tang fills my mouth. I don't like her

comparing catching prey to changing fate. I'm not trying to kill someone. "Are you saying that fate has an order, one that must play out before it can be tampered with?"

"Fate has an order, yes, but think of it, rather, as an order of harmony and balance. That balance must hold or the Changer of Fate cannot change anything."

I start to understand her meaning.

Although the Red Card foretells that I can change fate, I'm only able to do that if I hold the rest of my fate in balance. Which means I must also follow through with what the other cards have divined for me. . . .

The Midnight Forest for a forbidden choice. That must mean entering the Forest Grimm wearing the red cape.

The Pierced Swans for a love that's either true or star-crossed. Axel and Ella flit to mind. That card describes them perfectly. They're necessary to my journey.

And finally the Fanged Creature for my untimely death— how my own fate must end after I change fate. There's no other alternative.

This is the story of how I save my mother.

And, as it has been from the beginning, this remains the story of how I die.

CHAPTER 6

hat night, after Grandmère has fallen asleep, I take the shears from her sewing basket and cut eight inches off the length of the red hooded cape. I hem the raw edge, as well as the edge of the strip I've cut away. I tie the cape around my shoulders and stuff the strip in a pack I've prepared with food and supplies.

My heart pounds in a flurry, a drumroll to a battle march. *You're doing the right thing, Clara.* Now is the best time to leave. Over the last several days, in preparation for the lottery, I slaved in the pasture and cottage, tending to every chore I could think of to ease Grandmère's workload if I was chosen.

Our farm hand, Conrad, will help her as well. And when I return—no, when *Mother* does—she can also help like she once did. Running the sheep farm will be easier after I find the Book of Fortunes and use it to lift the curse off Grimm's Hollow.

I leave a note on the kitchen table and hurry into the darkness outside. I don't light my lantern. The crescent moon is just bright enough to illuminate the path leading to the Dantzer farm.

Axel lives in a small house, once meant for dairymaids, on the north end of the property. The Dantzers fixed it up to serve as his first home with Ella. The two of them never got the chance to share it, but it's his now. He doesn't have any other family he's willing to live with. His mother died giving birth to him, and his father was a merchant from the lower valley. One winter, he left Axel in our village with his uncle while traveling through the dangerous pass between the Ottenhorne Mountains.

That was before the curse, but the mountain pass may as well have been cursed anyway. An avalanche struck, and Axel's father never returned.

My friend lost someone before the people of Grimm's Hollow had any Lost Ones of their own, and his uncle, a drunkard, was lost long before he ever took Axel in.

I rap on his door. Axel doesn't answer. I sneak over to the east-facing window. The shutters are open. His bed is tucked length-wise against the windowsill. The scarce moonlight shines in on him, casting a faint silvery sheen across his tanned skin. He's sleeping without a shirt on and has an arm draped over his face.

I jostle his shoulder. "Axel." Why am I whispering? No one from the big house will hear me unless I shout. "Axel," I say louder, and shake him again.

He mumbles, eyes closed, and swats my hand away.

"Wake up."

His eyelids flutter, but don't open. I jostle him harder. He grunts.

This is ridiculous. I had no idea he was such a deep sleeper.

I set my pack down on the grass, along with the unlit lantern, and hoist myself up on the windowsill, hissing as my crooked spine twinges. I slip inside the room on his bed. I'm wedged between the wall and his body. Carefully straddling my legs over his hips, I try to crawl over him before he—

His eyes jerk open. He flinches, grabs me, and flips me over on my back. I gasp, pinned between his knees. His chest and ab-dominal muscles flex above me. I'm stunned, dizzy, disoriented. My skin flares with heat.

He blinks twice. "Clara?"

I can't locate my voice.

"What are you doing here?" he rasps. "You can't sneak up on me in the middle of the night like that. What if I'd hurt you?" His eyes linger on my parted lips. I'm not breathing. "I *am* hurting you!" He hastily shifts his weight off me and helps me sit up.

I gulp in air and let the night breeze cool my face. I pull at the strings near my neck, trying to get cooler, and the cape falls off my shoulders.

Calm down. Axel wasn't hurting me. I wasn't suffocating, just startled. "You're very quick . . . and strong," I say. Possibly the stupidest words that have ever tumbled from my mouth. "I couldn't wake you up, so I—"

"—thought you'd sleep with me?" His grin slips, and he winces. "That didn't come out right." He scrubs a hand over his face. "Do you need a drink of water? I need a drink of water," he mumbles.

When he stands, the blanket slides off his body. He's wearing thin linen pants that bunch at his knees and hang low on his hips. As he walks to his dresser, I can't stop staring at the dimples that mark both sides of his lower spine.

He lights a candle and pours water from a pitcher into a mug. "Are you going to tell me why you came here?" He returns to the bed and pulls up a stool to sit beside me. "Clearly it couldn't wait until tomorrow morning." He chuckles, passing me the mug.

I take a long drink and try to collect my thoughts. I'd rehearsed everything I was going to say to him, but now my mind is scrambled. It might help if he put on more clothes. I've never been in a boy's room before, except Conrad's, but he's three times older than me and smells of cheese and sheep. Axel is only two years older and smells of pine needles and wood shavings.

"My map," I say. "I need it back."

His eyes narrow, traveling from me to my fallen cape. He rises and kneels on the mattress, peeks out the window, and then groans. He's seen my pack and lantern. "Are you out of your mind?" He whirls on me.

"Just listen before you—"

"You barely made it out of the forest alive this morning!"

"That was a lifetime ago. Everything's changed!"

"No. It won't change until the next lottery—and then only if you're incredibly lucky. You can't enter the forest without its permission."

"I drew the Red Card, and I have the red cape." My words trip over each other in my excitement, though it sounds more like desperation. "They're made with red rampion."

"What in Grimm's Hollow are you talking about?"

"Come with me." I clasp his hand and scoot closer. "I made a scarf for you from my cape."

"A scarf in the summertime?"

"Wear it as a sash then. It will protect you."

"Slow down, Clara. Nothing you're saying makes sense."

"The red rampion is the key to entering the forest. I tested it today. The forest let me cross the border. Ask Henni. No, don't ask her. She won't want me to go. But *you* need to come." I take his other hand. "You and Ella, you're the Pierced Swans. You're necessary."

"Is this about a card reading?" He shrinks back. "You can't stake your fate on your grandmother's fortune-telling."

I *can*, actually. Grandmère's readings have never proven to be false. But Axel isn't a strong believer in destiny. Losing his father and then being left in the care of a negligent uncle has robbed him of any convictions that fate can hold significance.

"It's more than that," I reply. "My mother made me this cape. She dyed it with red rampion, don't you see? It took me until now to figure out that she left me what I needed all along to save her. It's been in my cottage, just waiting for me all this time." I squeeze his hands. "Come with me, Axel."

He exhales and pulls away, dragging his fingers through his mussed hair. "I don't know. . . ."

"What do you want more than anything?" I lean forward. "What have you wanted every waking moment since last summer?"

His gaze drops, latching on to a lock of my dark hair, which has spilled across the front of my shoulder. My *bare* shoulder. The loose neckline of my dress has slipped askew. My cheeks flush, and I pull the dress back into place.

Axel swallows. "I want Ella back," he whispers, his eyes gradually lifting to mine. "I want her home again."

My heart tugs. I feel his longing as if it's my own. We're bonded in that way, each of us missing the person we love the most. "And I want my mother back." I uncurl my fingers, opening my empty hand for him. "This is our chance, Axel. Come with me."

His brows pull inward. The corner of his lower lip catches between his teeth. The night breeze flits across my collarbone as his fingers slowly slide across the small space between us. They skim across my wrist, my palm, and knit together with mine.

A rush of tingling spreads up my arm, and my chest expands, trapping its warmth.

I drew the Red Card, I have the red cape, and I have Axel.

Together, we're bound to succeed.

He draws a steeling breath and nods. He packs a bag, gives me my map, and wraps the red strip I made him around his neck—a scarf for now. He closes his shutters and leaves a note for the Dantzers on his bedside table.

We creep out of the house through his front door, close it behind us, and cross the pasture to the trees bordering the Forest

Grimm, the spot where Ella entered last summer. The Dantzers have made a small monument of stacked stones for her, almost like a grave marker.

Just beyond it, Axel pauses at the line of ashes and stares up at the trees. I sense the history of this place pressing down on him, palpable like the heavy air before a thunderstorm. I reach for his hand. "We're going to find her. This is going to work."

His gaze remains on the trees and their strong branches, sleeping giants for now. "Because of a red flower?" He shakes his head, and a slight tremor runs through his fingers. "How can it be that simple?"

"Trust me."

"It's the forest I don't trust."

I give his hand a tug, and his eyes finally drift to mine. "Everything has aligned for our success on this journey. I've seen the signs." The Red Card was drawn for me on the day I discovered the red rampion, the same day I also realized my cape was dyed with it. That can't be coincidence.

A smile touches his lips, softening the tight edges around his mouth. "You and your signs."

I shift on my feet to steady myself, unsure if his mocking errs on the side of exasperation or tender amusement. Faith in superstitions is in my blood, perhaps a relic of Grandmère's family of fortune-tellers. She taught me many omens, and villagers have shared their own beliefs with me as well. I collect them in my mind like I've collected knowledge of the forest. Both will guide me on this journey. "Trust me," I tell Axel again.

"I'm trying."

I straighten my spine, at least as much as my S-curve will permit. "On the count of three, then?"

He exhales roughly and shakes out his shoulders. "Fine."

"One."

Now it's my fingers that are trembling.

"Two."

Cold sweat flashes up my neck.

"Three."

Our linked hands squeeze tight.

Together, we cross the line of ashes.

Our shoes touch the ground of the Forest Grimm.

I don't breathe for the longest moment. When I do it comes in little gasps, as tentative as my tiptoeing as we wander in deeper. Five feet, ten feet . . . fifteen yards, twenty. The branches don't lash at us, the roots don't writhe, and the earth doesn't open to swallow us whole. Our astonished gazes collide as we continue forward without incident.

When we're a quarter of a mile past the border, Axel's rigidness melts away. He breaks into warm laughter. "Red flowers, hmm?" He shoots me a grin, one that has melted many hearts in Grimm's Hollow. His natural charm is a weapon he has no idea he's wielding. If he did—if that charm came with arrogance—it would have little effect on me. "You're a wonder, Clara Thurn."

I return his smile, rolling my eyes a little at the compliment. I found the rampion because of good luck and that was all. Still, his words lift a bit of heaviness from my shoulders. Luck is rare these days, a gift not to be discounted.

A breeze swirls by us, nudging our backs and urging us onward. In that whisper of wind, I hear the beckoning of my mother, not a stifled cry or a shudder of rage, but a haunting song, a breath of welcoming.

It's only my imagination, I'm sure, but I want to believe she knows I'm here. I'm wearing the red cape she made for me, and I've come to bring her home.

The Lost will be found, I promise.

CHAPTER 7

I f magic had a smell, it would be this forest. Though the night is black, it teems with a greenness that hasn't filled my lungs for three long years, ever since the curse brought on the drought in the village. I've forgotten what it's like to breathe *life*.

There's no brittle and bitter scent of death and decay here, like there is in Grimm's Hollow. The air is lush and tastes of growing things—trees and flowers and grass—all that thrives and is beautiful and doesn't die prematurely.

Maybe nothing dies in the deep reaches of the Forest Grimm. Maybe nothing grows old here. Perhaps Mother won't have grown any older when I meet her again. She could be vibrant and radiant, nothing like her tattered rose-red strip of wool on the Tree of the Lost.

Axel touches my arm, and I pause on the overgrown footpath. "Can I take a look at your map again?"

I pull it from my pocket and pass it over. As he unfolds it, I hold my lantern near him. Once we had traveled deep enough in the forest and were certain the Dantzers couldn't see the lantern's light, we lit the flame.

We study the map together. The only strategy I've come up with for finding my mother and Ella, along with *Sortes Fortunae*, is to travel from landmark to landmark, then pick our way back home again through the same chain of places. That way we don't become Lost.

The first landmark we're looking for is a tree house built in a maple. From there, we should be able to find the path to Whisper Falls.

The last half of the riddle from the page that *Sortes Fortunae* left behind flits through my memory:

Falling water
Lost words found
A selfless wish
The curse unbound.

Whisper Falls seems the obvious spot to begin our search for the Book of Fortunes, with the riddle's mention of falling water.

"Hmm." Axel's gaze lifts from the map. "We should be close." He scratches at the corner of his jaw and glances around. "Can you shine the light up there?" He reaches across me to point to a tree on my left.

I raise my lantern. I wish it were brighter. It doesn't travel any farther than a few feet ahead, which makes the tree house that much harder to find.

The thin crescent moon isn't doing us any favors either. Its crack of shining silver barely peeks through the dense canopy of the forest.

I squint at where Axel is looking, but I can't make out anything except two fat branches. I can't even tell the shape of the leaves to know if they belong to a maple. I certainly can't find anything to indicate a tree house. "Do you see something I don't?"

He crosses in front of me and moves closer to the tree. He's standing in the pool of lantern light now. It clings to his golden hair and broad shoulders and embraces him in a warm amber halo. He plucks a leaf and examines its edges and texture. "It's a sugar maple."

I nod, though my map didn't specify which kind of maple the tree house was in. "Did the Dantzers mention a sugar maple?"

What little I know of the tree house I learned from Henni. When her father was young, he built it a couple of miles from his family's dairy farm—the farm he later came to inherit. This was back when the forest welcomed villagers, of course. Before the curse, Grimm's Hollow seemed almost a part of these woods. People would venture in and out as they pleased.

"No." Axel ducks under a low-hanging branch and touches the tree trunk. "But I've been to this tree house before."

I cock my head. "You never told me that." I follow him, keeping him bathed in my lantern light.

"Here it is." He steps toward a trunk with ladder boards nailed into it.

As if climbing them, my gaze travels upward. I finally make out the rough shape of the tree house above.

Axel walks around to the other side of the trunk. "Ella showed it to me."

"Really? I didn't realize you two were close before the curse fell."

He nods slowly, picking at a gnarled knot of wood. "This is where we . . . where everything began between us."

"Where you first kissed her, you mean?" I drift closer.

"More like where *she* first kissed me."

"You didn't kiss her back?"

He scratches his neck. "I did. I was almost sixteen, so . . ." He shrugs a shoulder. "Ella was hard to resist."

I want to ask what it was like, kissing someone, but that's the kind of question I would ask Henni, not Axel . . . though Henni wouldn't be much help since she's never kissed anyone either.

I came of age more than a year ago, but most boys in Grimm's

Hollow are still wary of me. Not only am I the granddaughter of a foreign fortune-teller, I'm also the daughter of the first villager to became Lost. But it doesn't matter. I don't care about boys. Pining for romance is for other girls in the village. My future is a book that will never be opened. My life's purpose is to save my mother. I don't look past it. I won't *live* past it.

Under the weight of my lingering stare, Axel paces away from me and blows out a measured breath. "Should we camp here for the night?" He kicks at the packed earth between the exposed roots of the maple.

"I could sleep in the tree house," I offer. "Or you could."

He shakes his head. "Most of the boards had rotted last time I was here. It will only be more dangerous now."

"Oh." My gaze falls to the only flat and suitable spot for sleeping, a six-foot square of ground, which feels much too cramped for lying right beside a boy all night.

I fold my arms across my stomach and shift backward. I didn't think through all the implications of going on this journey with Axel.

His eyes make quick work of the way I'm standing with my shoulders curled inward. "How about you take this spot?" he says, and scoops up his pack. "I'll find another."

"All right." I breathe a little easier. "Here, you'll need the lantern." I pick it up for him.

He waves a dismissing hand and dredges up a grin. "I'll manage." Visiting the spot where he first kissed Ella seems to have put him in a somber mood. "See you in the morning."

I watch him amble away, his form growing dimmer as he moves out of the light. My heart does a funny little skip. "Don't go too far!"

He waves again, a silent *yes*.

I shuffle from foot to foot, fighting the urge to call him back again. Just because I didn't want him to sleep beside me doesn't mean I want him sleeping anywhere else.

I heave a sigh—one that's far too dramatic for my liking—and finally resign myself to letting him go for the night.

I untie the bedroll I've strapped to the top of my pack and lie down on it, using my cape as my blanket. I let the lantern burn for a few more minutes. I know I'm wasting precious tallow wax—I've only packed a handful of candles—but I can't make myself extinguish the flame just yet. What if Axel decides to come back? Will he need the light to find me?

Relax, Clara. He'll find me easily enough come morning.

I douse the lantern and curl into a ball, but sleep still eludes me. For one thing, my crooked spine is already missing my mattress back home. No matter how I shift, I can't get comfortable. But worse, the reverent elation I felt about being in the forest is gone now that I'm all alone. This is the place that stole my mother, the place that stole Ella from Axel, the place that killed lottery winners and leeched moisture from Grimm's Hollow.

And I'm inside its clutches now, past its gaping jaws and within its dark belly.

This is the place that's going to kill me.

I shudder and burrow deeper in my cape. The trees rustle, whispering death threats. Blades of grass sing discordantly. Night insects buzz and nip and bite.

I made a terrible mistake letting Axel leave.

I'll never sleep, I'll never sleep, I'll never . . .

Something shines in my eyes. Sunlight. It peeks in through the slim crack between my bedroom shutters. Am I dreaming? Groggily I sit up, my eyes mostly closed. My internal clock tells me it's time to stoke the fire in the kitchen, prepare a bowl of porridge for Grandmère, and gather eggs from the henhouse.

My eyes fully open, and I gape, looking around. Blinding green surrounds me, a dreamscape of trees and shrubbery and vibrant wild grass.

I'm not dreaming. Where I am and how I came to be here slams back into my mind. Memories of last night crash in right afterward.

I shiver and tighten the strings at my neck. I fold the red hooded cape closer around me against the cool morning air. The towering canopy blocks out most of the sun. But the chill of the forest doesn't account for the ice forming at the base of my spine and slithering up my back. Something isn't right, and my sleep-addled brain can't place why.

I look directly above. I'm beneath a maple, but it isn't a sugar maple; it's a red maple, and no weathered boards are nailed to its branches.

I'm not under the tree house anymore.

I don't know where I am.

I scramble to my feet. "Axel?" I whirl and scan the forest. His spruce-blue vest, red scarf, and tousled head of hair can't be seen in any direction.

"Axel!" I call louder. He doesn't answer back.

My heart kicks a heavy beat.

He's lost. I've lost him.

No, I'm lost.

Lost.

Lost, like my mother.

CHAPTER 8

A xel!" My voice is hoarse from shouting. At most, an hour has passed since I found myself alone. I cling to that fact like it's my only tether to reality. Everything else is unfathomable. How could I have woken up somewhere else?

Some people are prone to sleepwalking. Maybe that's what Ella was doing when she wandered into the forest on the eve of her wedding. Henni said she used to sleepwalk on occasion. But I've always been settled in my sleep. Mother said even as a baby, I didn't whimper or wiggle after she laid me in my cradle.

"Axel!" I cry again. I'm definitely whimpering now. We weren't supposed to be separated. This wasn't in the cards. He and I were supposed to find Ella, and then the two of them as the Pierced Swans were going to help me find *Sortes Fortunae* and my mother.

How will I find her now?

I turn to my right, changing directions, and race faster. I can't wander too far from my starting point. It could be closer to the tree house than I think. My pack thumps against my back, which only makes my spine throb worse. The lantern clanks and rattles, hooked on one of the straps.

"Axel!"

A blackbird launches out of a pine and flies away from me. *Tchup, tchup, tchup.* Another bird calls from the same tree. Also a blackbird.

Two blackbirds perched together is a sign of good luck. But now that the second bird is alone, is that luck gone?

I hear my name in the distance, so faint it sounds like an echo from an impossibly deep well. I probably just imagined it. I turn in a circle and listen more intently.

A few seconds later, the voice comes again, clearer, louder. "Clara?"

My pulse jumps. "Axel?" His baritone register strikes a chord of familiarity in the very center of my chest.

"Clara!"

It *is* him. I spring toward the direction he's calling from.

We keep shouting each other's names. I zigzag around the trees, coming closer and closer to the sound of his trampling boots and frantic voice. Finally I see him. He's thirty feet away at the end of a small clearing.

He bolts toward me. I sag with relief and stumble nearer. My legs have turned to molasses. I'm laughing, maybe crying. My emotions are scattered. I'm an utter mess.

Axel throws down his pack, and I drop mine. He catches me in his arms. My cheek presses to his chest. His rapid heartbeats thunder against my ear. "I thought I'd lost you," he pants.

"I'm so sorry." I close my eyes, savoring how solid and real he is, the way his natural woodsy smell is undercut with musky perspiration. I drink it in, everything human about him that reminds me I'm no longer on my own. "I never sleepwalk. I don't know how it happened."

He pulls away. A small crease forms between his brows. "You woke up in a different place too?"

"Yes. The tree house was gone, and I— Wait, where did *you* wake up?"

He gives a slight shake of his head. His hair glistens with

sweat. "All I know is I wasn't anywhere near you, even though I'd set up camp only two trees away."

He was that close? I wish I'd have known. I wouldn't have been so anxious last night.

"I thought I might have sleepwalked too," he adds.

Unease trickles through me and spoils the last of my relief. What are the chances that both of us sleepwalked during the same night? It's too far-fetched . . . and yet it makes sense. Did the same thing happen to the Lost Ones? Is that why they never found their way back home?

"We need to camp together from now on," Axel says.

He stole the words from my mouth. "And we should tie our wrists and ankles together."

"Good idea."

We gradually compose ourselves. He combs down his hair, though it remains stubbornly tousled, and I smooth the skirt of my homespun dress. It's a shade of cornflower blue that's weak and faded, but my cape is rampion red, the color of strength. At least it is to me. I just need to remember that next time I let myself get rattled so easily.

I'm meant to be here—the forest has allowed it—and my time in this world isn't over yet. I won't let it be until I've played fate's game and saved my mother.

Axel slings his pack over his shoulder, and when I grab mine, I also pull out my map. I scan what should be nearby landmarks—the creek that forks off of Mondfluss River, the canyon with limestone cliffs, the thin ribbons of water at Whisper Falls.

"Where should we head now?" Axel asks.

"Back to the tree house?" I suggest. "We're not going to find anything unless we know where we're starting from."

"I don't know." Axel picks at his lower lip. "I've been looking for the tree house for over an hour, without any luck."

"That doesn't change the fact that it's our best chance at finding the footpath again. We need it to lead us to Whisper Falls."

He shrugs with a little huff, which I interpret to mean: *All right, but I think this is a waste of time, and I'll be saying "I told you so" sooner than later.*

I don't let it dissuade me.

We set off, choosing a direction that should be south according to the eastward morning sun. Grimm's Hollow is also south of the Forest Grimm, which means the tree house should be somewhere that way.

Unfortunately with the thickets, undergrowth, and boulders we have to skirt around, we can't forge a straight path, and by the time the sun climbs to shine directly down on us, I've lost sense of which way we're going. It can't be south anymore. We would have reached the ash-lined border of Grimm's Hollow already.

I silently curse myself for deciding to start our journey in the darkness last night. Nothing around me looks familiar. I wouldn't know if we were anywhere near the tree house.

The hours lag on. My uneven hips and S-curved spine are smarting from our nonstop walking, not to mention my panicked racing around earlier in the day. The sun falls westward—the direction I now realize we've been traveling in. I grumble and pull out my map again. Axel has the gall to smirk with his unspoken *I told you so.* He takes a swig from his waterskin and offers me a drink, but I set my jaw and pretend I don't see it.

He elbows my side and chuckles. "Just forget about the tree house, all right? We're bound to stumble across something on your map soon enough, and it will set us on the right foot again." He nudges his waterskin into my hand. "Take a sip. You haven't drunk anything all day."

I relent and allow myself a couple of swallows. Along with my struggle to find any landmarks, I'm growing more and more nervous about finding water. We haven't come across any today, not even a trickle of a stream. If we had, I would have followed it back to its source, which might have given us our bearings again.

I finally heed Axel's advice, and we abandon our search for the tree house. We pause to eat a simple meal, rationing the bread and sheep cheese I've packed, then cut northward. I keep my eyes peeled for any signs of humanity. Grimm's Hollow has lost sixty-seven villagers in this forest. If we find any, we have a duty to help them too. The mantra from Devotion Day rings through my mind, the words said to each lottery winner: *Save our village. Save our Lost.*

But Axel and I should have seen some evidence of the Lost Ones' existence by now . . . campsites, makeshift shelters, even deserted settlements. Surely some villagers had banded together and devised ways to survive. But if they did, they're invisible to me. As the day whittles away hour by hour, and the sun droops past the wooded horizon, giving way to twilight, we find nothing to prove that anyone other than ourselves has ever traveled through here, not even as much as a scrap of fabric caught on a bramble or a faded set of boot prints.

Don't be discouraged, I tell myself. Our journey has just begun. Grandmère drew the Red Card for me, a card she's never drawn in any other reading. That has to mean enough luck is in my favor to help me succeed.

As the dark of night thickens, the magic of the forest intensifies. The green fragrance in the air heightens, sharp with pine and spruce. Fog collects along the ground, ebbing and flowing like a sea of smoke. And wind whistles from lofty tree branches, singing haunting melodies.

Half of my senses prick with warning, while the other half fall under a spell of wonder. I'm in the forbidden place I've longed to be since it captured my mother.

The Forest Grimm has always held a special allure for me. When I was younger, back when Father was alive and Grimm's Hollow wasn't cursed, I crossed the forest border with him one night to find a missing lamb. The forest must have felt the desire of our hearts because it assisted us. Branches swayed in the wind, pointing the way, and night flowers bloomed, attracting fireflies to illuminate our path. Soon we found the little lamb.

The world was once rampant with magic, Father said. It filled the water, the air, the earth, and everything that grew upon it. Magic worked in harmony with people and helped them live a peaceful existence. Even some people were magic, like Grand-mère is with her fortune-telling. But as magic became abused or forgotten, it hid itself deep in the earth or far underwater or high in the unreachable heavens. Only pockets of magic remain in the world—special places that haven't been neglected and are still reverenced by their inhabitants. The Forest Grimm was one of those pockets, Father said, a place where enchantment re-mained.

The murder that happened in Grimm's Hollow was a terrible offense to the forest, especially since the unknown killer used the forest's greatest gift—the Book of Fortunes—to make a wish to end another person's life. The forest's magic didn't just hide itself away afterward; it turned against the village and cursed us.

When the book is found again—when I find it—I'll need to make a selfless wish to break the curse. And what could be more selfless than a wish to save my mother?

Axel comes to a halt. "I think we've found the path—at least one of them."

"Thank goodness." I massage my aching back. Maybe we can camp soon. I glance around us and frown. "Where is it?"

He kicks at the fog, which curls back like a receding wave and uncovers a trail about two feet wide. I can't tell how far it stretches into the distance. I pull out my flint kit and light the candle in my lantern. Axel gives the fog a firmer kick, and more of the white puffs scatter. Before they thicken again, I catch a clearer glimpse of the trail.

"It's red," I gasp. Not an earthy red, like iron-rich soil, but a vivid and shimmering red. "Nobody ever mentioned a red trail like this before. It looks almost metallic."

Axel stomps on it. "It can't be metal. It's too soft."

I lean my weight onto it. It has a cushiony give, like a layer of mulch or cut grass.

My stomach quivers. "Do you think the forest could have changed after the curse?" When I made my map, all the villagers I interviewed shared what they knew of this place, but that knowledge could be outdated. No one has been here since before three years ago—no one who has returned, anyway.

"Sure," Axel says. "Think of how Grimm's Hollow has changed. Besides, the magic of the forest can do just about anything."

He has a point. That magic made a book that grants wishes. It makes trees move and the ground shift and the wind howl. I've seen it do that much and more to ward off lottery winners. Creating a new red path seems like child's play in comparison.

"But can we trust it?" I tap the path with the toe of my laced shoes, as if doing so is a better test than Axel's stomping. "We have no idea where it leads."

He lifts a broad shoulder. "I think if the forest had a mind to attack us, it would have done so by now. Plus, we're protected." He gives my cape a playful tug.

The wind in the high branches whistles again, but the melody has changed. It's shriller now, wilder. I don't know if that's a good or bad sign, or even a sign at all. The only superstition I recall about the wind is that you shouldn't whistle back at it. Doing so tempts it to grow more dangerous.

"The red rampion can't protect us from everything," I counter, thinking of the Fanged Creature in Grandmère's fortune-telling deck. That card spells my death, a death I've accepted since I vowed to save Mother from her own fortune when I was nine years old.

Axel groans, the good mood he's maintained for most of the day starting to crumble. "C'mon, Clara. Take this gift for what it is—the only promising landmark we've come across all day. The forest is finally throwing us a bone. Give it a chance!"

I scrutinize Axel's face in the lantern light. From his pinched brows to his weary eyes, there's no mistaking his exasperation with me. I crack a smile. "I predict you're going to hate me within a week."

He snorts. "I could never hate you. If I strangle you in your sleep, just know it's coming from a place of love."

I swallow a bubble of laughter, but it pops in my throat when he says "love," and a noise between a hiccup and a giggle tumbles out instead. I shove past him to mask my embarrassment. "Let's take your stupid path then."

He grabs me by my pack. "Not tonight, Clara." He hauls me backward. "No more traveling in the dark. We need to pace ourselves and get some rest. You don't want to see how grumpy I am when I don't get enough sl—"

A sudden gust of wind cuts him off. It rips through the air and funnels down from the treetops. The fog scatters. The red path writhes. My cape flies about me like a flickering flame. I clutch the strings around my neck to keep it anchored.

Before I can catch my breath, a second burst of wind seizes us. Its shrill pitch deepens to a resounding howl.

I lean into Axel for support. His arms cinch around my torso. His head tucks over mine, and his scarf flaps wildly.

The wind lashes out again with another howl, but this blast

is short-lived, dying as quickly as it started. I release a tremulous exhale and look up to meet Axel's wide eyes. At the same time, we break into nervous laughter.

"What was that?" he asks.

"I don't—"

A third howl splits the night. The *still* night. The wind is gone.

My smile falters. Axel's arms go rigid around me. "That sounded close," he whispers.

Too close. I cautiously pull away and glance over my shoulder. Twenty feet in the distance, standing beneath the lower branches of a silver fir, is a wolf.

Its eyes shine like plates of glass reflecting the lantern light. In the dim glow of my candle, I make out the animal's massive size—twice as big as common breeds.

A Grimm wolf.

Goose bumps crawl up the back of my neck, and my heart lurches faster. People from the lower valley don't believe in Grimm wolves, but those in my village know better. Sightings are rare, but everyone is acquainted with at least someone who's seen one. For me, that was my father.

One night while he was tending our flock in the pasture, a Grimm wolf crept out from the mist and slipped among the sheep without disturbing them. It was like the animals were hypnotized. Father raised his staff, trying to make himself look taller to scare the wolf away, but it wasn't fazed. The mist grew thicker, and when it dissipated, the Grimm wolf was gone, having taken two lambs with it.

The forest couldn't always help us. Just like the red rampion can't protect Axel and me from everything here, the forest also couldn't protect Father's lambs from the Grimm wolf.

If there is more than one kind of magic in this world, perhaps the two forces can't oppose each other.

"Stay calm," I whisper to Axel, keeping my eyes on the beast. "Don't turn your back on it." I'm a shepherd's daughter. I know a thing or two about dealing with predators. "Whatever you do, don't—"

"Run!" someone shouts. A woman. *Mother?*

I bolt ahead without thinking twice. I can't help it. What if it's really her?

Axel curses and springs after me. I follow the red path. It twists and turns like a river. I frantically scan the looming dark for any sign of Mother's dark hair, fair skin, and willowy form. I can't breathe, or I would shout for her. Fear has stolen my voice. The wolf has to be chasing us. Any predator would attack someone foolish enough to run.

But I can't stop now that I've started, so I race faster. Axel keeps up beside me. We're a clatter of packs, gear, and thumping boots. Nothing like the grace of a wolf. Wolves run with stealth and silence—Grimm wolves even more so. The beast will be upon us any moment. Its claws will rip out our throats. And Axel is a step behind me. The wolf will seize him first.

I reach for the blade strapped to my pack. Just a whittling knife. What was I thinking? I should have brought an ax.

I unsheathe the blade. Three feet ahead, the red path curves where it meets the girth of a giant oak. I plant my feet and spin around. With any luck, Axel will run past me and take cover behind the tree. Instead, he barrels into me. I lose grip of my lantern and knife.

The lantern crashes to the ground. My knife tumbles after it. The air whooshes from my lungs, and the candle flame sputters out.

I skid backward and try not to fall over. Something collides into me from behind. For one terrifying moment, I think it's the wolf, but there's no fur, no fangs. A wet face presses into my neck.

"Don't let it eat me!" a woman cries.

No, not a woman. Not my mother. Just a girl.

My chest rises as I take in her scent of fresh milk and dandelions. "Henni?"

CHAPTER 9

I gape at my friend—my friend who never attends the lottery because she's so frightened by the Forest Grimm—and here she is in the heart of it. I can barely see her in the darkness. She's mostly a silhouette and two glimmering pupils. I fumble for words. "How did you—?"

Axel grabs me by the arm. "Doesn't matter. Climb!"

Before I can summon a response, he hoists me up, practically throwing me at the first branch of the oak. It's seven feet off the ground. I clumsily latch on to it and swing myself upright. Henni yelps as Axel boosts her up right after me. She has a harder time getting on top of the branch. I yank her from above and Axel pushes her from below.

"Hurry!" I grunt. It's a miracle the Grimm wolf hasn't attacked Axel yet.

Henni finally scrambles onto the branch. Axel leaps for the tree next, and in a blur of agile movements I can't make out in the night, he grabs the branch and swivels his body until he's sitting on top of it. "Higher," he shouts.

The three of us clamber up the oak. Henni and I struggle with our skirts, but they're the least of my worries. Thoughts of the wolf consume me. It's true that wolves don't climb—their claws aren't retractable like the ones foxes and cats have—but wolves *do* have powerful hind legs. They jump. And a Grimm wolf, no doubt, has even more skill at it.

I strain my ears to catch any sounds from below. Snarls or

growls or heavy thuds from lower branches. But I can't hear anything above the huffs and ruckus of our scraping shoes and the leaves we rustle.

"Ouch!" Henni cries as I step on her fingers.

"Sorry!" I adjust my footing. She's one branch below, but I can't see her in the dark. I may as well be climbing blind. I paw at the air, searching for another branch to pull myself up with, but my hands hit a barrier. It isn't rough like bark or leathery like leaves. It's thready and netlike. Almost like a web, but stronger.

I shuffle to the trunk of the maple and pick my way around it. I gain new footholds and try to find a spot to get past the strange net. I finally feel an open space, and I reach through it, grappling for a branch. At last my fingers graze one. I lift on my toes and—

Crack!

The branch I'm standing on breaks. I scream and plummet. My cape flies in my face. I claw out to grab anything.

"Clara!" Just as Axel shouts my name, my back hits something springy, like a knitted blanket.

I rebound into it, bounce a few more times, then lie stunned and sprawled out.

Axel calls my name again. His voice is close. I can't have fallen far.

"I'm . . . all right." I peel my cape off my face and sit up. My back smarts at the base of my crooked S-curve, and I suppress a groan. My hands prod over the blanket-like thing that caught me. "I landed on some kind of net." Apparently there's more than one in this tree.

Axel makes his way down to me, and Henni descends after him. In the time it takes for them to reach my tier of branches, I feel more settled. I've absorbed the quiet from below and separated it from my friends' noises above. The wolf isn't in the tree. We're safe for now.

"Here." Axel reaches to help me off the net. My eyes have adjusted to the darkness, and I make out his shadowy features three feet away. I'm in the center of the net, which is about eight feet wide, room for all of us if it's strong enough.

I cautiously stand and grab a higher branch to support my weight.

"What are you doing?" Axel asks.

"Testing the net." I bend and straighten my legs a few times, pressing my weight into it. The net bounces a bit, but holds firm. If anything, the crash of my fall should have broken it. I suppose that was test enough. "We should all sleep on this tonight."

"We should *what*?" Henni squeaks. Her silhouette shudders behind Axel.

"We're safe from the wolf up here," I explain. "And we can get some sleep if we have a place to lie down. This net will do."

It takes some more convincing, but after a few minutes Axel and Henni relent and join me. We settle down together and nibble on some provisions in our packs, a kind of midnight supper.

I only manage a few swallows. My stomach is still coiled tight from our near-encounter with the wolf. And Axel's too distracted to eat much himself, his eyes peeled below as if he expects the wolf to materialize from the darkness at any moment. As for Henni, I have no idea how much she has eaten of her cheese wedge. Her back is turned to me.

At first I think she's just examining the tree, seeing the dim strokes of its branches with her artist's eye, but then she suppresses a small noise that sounds like a sob. I scoot around to see her face. A sliver of moonlight shines down through the leaves and glistens on her gathering tears.

"Oh, Henni," I murmur gently, taking her hand. She's the

most timid and sensitive person I know. This is no place for her. "Why did you come?"

She sniffs. "I couldn't be left behind again."

Again? Is she talking about her sister? "Ella didn't leave you on purpose."

"What if she did?" A fat tear leaks from the corner of her eye and slips down her cheek.

On my other side, Axel's body goes very still, like he's holding his breath.

I squeeze Henni's hand. "Why would you think that?"

"It doesn't matter." She shrugs and blows out a long breath to compose herself. Wiping her eyes dry, she abruptly sits taller. "Guess how I entered the forest."

My brows lift at the sudden change of topic. But I *have* been wondering about that. "How?"

She slides her hand into her dress pocket and pulls out a clutch of tiny flowers. I can't see their color in the darkness, but I breathe in their herby-sweet smell. Red rampion. "I used your trick to cross the line of ashes," she says, and her teeth flash as she briefly smiles.

I lean closer to touch the flowers. They're crumpled and withering, barely hanging on to the stem, and the tiny parsnip-like roots feel dry, already leeched of moisture. "That was very brave of you," I say, but my lips press together against adding *and foolish*. I don't want to upset Henni when she's finally cheering up. "How did you know you would find us before these wilted?"

"Would that have mattered? It's not as if the rampion that was used to dye your cape is still fresh from the plucking."

She has a point. The truth is I know very little about the magic of red rampion—how much is required to offer protection, how long that protection lasts, and why it's even protective in the first place. What makes it special to the forest? Still, wearing rampion that's dyed into cloth seems more secure than carrying it in a pocket where it can shrivel to dust.

"Besides, I wasn't too far behind you," Henni adds. "Your grandmother showed me your note this morning, and when she realized you weren't with me, she checked Axel's home. I went with her, and we found his note too. I knew you two couldn't have traveled that far here at night. Plus Axel leaves heavy tracks. Always has." She grins. "Whenever he and Ella used to sneak—"

"Did your parents see my note?" Axel cuts her off. The lines of his shoulders are stiff, and his voice strains tight.

Henni pauses for a moment. "Mm-hmm."

He scrutinizes her. "And they weren't upset?"

"Not in the least. They were hopeful. I told them about Clara's red cape, and that you would be safe with her, even though I didn't exactly know how. Maybe you two would have to hold hands or—"

"We didn't hold hands," I blurt. Heat flushes into my cheeks. I really hope she didn't tell them Axel and I might have to do that this whole journey. Mrs. Dantzer has always been a little uneasy about my close friendship with Axel.

"There was no need," he adds, flapping one of the ends of his scarf. "Clara made this for me."

Henni takes a harder look at it. "Oh, I see. Well, that was clever of you to cut it from your cape, Clara."

It doesn't feel particularly clever, but the compliment spreads a little warmth through my chest all the same. Henni has a gift for making other people feel special like that.

Truth be told, I'm worried she might be a burden on this journey. Grandmère didn't draw the Daisy Chain in my reading, the card representing friendship and sisterhood. Does that mean Henni can't offer anything essential to my quest like Axel and Ella can as the Pierced Swans?

As much as I love Henni, will she just be an impediment?

"I'll make a scarf for you too. First thing in the morning." I muster a smile and try to scatter my doubts. I need to accept that Henni is here now. I can't waste time or the progress we've made on our journey by escorting her home again, and I wouldn't let her go alone. "Meanwhile, don't lose those flowers."

She slips the red rampion back into her pocket. "What if you made me a kerchief instead? I brought a sewing kit."

"You brought a *sewing kit*?" I arch a brow.

"Just a needle and thread and a small pair of shears. You never know when your skirt might tear or your socks need darning."

I burst into laughter and throw my arms around her. Only Henni would have thought to bring a sewing kit into the Forest Grimm. "Of course I'll make you a kerchief."

We prepare for bed and hang our packs on nearby branches, then lie down side by side. I position myself in the middle of my friends. The slight give of the net has Axel and Henni rolling into me, but I don't mind. Their pressure is comforting, and our bodies keep each other warm. Maybe it will be nice having Henni here. For the moment, three people feels safer than two.

None of us falls asleep right away. If my friends' nerves are anything like my own, they're still prickling from our race from the wolf. "Do you think we should tie our wrists and ankles together?" Axel asks, reminding me of my suggestion this morning.

I consider it for a moment, not keen on the idea of being separated again. "I think we're all right up here. If we manage to sleepwalk out of a tree, we should quit this forest and join a troupe of acrobats."

His breathy laugh warms the crown of my head. "As if you'd ever quit this forest without finding what you came for."

A smile flickers across my lips. The way he talks, he makes my stubbornness seem admirable. Grandmère has never seen it that way. Whenever she caught me poring over my map or throwing a pining gaze at the forest, she chided me for wasting my time. I felt the fear behind her words, though, her worry that I would meet the fate she foretold in this place.

But I *will* meet it. Axel is right. I'll never quit this forest. After I find my mother and *Sortes Fortunae,* these woods will be the end of me. My untimely death is necessary, part of what fate requires to stay balanced.

The branches creak with our weight, and the net gently sways, finally rocking us to sleep. It isn't quite dawn yet when I awaken, but I feel the promise of the sun in the way the oak leaves start to take crisper form in my vision. I shift, and my back twinges. The S-curve in my spine wasn't helped any by the bend of the net. I need to get out of this tree.

I grab Henni's pack and my own and carefully step over my friends, picking my way out of the net. It looks stranger in the growing light, some kind of ruddy shade and unlike any rope I've ever seen. Did any of the Lost Ones make it? What would they have used to fashion it?

I descend the maple—a much easier chore than climbing it at night—and once I reach the lowest branch, I pause, waiting several minutes for any sound from the wolf. Finally convinced she's gone, I throw down the two packs and jump to the ground, grunting when my shoes hit the hard surface. The shock of it zings up to smart my back. I hiss and rub my spine. I have to be more careful or I'm going to cripple myself only two days into this journey.

I retrieve the lantern and the small knife I lost last night and strap them onto my pack again. From Henni's pack, I retrieve her small sewing kit—a rolled strip of fabric with little pockets for the items she mentioned, as well as a thimble and three small spools of thread. I'll work on making her kerchief while I wait for her and Axel to wake up.

Taking care that my cape never leaves contact with my body, I untie the strings at my neck and spread it across my lap. I cut another length away from the bottom of the cape and hem the raw edge before tying the cape around me again. It reaches my upper thigh now. It's a good thing I don't have any more friends, or I might end up with only a bib left to wear.

As I'm finishing the final stitch of Henni's kerchief, she and Axel hop down from the tree. She breaks into a wide smile. "Is it done?"

I nod and hand her the kerchief. "Unless you want to add some embroidery. I thought about stitching on a flower or two, but you know my skills are lacking. It's a miracle I can hem a straight line."

"No, it's perfect!" She quickly wraps it over her head and ties it beneath her chin. Between the kerchief and the way she wears her hair in two braids, she looks even younger than her age of fifteen.

The pit of my stomach twists. I need to make sure she stays safe in the forest. Henni rarely ventures away from her dairy farm unless she's collecting ingredients for paints or running little errands for her mother. She's not used to hard labor in the outdoors, like Axel, and she hasn't prepared like I have to be here.

"Thank you, Clara." She bends to kiss my cheek before she wanders away to inspect a bed of wood sorrel that's flowering bright yellow.

As I roll up her sewing kit and return it to her pack, Axel stretches his arms and yawns widely. I bite down on a smile when I see a tuft of his golden hair sticking straight up in the back. Somehow the cowlick makes him even more charming. "I don't know about you two," he says, "but I'm starving." He carried his own pack down from the tree, but he doesn't look inside it.

Instead, he eyes my pack and Henni's and plops down on the ground beside me. "Please tell me you've brought a leg of roast mutton."

I stifle a snort. "Yes, along with gooseberry pie and pickled beet salad."

"Don't torment me." He groans and collapses on my lap. As he rolls onto his back and nestles his head on my crossed legs, my stomach grumbles.

"Seems you're the one tormenting me." My mouth waters at the thought of roast mutton. It's a dish Grandmère and I only eat sparingly. Every year since the curse, fewer lambs are born. It's better that we survive off sheep milk and cheese and barter for what we can with our Thurn wool.

"Well?" Axel closes his eyes, continuing to languish on me as his human cushion. "What's for breakfast?"

I flick his shoulder with a finger like I'm shooing away a bug. "You know very well what's for breakfast: the same food we nibbled on yesterday. Sheep cheese and Hollow bread." The latter is what the villagers of Grimm's Hollow learned to bake in lieu of our region's customary dark-grain bread. How I miss its lovely aroma in the kitchen of my cottage. Hollow bread is a paltry replacement made from the grains we can rummage—mostly barley—mixed with lentils, beans, and a fair amount of sawdust. "Would you like me to hand-feed it to you?"

He grins lazily. "It's like you read my mind."

I wrap my finger around his cowlick and give it a hard yank.

"Ow!" He laughs and rolls off my lap. Opening his pack, he tosses me a stick of beef jerky. "Here. Enjoy the spoils of Gerdie."

I take a bite while trying to summon a bit of reverence for one of Henni's favorite dairy cows. The Dantzers only eat them when they die on their own. "Poor Gerdie."

Axel takes out a stick for himself. "So what did you make of that net?" He leans back on his elbows. "Who could have made it—and what did they make it with?"

I pick apart the jerky. "I've been wondering the same thing."

"My dad used to sell silk on his merchant wagon." Axel squints up at the tree. "That's what that net felt like—bundled threads of silk."

I chew on my lip. Nets of silken threads in the Forest Grimm? It doesn't make any sense.

Axel pulls out another piece of jerky and looks over his shoulder. "Hey, Henni!" He takes aim to toss it at her.

"Don't tell her it's Gerdie," I hiss.

"She already knows it's Gerdie," he whispers. "All the jerky is Gerdie." He throws the stick. "Catch!"

I wince, anticipating Henni's reaction. But she doesn't even look our way. The jerky falls just shy of the red path she's standing on, fifteen feet from us. She crouches and gingerly touches the path, then recoils sharply. "It's hair!"

Axel's brow furrows. He barks out a laugh. "Hair?"

Henni stands and jabs a finger at the path. "Hair!" Her shoulders lurch like she's going to vomit.

The curve of Axel's smile slackens. "Clara," he says quietly, "you don't think the net is also made of—?"

"Yes." A bitter tang fills my mouth as the horrible reality sets in.

We spent the night sleeping on a web of human hair.

Axel violently shudders. I force a half-chewed bite of jerky down my throat. Among the great mysteries of this world is the fact that hair is exquisitely beautiful when attached to someone's scalp, but once it's not, it's entirely revolting.

"Where did it come from?" Henni stumbles backward. "How can there be so much of—?"

She cuts herself off with a scream. The red hair writhes to

life. In a flash, it tangles around her ankles and jerks her flat on her back.

Axel and I spring up. "Henni!" I launch for her.

The red hair coils rapidly around her body and forms a tight cocoon. Her legs are wrapped first. By the time I reach her, one of her arms is pinned to her side and the hair binds her stomach. I grab her free arm, but the hair is too strong. I can't budge her loose.

"Get Henni's scissors!" I yell at Axel. "Or my knife! Something!"

He's already fumbling through his pack. He withdraws a knife with a black hilt. Tosses it near my feet. I snatch it up. Start hacking at the hair. Two inches fall away near Henni's shoulders.

I'm not fast enough. The hair is at her neck. *Hack, hack, hack.* It's coiling over her chin. She releases an ear-shuddering scream, cut short by more hair gagging her mouth.

Hack, hack. My hand shakes. Henni's eyes are saucer-wide.

A few yards ahead, a ripple runs through the red path, racing toward Henni. I drop the knife. Clutch her cocooned body. Desperately try to hold her in place.

As if sensing me, the path gives a hard yank. The glossy hair slides out of my grip . . .

. . . and Henni is dragged away.

CHAPTER 10

I bolt after the red path in the direction it's pulling Henni.
"Let her go!" I don't know who I'm shouting at. The forest?
Does that even make sense? How would it have created a
path of human hair?

Axel catches up with me, chasing the path too. We're careful to keep off the hair. We can't help Henni if we get tangled
up too.

Her wrapped body is out of sight. The hair is moving faster
than we can run, a rapid river of glistening crimson. My heart is
in my throat. This can't be happening. I can't lose my best friend.
The Dantzers can't lose another daughter.

Strands of hair branch off the path and snake up trees, no
doubt where more nets are strung up. It's all a giant trap, but why?
To what end?

I'm sprinting faster than I have in my life. My lungs burn.
My cape flaps wildly. I'm still not fast enough. The last of the
red path appears, coursing from behind us where the hair ends.
In a few blinks, it flashes past us and zooms ahead, zigzagging
between the trees.

"Hurry!" I call to Axel, though he probably can't move any
faster with the three packs he's hauling. "We can't lose the path!"

But it's too late. The last of the red hair slips around the exposed roots of a pine, twenty feet away, and falls out of sight.

"No!" I race after it, but when I reach the pine and look beyond, my chest sinks. The path, the hair, my hope of saving Henni—it's all gone.

My eyes burn. I scrub at an errant tear and fist my hands. I break into a run again. Enter a thicket. Fight my way past a tight clutch of branches. Kick through the tall grass.

There's no red anywhere, none except for my cape and Axel's scarf. A sob rises in my throat. I push it down and release a cry of frustration.

"Clara, stop." Axel grabs my arm, but I shrug him off and keep wrestling my way through the thicket. "Stop!" He drops the packs and takes me by my shoulders, spinning me around to face him. "You don't know which direction the path went. Getting yourself more lost won't help Henni."

My glare is razor sharp and filled with enough fury to burn this forest to the ground. But Axel's eyes are gentle and rimmed with understanding. The blue in them aches for me, or maybe with me. I grind my teeth together. Empathy won't help me right now. "We can't just do nothing!"

"I know, but we need to think, and you need to take a breath. Where's the careful girl who spent years making the perfect map of this forest?"

"The map that hasn't helped us once?" I bite out.

"That's beside the point. All I'm saying is keep your head."

I exhale roughly, my blood hot. I know he's right, but he doesn't understand. In all my meticulous planning, I always meant to travel here alone. Bringing Axel was one thing—his role was foretold in Grandmère's cards—but Henni's involvement was never accounted for. "She—" My throat closes. Moisture clouds my vision. "She wasn't supposed to come here." *She's not the one supposed to die.* "What if she's already . . ." I cover my eyes, and my shoulders hitch with a silent sob. I try to turn away, but Axel doesn't let go of me. He pulls me into his arms and runs a soothing hand down my hair where it pools into the hood hanging from my shoulders.

"Henni isn't dead," he says firmly.

"How do you know?"

"The same way I know Ella isn't dead. The same way you know your mother is still alive."

"Does that mean Henni is Lost?"

"Maybe."

A tear seeps out from the corner of my squeezed-shut eyes. Lost is dead if you never see a person again. And we haven't found another soul in this forest. "How do we find her?" *How do we find anyone?*

Axel thinks for a moment. "We go back to where we last saw the red hair. It would have left an imprint on the ground, like water does after it dries up in a riverbed. All we have to do is . . ."

He trails off as a distant melody flits through the late-morning air. I pull away from his chest and turn my ear to it. Someone is singing. A woman. It can't be my mother. Her voice was lovely, but never that beautiful. Henni's isn't either.

I meet Axel's questioning gaze and break into a cautious smile. Warmth trickles through my limbs. "We're not alone," I whisper, as if speaking any louder might scare the woman away.

The corner of Axel's mouth lifts. "See? I knew something would finally work in our favor." He hands me my pack and keeps hold of his and Henni's, adjusting their straps on his shoulder. We change directions in the thicket and follow the sound of the voice.

Ahead, the trees start to thin where the thicket breaks apart. Shafts of sunlight slant toward us, motes sparkling in their beams like golden fairy dust. The woman's voice comes clearer now. I capture some of the words she's singing:

Dearest, come back to me
The honey is golden
The flowers are red
I'll fend off the murdering wolf.

I don't recognize the tune, but it's in a minor key and beautifully haunting, like a lullaby or a plea for a lover to return.

I drift toward the sound, my mind whirring with whom the villager could be. Not Ella, or Axel would be rushing ahead and leaving me to chase him.

I toss him a glance. "Who do you think—?"

Something tickles the side of my face. I move to brush it away, but it sticks to my fingers and hair.

I've walked through a spiderweb.

I gasp. A sign of good luck. It means I'm about to meet a friend. I grin and hurry faster.

We emerge from the thicket and enter a wide clearing surrounded by colossal fir trees. A tower soars above them, perhaps once a watchtower. Its stones are ancient and covered in lichen, moss, and ivy.

No one in the village told me about a lone tower here, but the Forest Grimm is said to hold the ruins of a stone fortress. Centuries ago, a great battle took place deep in the heart of this mountain range. No one remembers the cause of the war or who fought whom. Borders of countries were different back then. But according to legend, every soldier who died here became a tree, and this dense forest took root from their blood, flesh, and bones.

It's the kind of frightening story that always thrilled me, like the ones Grandmère read when I was a child, but also the sort I never believed. A tree could never have been a person. But some of the tale could be true. A battle could have taken place here long ago, and a fortress could be hiding somewhere in this forest. Even before the curse, villagers were careful not to wander too far in these woods for fear they wouldn't find their way back home.

Axel comes to my side. "Look." He points in the distance.

I've been so caught up in the tower's height and ring of crenellations that I haven't seen what he has spied until now—a ribbon of red along the ground. It's winding its way toward the base of the tower, about fifty yards from us.

My pulse trips faster. Maybe Henni isn't Lost after all.

We rush to the tower. It has no doors on the near side. When we round its far side, we find no doors there either. The only opening is a high window. Like a waterfall rushing backward, the red hair rises up the tower and pours into the window instead of spilling out from it.

"Henni." My breath catches. Her cocooned body has almost reached the window. I tug against the red hair, but I can't stop it from climbing. On impulse, I jump into it. I wrap my arms and legs in the hair and let it pull me upward. I can't lose Henni.

"Clara!" Axel reaches for me, but I'm already too high. His fingertips skim the toe of my shoe as he leaps for my ankle.

"It's the only way up!"

He curses but follows after me, weaving himself into the hair as it rises up the tower.

Henni's muffled scream pricks my ears. Her nose and eyes are exposed, never having been wrapped in the hair. I suddenly see what she does, a creature crawling spiderlike out from the window and tangling in the red—no, the creature is the source of the red. It's her hair. She's . . . she's *human*.

Headfirst, the woman travels down her own hair, her arms and legs fastened around it as she rapidly slithers lower, descending faster than her hair is ascending. I gape, struggling to understand how she's accomplishing the feat.

I spy a large hook at the side of the window. A chunk of her hair is looped around it, forming a tether in case she falls. While some of the hair is anchored to the hook, the bulk of it continues to rise, being sucked up through the window. Perhaps the tower contains a pulley system that draws up her hair.

The woman is clad in black from her long-sleeved, form-fitted woolen shirt to her slim woolen leggings. Her feet are bare. Her face is feral. That animalistic expression is why I didn't recognize her at first.

"Fiora?" Disbelief scrapes across my voice.

Hanging in the hair on my left, Axel shakes his head. "It can't be."

Fiora Winther was one of the first villagers to be Lost in the Forest Grimm, only four months after my mother went missing. She was always reclusive, like her hermit father, but unlike him, she did venture from home when necessary. She came to our sheep farm on occasion to purchase spun wool or to barter her services for it. Fiora was a weaver, and Mother said she had an impressive loom that had been passed down over generations in her family. She had to be in her late twenties, and she'd been weaving since she was young. From all the nets in the trees, it seems like she is weaving still.

"Imagine her hair is tucked back in a cap," I tell Axel. Fiora was always a little shy of her stark red hair.

"And imagine it isn't several miles long?" he adds dryly.

I shrug with a bewildered nod. I have no idea how to explain its excessive length. But it doesn't matter. What matters is helping Henni. "Fiora!" I shout.

Continuing her descent upside-down, she has just reached

Henni's wrapped body. She clutches it possessively and peers at us below. I can't make out her expression. We're a quarter way up the tower, and she's only a few feet beneath the high window. The moment she hears me call to her, the red hair stops rising. "There is no one here by that name," she calls back. Her tone is savage and guttural, nothing like the rich soprano of her singing voice.

"I don't think it's her," Axel whispers.

"Who else could it be?" No other person in the village has that shade of hair. Maybe Fiora is guarding her identity for some reason. It might help to know that I'm not a stranger. "I'm Rosamund Thurn's daughter, Clara," I yell.

"I don't know you. Let go of my hair!" She shakes it hard, and Axel and I jostle and slam against the tower. I slide down a few inches and tighten my hold.

"Wait!" I shout as Fiora reaches to shake us loose again. "You may not remember me, but I remember you. I know you are Lost."

She freezes, her limbs harsh black lines in the distance. "You know what I've lost?" Her voice hitches, lifting a note.

Not exactly what I meant, so I hesitate to answer.

"Say yes," Axel hisses. Sweat beads at his temples. His grip on the hair isn't as secure as mine, and we're thirty feet off the ground. If he slips, he won't survive the fall.

"Yes!" I tell Fiora.

She stalls and crouches over Henni. Again, I'm reminded of a spider in the way she suspends upside down with her arms and legs bent at sharp angles. "Then you may join me," she finally says. She grabs Henni's cocooned body and takes it with her, climbing back up her hair. Fiora has become impossibly strong. Another mystery like her abundant hair.

She drags Henni in through the window. Fiora doesn't look

out to spare us another glance, but her red hair draws upward again, bringing Axel and me with it.

We glide up the tower. The closer we come to the window, the more my stomach tangles into hard knots. Once we make it inside, there's no getting out again, I realize, except by Fiora's hair.

It's all right, Clara.

I walked through a spider's web before we came here. I had my sign of good luck.

Or was it?

What if the web didn't mean I was about to meet a friend?

What if it meant I would be caught by a spider?

CHAPTER 11

There is no pulley in the stone tower. In fact, there is not much of anything besides Fiora's river of hair. When Axel and I crawl into the round room, I expect it to be stuffed to overflowing with her locks of red. But compared to how much I know of it exists, only a modest amount lies within.

The hair coils on the floor in a fifteen-foot circle, filling the span of the room as it spins like a whirlpool. Fiora isn't even touching it anymore. The hair moves as if it has a mind of its own.

Across the room is an open hatch on the floor, leading to whatever space exists below. The excess hair glides into it as more locks spill in from the window.

Fiora drags Henni inside a large fireplace to my left. Thankfully no logs are burning—the fireplace is empty—but that doesn't ease my nerves. The stonework surrounding the fireplace has been carved to look like the giant face of a wolf, and the opening of the hearth forms its gaping jaws.

The Fanged Creature from Grandmère's deck flashes to mind, except that that card represents *my* fate. Henni shouldn't be the one in danger. Nothing is going as I expected. The world is muddled and topsy-turvy, and my fortune is snarled up with it.

"I did not say the boy could enter." Fiora glares at Axel. She's settling Henni's cocooned body against the fireplace's inner corner, positioning my friend so she's sitting upright. Fiora crouches beside her like a vicious guardian.

I angle closer to Axel. "But he also knows what you lost."

Not missing a beat, he grins, his natural charm on full display. "Axel Furst," he says, introducing himself. "We never met in the village, but Ella told me you wove the muslin for her wedding veil."

Fiora angles her head, studying him with her cunning hazel eyes. If anything he's said rings a bell, she makes no sign of it. "I am Rapunzel. And if you know what I have lost, you may stay."

"Rapunzel?" Why would she call herself that? "Is that your middle name?"

Fiora's sharp gaze slices into me. "Rapunzel is my only name. It's what I *am*."

I sneak a glance at Axel to see if he has any clue to what she's talking about, but from the lines wrinkling his brow, he's just as confused as I am. His eyes seem to say, *I know what this woman has lost—her mind.*

Maybe she has. Maybe that's what nearly three years in the Forest Grimm does to a person.

I think of my mother and immediately regret the thought.

"Make yourself comfortable," Fiora says in her guttural, animalistic voice.

I scratch my arm and peek around the room as if a pair of chairs might suddenly materialize. With no furniture to sit on, Axel and I awkwardly settle on the carpet of hair, which continues to writhe as the last of it slips in from the window.

Eight feet away, I meet Henni's hyper-alert gaze and give her a small nod, my silent promise to help her escape this predicament. "Why doesn't the tower have any doors?" I ask Fiora, keeping my tone light and conversational. I school my features against the pain flowering through my crooked spine. Now that some of my adrenaline is wearing off, I feel the toll that all my racing and climbing has taken on my body.

"It once had doors." Fiora tucks a few stray hairs back into the coil around Henni's legs. "But I sealed it off with mud and stones."

"Why?"

"So I wouldn't lose anything," she replies, as if the answer is obvious. She returns her focus to Henni and leans closer, studying her eyes with rapt attention. A shudder chases through Henni's body.

"She isn't what you lost." I resist the urge to launch forward and peel her away from my friend.

Fiora whirls and bares her teeth at me. I can't help flinching. They aren't sharp like the incisors of the carved wolf hanging down from the mantel, but her expression is just as disturbing. "She's mine unless I say differently!" she spits out. Her words reverberate into the pitched ceiling.

"Clara, the hair," Axel whispers. He throws a pointed look at my left hand. Locks of red are sliding around my wrist like a manacle.

I quickly shake them loose and take a long breath to calm my nerves and regain my composure. "Her name is Henrietta Dantzer," I explain to Fiora. "Her parents own a dairy farm in Grimm's Hollow. Maybe you remember Ella Dantzer? Henni is her younger sister."

A hard crease forms between Fiora's scarlet brows. I've only confused her further. "She feels like what I lost," she says, setting a hand on Henni's wrapped-up shoulder. "My hair . . . it senses things."

"Does it?" I swallow, even more uncomfortable with sitting on the red hair now. It undulates on the floor like a sea monster's tentacles. "What does Henni feel like to you?"

Fiora searches for the right word. "Innocence?"

"You lost your innocence?" I ask gently.

"No!" Her limbs tense. A thick band of hair latches around

my knees. Then, just as suddenly as Fiora fired to anger, the hot emotion withers away, her posture wilting with it. "Maybe." She looks around the room like she's fighting to remember something else, and I discreetly wiggle out of her hair, which has loosened its grip. "But I think I lost more."

"Perhaps you had friends here," Axel suggests.

"Friends?" Fiora slithers a few inches closer to him. At his back, her hair crests like a wave and scoots him nearer. "Do you know their names?"

"Y-yes," he stammers, unnerved as more red locks nip at his legs, like a litter of kittens rooting for milk. "We, um . . . we all do." Flustered, he gives me a pleading look, unable to summon any of them in his current state.

I scour my brain to help. "There is Kasper von Weyler, Madlen Sommer, Ernst Engelhart." I rattle off names of some of the prominent Lost Ones, people Fiora might have known in Grimm's Hollow.

Her hair tugs me closer so I'm sitting beside Axel again. We're now five feet from her and Henni, where they perch inside the jaws of the wolf.

"And there's someone very special," I continue. "Rosamund Thurn." My heart strikes my rib cage with a painful thump, and my hand drifts over my pocket. Past the cloth of my dress, I feel the shape of the acorn and squeeze it tightly. "Rosamund looks like me, but she's taller and older and much more beautiful."

Axel makes a small noise that sounds suspiciously like a scoff. "What?" he says, put on the spot as I frown at him. "You don't give yourself enough credit." He waves a hand at me, the tips of his ears flushing pink. "You're pretty, Clara. You have to know that."

A flush of my own warms my face. *He thinks I'm pretty?*

Fiora creeps nearer, and her gaze darts between us. I roll

back my shoulders as if I can shrug off its intensity. "Rosamund worked with wool like you, and she—"

"I do not know this Rosamund!" Fiora snaps. A loop of her hair lashes over my mouth and binds it closed. "But the two of you . . . you also feel like what I lost."

I struggle to pull the hair free. Axel reaches to help. Once his fingers meet my cheeks, Fiora sighs, and her red hair falls away. Axel is left touching my face, one of his thumbs on my lower lip.

"Love and longing." Fiora tilts her head, slinking closer in her spiderlike stance. "That is what you two feel like."

If I wasn't blushing before, I'm sure I'm just as red as Fiora's hair now. "No, no, no." I burst into nervous laughter and pull away from Axel. He drops his hand at the same time. "Axel and I— He already has a— He should be married!"

"A year ago," Axel adds, scrubbing his palms against his trousers. "But I never— That was before—"

"He's like a brother to me," I cut in. "Or a cousin. Or someone distantly related who's just—"

"A really good friend," Axel finishes.

"We're both really, really good friends." I nod again and again, unable to stop my chin from bobbing. "Friends who love each other—because friends can love."

Where is Fiora's hair to bind my mouth shut again?

Behind Fiora, Henni's eyes bulge at me like I'm the one who's lost my mind.

Fiora's lip curls back into a snarl. "If you are not what I lost and you cannot help me find it, then I have no use for you." Her hair whirls around me and Axel and drags us toward the window. He clambers for our packs and hastily scoops them up.

"Wait, you should come with us!" I claw toward Fiora and

Henni. I owe it to my village to save as many Lost Ones as possible.

"I cannot leave my tower." Fiora's expression hardens. "What I've lost will come back. The forest moves, but my tower remains. It is the only way to find me."

The forest moves?

A brighter flare of panic surges through me. What if Axel and I weren't sleepwalking when we woke up in different places? What if the earth and trees shifted and separated us instead?

I fight the urge to barrage Fiora with more questions, but there's no time. Her tide of red hair already has Axel at the window. He braces himself against the stone frame so he isn't hurled outside.

I turn desperate eyes on Fiora. "You've forgotten about Henni! She needs us to stay!"

The hair coiled around Henni tightens, and she gives a stifled cry. Fiora skitters backward to crouch close beside her prey.

"She's the one who truly knows what you've lost," I go on in a rush, clamoring for any reason that can stall Fiora. "But she won't tell you unless we remain nearby. She's too shy, and we're her friends."

Fiora looks to Henni for confirmation, and Henni nods rapidly.

The hair fighting Axel and me lets up and settles back into its eerie writhing. Axel stumbles away from the window and catches his breath.

I slip closer to the fireplace. Its wolf eyes bore into me. "You'll have to loosen your hold on Henni so she can speak, of course," I tell Fiora.

The red hair unravels around Henni's mouth.

"She'll need to be completely unwrapped." I keep my voice

even. "Henni has a delicate disposition. She only complies when treated with gentleness and respect."

Fiora's hazel gaze sharpens, and her red hair whips near my face. A warning. I exhale slowly through my nose. "Rapunzel," I say, calling Fiora by the name she now claims, "please let down your hair. Release my friend."

A spasm scuttles through her brow. "And if I do, she will reveal what I have lost?"

"Yes," I promise. Henni's forehead shimmers with sweat. I've put her in an impossible situation. She's probably racking her brain for something useful to say to Fiora, so she can succeed where I've failed. With any luck, she won't have to say anything.

I dart a glance at Axel, and he nods, creeping backward toward the flickering end of Fiora's hair. It skims the outer edge of the whirling red circle.

Fiora stands tall. Her flaming hair billows down the length of her body. She extends a hand to Henni. The cocoon binding my friend loosens and drops away.

Henni pushes to her feet on shaking legs. She accepts Fiora's hand. Fiora doesn't let go. She steps disturbingly close. Their noses are almost touching.

"Henrietta Dantzer," Fiora says, "you will tell me what I have lost." A threat, a plea, a prayer.

Henni's face leaches of color. "You . . . um . . . you've lost . . ."

"My friend would have an easier time if she were closer to us," I tell Fiora as I inch backward, nearer to Axel. "I warned you she was timid."

Fiora reluctantly lets go of Henni's hand. Henni treads away like she's tiptoeing on razor-thin ice. Ribbons of red hair slither after her.

From behind me, Axel slips a knife into my hand—*my* knife from the small size of its hilt.

My heart kicks faster. My gaze flits to the wolf's eyes and sharp teeth above the fireplace. *Remember your role,* it seems to say, as if it's the Fanged Creature come to life. *I mete out death, not you.*

Henni reaches my side. A small whimper escapes her.

I pull her into a one-armed hug. "It's all right." I rub her back as I toss Fiora a calm smile.

She watches us unblinkingly, her body tensed.

"Go on and tell her," I urge Henni.

Her knees knock against me. "Um . . ."

I shoot Axel an urgent look. Whatever he's planning can't wait another second.

In a rush, he loops the end of Fiora's hair several times around his wrist. "Hold on!" he hisses.

"To what?" Henni blanches.

"Anything!"

She clutches me tighter. Axel grabs me by the waist. He wraps a thick band of hair around Henni and me. He jerks us to the window.

"What is this?" Fiora's hair fans wildly behind her. "You promised me—"

"You've lost yourself," I confess. "I'm sorry. We don't know how to help you."

A cry of unadulterated fury rips out of her throat. Her hair thrashes like venomous snakes.

Axel quickly wraps more hair around the hook at the window.

A separate lock of red strikes Henni. It swiftly coils around her neck. I grab it and cut it away.

Axel drags us onto the window ledge. A storm of hair flies after us. I hack at anything red. Fiora charges forward. Her eyes are pits of hellfire.

"Jump!" Axel shouts. I try to, but my shoes are already lifting off the ledge. He and Henni have done all the work. We hurtle backward. Time seems to slow.

Fiora reaches for Henni's neck—this time with her bare hands.

My knife whips up. Raw instinct takes over.

I throw the blade, and we tumble from the tower.

CHAPTER 12

ir rushes past me. All my blood is in my head. My thoughts race and trip over each other.

The hair is too long. It won't catch our fall.

We're going to die. We'll be dead like Fiora.

Dead? Did I kill her?

I'm cursed.

I'm the curse.

As we fall, we swing toward the tower. *Slam!* Our three bodies smack the stones and crash in a tighter tangle of hair and limbs.

"Grab the ivy!" Axel shouts as we continue falling. He clutches a vine, and I scramble to do the same. Henni tries, but it's out of her reach.

The ivy slides through my grip. Axel loses hold of it too. We grope for more clusters. The effort slows our descent. We're no longer in a free fall.

"Liars!" Fiora calls down at us. "I'll kill you for deceiving me!"

She's still alive. A flood of relief washes through me. I'm not a murderer.

The ivy thins. Axel claws at the tower. I reach for a thick patch of moss. We're more than halfway down. Fiora crawls out of the window in a headfirst descent.

She doesn't make it far. She cries out and clutches her upper arm. I can't see the blood among the red of her hair, but I know she's bleeding. I remember where I lodged my knife.

I can't keep hold of the moss. Our plummet quickens. Fiora

climbs back to the windowsill. Grabs the hair on the hook with her uninjured arm. She yanks with her incredible strength.

Henni yelps as we jerk to an abrupt stop. Axel curses. We're fifteen feet from the ground. A dangerous drop. A fall that could break arms, legs, backs, necks. But we have to risk it. I glance at Axel. He surveys the ground and gives a small nod. He's in agreement with me.

Fiora starts tugging us up by her hair. I no longer have my knife. Luckily Axel has his—and he's already thinking ahead. He throws down our packs and saws his blade through the hair encircling the three of us.

I catch Henni's eye. "Keep grabbing for ivy, moss, and stones to slow your fall."

"You'll land fast," Axel adds. "Protect your head, keep your muscles loose, and bend your—"

Henni shrieks as she drops. I'm also slipping loose. I grapple for the hair, for Axel, for anything. I don't want to crash on top of her. But my fingers throb. All my strength is spent.

I drop. My cape flies in my face. I wrestle with it, blinded. Panic closes off my lungs. A cog in my brain whirs just in time to remind me of Axel's instructions. I loosen up. Tuck my arms around my head. Bend my—

I land in a heavy thud and flop to the side, groaning. My muscles pang. Bones scream. My crooked spine throbs relentlessly. But nothing snaps or breaks. I gingerly sit up and pull my cape out of my eyes.

Henni crawls out of a big leafy bush that broke her fall. Lucky girl. But where is—?

"Watch out!" Axel yells, still hanging in the red hair. He lets go, and I scamper away just before he hits the ground.

His landing is a thing of beauty—agile, fluid, acrobatic. Nimbly, he rolls up to his feet and brushes the dirt from his trousers and sleeves.

I gawk at him, a little dizzy in the head. "You should perform for the village."

He doesn't pause to chuckle or even grin. He grabs our packs. Tosses one at Henni. Yanks me up. "Are you all right?" I open my mouth to say yes, but he doesn't wait for an answer. "Run!" He shoves me in the back, unwittingly jostling my sore spine. I clench my teeth against the pain, and we race away.

Fiora's hair blasts from her tower window, a starburst of red.

A string of foul words tumbles from Axel's mouth. We pick up speed and launch in a different direction from the way we came.

I scan the landscape for a means to protect ourselves, but all I find are trees. Climbing them won't help. Fiora's hair is too adept in branches.

Strands of red flood after us, a blinding deluge of crimson. They'll reach us all too soon.

The ground dips like we're headed toward a gully. A faint roar rises on the air. *Water.*

Axel and I exchange a desperate glance. "A river?" he asks.

I nod, though I can't be sure. "It could move faster than Fiora's hair."

We alter course and aim for the rushing sound. It's growing louder. Hope surges through my breast.

A flash of red lashes out at Axel. He whirls and tries to knock it aside with his pack, but the hair swiftly latches on to the straps and tears it away from him.

He lunges for it, but I grab his arm. "Let it go!"

Henni screams. She's fallen to the ground. A lock of red hair has her shackled by the ankle. Axel draws a knife from his belt. Cuts her free.

"Keep running, Clara!" he shouts as he helps her up.

I do as he says, but only because the river sounds close. I'll find a safe place for us to enter. A bank or a shallow spot of—

Fur and teeth crowd my vision. A large creature springs into my path. I gasp and jerk backward. My heart pounds a hailstorm in my chest.

The Grimm wolf.

She's seven feet away. Fangs bared. Hackles raised. Tail stiff. An attack stance. She gives a low, throaty growl that reverberates through my bones.

I shouldn't run from a predator, but Fiora's hair is too close. It hisses through the grass like a nest of snakes.

I bolt left and cut a diagonal line for the river. I don't want the wolf seeing my friends. She might chase them instead. I have to draw her away.

She snarls and leaps after me.

I race as fast as I can. The river comes into view. A tree with a low branch hangs over the rushing whitecaps. I charge for the tree, grab the branch, and lug myself onto it. Wolves aren't afraid of the water. The tree is safer.

The Grimm wolf pounces for the branch, and her jaws snap at me. I scramble toward the end of the limb. It looks sturdy enough to hold me. Maybe I can—

Crack! The branch breaks in the middle. I'm submerged in icy water and paw wildly for the surface.

I emerge and cough for breath. The Grimm wolf remains on the bank, but I barely catch a glimpse of her. The current is too fast. My cape drags me under. I kick hard, struggling to rise again. My grappling hands finally seize the fallen branch. I pull my head above water and drape my arms over the limb. The rapids wash me farther downstream.

"Clara!"

Axel.

I manage a glance behind me. He and Henni have also jumped in the river. They're a few yards behind me. Fiora's hair thrashes after them, but I was right about its speed. It isn't as fast as the water.

My friends catch up to me on the current. I share the branch with them. It's eight feet long and buoyant enough to keep the three of us floating.

I choke on a mouthful of water and spit it out. My body shakes, but my blood rages hot. I imagine the Grimm wolf watching from a distance and grind my teeth together.

I'm not dying today.

CHAPTER 13

I hang my soaked dress on the branch of an ash tree near the riverbank. If I squint and stand back, the linen doesn't look wet anymore. It's easy to imagine the skirt and sleeves are longer, the cornflower blue isn't faded, and my mother's necklace of rose-red glass beads hangs above the laces that tie the front of the bodice together.

I picture Mother in this same dress that used to be hers. The top half of her sable hair is twisted away from her face and fastened at the back, the same way I wear mine. She smiles with her head tipped to the side. Her gaze sees through me, understands me.

Do not fret, dear heart, she seems to say. The words she told me as a child before giving me the acorn from the Grimm oak. It's what I continue to imagine her telling me. She doesn't want me to worry. She believes I'll find my way through any challenge. I can find her, save her, and then she can return home.

But how?

A twig snaps to my left, and I startle. But it's not the wolf, only Axel.

He grins, though his brows draw together. "Are you all right?"

I nod and massage my lower spine. My S-curve has had too many adventures lately.

"How is your back holding up?" Axel asks.

"It will be fine as long as we can take a small break from falling down towers, racing away from wolves and violent hair, and swimming through rapids."

"I could do with a break from all of that too." He chuckles, and I try to avert my eyes from his bare chest, and the way the taut muscles of his abdomen flex as he laughs.

The only thing he's wearing are his cropped linen pants, undergarments that are wet like the chemise I shiver in beneath my red cape. He also keeps his red scarf looped around his neck. Whether our red rampion–dyed clothes are drenched or dry, we don't dare to remove them. What if the forest will expel us, even though we're well past the border? Or we become Lost without the rampion's protection? Can it even help against that possibility?

I wish Mother had written a letter to explain all the rules of the red flower when she hid the cape inside her mattress.

"Let me help," I say to Axel, and break off twigs from the ash tree with him. We need to keep the campfire burning. It's been hard to find any wood in the forest that isn't green. There are no fallen branches or dead trees here. This ash is the only one we've come across. The trunk is split and most of the limbs are charred. It must have been struck by lightning.

An hour ago, when we first saw the tree, we finally dragged ourselves out of the river after floating down it for several miles. A dead tree represents either death or running out of time, but the thought of sleeping in the warmth of a fire tonight overshadowed any of my worries over bad omens. I already know I'll die in the Forest Grimm, and I could tell myself I'm short on time without a leafless tree to remind me.

Our food supply is running low, not helped by the fact that Axel lost his pack and that I wasn't planning on another person joining us on this journey. Henni may have thought to bring a sewing kit, but she didn't plan much in the way of edible things, just a couple wedges of cheese and a crust of Hollow bread— similar to what I've brought but in far less quantity.

Now, thanks to the river, both of our bread supplies have

turned to mush. At least we have plenty of drinking water, though I haven't taken a sip since we came ashore. I drank half the river trying to navigate the rapids.

"I think I'll sleep over here tonight," Henni announces. She's twelve feet away and hiding behind a large shrub. "I'm not so c-cold."

"You'll do no such thing." I stride to the campfire between her shrub and the ash, and set down my bundle of twigs beside it. "Your teeth are chattering so loudly, everyone in Grimm's Hollow could hear you. Besides, the sun is setting. The air will get even cooler."

"But I'm only wearing my chemise," Henni hisses.

"Same as me."

"You have your cape! I only have my kerchief. I'm indecent!"

"Don't worry, Henni." Axel ambles over to join me by the campfire. "I'll keep my back turned for the rest of the night. You have my word."

The shrub rustles as Henni deliberates. "What if you hear a sudden noise in the forest, and you accidentally peek?"

Her voice is wobbling now, and with Henni, a wobble is just short of a sob. She's had a hard enough day as it is without having to worry about privacy. An idea pops to mind. "What was that?" I glance at Axel, who has said nothing. "That's a wonderful idea!"

"What is?" he murmurs.

"Henni, Axel has just offered to wear his scarf as a blindfold."

"He did?"

"I did?"

I clap a hand over his mouth. "Whatever makes you comfortable, he says."

"Oh, thank you, Axel." Her wobble fades away. "You're a true and honorable friend."

"The most honorable I know," I whisper with a wink, and unclamp his mouth.

His eyelids narrow, and he shakes his head at me. "You're an evil person, Clara Thurn."

I grin, banishing his halfhearted insult with a wave of my hand. "I'm sure you would have offered her the same." I reach for the scarf around his neck. "I just beat you to it."

I untie his scarf, careful to keep it touching his body as I spin him around and wrap the wool around his eyes. He grumbles, but I don't let it ruffle me. I see the curve at the corner of his mouth, a smile he's fighting to tamp down. Besides, Axel truly is the most honorable person I know. I'm sure he's happy to help Henni be at ease tonight.

I guide him to sit by the campfire and settle beside him. Reassured he's blindfolded, Henni emerges from behind her shrub to join us. We share our mushy bread, nibble on wet cheese, and let the heat from the flames dry our undergarments and river-cold bones. I silently bless the waterproof pouch that kept my flint kit dry so we could light this fire in the first place.

When the stars freckle the sky and the horns of the waxing crescent moon point down at us, fatigue gets the better of me and loosens my tongue. "I could have killed her," I murmur.

Axel stops sharpening his knife against a river stone, a dangerous activity for any other person who couldn't see, although he makes the task look effortless. "Fiora?"

I nod, though I'm starting to think of her as Rapunzel. The Fiora I knew wasn't anywhere to be found in the hostile woman we met in the tower. "My knife could have hit her heart or throat or—" I swallow and wrap my cape tighter around myself.

"She was trying to kill me, Clara," Henni says, touching her neck with her fingertips. She's sitting across the fire from me and Axel, still keeping a little distance from him. "You saved my life."

I force a fleeting smile. She's only trying to comfort me. I'm sure Henni is grateful to be alive, but I know her sensitive heart. If I had indeed killed Fiora, Henni would have cried for days. And when she had later returned to Grimm's Hollow, she would have painted a portrait of Fiora and given it to her father. She would have spent the rest of her life feeling guilty that her life was spared because another person died.

"You did the right thing," Axel says, also trying to reassure me. "And because you have a good soul, Fiora didn't die. Your blade flew true and matched your intent."

That sounds like a fabrication in children's stories with dragons and warriors and good always triumphing over evil. I don't know if I believe in it, but I like it. "So now I'm good and not evil?"

He cocks a grin. "You were never evil."

"Even if I think you look ridiculous with that scarf over your eyes?"

"Perhaps a little evil."

I laugh and bump his shoulder with mine.

Henni sits up taller and ties her kerchief around her wrist. Her hair has dried, and she starts braiding it into two plaits. "I think I've figured out why Fiora calls herself Rapunzel. Well, maybe not *why* she does, but I at least understand the connection."

Axel turns his ear to her, and I lean forward, swatting away a snapping ember.

"Rapunzel is another name for rampion," Henni goes on. "It was used in the old language. I read about it once in a book about herbs."

Leave it to Henni to know all the unusual names for plants in her avid quest to find the perfect paint ingredients. "I suppose that makes sense. Fiora's hair is the color of rampion—at least red rampion."

"Perhaps rampion is what made it red to begin with." Henni ties the end of her first braid.

"How do you mean?" Axel sets down his knife and stone.

"Well, the same midwife who delivered Fiora also delivered Ella and me, and she told Mother how *Fiora's* mother saved her pregnancy. Mother later told me the story."

"I'm already confused," Axel says.

Unfazed, Henni continues, lost in the memory. "When Fiora's mother was in danger of losing the baby, she went into the Forest Grimm and ate rampion. It helped the baby keep growing in her belly."

"Red rampion?" I ask.

"It had to be, although the midwife didn't say."

I think about it for a moment. "That was about the time that Fiora's mother made her one wish on *Sortes Fortunae* as well."

Axel and Henni don't comment, probably because they wouldn't know either way. The only reason I do is because of my obsession with the Book of Fortunes, always the means I've counted on to save Mother.

The council chamber in Grimm's Hollow holds a register of wish ceremonies, and I've visited there countless times to read it. It lists the villagers who have used their one wish on *Sortes Fortunae,* as well as the month and year of the occasion.

I used to dream of the day my own name would be written in the register, a kind of legacy I could leave behind after I died and Mother lived, my mark that my life meant something, even if I couldn't share what it was that I wished for. Wishes themselves aren't listed in the register. Everyone must abide by the rule that wishes remain secret.

"Maybe the wish Fiora's mother made was how to save her

baby," I muse, "and the book told her to eat red rampion." That makes sense. The Forest Grimm made the Book of Fortunes, and red rampion is also strongly connected to the forest's magic.

Axel shakes his blindfolded head. "If Fiora's mother told the midwife what she had wished for, the spell would have been broken. *Sortes Fortunae* would have reversed the wish, and Fiora would have died."

"What if Fiora's mother didn't tell the midwife?" Henni combs her fingers through the other half of her hair. "What if the midwife just saw her do it—return from the forest with the rampion and eat it?" She lifts a shoulder. "Whatever the reason, Fiora lived, and her hair is the same shade of red as your scarf and my kerchief and Clara's cape."

I gaze at the hair Henni hasn't started braiding yet. It looks so much longer when she wears it down, which she rarely does. "The rampion could have also made Fiora's hair grow long in the forest, just like it helped her grow in her mother's belly. The rampion's magic must be stronger here."

This is all speculation, of course, but for the most part, it adds up. I gnaw at my lip, still puzzled by one last mystery. "The only thing I don't understand is that red rampion is supposed to be protective. So why hasn't it protected Fiora *now*—as a woman? Here, in the forest? You saw her. She isn't the same person."

Fiora's words echo through my mind: *Rapunzel is my only name. It's what I am.*

Henni's brows scrunch up. "Maybe the red rampion isn't protective forever. Fiora has been in the forest for almost three years now. She's a cursed villager just like the rest of us. The forest must have figured that out at some point."

"You said it yourself last night, Clara," Axel adds gently. The firelight catches the sculpted lines of his jaw and the soft divot of an almost dimple on his chin. "The red rampion can't protect us from everything."

A finger of ice slides up my spine, despite the heat from the campfire. I shiver and burrow deeper in my cape.

Our conversation dwindles. With nothing more than our worries left to keep us awake, we stoke the fire one last time and prepare to go to sleep. Since Axel lost his bedroll along with his pack, the three of us lie down crosswise on the two remaining bedrolls and let our legs drape onto the grass.

I position myself between my friends like I did in the tree net, but this time my reason is to spare Henni the mortification of sleeping beside a boy while she's clothed only in her chemise, even if that boy is blindfolded.

I use a rope from my pack to tie our ankles together, my left one to Henni's, and my right one to Axel's. None of us wish to wake up in the morning separated from each other. We also consider tying our wrists together, but that seems excessive, and we'd like to be able to move at least some of our limbs in the night.

Axel and Henni fall asleep before I do. I fidget with the strings of my cape, unable to shut my eyes. The moon has shifted, and the dead ash tree blots out its light and paints eerie shadows in the forest beyond.

You're running out of time, Clara, I feel the ash telling me, unwilling to let me find comfort within the reach of its bad omens. *And the rampion can't protect you forever.*

CHAPTER 14

I wake up with my nose pressed to something soft and warm that smells of the breeze from the Forest Grimm when it wafts past the hedgerow of my family's sheep pasture—air that is clean with green wood and sharp with mountain pine.

Eyes closed, I breathe in deeper and discover subtler notes, honeyed and musky like beeswax, but also earthy like cedar oil rubbed into leather.

I sigh and open my eyes . . . and find my face nuzzled against Axel's bare chest.

I jerk upright and swipe the drool from the corner of my mouth.

Henni stirs, but not Axel. He's stone-cold asleep and lying on his side, still wearing his blindfold. The ends of his scarf are tangled around his face like he had a fight with them in the night. My fingers itch to smooth them down and, while I'm at it, trace the strong line of his jaw. Is his skin as warm there as the rest of his body?

My eyes drift over the length of him and linger at the ligaments near his hip bones. They dip at an angle and slide under the low-slung waistband of his linen pants.

Henni stirs, and I flinch slightly, tearing my gaze from Axel's torso. "Henni." I nudge her fully awake. "You should change before Axel wakes up. We ought to give him back his eyes today."

She doesn't need to be told twice. I untie the rope binding

our ankles, and she scurries off to grab her dress from one of the ash branches.

"Um, Clara?" she says after a few moments. "The shrub I undressed behind yesterday . . ."

"Mm-hmm?" I catch myself staring at Axel again. There's a pink mark on his chest from where my cheek pressed against it. It's shaped like half a heart.

"It's gone."

A good five seconds pass before I register what she said. I look to where the shrub was, on the other side of our campfire's charred remains. But it's no longer there.

A horrible sinking sensation trickles inside me like molten lead. I turn my head slowly and take in the rest of our surroundings. The dead ash tree and the river are still here, but nothing else looks the same. There's no copse of aspens behind the ash, no lone willow across the riverbank, no purple marsh orchids peeking up from the wild grass.

Fiora was right. The forest moves.

Which means my map—the map that was soaked in my pack but remained miraculously legible, the map I spread out last night to dry and pinned down with rocks so the breeze wouldn't steal it away—is completely obsolete.

No, no, no.

My breath goes shallow. I rub my hands down my face and rock back and forth. I thought I was close to finding our bearings. The river was a strong landmark. I hadn't solved which river it was—the Forest Grimm has three—but now I never will.

How will I find you, Mother? How will I point the way home?

"What's wrong?" Axel's voice croaks, groggy with sleep. He's peeking at me from a gap beneath his blindfold.

Henni gasps and darts behind the ash tree so she can continue changing in private.

I slide the scarf from Axel's eyes, slipping it up off his forehead. "You don't have to wear that anymore."

He takes in my miserable expression and pulls himself up on one elbow. I imagine what I must look like, my green eyes rimmed in red, my dark hair wild and tangled, and all the glow of hope in me lost.

"Bad dream?" he asks gently.

I choke on a humorless laugh. "I wish. Give me a nightmare. Dreams end. I can't wake up from this." I wave a hand at the surrounding forest.

His mouth parts as he absorbs all that has changed in the night.

"This is how they became Lost." I tuck my knees to my chest. "My mother, Ella, Fiora . . . every villager who disappeared here." I shake my head as pain crushes my heart. "How did I think it wouldn't happen to us?"

"Hey, now." Axel sits up and shifts closer, wrapping a strong arm around me. "We found a river. That isn't nothing. For one thing, it didn't move while we slept. That means we can depend on it for navigation. Plus we can drink and fish from it, which will keep us alive."

"I didn't come here just to survive."

He holds me tighter. "We'll find your mother, Clara."

I tuck my head sideways into the crook of his neck so he won't see my gathering tears. "How?"

"Put yourself in her shoes. She would have eventually found one of the rivers, like we did, and she would have stuck by it for the same reasons we're going to."

I gently bite at my lip, thinking through what he's saying. "Each of the rivers intersects with another at some point in the forest. In the northwest, Snow River feeds into Bremen River, and in the southeast, Bremen River feeds into Thrushbeard River."

"Exactly. We'll use the rivers as our new trail. If we stick to them, we'll eventually find everyone we're looking for."

"But Fiora wasn't by a river," I point out.

He shrugs. "She was close enough to one. Anyway, we shouldn't use her as an example. We all agreed she wasn't herself."

I give a small laugh, then immediately pinch my lips together. It isn't Fiora's fault that the forest drove her to insanity. Maybe I can still save her. Her strange hair and its magic must be somehow tied up in the curse. If I can find *Sortes Fortunae* and use my one wish to break it, perhaps Fiora's hair will return to normal and she won't be so violent.

"Finding the Lost Ones might not be the hard part," I concede. "The bigger problem is that none of these rivers lead back to Grimm's Hollow. How will you take everyone home?"

"We."

I give him a blank look.

"How will *we* take everyone home, you mean."

"That's what I . . ." I shake my head. "Yes, of course." I haven't told him about all the cards in my fortune. He only knows about the Pierced Swans and the Red Card, not about the Midnight Forest and the Fanged Creature.

He doesn't know I'll have to die.

He presses a kiss to the top of my head, and a shower of warmth prickles over me. I curl my toes in the grass against the urge to nuzzle closer to him. I remind myself what I told Fiora about Axel: *We're both really, really good friends. Friends who love each other.* I can't let his charm deepen my feelings. He's destined for Ella, and for reasons only fate knows, I need them as a pair to help me fulfill my journey.

"We've gotten this far," he says. "We'll figure out the rest when we get there."

I close my eyes and pretend I have more than one wish, and that I don't need the Book of Fortunes to grant it.

I wish that Axel is right.

CHAPTER 15

here are faces in the trees. They start to catch my attention toward the end of the second day as we continue following the river downstream. It's that time of evening when the light is scattering to dusk and it's easier to believe things I wouldn't think possible if the sun were still shining.

At first I wonder if my eyes are deceiving me. I'm tired and hungry and worried that we haven't seen another Lost One since Fiora. Maybe I'm inventing people out of sheer desperation. But why would I imagine their faces warped and their expressions twisted in agony? The knots and ridges on the trunks are their howling mouths, wrenched brows, and terror-stricken eyes.

Axel and Henni must not see them or they would have said something. I'm too afraid to speak about the faces myself for fear I'm descending into madness like Fiora.

When we go to sleep that night, we don't light a campfire. We're out of deadwood. "Deadwood" takes on a whole new meaning now that I wonder if dead people have become the trees. Ironic since those trees are alive, except for the ash struck by lightning. Or perhaps I'm wrong. Maybe the people in the trees are still living but trapped behind the bark.

Are any of them my mother?

The next day, my friends and I don't speak as much. Until now, any silence between us has been comfortable, but now the quiet strains, tearing stitch by stitch at the seams holding my confidence together.

The tormented faces aren't in every tree we pass. They like to hide behind unscathed oaks, proud larches, and noble firs. They're in the fringes of my vision, like they want me to turn and take a double look at them. I try not to. I trap my gaze on the river and will myself to believe my mother still has flesh and bones.

On the fifth day that we follow the river as our trail, we run out of food. We try to forage for berries, but all we come across are those from nightshade, lily of the valley, and black bryony—all poisonous. Some of the faces in the trees have crooked smiles now.

"We need to fish tomorrow," Axel says.

So far we've avoided fishing because it means a delay in traveling, and none of us are keen to eat fish raw, but today Henni had the thought of using pine cones to make a small campfire for cooking. Pine cones are normally only used as kindling, since they don't burn for long, but Axel suggested coating them in pine sap to help them burn longer. Hopefully long enough to bake brown trout.

I wake up the next morning to find Axel has already untied his ankle from mine. He's sitting six feet away and struggling to thread one of Henni's needles. I smile as I watch him. When he concentrates, he sticks his tongue out a little, and it's unabashedly adorable.

I prop myself up, one leg bent and the other straight; I'm still roped to Henni. The air is brisk, so I draw up my hood against the chill. "Are you sewing me a new dress?" I tease Axel.

He nods without blinking, keeping his gaze fixed on the eye of the needle. "It will have ruffles and bows and all the puffy bits girls like."

"Puffy bits?" I snort.

"Sleeves, skirts . . ." A grin flits about the corner of his mouth. "Don't pretend you don't know about the puffy bits."

"The only puffy bits I want are the ones I can eat." My stomach releases a timely growl, and I untie myself from Henni. "Please tell me we have pastries for breakfast."

"How about fish? This is going to be a hook once I bend the needle, and Henni's thread will be the line. All we need is a sapling for the pole."

"So then I don't get my dress?"

Ignoring me, he growls at the needle, muttering something unintelligible. "Care to help me thread this? I've been at it for the last quarter of an hour."

I crawl over and take a closer look. The movement sends a twinge of pain through my spine, but it fades as I adjust into a more comfortable position beside Axel. "That's because you need to lick the end of the thread."

"Lick it?"

"That really didn't occur to you?" A laugh tumbles out of me.

He struggles to come up with an excuse. "Well, it would have if I wasn't starving. My brain has started to eat itself."

I wiggle closer and give his arm a poke. "If you thread that needle, I'll tell you a secret," I say like it's a dare.

The blue of his irises narrows to suspicious slits. "What kind of secret?"

"The kind that will help fill your stomach faster."

He harrumphs like he doesn't believe me, but then relents, muttering, "Fine." He licks the thread. It slips through the eye of the needle with ease. He groans and laughs at himself. "I should have asked you how to do that forever ago."

"Or you could have asked if I'd brought any fishing tackle."

He freezes. "You didn't. You couldn't have. I know everything in your pack."

I rock back on my haunches. "You never peeked in my pocket tin?"

His mouth drops open. "The pocket tin? But it's painted with a woman dancing under the moonlight," he sputters. "I thought it was filled with . . . things girls need."

"Things girls need?"

"For personal reasons—personal times!" He waves a vague but exasperated hand through the air. "I don't know what you keep in there! It's none of my business!"

I throw my head back and roar with laughter.

Henni wakes up, her nostrils flaring with a wide yawn. "What's so funny?"

"Axel is," I answer promptly. He shoots me a glare, but his lips clamp against trying not to laugh with me. "He thought my tackle kit was a tin of 'things girls need.'"

He throws his arms up. "Paint a fish on it next time!"

"Girls can fish too, Axel." Henni levels him with a bleary-eyed stare, completely misunderstanding our conversation.

I'm laughing so hard now my stomach aches and I can barely sit upright. "You two are priceless. Never change."

"That's it. I've had enough." Axel rises from the ground. "I won't be laughed at another moment. Time to drive this madness out of you." He flashes a wicked grin.

"What are you—?"

He charges at me with his needle. I yelp and jump to my feet. He chases me around the clearing we've camped in, feigning like he's going to stab me. It doesn't stop me from laughing. I'm practically cackling now. "I'm not your pincushion!" I yell.

He's getting closer. He's always been the faster runner. But being small has its advantages.

I duck through a narrow gap in the underbrush and scramble out the other side. I'm farther from the river now, and the dense forest looms beyond. I race forward recklessly, a broad smile on my face.

It's the most wonderful release to let my worries fly away for a moment and pretend I'm just an ordinary girl playing with a charming boy in a forest that's not enchanted or haunted or destined to kill me.

I rush past a few trees and weave around them, looking for a trunk thick enough to hide behind. Twelve yards ahead is the perfect tree—a sprawling sycamore. I bolt for it.

"You can't escape me!" Axel shouts. His voice is closer than I expected. I hurry faster.

I'm almost to the tree. I squeal, giggling like a child. I'm just about to dash behind the trunk, when Axel's hand grazes my shoulder. Startled, I shriek and spin around. He collides into me, and we tumble to the grass.

He's lying on top of me, the full pressure of his body flush against mine, chest to chest, hip to hip, legs to legs. We pant, laughing for a moment, a tangle of red with my cape and his scarf, which has fallen across my eyes. "Is this your revenge for the blindfold?" I demand.

"Maybe." He chuckles and pulls it off my face. "But your eyes are too beautiful to be hidden, Clara."

My breath catches in a tiny hiccup. The last of my laughter dies in my throat, swallowed by the sudden skipping of my heart. His blue eyes are shaded by his tousled locks of golden hair. He's gazing at me in a way he's never looked at me before, and the weight of it is heavier and warmer than his body.

Before I know how to react or what to think or feel, or even how to draw air back inside me, he presses his lips to each of my eyes, first the left one then the right, and it's the gentlest, feather-soft, impossibly tender touch. It's sunlight and rainfall and dusting-sugar snow. It's every season and range of feelings wrapped into one powerful sensation. I shiver with it, the flurry rushing up my spine and across my shoulders and down to the tips of each finger . . . fingers that tug at his sleeves and pull him closer, even though we're as close as we've ever been.

His mouth hovers lower, but then he swallows and draws back, his gaze searching my face like he wants to make sure he hasn't crossed some kind of boundary with me, some line of ashes around my heart that I don't want him to trespass. But if there is one, I can't find it. My mind is underwater. My pulse thrashes through every hidden space of my body. Why has he only ever been a friend to me? Why have I never allowed him to be more? The reason is too slippery to grab hold of.

His eyes slowly lower to my lips again. I arch my back, desperate to reach him. I want his kiss more than I've ever wanted anything. I want his mouth on my mouth and his hands in my hair and the heat of him to envelop every inch of my skin.

"Axel." His name tumbles from me in a murmur I didn't mean to utter. I can't help it. I'm trembling, yearning, aching for him. Something I've kept asleep in me is wide awake now, a storm of emotions and sensations I don't understand. The only truth is I want more.

He caresses my cheek with the back of his fingers. He bends his head toward mine. His lips are close . . . so close I feel his breath fan my face.

A flicker of red teases the corner of my vision. It isn't my cape or his scarf. Some dread feeling inside me beckons to turn to it, to capture it fully with my eyes.

I give in to the almost palpable urge. It's stronger than even my hunger for Axel.

I turn. Look. What I see crashes down on me harder than a mountain avalanche.

A veil. Caught in the woody fingers of the sycamore above.
A veil of gauzy red muslin.
A wedding veil.
Ella's veil.

CHAPTER 16

"What's wrong?" Axel asks. When I can't muster any words, he turns to see what I'm staring at. Every muscle in his body hardens to marble. He slips off me, and I sit up at once, putting six inches of clean space between us.

Ella.

Beautiful and graceful Ella. Axel's true love Ella. Axel's intended bride Ella.

She didn't exist when his lips brushed my eyes and his fingers stroked my cheek. But she's everywhere now. In this tree, in *every* tree, every blade of grass and flower petal. She's this very forest for Axel. He came here for her. How could I have forgotten that, even for a moment?

"What are you two doing?" My shoulders wilt at the sound of Henni's voice. Ella is the very forest for her too.

"We . . ." My voice is cracked glass. Henni looks at me like she doesn't know me. She's carrying our packs as if Axel and I were going to run off without her. "We fell."

I fell. I wanted Axel just now. I wanted him more than I thought I'd wanted anything. But my head was muddled and my blood was on fire. How could I want him more than the reason I came here?

For me, this forest is my mother. She's the one I'm destined to save. She's why I've lived as long as I have so that she can live longer.

"We found Ella's veil." Axel stands, his posture soldier-stiff. "Clara found it, that is."

Henni doesn't move. Doesn't act surprised. Doesn't say anything. She's been my best friend for as long as I can remember, and now I can't read her at all. I don't know if she's shocked or angry or hurt or even indifferent. Did she see me almost kiss Axel? Or is something else bothering her? Is she worried something terrible has happened to Ella?

"I'll get the veil," I tell her. I push to my feet and shift farther away from Axel. "You can give it back to Ella once we find her."

Henni's expression remains flat and unresponsive.

I turn to the trunk of the sycamore. I search for a knot or a low branch, something I can use to start my climb. In the whorls and lines of the bark, a pair of accusing eyes glares back at me. I jump with a sharp gasp.

"Clara?" Axel closes the distance between us by a step.

I mask my reaction, pretending I just got a twinge of back pain. "I'm all right."

No, I'm losing my mind.

"I can lift you up," he offers. He moves closer. His steps are cautious, his voice tentative.

"I can do it."

"You should at least—"

I flinch when he touches my shoulder.

"—tighten the strings of your cape." His hand falls away. "They're coming loose."

I don't tighten the strings. I climb the tree as quickly as possible. I can't bear to feel Axel's nearness. Even the air is full of him, charged with lightning energy that raises the hair on my arms.

The red veil is four tiers of branches up the tree. It hangs by two budding offshoots of a sturdy branch, like a sheet held by clothespins. It's as if the sycamore is mocking me, holding a blatant reminder on display of the girl Axel loves.

And I'm glad he does, I remind myself. I need the Pierced Swans to come together if I'm going to be the Changer of Fate, and I have to be or this whole journey is in vain.

I reach the veil and quickly pluck it away. The red muslin is cool to the touch, but it may as well be blistering hot for how difficult it is to hold against my skin.

I descend the tree as fast as I climbed it. I present the veil to Henni like a peace offering, even though I can't pinpoint why I feel the need to make amends.

She shuffles back as I approach, though her shoulders hitch up when she finally looks at the veil. A little squirm runs through her, but then her jaw hardens. She drops my pack on the ground. "You can carry the veil."

It's the last thing I want to do, but I press my lips together and nod. I kneel and stuff the veil inside my pack, then fidget with the cinch, my eyes lowered. "Can we go for a walk?" I ask. Walking is all we've been doing for days, but maybe if Henni is alone with me she'll tell me why—

"Clara, don't move!" she whispers. My eyes snap up. What could have happened so suddenly? Henni is shaking, and her face has gone ashen. Her gaze fixes on something behind me.

I break into a cold sweat. It could be anything. A lock of red hair snaking after me. Trees with faces creeping up in broad daylight. But I know it isn't. I know it like I knew the Fanged Creature would always be in the cards Grandmère drew for me.

I slowly pivot on my knees. I can't have my back to a predator.

Across the thirteen feet separating us, the eyes of the Grimm wolf are riveted to mine. Everything in the way she holds herself shows sheer dominance. Her head is stretched high, her neck arched, her ears perked and stiff. Her stare is direct and pointed, and her irises have an unnatural violet cast.

She's following me, hunting me, the harbinger of my untimely death. And she means to deliver it.

Axel hasn't seen her. He's in the path between the wolf and me. With his head downcast and his posture withered, his hair falls in his eyes. He scuffs one of his boots against a gnarled root of the sycamore.

"Axel," I hiss. He doesn't hear me. He's probably thinking of Ella and feeling even guiltier than I am.

"Axel!" My voice bleats a fragment louder. Still, he doesn't look up. His head droops even lower. His neck is horribly exposed. The Grimm wolf's jaws could sink into him in an instant. If she senses he's in the way of what she wants—me—she'll kill him and toss him aside for the vultures.

The wolf's legs tense. Her fur bristles. She's readying to make a move.

"Axel!" My voice cracks with my whisper-shout.

His head jerks up. The wolf bares her canines. Axel turns to follow my gaze. It happens too fast. There's no time to warn him to act slowly. He jumps at the sight of the wolf.

The wolf springs.

"Stop!" I lurch to my feet. My cape snags on my knee. It ripples off my shoulders.

A sycamore root lashes up from the ground. Coils around my waist. Yanks me in the air.

"Clara!" Henni screams. Axel whirls back to me. The wolf knocks him aside and lunges, eyes latched to mine.

The root throws me ten feet away from the tree. I land on my side. Scramble for my cape. No, I need a weapon. The wolf is almost upon me. I grope the ground for a stick, a rock, anything.

The earth rumbles. In a flash, it rises and shoves me backward. A thick branch swings for my face. I roll away, gasping for breath. The forest is trying to expel me. Kill me. Unless the wolf kills me first.

She leaps at me, jaws wide. Another branch swoops. Tethers to my right arm. It snatches me from the wolf's path.

I'm twenty feet in the air now. A deep groaning thunders from the ground. The sycamore completely pulls itself up from the earth, its roots surfacing like great legs.

My friends race around the tree and try to reach me. Henni has my cape. Axel wields his knife. The wolf prances below me, jaws snapping. She's waiting for me to drop.

The branch that holds me retracts like a coiled-tight spring. It's going to release any moment, shoot me like an arrow from a crossbow.

I clamber with my free hand and grab an offshoot of the branch. I bite it hard. I'd rather fall than be thrown.

The branch jerks, dropping me at once. I catch another branch as I plummet. It spasms and writhes out of my grip. I tumble down farther, grabbing branch after branch, clumsily breaking my fall with whatever I can.

I'm at the lowest tier of branches now. I desperately hug the trunk to keep hold of the tree. The wolf growls below me, pacing.

Henni sneaks up. Balls my cape and hurls it at me. I let go of the trunk to grab it. The branch I'm on bucks wildly. I'm knocked sideways. I can't catch the cape. It glances off the tree. The sycamore rocks and twists. I grope for the branch, but miss.

I fall. Hit the ground. My crooked back seizes. Henni shrieks my name.

Flashes of the wolf and Axel streak through my vision. His knife is raised as the wolf pounces for me. She snags the skirt of my dress in her teeth.

Axel flings himself at the wolf. A root lifts to trample me. It hurls him aside in the process. The wolf drags me a few feet away. I claw at the ground, but the wolf is stronger.

Past the tall grass, a large burrow hole comes into view. The wolf yanks me inside of it. I desperately cling to the earthen walls of the opening. "Axel!" I cry. "Henni!"

Above me, a massive root overshadows the hole and lowers like the foot of a giant.

With a deafening stomp, it slams down and seals me inside with the wolf.

CHAPTER 17

’m in the den of the Grimm wolf. She's brought me here to feast on me. I can't see anything in my stifling surroundings. The darkness is absolute. I muffle a cry as the wolf drags me deeper into her burrowed tunnel.

I wasn't supposed to die like this. Not without saving my mother first.

Thin roots slide over my face like spider legs. I claw at them, trying to find something to hold on to, but they break away in clusters and rain dirt over me.

The tunnel levels out. The wolf is now dragging me horizontally. My shoes are in her mouth, my ankles in her jaws. I try to kick, but I can't wrestle free. I twist up to punch her snout, but the tunnel abruptly narrows. I'm knocked flat on my back again.

Reserve your strength, Clara. Soon this tunnel will open to the heart of the den. I'll have room to properly fight—or quickly die.

I don't know how long or far the wolf takes me. Time is a blur of frantic heartbeats and rampant heartache. What if I never see Mother again? Or Henni and Axel?

What if I'd let him kiss me under the sycamore tree?

At last, the tunnel opens, but not into a closed den. There's light here, although it's heavily shrouded by cloistering spruce and pine. We're aboveground in a hollow of the forest. The air is cool and damp, and red-spotted mushrooms surround the edges of the grassy slopes. We must be near water.

Something whistles past me. A spear. The wolf drops my ankles and dodges it. I hurriedly push to my feet. The wolf comes at me again. Another spear darts from the shadows. The wolf ducks, and the spear whooshes by her.

"Have you come to join my menagerie?" an airy and high-pitched voice calls. A woman steps out from the shadows, but only partway. I can't make out her face. She's holding another spear, crudely made from a stick and what looks like carved bone. "I would love another friend."

I don't know if she's speaking to me or the wolf, so I press my lips shut.

"Last chance." The woman takes aim at the wolf.

The wolf snarls and draws up to her full height.

The woman doesn't shrink away. Her slim fingers tighten around her spear shaft. She throws the spear, fast and fierce. Somehow the wolf is faster. She springs away and darts out of the hollow. The woman chases after her, leaving me alone.

I remain tense for several moments, expecting the wolf to leap out from the dark thickets and return for me, but none of the trees stir with sounds of her.

A huge breath of relief purges from my lungs, though a pinch of anxiety remains trapped inside. Who was that woman? Not my mother, that's a certainty. I only caught a shadowed glimpse of her, but it was enough to sense the difference. Mother has an unbridled spirit that manifests in every movement. This woman was more polished and graceful. I saw that even as she sprinted away.

I think of any Lost Ones who might have such a bearing. Could she be Ivana Hirsch or Marlis Glathorn? I shift from foot to foot, awaiting her return. She *will* return . . . won't she? I imagine she'd be glad to find another soul in the forest.

The woods remain silent except for the sound of a thin breeze hissing through the leafy branches and wild grass of the hollow.

My anxiety ratchets up a notch, a clock wound too tight. If the woman doesn't return, what will I do? How will I find Axel and Henni? The burrow hole the wolf dragged me through is sealed off on the other end.

I reach to close the front of my cape—it's become a kind of shield—but my hands grasp nothing. The cape is gone, I remember. I never tightened the strings like Axel warned me to.

I wrap my arms around myself, feeling naked. I pace the hollow, rub my sore spine, and crane my neck to spy any exit that looks promising—a worn path, a stream, even a deer trail—but I can't see anything in the surrounding thicket. *I'll count to a thousand,* I tell myself. *Then I'll venture off on my own.*

When I reach 793, something flickers in the corner of my vision. I slowly revolve, bracing myself for the worst. But no gray fur flashes from behind the trees. It's not the wolf. It can't be the woman either. The person racing by is too short.

It wouldn't be a child. No children were ever Lost. The Forest Grimm had the kindness to spare them that fate. All the Lost Ones are sixteen or older. Old enough to make a wish on the Book of Fortunes, if that were still possible.

I creep forward. "Hello?"

The little person halts and hides behind a pine tree.

"Do I know you?" I rock forward on my toes to step closer. "I'm Clara Thurn from Grimm's Hollow."

No response comes. Maybe it's not a person, but an animal . . . an unusually large hare that I mistook for someone with two legs. I'm about to turn away and leave the poor creature in peace when a small voice finally peeps, "Mama says I shouldn't speak with strangers."

I stifle a gasp. It *is* a child. A boy, from the clear tenor of his tone. I inch nearer. "No one is a stranger in Grimm's Hollow."

"We're not in the village."

"But surely you're from there." The other mountain villages aren't within walking distance.

Behind the pine, a head pops out covered by a mop of glossy brown curls. Two large hazel eyes clap on mine. He's a beautiful thing, from what I can see of him, like a fairy child from Grandmère's book of children's stories.

I'm ten feet away now, but I still strain to see him clearly. His form is blurry in the shrouded daylight. From his height, I'd guess he's seven or eight years old. I can't remember ever seeing him in Grimm's Hollow, though something about him feels familiar.

His lips mash together as he studies me without blinking. "Do you still know the way back home?"

"Yes." *Kind of.* "I'm the tiniest bit lost at the moment."

He shuffles out into the open, his shoulders slumped. "That's what they all say."

"They?" Has he met other villagers in the forest? "Was that your mother who chased after the wolf just now?"

"Mama was afraid of wolves." He idly kicks at the wild grass, but he's so slight in build that he barely stirs the blades. "What happened to your red cape?"

My fingers clutch the base of my neck where the cape's strings should be. "How do you—?"

"Red for rampion. Red like the color of roses." His voice falls into a singsong rhythm, like he's reciting a nursery rhyme.

"You know about red rampion?" I squint harder, still struggling to see him better. It must be my vision that's hazy, not the light, because the boy remains slightly out of focus.

He nods and hops over a stone. "The first to grow forever holds the seed of magic. That's what he told me."

"He?"

"The oldest tree. He says he was once a man, but no one besides me believes him. No one hears him like I do."

The haunting faces I've been seeing in the forest jump to mind. Perhaps I didn't imagine them after all. "Red rampion was the first to grow? Is that what he meant? Grow where?"

"The Forest Grimm, of course. I know a poem about it. Would you like to hear it?"

"Um . . . yes." I'm having a hard time keeping up with everything the boy is saying. I'm too distracted by his restlessness. He doesn't hold still. He circles me, jumps to swat dragonflies, and scours the ground like he's searching for insects.

"I learned this all by myself," he says. "But I guess I couldn't help it. The oldest tree wouldn't stop saying the words." He puffs out his small chest. "Are you ready?" I nod.

When magic kissed the earth, it grew a red flower,
Which woke up the land and granted it power.
But a curse be upon those who wrong this domain,
For when blood soaks the soil, magic shall become bane.
Forgiveness comes slowly after such insurrection,
But the first to grow here will offer protection.

The boy stares at me expectantly after he finishes, the edges of him continuing to blur and streak in my vision. "Didn't you like it?"

"I . . . yes."

"You didn't clap. And 'insurrection' is a big word."

"S-sorry." I give him a round of applause, but it's faint and clumsy. My hands have started shaking. I finally recognize the boy. I saw a miniature portrait of him once, in Axel's uncle's house of all places. It sat in a dusty corner beside another framed picture, this one of a woman, Axel's aunt. She had passed away years before Axel came to the village. "Are you Oliver Furst?"

"No one calls me Oliver." He wrinkles his nose. "I'm just Ollie."

"Ollie," I repeat, speechless. I see too much of Axel in the boy now, how his hair might have been curlier like Ollie's as a child, even though Axel's hair is golden and Ollie's is chocolate brown. Their eyes are also similar, just different colors.

The two of them are cousins—a cousin Axel never met because by the time he came to live in Grimm's Hollow with his uncle, Ollie was already dead.

Icy frost stabs my veins and raises gooseflesh on my arms. The boy I'm looking at . . . he's a ghost. "How long have you been in the forest?"

Ollie leaps at another dragonfly, but doesn't disturb it. His hand passes right through the bug as it whizzes by. "I don't bother counting days anymore."

"Is your mother here with you?"

His mop of curls bounces as he shakes his head. "Just the tree people, but you have to die here to become one of them. Mama died in the village. Me too. We caught the blood cough."

Consumption. It took six villagers when it swept through Grimm's Hollow thirteen years ago. I was only a small child back then, and my family was spared the sickness. I don't remember the epidemic, only tales of it. I don't remember Ollie either. Did we ever meet? I would have been four years old when he passed away. "Why are you here if your mother isn't?"

He releases an exaggerated sigh. "You ask a lot of questions."

A smile works its way to my lips, despite the fact that I'm speaking with the spirit of a dead boy. "My father once said that's what my epitaph will read one day: *Clara Thurn. Asked a lot of questions.*"

"Epitaph?" Ollie's little mouth purses. "What is that?"

"Words on a gravestone."

"Oh." He kicks through the grass again, but can't make it rustle. "I've never seen mine."

I have. I've seen every grave marker in Grimm's Hollow. Before I made my peace with death, I used to wake in a cold sweat from nightmares of being trapped inside a coffin underground. I chased the fear away by visiting graves, which I found to be calming places. Most burial sites are on people's lands, but some, like Ollie's, are in the common graveyard on the outskirts of the village square. "You were buried beside your mother."

He slows his traipsing and picks at the worn edge of his suspenders. "I wish I could rest with her."

"Why can't you?"

"I did a bad thing." He lowers his head and stares at his shoes.

"It couldn't be so bad." I drift closer and kneel in front of him, wishing his blurry form were solid enough for me to wrap my arms around. "You're just a boy."

"Boys can steal pennies." He sniffs. "I stole two of them. Mama told me to give them to a poor man, but they were just enough to buy cookies on the next market day, so I buried them in the forest to save for later."

I tilt my head, understanding how this story must have ended. "And before market day came, you caught the blood cough?" I ask gently.

His hazel elfin eyes lift to mine. I didn't think ghosts could cry, but unless it's a trick of his blurred appearance, his eyes are gathering tears. "The fever made me forget where I buried the pennies. I still can't remember. And my fingers can't dig up anything." He thwacks the grass to prove his point, and his hand sails through the tufts without bending the blades. "How will I rest unless the pennies are given to the poor man like I promised?"

My heart squeezes. Soon I'll be dead like Ollie. I'd hate to have any unfinished business that tormented my spirit. "Maybe we can help each other. I'll keep a lookout for your pennies, and you can help me search for *Sortes Fortunae*."

His frown deepens. Is he confused?

"The Book of Fortunes," I prompt. He probably died too young to remember its significance.

"I know about the book." His voice adopts a glum tone. He turns away and heads back for the thicket. "Everyone's looking for it and no one ever finds it."

"But do *you* know where it is?" I spring up to follow him, wincing as the sudden movement sends a spasm of pain through my S-curve. "I promise to help you find your pennies."

"That's what they all say." He walks past the tree line of the hollow. "But then people forget who they are or they die here, and it's too late." He tosses me a weary glance. "I thought you would be different. Magic touches rare people, just like it touched this forest. The woman in red said you might be one of them. But you're already lost."

My mind swirls with all he's just said. "Woman in red? Was her name Rosamund?" My stomach flutters with irrational hope. The chances are next to nothing that she's my mother. How could she be when Mother journeyed into the Forest Grimm wearing a green dress? But then I think of the strip of red wool on the Tree of the Lost in Grimm's Hollow. Grandmère and I chose it because it's Mother's favorite color.

Ollie jumps over a protruding root as he advances farther into the thicket. "Red for rampion. Red like the color of roses. Watch for the girl in the red cape."

"Who taught you that?" I scramble after him. "The man in the oldest tree or the woman in red?" It could be someone else for all I know, but Ollie doesn't bother to say. He just weaves into a dense copse of aspen, too clustered for me to squeeze through. Even if I could, he's already starting to vanish between the shafts of sunlight. "Wait! Will I see you again?"

He shrugs a ghostly shoulder. "There's a girl who lives in this hollow. You should be nice to her. But if she offers you stew, tell her to taste it first."

"Wait, please don't go! At least help me find my friends."

He turns around, his body barely visible with its growing transparency. "Oh, and don't leave here without your cape."

"Ollie!"

It's too late. He fully disappears. The space where he slipped between the trees has become only mist and motes.

CHAPTER 18

I clutch the trunk of a slim aspen, my mind reeling. The moment Ollie vanishes, I start to doubt my encounter with him. No one I know has ever been visited by a ghost, not even Grandmère, and she of all people might have experienced such a curiosity. But perhaps the old woman doesn't tell me everything.

I turn in a slow circle, unsure where I should go: return to the hollow—Ollie said I shouldn't leave here without my cape—or journey blindly back into the forest and hope I somehow meet up with Axel and Henni.

I fist my hands and force myself forward, leaving the hollow behind. It's not as if I can just wait for my cape to miraculously return to my possession. I'll have to test my luck without it and attempt to find it on my own.

This section of the thicket isn't as deep as I first imagined. After I pick my way through a few more yards of clustered trees, I spy another hollow—or perhaps the same hollow, just divided by the thicket.

I duck under a branch and emerge into the clearing, but before I'm even standing straight and can take in my surroundings, a woman captures my full attention. She's eight feet ahead and standing in the shadow of a large oak bordering the hollow. Unprepared to meet another person so soon, I startle.

"Are you cold?" she asks. Her voice is breathy and rhythmic, like air and water coursing together. "Come and rest in my home.

I've been waiting for you. I have furs to warm you. I will make you comfortable."

She glides forward a step, and the silky shadows slip away from her face. She's not so much a woman as she is a girl, I realize. Her hair is stringy and falls to her waist in a tangle of russet waves. Dirt smudges her skin, and her dress is even dirtier, black in places where it isn't brown.

I don't recognize her from the village. Could she be another ghost like Ollie? He mentioned a girl in the hollow, but he didn't say whether she was dead or alive. I squint at the edges of her. They aren't blurry like Ollie's. "Was that you who threw a spear at the Grimm wolf?" I ask.

She dips her head in a queenly way. "You may call me Cinderella," she replies. "And sadly the wolf escaped me. A shame. She had such beautiful fur."

My jaw drops. I stare past all the wildness of her and take in her doe eyes, dainty nose, and elegant bearing. I envision her with cleaner hair—light chestnut instead of russet—and fresh glowing skin. I see her dress as it once was, no longer grimy but wedding-white and trimmed with ribbons and fine embroidery. All she's missing is her red veil, the veil I found in the sycamore. The veil I left behind in my pack.

"Ella?" I gasp. I rush forward to embrace her. We were never close friends, but it doesn't matter. I'm brimming with Henni's joy and Axel's happiness, as well as my own relief that I've found another Lost One in the forest.

Just as I'm about to fling my arms around her, she jerks back stiffly. "I apologize," she says, affecting a smile. She smooths her hair as if she's pinning a lock into an immaculate coif. "I always welcome strangers, but I'm not accustomed to embracing them, nor hearing them call me by informal names."

I stagger on my feet for a moment. I don't understand. Ella is her full name. It isn't short for anything, like Henni is for Henri-etta. In actuality, it's Cinderella that's her informal name. The villagers started calling her that once word spread about how she became Lost. But how did Ella learn that name for herself after she had already left the village?

"Sorry if I've offended you." I bury the sting that she thinks I'm a stranger. She should have remembered that I'm her sister's best friend. "I'm Clara Thurn from Grimm's Hollow." I wait a beat, but she still shows no signs of recognition. "Thank you for saving me from the wolf."

Her smile relaxes, and she dips her head again into another graceful curtsy. "I'm delighted you have come, Clara Thurn." She turns and glides deeper into the hollow, angling her head at me in a silent invitation to walk beside her. "My menagerie keeps me company," she says, "but people are altogether more interesting, don't you think?"

"Yes," I readily agree as I join her, though I haven't given it much thought—and what does she mean by "menagerie"? Still, being agreeable is my instinct with Ella. She was always the older sister I was trying to impress, the more confident version of Henni.

"Welcome to my home." She flourishes a hand to indicate our surroundings, like we're standing in the foyer of a great house. And although the hollow isn't a man-made structure by any means, it's more beautiful than any I have ever seen. Lush ferns, close-knit spruce trees, and red-spotted mushrooms surround us, as well as a rocky outcropping with water trickling down its face. The water feeds vines that droop with blush-pink and silver-blue flowers. White butterflies dance around them in a sparkling flurry.

I breathe in deeply, capturing the heightened smell of the forest. It's floral and crisp and earthy all at once. It's as if most of the magic of the Forest Grimm has descended on this place. No wonder Ella has made it her home.

Little creatures and small animals gather around the edges of the hollow. Squirrels and rabbits and ducklings. They must be attracted to the magic too. Even a fawn has nestled in the grass. Beside the fawn, a dove spreads its wings to take flight . . . though it never leaves the ground. I blink, taking another look. Its wings remain frozen and outstretched. The fawn also doesn't turn her head toward me like deer do when someone new approaches.

Dread seeps inside me. I stare more closely at all the animals, and the smell of the hollow turns bitter like tea steeped for too long. The animals aren't alive. They're dead and stiff and horribly preserved. This is the menagerie Ella was referring to—the collection that keeps her company.

I force a swallow to drown the bile rising in my throat. I need to calm myself. This isn't as unnatural as it seems. Ella's father was known for his own collection of mounted animals. When a dairy cow died, he would tan its leather, and that led him to tan the skins of other creatures. He would stretch them over plaster models so they could retain their native shapes.

The parlor of the Dantzer home held most of the animals, though Henni never grew accustomed to them. Their beaded eyes were always watching her, she said, so she preferred to bide her time in the kitchen or the workshop her parents let her use for painting.

But maybe Ella was different from her sister. Maybe she enjoyed the parlor. Maybe she even helped her father in the tannery as he preserved the animal skins with arsenic.

The forest clearly doesn't serve as an adequate tannery, however. These animals look nothing like those in the Dantzer household. They're distorted and roughly stitched together without a model to hold them up correctly. It looks as if they've been stuffed instead, because dry leaves and dead grass are poking out between their seams.

The eyes are strange as well. They aren't painted beads, like those in Ella's father's collection. These are made of seeds and nuts, sometimes mismatching, which lends them the lopsided and twisted appearance of the animals. All in all, they're freakish, like something from a nightmare.

But who am I to judge Ella for creating them? She must have done so to make this hollow more like her home, and she probably ate the meat to survive. She was only trying to endure this place all by herself.

"What was that?" She leans closer to an owl with a crooked beak as if it has just spoken. It's perched on an exposed root beside a gathering of field mice that stand on their hind legs like miniature people. "Yes, she is beautiful," Ella tells the owl before she turns to me and whispers conspiratorially, "Watch out for Klaus. He's a notorious flirt."

I'm caught between an amused smile and a pained one, unsure if she's joking.

A branch of a weeping willow rustles. I startle, but realize it's only billowing from the breeze. "Do the trees ever move in here?" I ask. "Or anything else?" I sneak a wary glance at a particularly thorny bramble. I'm not keen on being attacked again without my cape.

"The forest won't harm you in my hollow." Ella strokes the willow branch like it's the mane of a domesticated cat. "We made our peace long ago."

She sounds almost as if she's resigned herself to living in these woods. "But you *do* want to leave?"

"Do I?" She tilts her head, considering the question as if it's a profound one. "I cannot leave if I have not yet been found."

"But . . . *I've* just found you."

"No, I found *you*. I saved you from the wolf, as you said." She abruptly turns to address two stuffed squirrels that are posed with linked tails. Their teeth hang crookedly from disfigured mouths. "Hush now," she chides them. "It isn't polite to make fun of people. Clara can't help it if she's confused. The forest can riddle the senses."

Indeed it can, and Ella seems to be a prime example. At least she has more of her wits intact than Fiora. She's just a little . . . well, lost. Which gives me hope that my mother might still be herself when I find her.

She bats her lashes once, then twice, looking me over from head to toe. "Why, you're shaking, Clara Thurn, and your waist is as thin as a reed."

I glance down at myself, surprised to find that I truly am shaking. I've grown so accustomed to my hunger that I hadn't noticed. "Food has been lacking," I confess.

"Then you must come to my kitchen," she says warmly. "I have plenty to share." I follow her to one side of the hollow. Just past the trickling water of the rocky outcropping is a dry spot of bedrock that juts out to serve as a table. On it rests an assortment of mushrooms, tubers, wild roots, and greens, as well as utensils carved from bone—all natural things Ella could have found or made in the forest. But at the back of the table are things that must have been brought here: a neat row of spice tins and corked bottles filled with powders and dried herbs. There's even a small collection of salt-glazed stoneware, including plates, bowls, and mugs.

On the ground beside the table is a copper traveling kettle filled with bubbling stew. It's perched on a bed of stones atop a low-burning fire. Next to it lie stacks of chopped dry wood, and in the distance larger stacks of green wood are in the process of seasoning. A gleaming ax leans against them.

"Where did you get all of these things?" I ask, my mouth slack. According to Henni, Ella entered the forest with only the wedding clothes she was wearing. I've kept that tragically romantic picture in my mind, and it didn't include her holding an ax in one hand and a kettle in another while she also lugged a satchel of cooking gear on her back.

"They are gifts, of course." Ella picks up a knife—a steel knife, not one of her bone-carved creations—and slices into a mushroom. "You're not my first visitor, Clara."

My brows rise. Then maybe—"Did you ever meet my mother? Rosamund—Rosamund Thurn," I add hastily. Ella may have forgotten me, but no one could forget my mother. Like Ella is to Henni, my mother is the bolder, lovelier version of me. She would have made an imprint.

"I can't hold space in my head for names." Ella scoops up the diced mushroom. "They're far too slippery."

"But Rosamund looks like me and—"

"I don't remember faces either."

"But she—"

"Eat, Clara." Ella *tsk*s. "Be my guest while you still have a name and a face to me."

I resign myself to silence as she tosses the diced mushroom in the stew and gives it a stir before ladling me a bowlful. She doesn't dish up a bowl for herself. Instead, she gestures for me to sit on a carpet of overlapping furs in the center of the hollow. I reluctantly do so, even though I'm far too restless. Ella joins me, sitting a little too close for comfort.

Her pupils are dilated and she languidly leans to the side and rests her weight on one arm. She's waiting for me to take a bite, I realize.

I glance back at the mushrooms on the table again. None are poisonous like the red-spotted variety growing around the hollow.

Still, I hesitate, remembering what Ollie said: *There's a girl who lives in this hollow. You should be nice to her. But if she offers you stew, tell her to taste it first.*

"Aren't you hungry as well?" I ask. "Perhaps we can share." I hold out my bowl.

Her doe eyes narrow, and she angles away from me. "You didn't meet Ollie, by chance, did you?"

"Ollie?" I repeat, like I'm unfamiliar with the name. But I don't fool Ella.

She *tsk*s again and mutters, "That little devil. I know he means well, but if he goes on scaring away all of my guests, how will I make any friends here?" Her immaculate posture droops as she casts her gaze about the hollow. "I will admit, my menagerie can get tiresome."

"But why would Ollie want to scare people away from you?"

Ella sighs like she doesn't know where to begin. "Tell me, Clara Thurn of Grimm's Hollow, am I the first person you have met in this forest, aside from little Ollie?"

I twist my fingers in my lap. "There *was* another woman, Fiora—Rapunzel."

She leans closer. "Ah, and I can see in your eyes that she was a dangerous sort of person, yes?"

I blink away the image of Henni being dragged through the forest cocooned in Fiora's fiery red hair. "She *did* have a penchant for strangulation."

"There, you see!" Ella spreads her arms wide. "You never know when you might encounter a friend or foe here, and I have learned to protect myself." She takes up my spoon and dips it into the stew. "Do you know what I can also sense when I look in your eyes, Clara?"

I think of Axel and the warm pressure of his body under the

sycamore, how I forgot everything I'd been working toward in my desperation for his kiss. "What?"

"You are the sort of person who will be a friend." She brings the spoon to her mouth. "You have nothing to fear from me." Her throat contracts as she swallows a bite.

My nerves settle. She passed Ollie's test; the stew is safe. I look into my bowl, and my stomach rumbles at the sight of all the fresh vegetables swimming in the herb-clouded broth. "This *does* smell amazing."

"Thank you." Her cheeks flush a lovely shade of pink. "I've worked hard to make it pleasing."

I spoon up a bite and tip it into my mouth. Once it meets my tongue, I close my eyes as an involuntary moan escapes me. The mushrooms taste like rare truffles, and the stew is seasoned to perfection. I can't remember eating anything half as delicious in my life, though I suspect that's mostly due to my starvation.

Ella beams. "I knew you'd like it."

"It's exquisite!" An easy compliment to give when all my tongue can remember is the taste of Hollow bread.

I gobble up half the bowl, nearly forgetting to breathe in my haste to stuff it inside me.

"Careful, dear." Ella laughs. "Your stomach will cramp if you eat too quickly."

I force myself to chew my next bite before swallowing it, laughing with her as I wipe a bit of broth trickling down my chin. I bet when Ella eats she never spills a drop on herself. She's a model of refined elegance. Even with the wildness of her hair and the smudges of dirt on her skin, she's a vision of rare beauty. Her lashes are long and dark, and her lower lip protrudes in a natural pout that makes her look as though she's ready to be kissed at any moment.

How many times has Axel kissed her?

I set down the bowl. My stomach does indeed start to cramp, though perhaps it's because of what I'm about to say. "You might remember one name from the past." Nervous energy shoots through my fingers and toes. "Axel Furst."

As soon as the words are out of my mouth, I wish I could take them back. I feel like I've exposed a great secret, although I'm unsure why.

Two delicate, perfect lines form between Ella's brows. "Axel," she repeats, and the pulse at the base of her throat flutters. "Is he a prince?"

I almost laugh, but then I picture Axel haloed in sunrise-gold and walking with my father among the sheep in our pasture. I remember him whispering *We'll find your mother, Clara.* I feel the gentle press of his mouth on the crown of my head and against my closed eyes. "Maybe."

Ella smooths the skirt of her wedding gown that she's spread around her furs. "I am waiting for my prince to come. Perhaps it's him."

"Perhaps," I reply, but I know it's him. He's the other half of the Pierced Swans to Ella, their curved necks forming the heart on Grandmère's painted fortune-telling card. "You said you couldn't leave here until you've been found," I remind her. "Did you mean found by your prince?"

Moisture collects in Ella's eyes, and she nods, her gaze traveling away and growing distant. "I lost him, you see. And I lost my veil. I did what the book asked . . . I had the woman dye it red. I thought it would protect me and my prince, hold us together." A tear rolls down her cheek. "But we lost each other anyway."

"A woman dyed your veil red?" I shift closer. "What woman? My mother—Rosamund Thurn?" Mother had experience with using the rare red rampion as a dye. But then how could she have helped Ella? Ella's wedding was supposed to be a year ago, and Mother went missing three years ago.

Ella shakes her head at me, like a mother does with a child who will never learn. "Names, Clara. They are too slippery. All I have space for are heartbreak and hope. And my prince . . . he is both."

Again, the pressure of a great secret bears down on me, although I've already given her Axel's name. But Ella doesn't remember that he's the boy she's been waiting for, and she doesn't know that I've found her red veil. I'm in possession of the answers she's been yearning for.

I should tell her about her part in breaking the curse. The Pierced Swans were in the cards Grandmère drew for me, just like the Fanged Creature, the Midnight Forest, and the Red Card. And Grandmère warned me that fate must be held in balance or the Changer of Fate can't change anything.

Ella and Axel, as a pair, are somehow essential to my journey, whether they're truest loves or star-crossed lovers. I know that—I truly believe it—but a selfish part of me wants to run away from this hollow and burn Ella's veil as well as the memory of Grandmère cards. I want to escape with Axel to the lower valleys where curses don't exist and fate isn't a word and a future can be whatever a person desires.

I wring my hands together and take a steeling breath. My role as the Changer of Fate is tied to saving my mother. I choose her. I'm always going to choose her. "What if I told you that Axel came with me on this journey, and we found your—?"

"Clara?"

My heart stops at the sound of his voice. I look past Ella to a thick line of spruce trees, opposite the direction I came in.

Axel emerges with Henni. He's holding my pack, and a slip of Ella's red veil peeks out from the top.

His eyes latch to mine. A mixture of wild emotions crosses his face. "Are you hurt?" He takes a step closer. "Did the wolf . . . ?" His gaze roams over me. "We found her tracks and followed them here and—"

"I'm fine." I dredge up a smile. He hasn't noticed Ella other than a cursory glance at the back of her head. And she hasn't turned toward him. She's taking shallow breaths as she stares at me with large and frantic eyes. It's like she's worried that by looking at him she'll break the illusion of what all her senses must be screaming—that her prince has finally come. "She has been taking care of me." I gesture at Ella.

Axel goes still . . . as still as the creatures in Ella's menagerie. But Henni takes a cautious step forward. "Who has been taking care of you?" Her voice quivers with desperate hope.

I swallow and meet Axel's gaze, trying to capture the river-blue in them and the last scraps of tender affection he might ever feel for me. "She calls herself Cinderella."

CHAPTER 19

As graceful as a dancer, Ella stands and pivots to face Axel and the twelve feet dividing them. Henni gasps and presses a hand to her chest. Axel's arms go limp. My pack slides off his shoulder and thuds unceremoniously on the ground.

"You're alive," he says. "I knew you would be—I felt it, I never gave up hope—but still . . ." He drags his hands through his hair, then down his face, and covers his nose and mouth. He takes a long shaky breath. "I found you."

My eyes blur as I watch him and his happiness. I try not to dwell on how he's looking at Ella. Instead, I turn my thoughts to my mother. Is this how I'll react when I find her? Or will I burst into tears? Perhaps laughter? My chest aches, imagining it.

Axel rushes to embrace Ella. As she did with me, Ella stumbles back before he can touch her. Axel grinds to a halt. The muscles in his throat tighten. "I'm sorry, Ella."

"Cinderella." Her rebuke isn't cold, only insistent, like her new name is also one of the only things she can hold space for and must cling to for a sense of sanity.

Axel's forehead wrinkles as he contemplates her. "I'll call you Cinderella if that's what you want." He fills his chest with another deep breath. "I'm sorry, Cinderella. I'm sorry I couldn't save you when you entered the forest."

I picture what he must be remembering, although I wasn't there: Ella in her wedding gown and red veil, walking dreamlike beyond the forest border on the eve of their wedding day, and Axel powerless to stop her as the trees barricaded him.

"I'm sorry you've been separated from your family for so long. I'm sorry . . ." His voice breaks. He lowers his gaze to his weather-worn boots. ". . . for everything."

"I'm sorry too," Henni says, tearing my thoughts from Axel and Ella's reunion. This moment must be overwhelming for her as well, even though she's been quiet until now. It's like she's stunned to the point of near paralysis, clutching the trunk of a young aspen for support, like her knees are on the verge of buckling.

Oblivious to Henni's words and state of shock, Ella doesn't bat an eye at her sister. It's as if she can't even hear her. Instead, she tilts her head at Axel, who consumes her focus. She walks around him tentatively, examining his clothes and height and everything about his appearance. With her slim, long fingers, she reaches up and touches his cheek, the line of his jaw, the column of his throat. I feel her trying to remember him in ways that go deeper than the recesses of her mind, and that undertaking is intimate, personal, private.

Henni, even rattled as she is, has managed to turn her gaze away. I try to look away too, but I can't. With each passing moment, I feel younger, smaller, and more insignificant as Ella's hand glides over Axel's chest and abdomen and down the side of his hips.

His brows knit and he holds his body taut, but he can't take his eyes off of her as she continues to explore him. I don't blame him. Her beauty is penetrating.

Her hand drifts back up his chest to his face, and her thumb brushes over his lips twice. "Will you eat some of my stew?"

Axel's brows jut up. "Your . . . stew?"

"Clara Thurn ate some. She enjoyed it heartily."

Axel's eyes dart to me. I shrug and place a hand on my stomach, which hasn't stopped cramping. "I may have overindulged myself. It was delicious."

"All right, then," Axel says to Ella. "If Clara had some."

Her hand immediately drops from his face. She sweeps away to her makeshift kitchen. Henni rushes after her, finally regaining her composure. "I'll help."

Ella doesn't spare her sister a glance, but she allows Henni's assistance in gathering the stoneware and utensils. In a daze, Axel retrieves my pack and comes to join me on the furs.

We're both quiet for a moment, the only sounds about us the birdsong in the air, the water trickling down the rocky outcropping of the hollow, and the clanking as Ella ladles more stew into bowls.

I realize that the wedge-lift in my left shoe has slid out of place. I untie my laces and shift it under my heel again, all the while struggling to think of something to say. My heart is thumping too fast. The only conversation Axel surely wishes to engage in must be about Ella—Cinderella—and I can't bring myself to say her name.

Axel is the first to break the silence. "You promise the wolf didn't harm you?"

"The wolf?" I tighten my shoelaces again. I'd forgotten about the wolf. "Other than a scare I never wish to repeat, yes, I'm unscathed. Ella threw spears and frightened her away."

"Ella threw spears? Huh." Axel nods, trying to accept this along with everything else he's coming to terms with. His eyes shift around the hollow, observing all the strange mounted animals. "So on a scale of madness, how do you rate her, zero being 'a bit confused from spending a year surviving on her own' and ten being 'ready to start growing long hair with Fiora and strangling people'?"

"I'd say she's a solid five."

He chews on his lip. "And would you say a five is reversible?"

"On a scale of one to ten, I'd give it a five."

He cracks a smile. "I'm really glad you're safe, Clara."

Warmth scuttles across my shoulders. "And I'm glad you found me . . . and Ella," I choke out. "You deserve every happiness."

His smile falters. He ducks his head closer to me. "Listen, about what happened between us earlier . . ." A vivid image of his mouth lowering to mine takes hold of me. "I wish I hadn't—"

"Did you bring my cape?" I blurt.

"Um . . . oh, yes." He rubs the back of his neck and reaches for my pack. He's loosening the cinch when Ella and Henni return, each of them holding a steaming bowl.

Ella passes hers to Axel. "Eat up, now. Henrietta tells me you three have been traveling for days, even sleeping together at night." Axel coughs, swallowing his first bite of stew. "Though Henrietta insists she only sleeps beside Clara."

"I also sleep fully clothed," Henni adds, "unless you count the night Clara blindfolded Axel." I give her a pointed stare, and she shakes her head, mouthing *What?*

Ella's gaze sears into me, her smile sweeter than honey. "And what about you, Clara? Do you sleep fully clothed when you're tied up to Axel?"

My cheeks scorch hotter than a blacksmith's forge. "Of course I do! I . . . he . . ." Another memory seizes me, more vivid than the first. My head nestled against Axel's bare chest, his intoxicating smell invading my senses. I blink and rock back slightly. "There's nothing improper about—Axel and I, we—" My voice echoes back in my ears, but slower than how I spoke.

Axel clears his throat. "What's in the stew, Ella—er, Cinderella? It's wonderful."

Smart. A change of topics is just what we need.

Ella opens her mouth to speak, but Henni beats her to it.

"What *isn't* in it, you mean. You should see her collection of herbs and spices and powders. It's practically an apothecary over there. Why, she even has arsenic!"

Axel gives a nervous chuckle. "Don't tell me you've poisoned us, Ella."

She smiles furtively. "The arsenic is for my menagerie."

"Of course." He laughs again, but it's genuine this time. "Well, you've truly made this hollow a home."

Henni grins at Ella. "Leave it to my sister to make anything beautiful." I get the distinct feeling she's trying to impress Ella, but Ella remains indifferent, not acknowledging her at all when she speaks. Ella must not remember Henni. Her attention remains fixed on Axel. Every time he takes another bite of his stew, her lashes lower and lift from his lips to his eyes.

"You are handsome like a prince," she concedes, as if she's been deliberating about him inwardly. "But I wonder if you are truly *my* prince. I wish I could be given a sign."

Axel resorts to another bout of nervous laughter. I almost mention the Pierced Swans card, but I doubt Ella could comprehend the importance or validity of Grandmère's fortune-telling, not in her state of mind. She probably doesn't even remember Grandmère. She doesn't seem to recall anything about Grimm's Hollow.

Or does she?

"Did you ever try searching for *Sortes Fortunae* in the forest?" I ask.

"Of course," she replies smoothly. Axel pauses, lips parted, his spoon frozen on its way to his mouth. Ella takes his hand and gently guides him to swallow another bite. "Why do you think I chose this hollow?" she adds, and then recites the last half of the riddle from the page that the Book of Fortunes left behind in the village:

Falling water
Lost words found
A selfless wish
The curse unbound.

"This place had all the signs. The dripping water, the palpable magic, even the red-spotted mushrooms, just like the ones that surrounded the pavilion where *Sortes Fortunae* used to be kept in . . . where it used to be kept," she amends, omitting the forgotten name of Grimm's Hollow.

I arch a brow, impressed at how much she's remembered. I sneak a glance at Axel and hold up four fingers, decreasing Ella in our scale of madness by a point. "But you never found the book?" I press, and scan the hollow to see if I could have missed it somewhere.

She shakes her head sadly. "Even if I had, I wouldn't have been able to make a wish."

Henni sets down her bowl. She's polished it clean. "You never told me much about your one wish."

"Didn't I?" Ella finally meets her younger sister's gaze. "Well, it was before the curse. You were practically a child."

Henni is speechless for a moment. We all are. Ella just acknowledged that she remembers some of her past.

"What did you wish for?" Henni asks on a hitched breath, careful not to break the spell of clarity over Ella.

Ella's doe eyes flit to Axel, and her head dips shyly. "I cannot share that."

"I mean, what did the book tell you to do?" Henni says, bringing up the one loophole in the rule against wish-sharing. As long as someone doesn't reveal their wish directly, they can tell other people what the book's instructions were to obtain it. Though in my experience, learning that was never very illuminating. Father said that *Sortes Fortunae* told him to shave his beard on a full moon and bury the razor in a neighbor's herb garden. I could never fathom how that helped him gain whatever it was he most desired.

Ella's eyes go unfocused. She runs a hand down the length of her hair. "I was told to prepare a wedding veil and have Rosamund Thurn dye it with red rampion."

My heart stops. My vision blackens around the edges. Ella's words ring discordantly, out of time and out of order. *Rosamund—Thurn—Rampion—Red—Rosamund—Red.* I stare at Ella, transfixed as her mouth shapes the words, then speeds backward to repeat them again.

"Mother?" I say. I smell the rosewater she dabbed on her wrists and neck, the lanolin she extracted from sheep wool for salves, the grassy scent of her apron from the abundant time she spent outdoors.

"What about your mother?" Ella asks.

"She's"—*Thurn—Rampion—Red—Red*—"Rosamund Thurn."

"Rosamund *who*?"

"The woman who dyed your veil," Henni says, nudging her sister's memory. "But why did you prepare your wedding veil so long before you were even engaged?"

My muddled head clears for a moment to ponder Henni's question. Ella's veil was already red before she entered the forest—she'd wanted it that color for her wedding day—which means Mother must have dyed it before she or Ella went Lost. At the latest, that would have been three years ago, before Mother went Lost herself . . . but that was also one and a half years before Ella and Axel became engaged.

Had Ella simply done what the Book of Fortunes instructed as soon as possible after she'd made her one wish, not knowing whom she would marry? Or was her eye already set on Axel as far back as three years ago, when they were both sixteen?

Had she asked *Sortes Fortunae* what might help her win his heart forever?

A sudden wave of fatigue washes over me. I struggle to think through why the book directed Ella to commission a veil dyed with red rampion. I don't understand the rampion's full power, but could its protective qualities be strong enough to hold a relationship together after it was already forged . . . or in Ella and Axel's case, after they were married?

Could their wedding vows have been that much more binding if said while she was wearing her red veil?

"Did you even know Axel that well before Rosamund became Lost?" Henni asks her sister.

"Axel?" Ella frowns.

Axel shoots me a concerned glance. I would hold up six fingers, but my hands suddenly have twenty, and I can't sort them out.

"Your prince," Henni explains, nudging Ella again. "And look what he's brought you." She opens my pack and pulls out what my mother dyed for me.

"A cape?" Ella looks nonplussed.

"No." Henni tosses it at me. I try to catch it, but my hand is too slow. The cape lands in my lap while my arm is still raised.

Henni digs deeper. She pulls out the long gauzy veil of red muslin. "This."

Ella's lips slowly pull apart in a shocked, perfect O.

"Don't you see?" Henni grins like she's just offered her sister a gift greater than any that *Sortes Fortunae* could ever grant a person. "He really is your lost prince."

At the foot of the mounted owl, the dead field mice clap their tiny forefeet together. "Lost prince, lost prince!" they cheer.

"My charming prince?" Ella gasps.

The mice are dancing now. "Charming prince! Prince Charming!"

The owl hoots, ruffling his feathers. The fawn rises and leaps about the hollow. It has two heads. The red-spotted mushrooms triple in size and radiate a sunburst-rainbow glow.

In a daze, I turn to Ella. She's wearing the veil already, just like I'm somehow wearing my cape. Did Axel tie it on me? "You . . . p-poisoned . . . me." My words slur in suspended time. She put more than edible mushrooms in the stew. She must have also used the red-spotted ones. They're known to paralyze people and put them in a sleep they might never wake up from. I watched her taste the stew, but perhaps one spoonful wasn't harmful.

"Not just you, Clara. I gave it to all of you." Ella smiles like she's revealed a great secret. "But don't think of it as poison. It's enlightenment. It's the Forest Grimm speaking to your soul." Her eyes grow abnormally large, and her irises shrink, leaving only dilated pupils—vast holes—in their place. "And what better time to be awoken than on my wedding day?"

Axel clutches his stomach. "I think I'm going to be sick."

"It will pass, my prince," Ella coos. "And once it does, your eyes will open and you'll see colors that never existed. You'll feel beauty and wonder and unbridled joy."

Where is my pack? I paw around for it. I have a kit inside with emergency supplies. It includes black powder from Grandmère's apothecary cabinet. When it's taken with water, it binds to toxins and lessens their effects on the body. I brought it in case we accidentally ate any bad berries or needed to make a poultice for a snakebite. I never thought we'd have to use it to protect ourselves from Axel's unhinged fiancée.

"You can't marry today," Henni tells her sister. "The journey home will take longer than that."

"I'm not waiting until then. I won't leave here until I wed."

I find the pack and dig inside the kit. My fingertips graze the corked bottle of black powder.

"But who will marry you?" Henni asks.

Ella gives Axel a bewitching smile. "My prince and I will marry ourselves."

That practice is legal, although rare. Our ancestors used to hold such ceremonies. But what does Axel think? When I turn to him, his face fills my vision and starts multiplying. His skin is a sickly shade of green. He needs my remedy. I try to grab the corked bottle, but my fingers have gone too lax and sluggish.

"Ella, don't be rash." Axel places his hand over hers. "This isn't the way you wanted to get married."

"I have waited long enough for you." She pulls away and stands tall. "We will marry before midnight."

Midnight—Midnight, my mind echoes.

Chimes reverberate in the air and ring twelve times. I don't see the clock where they're coming from—I doubt there is one—but they sound just like the chimes in the village square of Grimm's Hollow. It held a great clock, the pride of our townspeople's craftsmanship.

"There is a beautiful meadow beyond this hollow," Ella says. "We will have a ball there—a wedding ball."

Henni squeals in delight and claps. Twelve claps followed by twelve more chimes. "May I be your attendant?" she asks, careening from left to right as she tries to stand. The mushrooms are starting to take effect. "Everything will go well this time. You'll see."

Ella nods serenely, looking down her nose at her sister as she accepts her offer. Henni's eyes shine with tears of happiness. Then she clutches her stomach. "Oh dear." She races to a bush and vomits into it.

My fingers finally close around the corked bottle. Clumsily, I drag it out of the pack. "Axel," I try to whisper, but my voice amplifies, bouncing inside my head and around the hollow. "I've brought something that . . ." *Can help?* I frown. Why do I need to help him again?

"And you, Clara . . ." Ella reaches for me. I hesitate, unsure what to do with the bottle I'm holding. Why did it feel so important a moment ago? I covertly slip it in my pocket and set my hands in hers. "You shall be my guest of honor." She lifts me to my feet. "Look at yourself, dear. See how you've already dressed for the occasion."

My gaze lowers to what I'm wearing, and before my eyes, my faded cornflower-blue dress ripples away to reveal another dress in its place, the most beautiful dress I've ever seen.

It hangs off the shoulders, where billowing sleeves gather with ribbons above the elbows and wrists. The corseted bodice, tightly fitted at the waist, spills into an extravagantly bloomed skirt that trails the ground in smoky puffs. The fabric is like a cloud, and traveling down its sheer layers is every shade of blue. Frost blue, forget-me-not blue, periwinkle blue, robin's-egg blue, pansy blue, sapphire blue, midnight blue.

My cape has disappeared with my old dress, but a thin crimson ribbon encircles my waist and elegantly droops in a slender bow that rests against the folds of my skirt.

I spin full circle, watching the dress swish and sway as awe prickles through me. Petals flutter from the crown of my head, and I realize I'm wearing a wreath of red roses. Strangely, I can see myself from outside my body, and I appear a little older, more like my mother. My sable hair hangs down my back in loose waves, and the lashes around my green eyes are longer, thicker, darker.

Little scraps of paper flit down among the rose petals like

falling snow. My name is scrawled upon each of them. *Clara Thurn, Clara Thurn, Changer of Fate,* they whisper. Ollie's voice joins the chorus: *Magic touches rare people.*

The papers drift into two goblets that rest on the ground. Once the goblets are filled, they ripple away and transform into a pair of delicate slippers made of glass, one amber and one moss green. I blink, and the glass slippers are on my feet.

Ella's laughter rings in my ears. Her kiss presses to my cheek.

I don't want to look at her, so I keep staring at my slippers. "It's my turn to be chosen," I tell them and the papers they're hiding. My declaration feels important. It's something to do with the images flashing before me. An acorn. A fluttering strip of rose-red wool. The thin rope that binds my ankle to Axel's. A pair of white swans.

"I must ready myself." Ella's voice swirls around me. "This euphoria won't last beyond midnight, and before the spell breaks, I will see myself a bride."

CHAPTER 20

I don't know when it happened—the day has been a blur of dancing colors and bodiless voices—but the sun has set and the full moon hangs above me in a hyper-vivid blue sky.

I've been wandering through the woods, searching for something. I stumble up a set of natural stone stairs that lead into a large clearing, and I hazily realize I've found it.

The meadow ballroom.

The moon and stars descend closer, dangling by silver streaks in my vision like a chandelier and pendants on iridescent chains. They illuminate a dance floor of pillowy grass and abundant wildflowers. A shimmering pond rests in the middle. Lily pads float in clusters that bloom with jewels of pink and white.

Some of the surrounding trees unearth their roots and shrink to the size of people, becoming humanlike. They step out onto the dance floor in pairs and begin to twirl with their branchy arms twined around each other.

The forest strikes up a symphony of chirping crickets, crooning nightingales, and woodwind breezes. My beating heart adds the percussion.

I weave about the dancing trees, my glass-slippered feet picking up the one-two-three rhythm of their mesmerizing waltz. All I need now is a partner. A handsome maple offers me his hand, but I politely decline with a shake of my head and a curtsy. I want someone else.

I find him under a red-spotted mushroom that is taller than

my mother's Grimm oak. He's sitting propped against its white stem, his eyes glazed over. But once he sees me, those eyes focus and warm. He rises to his feet. His homespun shirt, vest, and trousers fade away into smoke, and I find him wearing a regal gold-and-ivory ensemble instead: a brocade high-collared frock coat, a silk waistcoat beneath, and velvet breeches tucked into tall, polished boots.

His hands take me by my waist, and he pulls me close so our bodies are touching. "Clara," he whispers, and my name on his lips has a taste and smell, like every summer evening bottled up in a heady blend of black-cherry wine.

I lean into him. "Dance with me."

His right hand drifts around my back, while his left hand clutches my right one and lifts our arms together. We start to spin and travel across the dance floor. The trees make way for us. The moon and stars keep us lit. They shine along our path and limn us in silver.

"Why are you crying?" Axel's voice is a tender murmur.

I'm crying? Only then do I feel the tears slipping down my cheeks. "I suppose it's happiness." But if that's true, why does a sharp pain slice through the center of my chest? "Don't let me go. I don't want it to end." Pain is better than losing him.

His hand withdraws from my back, and the ache inside me intensifies. But then he brushes my tears away and kisses my forehead. "I'm not going anywhere."

He folds me closer against him, and I lay my head on his shoulder. We sway to a slower rhythm and a purer melody, and then our feet lift off the ground. We float over the wild grass, the sparkling pond, the blooming water lilies. The trees in the meadow retreat to the borders of the ballroom and grow back into giants that frame us with boughs of pine needles and leaves of oak and maple.

"Do you have wings?" I ask Axel, dizzy from the beautiful weightlessness of how he holds me.

A soft chuckle vibrates through his torso. "I was going to ask you the same thing."

I stare at him and what I can see of myself. It's true that no wings expand from our backs, but his frock coat and my dress have sprouted silky white feathers. Swan feathers.

More tears trickle down my face. They slip in rivulets beneath my jaw and slide down my neck. *I'm not supposed to fall in love.* The Pierced Swans card was never meant to be about me. How could it be when Grandmère also drew the Fanged Creature? *It isn't fair.*

"What isn't fair?" Axel asks, and I realize I've spoken aloud. I can't keep my answer trapped inside me any longer. It's been eating at me since he kissed my eyes beneath the sycamore. If I'm being truthful with myself, it's been eating at me since he let me cry on his shoulder after we delivered the twin lambs.

"To love before death," I say.

His gaze penetrates mine, and though his eyes are overly bright and his pupils are dilated, his river-blue irises are unbearably soft and filled with sympathy. "What kind of life would it be otherwise?"

"But it shouldn't happen so soon."

"Love?"

"Death."

"We're not going to die in this forest, Clara."

He won't, anyway. And while I'm glad of that, it doesn't hold my heart together. "You will be so happy with Ella. You'll be a part of a true family again, just like you've always wanted."

He bows his head. "I don't want to hurt Ella or her family."

"Of course you don't."

"They've been so good to me."

"I know."

"I need to bring her back home. I promised myself I would do that."

"You don't have to explain." If he does, I know what he'll say next—that she won't leave here unless he marries her. "I understand what has to happen tonight."

"But you don't understand how I feel about . . ." He shakes his head and lifts his eyes to mine. They seem to reflect the pain inside me. "Clara, how am I supposed to . . . ?"

"Stop." I push my hand against his chest.

"I can't." He takes my face in his hands and tilts my head up.

We're no longer dancing, but we keep floating as the world spins around us. The stars zoom about and transform into fireflies. White feathers grow from the ends of my hair and climb Axel's shirt to fringe his collar.

His gaze lowers to my lips, and my heartbeat quickens, an unrestrained pulse thrashing through my limbs, fingertips, and toes. He's going to kiss me, and I'm going to let him, even if it's a kiss of pity or apology. I can't die without knowing how it feels.

My arms fold around the back of his neck, and I draw him closer. His breath heats my face. Our mouths are almost touching. I close my eyes. His lower lip catches the edge of mine, just a flutter of pressure. I shudder, murmuring, "Axel."

"Axel?" Ella's voice crashes into my awareness. Although it's soft and airy, it booms unnaturally through my head.

I rip out of Axel's arms and stumble backward, both feet planted on the meadow dance floor again. The world stops spinning. Ella and Henni have just emerged from the top of the stone stairs. They're standing beneath the natural arch of two trees that lean against one another.

Ella is twenty feet away, yet she fills my vision completely.

The feathers in my hair and skirt shrink and fade as I take in her ethereal appearance.

Her dress is entirely made of white feathers. They fan upward to cover her chest in a heart shape and spread out at her hips like wings. They cascade down her skirt in snowy puffs that sweep onto the wild grass.

Her pouted lips are petal pink, and her hair is pinned into a sleek bun with artfully arranged clusters of feathers that fasten above each ear.

Her bloodred veil is a striking contrast to all the white. It flows, hanging from the base of her bun down her bare back until it spills off her skirt and swirls in a long train that's triple the length it used to be.

In a distant corner of my mind, I'm aware that I'm hallucinating, that Ella must still be in her worn cinder-blackened wedding gown. But that isn't a comfort. She's a beautiful bride no matter what she's wearing, and she's going to be Axel's wife before midnight. It will cut me to the bone, but I have to let it be so. Otherwise she won't come home, and Henni's and Axel's hearts will break forever. It's better that mine does. My friends will be able to leave this forest once our journey is over, but my fate is destined to end here.

Ella glides toward Axel and me under the moonlight. Henni follows in her shadow, wearing a much simpler dress than her sister. It's a bruised shade of purple, and the skirt's length is juvenile in the way it only falls to her knees. Guilt nicks me when I catch Henni's eye. Her frown is as sullen as the last time she spotted Axel and me almost kissing.

But Ella seems to have forgotten what she walked in on a moment ago. Either that or she's an excellent actress. Her smile is serene, and her dancer-graceful arms are free from any tension.

There's only a hint of something darker and angrier in her slightly narrowed gaze.

She joins us where we stand at the edge of the pond, and her long-lashed eyes sweep over Axel. "You make a magnificent groom, my prince."

And he does. The rending ache in my chest tears deeper as I absorb how he's changed. He's now clothed fully in white like Ella. A cloak of white feathers drapes over one of his shoulders, and a crown of gold rings his head.

Perhaps the Pierced Swans aren't two people, but three, I realize. Axel and Ella are the pair who feel truest love for each other, and I'm the star-crossed bird floating above them with an arrow in my heart.

"Dance with me," Ella says to Axel, the same words I spoke to him earlier. "One dance and then we will take our vows."

He shifts on his feet. "Ella, I—"

"It's almost midnight. I lost you once on the eve of our wedding. I refuse to let that happen again. I won't be a tomorrow-bride any longer." She draws back her slim shoulders and lifts her chin high. "We will marry before the clock strikes twelve."

CHAPTER 21

here is no clock in this meadow, but Ella must hear its ticking the same way I do, the way we've both heard it tick for so long—me in my haste to save my mother, and her in her lost patience to wed the boy who was almost hers last summer.

"So many white feathers," I murmur, watching Axel and Ella sweep across the meadow in a new waltz, only now the forest's music is out of time. Ella is leading Axel faster than its tempo.

"White feathers?" Henni asks, coming to stand beside me.

"His clothes. Her dress."

"But Ella is in a golden dress." Henni stares at her sister with eyes that are glossy and wide, her pupils dilated just like Axel's and Ella's and also mine, I'm sure.

"Is that how you see her?" I wobble on my feet. Axel and Ella flip-flop in my vision. Where they were moving left to right, they're now moving right to left.

Henni says something, but the words sound strangely muffled. Then she repeats herself, her voice suddenly amplified like it's bouncing through a rocky canyon. "It's almost midnight! Gather round for the lottery!"

I startle. "Is it Devotion Day? Why didn't you tell me?"

I turn to Henni, but my friend's sweet face is gone. It's now the village clockmaker who stands beside me. He checks the hour on his pocket watch and clicks it shut. "How many times did you enter your name?" He cocks a thick brow at me.

Oh no. "You found out about that?" All the scraps of paper hidden inside my apron pocket?

His smile pierces through all my defenses. But it's Axel's smile now, not the clockmaker's. Axel is standing beside me, while another Axel dances with Ella. And there's a third Axel in the meadow—my Axel?—only this meadow is another meadow, the one on the outskirts of the Forest Grimm. The sun shines on his tanned skin. He's chewing on a piece of straw, and he pulls it from his mouth as he leans his head closer to mine. "Hurry. If we're quick, we can fix this."

"Fix what?"

"All those extra names. They have to come out of the amber goblet."

"But wait . . . I never put them in the goblet." *Or did I?*

The Axel beside me disappears, and a replica of myself takes his place. "You're hallucinating, Clara," the second me says. She's wearing my old faded dress and the cape dyed with red rampion. "It isn't Devotion Day."

"You're wrong. I'll show you." I crouch and try to slide off my left slipper, the one made of amber glass. I need to make sure seven papers are still inside it. I didn't count them when they fell in earlier. "I have to hurry," I tell me as I tug on the slipper. Why won't it come off? I fumble with a pair of laces I don't see, but I can feel. They shouldn't be there. My slippers have no laces. "I can't wait for another time to be chosen. Axel needs me."

"Don't you mean Mother needs you?"

"I . . ." *Isn't that what I said?* "Yes, of course."

The second me steps closer, and her red cape brushes my arm. "Do you really imagine Ella will let Axel leave her hollow after they're wed?"

My eyes turn to the pair of them dancing. Ella's head is on

Axel's shoulder the way mine was earlier, but her fingers dig into his back like claws.

"She won't abandon the place where she's learned to feel control over her life," second me adds. "She'll keep him drugged, and she'll harm anyone who tries to take him away."

"Maybe she won't have to drug him," I counter. "Maybe he'll want to remain here." Axel doesn't seem bothered by Ella's desperate embrace. His gaze is riveted to her, his expression ardent and earnest. "He loves her."

"You need him," second me insists. "He's necessary to your journey."

"Only if he's with Ella. Look at them. Could it be any more obvious that they're the Pierced Swans?" They twirl and twirl, a dizzying haze of flocked white.

"You see what you want to see, Clara."

I glare at the second me. "Then why are you here?"

"You want me to go?"

"Yes."

"Very well." The reflection of me transforms. She grows a few inches taller and several years older.

It's my mother now beside me, wearing the cornflower-blue dress and red cape.

I suck in a sharp breath, more startled by her than anyone else I've seen. I thought I remembered her exactly, but I was mistaken. I forgot how her green eyes are slightly closer-set than mine, and how her sable hair has threads of gray.

I had preserved her in my mind as young, the way I saw her as a child, but she's more like the Grimm oak she planted with her father, its leaves crisp and golden in the autumn once it had matured for many years.

"Did you keep the acorn I gave you?" she asks.

"Of course." My voice is a reverent hush.

"But did you keep its meaning?"

I'm not sure I understand, though I remember the last words Mother said to me before journeying into the forest: *The acorn was about your life, not mine.* "Oaks live hundreds of years. You told me they're almost eternal. The acorn reminds me that I can save you." I have my own reasons for keeping it.

"But that's not why I gave it to you, Clara. It was a gift meant to remind *you* to live. You haven't been doing that, not truly. Why won't you spread your wings?"

Is she really arguing with me about this? "You're the one who made me the cape. You wanted me to find you in case you didn't return home."

"You see what you want to see."

"I only want to see *you*." My voice cracks.

"And what about him?" Mother tenderly takes me by the chin and turns my head toward Axel. He's stopped dancing. Henni has ushered him to stand under the arched trees at the edge of the meadow where it meets the top of the stone stairs. Ella is standing fifty feet away, like a bride at the entrance of a chapel. The train of her feathered dress and her long red veil fan out behind her. "Do you think he really wants to marry Ella Dantzer? Or is he the sort of boy who would sacrifice his happiness just to bring her safely home?"

Flashes of memories play out before me like glimpses of a traveling troupe of actors, except the performers are people I know, and Axel—a copy of Axel—is the constant among them in their rapidly changing scenes.

First he's twelve, the age he was when his father died in the avalanche. He's plowing his uncle's field while the man shouts at him and swings a jug of ale like he's going to use it to beat him.

Now Axel's a little older, maybe thirteen. He's helping the young Trager couple who used to live near the Dantzer farm.

They're both sick with a fever, and he's repairing the roof of their small cottage. They offer to pay, but he won't accept their money.

The scene flashes, and now he's carrying the small Eckhart boy on his shoulders as his parents walk beside them to the village square. The mother is pregnant and the father leans on a crutch, nursing a broken foot.

Axel is everywhere in Grimm's Hollow, among everyone. Even reclusive Fiora Winther allows him to run an errand for her, passing him a sealed envelope to deliver.

And then Axel is with me. He's throwing tufts of wool in my hair to get me to laugh while I'm learning to shear sheep. Then he's racing me, each of us carrying pails of sheep milk. We're playing a game to see who can run the fastest without spilling a drop. Next he's teasing me. It's the first time I've danced with a boy at the harvest festival. Axel sneaks up behind us and pulls the ribbons loose in my braids.

Now it's the night I remember most, the night we helped the struggling ewe deliver her twin lambs. Axel keeps me anchored with his strength and buoys me with words of encouragement. There's no teasing from him then, no poking fun. When I burst into tears as we finish saving the second lamb, Axel's warm arms surround me and his hands smooth my hair.

"I think he's a boy who deserves a girl that can outlive this forest," I tell my mother.

"What if he is like you, and he doesn't know what he deserves?" She tips her head at me knowingly. "What if he has also forgotten how to live?"

The younger Axel fades away, and the Axel under the arched trees remains. Ella is only five feet from him now, mere steps from completing her advance down the meadow.

"You can put blinders on, Clara," Mother says, "but is it fair to allow Axel to make the same mistake?"

My jaw muscle tightens. "I shouldn't listen to you." It cuts me to say it, but it's the truth. "You're not my real mother. You're my mind warped with mushrooms."

I expect her to look offended, but she only lifts a dark brow and betrays a sliver of a smile, the way she did when I was little and tried to hide a pottery crock I had broken. "I'm still in your mind, Clara. I'm what you really want to hear deep inside you, otherwise you wouldn't have chosen me to say it." She starts to fade, growing transparent.

"Wait!" My heart slams faster. "Don't go!"

"Wake up, dear heart," she says, her voice firm but tender. "Fight. Live."

She vanishes.

One dry sob chokes out of me. But I don't allow another. I frantically search for a pocket I can't see. Somewhere beneath this illusion of a ball gown is my old dress. I finally find the pocket. My fingers dig inside and wrap around the corked bottle of black powder. I pull it out. Dump a good portion in my mouth and wash it down with pond water.

"Axel!" I wipe my face and spring across the meadow. "Stop!"

CHAPTER 22

As I run, the ticking of the invisible clock echoes louder. Or perhaps it's my heartbeat. The remedy hasn't hit my bloodstream yet. Ella is caught in a loop in my vision, speeding backward then hastening forward, retreating from and then advancing to Axel. But by the time I reach both of them, the loop breaks. Their hands are already clasped beneath the arched trees.

"Don't marry her, Axel!" I pant for breath. "Not unless you're doing it for the right reasons."

A few feet to my left, Henni frowns. "Clara, what are you—?"

"The right reasons?" Ella cuts her off, looking at me like I've lost my mind, ironic since she's the one who fed me her poison. "My prince is only made of right reasons. You don't know him at all."

Axel's brows strain together as he struggles to keep his eyes latched on her and not glance in my direction.

"Right reasons are only right if they aren't lies," I say.

"What are you implying?" Ella's voice remains overly feminine in its lifted pitch, airy tone, and exaggerated gentleness. It makes me feel all the more childlike in her estimation. "My prince would never lie."

"Yes he would, if it meant saving you and making your family happy again."

"Stop this, Clara," Henni hisses at me. "You're going to ruin everything!" Her bruised-purple dress darkens to a deeper shade of violet.

I forge ahead with what I came to say. "Will marrying Ella make you happy, Axel?"

Ella gives a delicate huff. "My prince is happy when those he serves are happy."

"I didn't ask you," I snap. Ella recoils as if I've struck her. I take a calming breath. She can't be as hypersensitive as she's acting. She's smarter than she pretends. She throws spears at wolves. She skins animals and stuffs them for pleasure. She brews poison to precision. We would all be dead now if she'd given us too much to eat. "Axel deserves more than just a life of serving other people."

"But that's what love is," Henni says.

"No, it isn't, not fully. Love is being someone's equal." I shift closer to Axel. "It's trusting them and confiding in them and being true with who you are around them and what you really feel."

"How cruel you are to insult him," Ella says. "My prince is—"

"He isn't a prince!" I've had enough of her painting him in a perfect light. "He's a boy who lost his father when he was twelve and was then raised by an uncle who could never be real family to him. All he's wanted ever since was to be part of a happy family."

"And he will be if you'll just leave us alone!" Henni grinds out.

I wince. Henni has never spoken unkindly to me. "It isn't my intention to hurt anyone. All of you deserve happiness. But happiness has to start with the truth."

I tread another step closer to Axel. His brow flinches. Ella's hands squeeze his tighter.

"Axel?" I say quietly, hoping he'll finally turn to me, but his gaze remains stubbornly fixed on his bride. "I'm not trying to force you to change your mind." My own mind is becoming more lucid, but I don't want to manipulate him while he's still in a delirium. "I won't say another word about this if you can look me in the eye and tell me you're marrying Ella because you love her. And I don't mean a friendly or compassionate love. I mean true love. The kind she deserves. The kind *you* deserve. If you can tell me that, then I'll be satisfied." *I will let you go.*

Ella turns to Axel, her chin lifted swanlike, her smile confident although a little stiff. Henni also stares at him, but her demeanor is fragile and desperate, one thread away from unraveling.

Axel holds Ella's gaze for a few more seconds—seconds that throb through me with the ticking of the invisible clock. Axel's white clothes, his cloak of feathers, and his gold crown start to flicker in and out of my vision. Beneath them I see flashes of his true appearance, his unwashed hair, the stubble growing on his face, his homespun and patched clothes, dirty from travel.

At last he breaks eye contact with Ella and stares down at their joined hands. He sways a little, still drugged, while I feel steadier on my feet. The remedy is starting to take hold.

He takes deep and labored breaths.

Look at me, I plead inwardly.

He licks his lips. Presses them together. Briefly closes his eyes. He inhales slowly and lifts his gaze to me. The blue has hardened to granite. He pries his rigid jaw open. "I'm marrying Ella because I . . ." His voice goes hoarse. He shifts his weight from leg to leg and clears his throat. "I love . . ."

"Say it." Ella pulls their clasped hands closer to her chest.

"I love . . ."

"Hurry, Axel," Henni pleads. "It's almost midnight."

"I know!" he says.

The tendons in Ella's neck pull taut. Henni bounces on her tiptoes. Will the spell really end right at midnight? Is Ella's poison that precise?

"Don't break my heart again." Ella's eyes water. "Say you love me."

"I . . ." Pain wrenches across his face. ". . . tried my best to love you, Ella."

The meadow hushes to abrupt silence. The strange symphonic music vanishes. There's not even a breeze or a breath to be heard. There's only the ticking that reverberates inside my mind. The clock hasn't yet reached twelve.

A small peep finally shatters the silence. It's Henni. She's softly crying. I move to comfort her, but she turns away and covers her face with her hands.

Axel kneads his brow with tense fingers and looks between both sisters. "I'm so sorry."

Ella has gone utterly still except for a tiny flare of her nostrils. She allows herself another moment, then draws her chin even higher, releases his hands, and takes a graceful step backward. Her mouth spasms with a tic before she purses her lips. "You will want to leave here then, I take it?" she asks him.

"I was hoping you would come with us," he says. "Your parents miss you, and I promised—"

"Will you share a drink with me before you go?" She cuts him off swiftly. "We will vow to be friends, if not husband and wife."

He blinks, caught off guard. "Of course. I *do* care for you."

"I'm so glad." Her voice is syrup-sweet. She turns to Henni. "The goblets, please."

Still a bit dazed, I glance down at my glass slippers, but of course Ella didn't mean them when she said "goblets," even if they are amber and moss-green like the ones for the lottery on Devotion Day.

Henni sniffs and passes Ella a pair of tin cups.

"I hope water agrees with you," Ella says to Axel. "I'm afraid my hollow lacks a winepress."

He musters a smile. "Water is fine."

She hands him a goblet and intertwines arms with him, holding her cup near his lips as he holds his near hers.

Chime, chime, chime. The first tolls ring in the midnight hour.

"Will you vow to always be true and faithful to me?" Ella asks.

Chime, chime.

Axel's brow furrows. "I thought we were vowing to be friends."

"Isn't the promise the same?" Henni interjects, looking hopeful again.

Chime.

"I suppose." Axel squirms.

"Then what is your answer?" Ella presses.

Chime, chime.

Eight tolls. Ella's white swan feathers are fading to black. I know it's just me seeing her that way—and I see what I want to see—but I can't ignore the dread roiling through my stomach.

"I vow to be your true and faithful *friend*," Axel replies.

Chime.

"That's not what I asked!" Ella stomps her foot.

Chime.

"You need to accept what I can offer."

Chime.

The moon and stars retreat higher, returning to the heavens.

"I will accept no such thing!" A vein bulges on Ella's forehead. "You will vow to be mine, and mine forever!"

"Ella, I can't."

Chime.

A shriek of pure rage rips out of her. Axel drops his cup and jerks backward.

My dread is acute now. Alarm bells ring wildly inside me. "Axel, Henni, we need to go."

Henni's mouth falls agape. "We can't just leave my sister!"

"She's dangerous."

"She's broken-hearted!"

I catch Ella slipping something from her sleeve. A small vial containing a steely gray substance. She empties it into her cup.

"What is that?" I inch forward. "What are you going to—?"

"It's for Axel." She tucks the vial away.

He shakes his head. "I can't take any vows."

Her eyelids slit. "Then. Just. Drink."

"Axel," I warn.

"I won't drink anything, Ella." He reaches for my hand. I reach for Henni's, but she steps back.

"Drink!" Ella screams. She lurches for Axel.

I reach to stop her, but only clutch a fistful of her veil. I yank it hard, and it tears free.

She gasps and whirls around, pinning me with a vicious glare. "Do you think I'll let any of you go?" She turns on all of us. "No one leaves me! I won't allow anyone to ever abandon me again!"

"What are you talking about?" Henni's face pales.

Ella stalks toward her. "Have you seen the faces in the trees of this forest?"

"I . . ." Henni swallows. "I thought I was going mad."

"I've seen the faces," I confess.

"Me too," Axel says. "Each of us must have thought it was madness."

"It's the dead." Ella's eyes sharpen. "The trees absorb them. They're the graveyard of the Forest Grimm."

"But you didn't . . . ?" Henni starts to shake. "None of the dead are there because of you, are they?"

Ella stands taller. Her swan dress is completely covered with black feathers now. "I won't allow anyone to abandon me."

She charges at Axel with her goblet. He throws his arm up to block her. The poisoned water splashes out. He ducks before any of it hits his mouth. Ella jerks up the hem of her skirt. Whips out a knife that's sheathed to her thigh.

"Run!" Axel shouts at me.

I grab Henni's hand. We race with Axel for the stairs. Ella's veil is tangled around my body, but its length has returned to normal. Henni's clothes also transform back to their ordinary state, and Axel's white feathers are billowing away.

We plunge down the steps. Ella chases us with her knife. Her monstrous wedding gown is losing its magic. The feathers shrink. The gown starts to fade to a stained cinder cloth.

I keep tripping on the veil. My left slipper catches in a crack on one of the steps. I lurch forward. I'm about to fall down the remaining stairs. Axel catches me before I topple. My left slipper pries off.

I spin to grab it, but Ella's knife flies at my face. I duck before it can swipe my cheek. Axel shoves Ella sideways. She lands in a bush next to the stairs. We hurtle down the last few steps. Axel keeps me balanced between the cumbersome veil and my only shoe.

As my friends and I make our final escape, I look back to steal one last glimpse of my slipper.

The amber glass fades, and its luminous facets turn dull and dark brown.

It's now only my scuffed left shoe.

The shoe with my wedge-lift inside.

CHAPTER 23

We rush through the hollow, grab our two packs, and race back the way Axel and Henni came here from the sycamore following the wolf tracks. The sycamore is near the river, and we need to keep using that unchanging waterway as our trail.

But the wolf tracks don't go far. They only lead us a short distance before they stop, running up against thickets, saplings, and brambles—obstacles Axel and Henni don't remember. Which means the forest moved during the meadow ball. It's the only explanation. As we hurry onward, I try not to lose heart. The river can't be too far away.

Axel guides us in the direction he's sure it must be in, but dense patches of trees and bushes prevent us from forging a straight path. We can't find the river, but thankfully we reach a thin stream that must connect to it.

Henni collapses on her knees and cups her hands in the water, drinking in huge mouthfuls. Axel and I crouch beside her and do the same.

"Can we sleep now?" She wipes the wetness off her chin. It's still nighttime. Even if we hadn't been drugged with mushrooms, we'd be tired, but I'm sure the stew we ate is worsening the effects. Shortly after we left the meadow, we stopped hallucinating, but then horrible fatigue set in for all of us.

Mine isn't as bad as my friends'—Henni has been stumbling on her feet, and Axel can't make it thirty seconds without yawning—but I've had a dose of black powder.

"Soon," I reply, and pull the apothecary bottle from my pocket. Now that we've found water and have put a fair distance between ourselves and Ella, I can also give them the remedy.

I uncork it and instruct them how to mix it into a slurry with the stream water. Henni makes a face as she tastes it, and Axel gags, but both of them manage to choke it down.

"I'm never eating mushrooms again," he groans. "I don't care if they're the safe ones. I've lost my appetite for anything that resembles a toadstool."

Henni rolls onto her back. "*Now* can we sleep?"

"Not yet." I rub my feet. They're only covered in thin stockings now—stockings that are already torn, filthy, and bloody from fresh cuts on my toes and heels. I removed my right shoe after we left the hollow and shoved it in my pack, entertaining some vain hope that I might get my left shoe back again, though the likelihood is next to impossible. "We need to get farther away. Ella can still track us here."

"Maybe we should let her." Henni stares up at the moonlight that splinters the forest canopy. Tears pool in her eyes.

"We can't," I say gently. "I'm sorry. I know this has to be difficult for you."

"Seems like it's difficult for only me," she murmurs, and though her voice is soft, her words lance sharp.

I suppress a wince. It's unlike her to be even the slightest bit unkind. "That isn't fair, Henni. Axel came on this journey to save Ella. You saw how he tried to persuade her."

"I saw how *you* tried to persuade *him*."

"I only meant to—"

"Clara was right to say what she did," Axel says, his words

given like a brother's—tough but caring. "Don't blame her. All of us are mourning Ella. She's not who she once was."

From where she's sitting, Henni whirls on Axel. "That doesn't mean we should abandon her!"

Axel takes a measured breath. "That's not what I was trying to say."

"We were lucky to even find her in the first place." Henni furiously wipes tears from her eyes. "How will we find her again? The forest will move and hide her from us."

"We're still going to save her," Axel promises.

"How?"

"The only way we can," I say simply. "The way we planned from the beginning. We'll find *Sortes Fortunae* and break the curse. It's because of the curse that Ella has gone mad, just like Fiora did. And it's because of the curse that the forest keeps moving. It senses anyone from Grimm's Hollow and tries to punish us. The red rampion only helps so much, and even then, it doesn't help forever." And why that is, I still don't understand.

According to Ollie and his poem, red rampion was the first to grow in the Forest Grimm, the first to wake up the land and grant it power. He also said red rampion holds the seed of magic. If it's that powerful, why is its protection limited?

"But what if we never find the book?" Henni stifles a whimper.

"We will," I say. I refuse to believe otherwise. I haven't given up faith in the Red Card Grandmère drew for me. To be the Changer of Fate must require enacting a reversal of fortunes for Grimm's Hollow, and how can I do that without making a wish on *Sortes Fortunae*? "And when the curse is broken, there's every reason to believe that Ella will be restored to the person she really is. The forest will stop fighting against all the villagers, and the Lost will be able to return home." It's how Mother will also be saved.

Axel lowers his head and traces a scratch on the back of his hand. "How many of them do you think are still alive?" he asks quietly. "How many did Ella . . . ?" He trails off, but the unspoken word hangs heavy in the air.

Kill.

Henni pulls her knees to her chest and hunches inward.

I force saliva down the dry lining of my throat. "Most of the faces in the trees have probably been there for centuries," I say, willing it to be true. "Those people must have died in the great battle long ago . . . and just like the legend says, they turned into trees." I think of what Ollie told me about the "tree people": *You have to die here to become one of them.*

"Either that or the trees absorbed them." Axel turns wary eyes on the forest. "That's the way Ella put it."

Ollie also said that people either forget who they are in the forest or die here. He didn't say "murdered here"—and dying in the wild can happen a number of ways—but being murdered could still be what he meant. Ollie isn't a fountain of clarity.

I sneak a glance at my friends. I haven't told them about my encounter with the ghost yet. I'll need to find a better moment— one where Henni isn't crying and Axel hasn't just almost married Ella for the second time.

"But Ella can't be the only one who . . . h-hurt the others," Henni stammers, dancing around the word "kill" again. "Fiora has to be responsible for some of those . . . those misfortunate in- cidents too."

"I'm sure she is," Axel says. "Fiora has been in the forest even longer than Ella. It must have made her madness that much worse."

They both look at me like they're waiting for me to agree, but I press my lips together and take a renewed interest in my sore feet. What Axel is saying makes sense, but I don't want to admit it, even to myself. Admitting it means my mother could be suffering a fate worse than Ella or Fiora. She was the first to go missing here.

But maybe she's fine. Although Ollie didn't confirm it, I'm still clinging to the hope that the woman in red is my mother, that she was the one who told him, *Watch for the girl in the red cape.* If she's looking for me, perhaps that means her mind is still sound.

But *how* sound? Does she truly remember me? Or is she like Ella, who only remembers a fractured version of the past? Ella recalls waiting for her prince, not a boy named Axel. Has my mother reduced me in the same fashion to only the girl in the red cape? Has she also forgotten my name and face?

Axel scoots closer to me. "We need to wrap your feet in something to protect them. I can tear off some of my shirt." He starts to unbutton it.

I almost choke on my own tongue. "Oh, that's not necessary." An unbidden image of him shirtless plasters itself in my mind. I've seen him bare-chested twice now. If he adds a third time to the mix, I might never think clearly again.

"Just the part I tuck in," he insists.

"I'll tear off the end of my chemise instead." I quickly reach beneath my dress and start yanking at it before he can do anything rash. I rip two long strips away and begin wrapping my feet.

"Here, let me help." He takes my left foot in his lap.

I open my mouth to protest, but the words die before they're spoken as he binds the linen strip around my toes . . . my arch . . . my heel . . . my ankle. My stockings only provide a thin barrier between his fingers and my skin, not nearly enough to mask how intimate and warm his touch feels. Shivers prickle over every inch of me. I'm drawing breath through tiny gasps of air.

He wraps my right foot as well, and by the time he finishes, dizzying flecks of black dance across my vision.

"There." He tucks the last bit of linen into place before he holds out a hand to help me up. But I don't take it. I can't touch him anymore. If I do, I'll likely pass out.

"Thanks," I blurt, and spring to my feet. I hurry ahead, my pack in tow, and continue following the stream. "We should keep moving," I call back to them.

"Wait a minute, Clara," Henni says. Something about her voice has a fresh edge of accusation. I turn to see what's the matter. She pushes up from the grass and nods at my pack like she's just noticed something. "You have Ella's veil."

I glance over my shoulder at the cinched top of the pack. A flash of red is peeking out. But why is Henni so upset? I wasn't trying to hide it. "I thought you saw me take it." Once we'd raced away from the stone stairs, I detangled myself from the veil and stuffed it away.

Her expression remains inflexible. "Why didn't you leave it in the hollow?"

I suppose I could have, but—"Ella said my mother dyed it with red rampion." It's another relic of her, like my cape. More than that, the veil feels like a clue. To what end, I don't know, but it's the closest I've come to finding anything connected to her since I set out on this journey. "Besides, Ella doesn't need this anymore. The wedding didn't happen."

My voice isn't harsh, but Henni gapes like I've burned the veil to ashes with my very words. "It can protect her!"

"Maybe it once did, but it can't anymore. It didn't even protect her from herself while she was wearing it in the meadow. Ella isn't going to change until the curse is broken, Henni."

"You don't know that," she snaps. "Maybe she just didn't wear the veil long enough. We have to take it back." She rushes for me, and I flinch backward. Axel quickly steps between us.

"We're not going back," he says firmly. "Clara is right. The only way to save Ella now is by finding the Book of Fortunes."

Henni's jaw muscle twitches. "Seems Clara is always right." She storms past us and takes the lead in following the path along the stream.

I release an exhale so heavy it threatens to collapse my lungs. Only a handful of people in this world truly matter to me, and Henni is one of them. I've never lost her good opinion before now, so the sting burns that much deeper.

Axel comes to stand beside me. "She'll come around," he says. "I think she's still suffering from the mushrooms."

That could be true, but she's also just been separated from her sister, and Ella is the whole reason Henni came on this journey.

As we start walking after her, Axel's fingers brush mine. A thrill of warmth surges through me, but I immediately stiffen and retract my hand. "I should . . ." I flounder. "Henni . . . she needs me."

Axel's brow furrows, but I hurry ahead and curse my pounding heart. I was careful about what I said to him right before he almost married Ella. I asked if he loved her, if marrying her would make him happy. But I didn't tell him how I felt about him, and I didn't ask how he felt about me.

I'm not going to live for much longer, so it's best that he and I don't grow more attached to each other. It isn't fair to cause him any unnecessary pain. Even if it makes my own pain cut deeper.

CHAPTER 24

Soon dawn descends, and the sun breaks through the foliage of the forest. As it rises, its light glistens like diamonds on the stream, but that gemstone illusion is all that sparkles in the water. No fish flicker, not even small ones. The stream is narrow and shallow, so I shouldn't have expected much, but my impatient belly gnaws and groans. Ella's stew did little to satiate my hunger.

We nibble on grass as we travel onward. Worse than being empty of fish, the stream has yet to lead us to the river, and the longer we walk, the more Henni's mood worsens. She hasn't spoken another word to me since she realized I've kept Ella's veil, and as the day wanes to nightfall, she doesn't show any signs of breaking her silence.

I don't know how to handle a resentful Henni—I've never had any experience with one—so I decide the best course of action is to give her some space. If I had to leave my mother behind like we did with Ella, I'm sure I'd be even more sullen. Though perhaps I am a bit sullen. I *did* leave my mother behind. The vision I'd had of her in the meadow ballroom felt so real. I desperately wish it had been. The space she'd filled in my heart feels all the more vacant now.

We make camp near the stream in a spot that doesn't seem to be haunted with any dead faces in the trees. As I lie down on my bedroll, the S-curve in my back throbs, and I lament the loss of my shoe with the wedge-lift all over again. This journey is going to be that much harder without it.

Axel takes his customary place, lying beside me on my right. Once I tie our ankles together, I turn to Henni, who always joins me on my left. But she marches to the other side of Axel and plunks down, binding her ankle to his without sparing me a glance. So much for the girl who was so modest a few days ago that she had me blindfold Axel.

In no time at all, she's lightly snoring. I massage the bridge of my nose, where a dull headache has been pulsing for hours. "She's never going to forgive me," I murmur to Axel.

"What about you?" His head turns a little toward mine. His tawny skin is tinted with violet from the cool-toned hues of the night. "Are you going to forgive—?"

"I'm not angry with her!" I whisper.

"I meant me."

"Oh." I wriggle to get more comfortable. "I'm not angry with you either. Why would I be?"

"I don't know." He manages to shrug while lying flat on his back. "I came very close to marrying Ella after I danced with you and we almost . . ." He exhales and rolls out a crick in his neck. "You probably think I've been careless with your heart."

"It isn't that."

He searches my face in the darkness. "Then why have you been avoiding me?"

"I . . ." The right words struggle to form on my tongue. It's so much easier to be indifferent to Axel during the day when we aren't forced to lie side by side, when I don't have to smell him and feel the heat of him and wonder how I'll find the strength to keep resisting him. He's waking up parts of me I buried long ago, parts I never allowed to wake up in the first place.

"Do you feel guilty that you persuaded me to not marry Ella?" he prods.

Again, I don't know how to answer. I didn't feel guilty at first about what I said in the meadow, but now I do a little, especially since Henni seems to hate me for it. But admitting that to Axel would be admitting how I feel about him, and I can't give him any more encouragement. Every time he's tried to kiss me in this forest, I've practically fallen at his feet. I have to keep my head and guard my heart. Guard his heart too.

"I was the one who broke off the wedding," he says. "It was my choice, and last night wasn't the first time I made it."

My lips part. "What do you mean?"

He drags his fingers through his hair and takes a long breath. "Last summer, on the night before we were going to marry, I told Ella that I couldn't go through with it. I realized I didn't love her, not the way I was supposed to, and it wouldn't be fair to her if I became her husband feeling the way I did."

I pick at the edge of my cape. "How did she take it?"

A small and miserable laugh escapes him. "Terribly. She said I'd ruined her life forever and that I could never repair the damage I'd done to her heart."

"Oh, Axel." I don't know what to say. I ache for both of them. I feel the pain Ella must have felt, and Axel's pain because of it.

"She wasn't full of rage like she was last night," he goes on. "It was worse. She was quiet . . . shattered . . . empty." He looks away, his gaze lifting to the stars peeking through the canopy. "I don't know if she was lured into the forest or if she went there willingly because I'd broken her heart."

I study his silhouette in the darkness, the way his chin quivers as he bites the corner of his lip. "And you never told the Dantzers what really happened between you and Ella?"

He shakes his head. "I was a coward. I didn't want to add to their pain."

"You weren't a coward." I slip my hand into his.

"Then what was I?" His eyes return to me.

"You were alone."

He swallows, nods tightly. "I still felt alone with them, even though they loved me."

"I know," I whisper. I always saw it in him. Behind his charming smiles and his unaffected air, he was a broken boy who yearned for his father the same way I yearn for my mother.

He threads our fingers together. "But I don't feel alone when I'm with you."

Radiant warmth blooms through my chest. I want to hold it there, guard it so it never fades. But I can't. Because I can never be who Axel needs me to be, someone he can always depend on. Someone he won't lose.

My eyes sting. "Please don't make this harder than it already is."

He shifts closer and smooths my hair from my face. "What's wrong, Clara? Really? Is this about that fortune-telling card you told me about—the Pierced Swans? Are you afraid we're star-crossed?"

"I . . ." Again, I can't give him a straight answer. Because now I know that *is* what we are, star-crossed through and through. But that's only half of what's keeping me silent. I never told him about the Fanged Creature, my impending death—the reason we're star-crossed to begin with. Even the Red Card can't undo my fortune.

Snatches of Grandmère's words course through my mind: *The Red Card does not change the meaning of the other cards, Clara. . . . Those fates are still required. . . . That balance must hold or the Changer of Fate cannot change anything.*

Axel's fingers drift down my face and cradle my chin. He gently lifts my head until I meet his gaze. "Why do you need a card's permission to tell you how to live your life?" he whispers.

My throat tightens as I try to keep my heart from rising. "Because fate never lies." Fate predicted my father's death. It sent my mother chasing after him, only to trigger her own misfortunes. Then it sent me after her, setting me on the course that's bound to kill me. I can't change how my story will end. I can only change hers.

Axel's brows flit together, and he smiles sadly, like he can feel just how deeply I've been hurting. "Do you remember when I told you on Devotion Day that you shouldn't tempt fate?"

I nod.

"Do you remember how you replied?"

I think back on that moment, how nervous he was that I'd cast my name into the amber goblet seven times, when my name shouldn't have been in there at all. "I said, 'Isn't it about time someone did?'"

He touches his lips to my forehead. "That's why your grandmother drew the Red Card for you, Clara. You're the person who tempts fate. You don't run away from it."

His words resonate, but I try not to let them take root inside me. I can't disregard my impending death in this forest. I can't let myself love him the way I want to—the way I wish I could show him. "I think I've lost all that bravery. I'm the one who's a coward."

"You're not a coward."

"Then what am I?"

His hand slides around to stroke the back of my neck. "Someone who thinks she's alone." His voice hushes to an earnest whisper. "But you're not, Clara." He brings me closer and presses one more kiss to the crown of my head. "You're not."

CHAPTER 25

We follow the stream for three more days, and it still doesn't merge into a river or grow any larger to make room for fish. I can't even find minnows or tadpoles swimming inside it. I'd eat just about anything right now. Thankfully the stream provides water to drink, but our bellies ache for something more substantial.

We gnaw on grass and the occasional edible flower, but we don't have arrows to shoot down birds or traps to capture squirrels or small creatures. Axel has taken to wearing his knife on his belt, but he finds no deer or rabbits to take aim at. I had relied on my map and fishing lures to keep us alive after we ran out of rations, but nothing in this forest has gone according to plan.

At the end of the third day, we consider turning back to look for the river we lost, but that's almost five days behind us now, and going that direction won't help us find any food, so we keep pressing onward, our eyes fastened to the stream as we search for any way it could be hiding *Sortes Fortunae.*

Henni has become religious about finding the book. Anytime the water trickles over a minuscule dam or a gathering of stones—anything that could be the falling water in the riddle—she gasps and points it out to Axel. But the Book of Fortunes still eludes us. It's never nearby, never tucked in the wild grass by the stream or buried beneath the water in a sunken chest like pirate treasure.

I doubt the stream is its hiding place—it's too obscure and insignificant—but I don't share those thoughts with Henni.

She's still upset with me. When I try to speak to her, she only answers with small words or curt nods, and whenever I dig through my pack or adjust its strap on my shoulder, I see her eyes narrow and her hands clench. She hasn't forgiven me for taking Ella's veil.

She hasn't forgiven me for anything to do with her sister.

I fear the only way to regain our friendship is to see Ella safely back home in Grimm's Hollow. But without the book and breaking the curse with it, that will be impossible.

"Perhaps we're going about our search the wrong way," I tell my friends when it must be noon from the angle of the sun. "What if we keep an eye out for signs of good luck rather than looking for the book directly? Those signs could lead us to *Sortes Fortunae*. I think Ella had the same thing in mind. She said part of the reason why she chose the hollow were its water and the red-spotted mushrooms."

Axel groans. "No more mushrooms."

"I'm not saying we need to eat them, but in stories they always promise good luck. Plus they were growing near the pavilion where the Book of Fortunes was once kept in the village. That has to mean something." I pause to rub my ever-throbbing hip and lower back. "And maybe they don't have to be red-spotted mushrooms. Any signs of good luck could lead us to the book. Four-leaf clovers, shooting stars, ladybugs . . ."

"Pigs are lucky," Henni says.

"A pig?" Axel chuckles.

I pinch him. This is the first time in days that Henni has spoken to me without stiffness in her voice, and I don't want him ruining the moment by teasing her. "Pigs *are* lucky," I say. "They symbolize wealth and prosperity."

"But where would we find one in the Forest Grimm?" Axel asks. "There aren't even wild boar here."

"You never know. Many farmers lost livestock in these woods since the curse."

Axel huffs. "Well, if we're ever so lucky to come across a pig, we're eating it."

"Not until it first leads us to the book." Henni thrusts up her chin.

Axel throws his hands up. "Fine."

The two of them have taken to bickering as the days wear on and our bellies grow thinner. They aren't genuinely fighting. Their tones aren't even raised. They're more like siblings who poke sticks at each other because they're bored . . . or starving.

Henni branches away from us, but stays within sight as she scours the ground now instead of the stream.

I smirk at Axel as we continue walking. "You're awfully possessive of this imaginary pig."

"Shh." He closes his eyes for a moment. "You'll shatter the illusion. I was just carving myself a thick pork chop. I can almost smell it, Clara."

I laugh. "Be sure to save me a bite."

"I'll give you all the best parts, even the cuts for bacon."

I laugh again, but my smile fades as I take in the sharpening edges of Axel's face, the hollowing beneath his cheekbones and temples, and the way his chin juts out harsher against the slope of his neck. He's withering away before me, and I'm sure I look as rawboned and undernourished. We desperately need a stroke of good fortune. I don't know how much longer we can keep walking hour after hour, day after day like this.

Axel absorbs my fallen expression. He takes my hand and squeezes it. "I hear that squirrels are even tastier than pigs. And as for luck, well, who decides what's lucky anyway? I say we do."

I catch myself softly grinning at him. I should pull my hand away. I usually do when he finds occasion to graze his fingers against mine. But I can't let go this time. He has a gift for finding silver linings, and that relentless hope is what has been sustaining me. "Are you saying you've figured out how to build a squirrel trap?"

"No. But tonight I insist on learning how."

He stays true to his word. An hour before sunset, we make camp early so he can begin his task. I help him break slim branches off the trees since there are no dry twigs on the forest floor, and he fashions them into a small cage, lashed together with sewing thread. Henni wanders around nearby us, still searching for any elusive signs of good luck. The day hasn't brought her any, and Axel's and my attempts have been just as fruitless.

I rub my sunburned brow as I cast my gaze about the surrounding woods. It's not that I thought *Sortes Fortunae* would be conveniently located close by, but I keep hoping the forest will throw us a bone, give us a sign that at least points us in the right direction. But we're tainted by the curse. These woods don't have any tolerance for those who come from Grimm's Hollow. I already feel their patience dwindling with us, despite the red rampion–dyed clothes we wear. It's like the forest is deliberately scaring the fish away and keeping the stream ribbon-thin. It wants us to starve and lose hope.

The only times it relents is when its guests have succumbed to madness. Then it makes a strange peace with them, like it did with Fiora and Ella. After those two became Rapunzel and Cinderella, the forest allowed them to live unharmed here. They were doing enough harm to themselves, I suppose.

"There." Axel sits back to assess his handiwork. "It's the ugliest cage I've ever seen, but I think it just might catch a squirrel."

I bite back a smile as I observe the cage with him. He wasn't lying about it being ugly. It's a wild contraption of haphazardly arranged sticks, somewhat resembling a box, with a little opening for a squirrel to squeeze inside. It's missing a trapdoor—we couldn't think of how to devise that part—but Axel plans to throw a handkerchief over the cage once it has ensnared a squirrel. I have one in my pack, and I've sewn little stones around the edges to keep it weighted down over the cage.

We have no food for the bait, so I reluctantly place the acorn my mother gave me inside the cage, with every intention to steal it back again after we've caught a squirrel.

The night is chilly, so we light a fire and enjoy its warmth while we still have energy to keep kindling the flames with pine cones. Axel watches the squirrel trap like a hawk, Henni roasts grass to see if it will be more palatable (it's not), and I remove the linen strips from my feet, wash them in the stream, and hang them to dry on a branch overnight.

My feet are sore and blistered, and my back hasn't stopped smarting. The willow bark I packed with my emergency supply kit only takes the edge off the pain. I entertain fantasies of stumbling upon a cobbler in this forest who can make me a pair of new shoes with a wedge-lift inside to slide under my left heel.

After waiting three hours and failing to trap any squirrels, the three of us heave a chorus of dejected sighs and resign ourselves to bed. In a hushed conversation, slightly heated on Henni's part, Axel persuades her to let me sleep in the middle of our trio tonight. He thinks he'll hear a squirrel if one scampers near the cage, and he wants to sleep on the outer edge of us so he can be ready to catch it.

We lie beneath a hazel tree, one I stare at for what feels like half the night, long after Henni has fallen asleep with her back turned to me and Axel is snoring quietly, despite his resolve to stay alert as our self-appointed squirrel hunter.

The hazel reminds me of the one back in Grimm's Hollow,

the Tree of the Lost that villagers hang tokens on to remember their loved ones. I picture the strip of rose-red wool I tied to the tree for Mother, and I whisper my never-forgotten promise: "I will come for you."

A breeze swirls, stirring an eddy of mulch through the air. My eyelids bat as I track the motion, hazily mesmerized. Another breeze whispers past me, and my vision loses focus. I'm lulled to the brink of sleep.

"Will you truly come for me?" a feminine voice asks. It's rich in tone, but weary and acerbic. My eyes snap open, and I look up. I startle to see a face that wasn't there moments ago protruding from the hazel's trunk. "I don't believe you anymore, Clara."

I gape at my mother, speechless. I have to be dreaming; I can't blame any red-spotted mushrooms for this vision. My mind, left to its own devices, is responsible.

Mother's beautiful face is reduced to bark and wood grain and warped knots. Aside from the fact that it's moving and animated, it's like the frozen faces of the dead people in the forest. "Am I too late?" My chest constricts against the hammering of my heart. "Are you still—?"

"Alive?" A fold of the bark arches where her brow should be. "For now. But you have forgotten me."

"I haven't, I swear."

"You're more preoccupied with finding *Sortes Fortunae* than you are your own mother."

"I have to break the curse. It will save you too."

"But will you really break it when you find the book, or will you wish for shoes or a suckling pig?"

"How can you say that? You know what I'm prepared to sacrifice for you."

Mother's woody eyes narrow, and her head cocks skeptically.

"But are you prepared to let your friends suffer? If it came down to it, Clara, would you save them or me?"

A wolf howls. The Grimm wolf? Has she found me again?

"I will save you," I promise Mother, though my words seem to scrape at my ankles where rope binds me to my friends.

"You're a terrible liar." Her face retracts into the scaly fissures of the bark.

"Wait!" I jerk upright. "I *will* save you!"

My words ring unusually loud. My eyes flash open. The night is darker now, and the ghostly glow that illuminated the hazel has disappeared.

I blow out a long breath, trying to shake away the sickly feeling of guilt inside me. That wasn't my mother in the dream. She could never be that harsh or cynical. She would never have expressed such doubt in me. I tell myself that, and yet her words sting.

A wolf howls from not too far away. I stiffen as my gaze lifts, following the sound to a high and steep rocky precipice in the distance. A large wolf—the Grimm wolf—is silhouetted against the waning light of an almost full-circle moon. I wasn't dreaming about her. She's really found me.

Another howl rips out of her. Shivers claw up my arms and neck like splinters of ice. That howl was portentous, filled with doom. It's either a threat or a warning—a promise of attack or a dark omen.

I would run—I would drag Henni and Axel away, even with our ankles bound—but the wolf can't reach us quickly from her high position. She wouldn't survive a speedy descent off that precipice. Still, I move to untie the rope binding me to Henni just in case . . . but it's already undone. And she isn't beside me.

My muscles tense. "Henni?" I yell.

Axel flinches and mumble-shouts, "Squirrel!"

A hysterical part of me wants to laugh—or cry—or dig myself

into a dark hole. My dream tried to warn me. Maybe the Grimm wolf did too. I'm responsible for my friends. I need to save them as well as my mother. But I've failed.

I jostle Axel awake, my hands rattling like I have the palsy. "Henni is gone!"

His bleary eyes sharpen and focus. "Gone? Gone where?"

"I don't know."

He hurriedly unties the rope at our ankles and lights our lantern. I grab my pack, and he grabs Henni's. My stomach twists. If she left us deliberately, she would have taken her pack. What's happened to her?

We circle our campsite and search for any fresh tracks, but they are too plentiful. Henni's shoe prints are everywhere. The whole time Axel and I were working on our squirrel trap, she was scanning our surroundings for any signs of good luck.

"Clara, look." Axel points to a strange trail that leads northeast and away from the stream: a path of shiny white pebbles that aren't natural to the environment. They're too perfectly placed— one every foot or two. "Do you think Henni left them for us to follow?"

"Maybe." I wouldn't put it past her. She could have collected them without us noticing, like she does with pine cones for our fires. "But if she didn't leave them, she still could have followed them, thinking they were signs of good luck."

"Are they?" Axel squints at them.

I scour my brain for any omens having to do with stones, pebbles, or moonlit trails, but nothing comes to mind. I steal another glance at the wolf watching above and swallow hard. "I don't know, but I think we have to follow it."

Axel fetches the squirrel trap. I take back the acorn and shove it in my pocket, and we set off after Henni. I hate leaving the stream. If this were a normal forest, I'd trust that the pebbles could lead us back to the water. But this is the Forest Grimm. It shifts when I sleep. It absorbs dead people into trees. It could open the earth to swallow pebbles in a fleeting heartbeat.

We'll probably never find the sure path of the stream again.

Are you prepared to let your friends suffer? I feel the nightmare version of my mother asking me again. *If it came down to it, Clara, would you save them or me?*

"I'll save you," I whisper, forging onward, and wrap my hand over the shape of the acorn in my pocket. "I'll save all of you."

As we pass out of the Grimm wolf's view, she howls one last time, her lone voice crying against the night. Whether she calls a warning or a threat, I'm sure it means one thing. . . .

Death is coming. The cards of my fate are all falling in line. And if I don't find the Book of Fortunes fast enough, the Red Card won't be able to help my mother or anyone.

Death will come in the form of the Fanged Creature.

And it will claim me.

CHAPTER 26

The pebbles catch the moonlight, shining our way into a moss-covered gulch that looks like a natural runoff for rainwater. With the way the trees grow on the sides of the gulch and how their branches curve to arch above it, it gives the illusion that we're walking through a dreamlike tunnel of leaves and lichen.

I'm holding Axel's hand. I'm not sure when it happened, if he reached for my fingers first, or if mine gravitated toward his, but I keep a firm grasp. I've lost one friend in the night, and I'm not letting another one slip away from me.

The gulch wends its way deeper into the thickening woods, and the air hangs heavy with moisture. It's going to rain soon. Axel's hair curls above his ears and the nape of his neck. Mine droops into dark, loose waves.

We haven't endured a proper rainstorm since we began our journey, only light sprinklings here and there, and while the village girl in me dances at the prospect of rain since it is scarce in Grimm's Hollow, the forest girl I have become is wary. The energy churning through the atmosphere feels like another bad omen. It's as if the Grimm wolf is still following me, her howls masked by the thunder stirring in dark clouds overhead.

Soon the pebbles lose their silver luster; the moon is hidden by the gathering storm. Only the flickering amber light from Axel's lantern guides us onward.

Just when I fear the pebbles will lead us nowhere, like the

stream we've been following, and the gulch will stretch on indefinitely, Axel nods ahead. "Look." Several yards in the distance, at the edge of the lantern's illumination, a natural incline leads out of the gulch. The pebble trail ends at the foot of it. "What do you think we'll find beyond there?"

I have no idea. "With any luck, Henni."

An unnerving sensation takes hold of me and raises the hair on my arms, a keen awareness that someone is watching us. I squeeze Axel's hand tighter as we walk forward and keep an eye on the trees cinching the gulch, looking for the silhouette of a tail or pointed ears. Has the Grimm wolf had time to catch up to us?

Lighting flashes. Thunder cracks. A figure steps out from the trees on the right ledge of the gully. I startle and clutch my hand over my heart.

Axel jerks to a halt. He raises his lantern to the trees, casting his gaze where I'm looking. "What is it?" he asks me. "Who's there?"

I stagger on my feet, still recovering from my fright. "Y-you don't see him?"

"Who?"

I stare back at the little boy with the head of floppy curls and large elfin eyes. The flickering lightning doesn't illuminate him any brighter than he already is. Neither does the lantern. He's not glowing exactly—no halo of light radiates from him like it does around fireflies—but he must be glowing a little, or else how could I see him in the darkness?

"Who's there, Clara?" Axel presses.

"I . . . He's . . ." Where do I begin? I never found the right moment to tell Axel about Ollie. In truth, I wondered if I should. Would mentioning him open old wounds about Axel's uncle—

Ollie's father? But now that I'm put on the spot, I can't be silent anymore. "Do you believe in ghosts?"

Axel shifts back and scrutinizes my face. "No." A vein pulses at the base of his neck, underlit by the lantern. "If ghosts were real, I would have seen my f—" His voice catches. He works his jaw muscle and clears his throat. "There are no ghosts, Clara. Not even in the Forest Grimm."

I nibble at my lip. What if he's right? What if I'm only seeing Ollie because I'm losing my mind like Ella? She implied she'd met the boy too. He'd been warning other villagers about her, she said. But was any of that true?

Ollie hops into the gulch. "It's not nice to say you don't believe in someone." He frowns at Axel, sizing him up. "Tell your friend I said so."

"I . . ." This is ridiculous. I don't have time for small talk with what may be a figment of my imagination. I just need to convince myself—and Axel—that Ollie is real so we can hopefully trust him. We could use his help to find Henni. "This isn't just my friend, Ollie. This is your cousin, Axel Furst."

The lantern wobbles in Axel's grip. Candlelight bounces around the gulch. "Clara, why would you—?"

"Axel spent some of his life growing up in your home." I talk over him, addressing Ollie again. "Tell me something that only the two of you would know from having lived there."

Ollie groans and throws his head back dramatically. "You're making me think too hard."

"Do you have something better to do?" I raise a brow.

He huffs just like Axel huffs when he's feigning exasperation. "Fine." He kicks at the ground and disturbs nothing. "There's a loose floorboard by the rocking chair where Papa hides his hard cider."

I repeat this to Axel, and his hands clench. "My uncle could have told you that if he was drunk enough," he says to me.

"But he didn't. And I'm not making this up." I tamp down a flare of hurt. "Do you think I want ghosts to be real?"

"That's not what I . . ." He exhales. "You know I trust you, Clara. But this forest . . . it does things to people. It could make you believe—"

"Humor me, then. Tell me what I should ask Ollie—something only you and he would know. Something your uncle wouldn't be aware of."

Axel scrubs a hand over his face and tries to think. After a moment, he begrudgingly answers, "There's an oak out back past the goat shed. Ask . . . *him*, or whatever it is you're seeing, what he would find if he climbed it halfway?"

I turn back to Ollie. He's jumping between a few pebbles marking our trail. "Well?"

Thunder ripples through the sky as he makes another leap. "Does Axel mean the knothole?"

I meet Axel's eyes. "He says there's a knothole."

Axel's mouth forms a skeptical line. "Any oak could have a knothole."

"Then think of a better question!"

"It's a special knothole." Ollie picks up a pebble, or at least goes through the motion of doing so. It passes right through his blurry-edged fingers. "It's where I keep my tin soldiers." He pantomimes throwing the pebble far down the gully.

I relay Ollie's answer, adding the last details as he shares them: "A set of nineteen soldiers," I tell Axel. "He lost one of the drummers."

Even in our dim surroundings, I can see Axel's face pale. "And the standard bearer in the set," he adds. "He was—"

"—missing his flag," I repeat Ollie's words as he finishes Axel's sentence.

Axel stumbles back a step, his eyes bulging. "Ollie is really here?" His gaze roams around us as if the boy is suddenly everywhere. "W-why? What does he want?" He tugs at his collar. "Is he upset with me? I stayed with his dad for as long as possible. Tell him that. But the man was too . . ." Axel cringes. "People say he wasn't the same after his wife and Ollie died. His grief made him angry and . . ." He backs himself up against the sidewall of the gully and takes several long breaths.

"It's all right." I go to him. "Ollie isn't upset with anyone but himself." And he's *real*! I want to pinch myself. I'm not delusional. "He's trapped in the forest because of two pennies."

I quickly fill him in on the story of how I met Ollie before I met Ella, and what Ollie told me about the coins he stole for himself when his mother intended them to go to a poor man. "Ollie buried them in the forest," I add, "but he can't remember where."

"Have you found them yet?" Ollie blurts. I startle to find he's standing right behind me.

"Well . . . no, I . . ." I shift, wiping a bit of sprinkling rain off my face. "We're deep in the forest. Don't you think you would have buried the pennies near the border of Grimm's Hollow?"

"So." He juts out his chin.

"So . . . that's very far away."

"Guess what moves when the trees do?"

I'm not sure what he's getting at. "Not pennies?"

"Wrong. Pennies can move because the earth moves. The tree roots stir up all the dirt, so my pennies could be anywhere in the forest."

It's logic befitting an eight-year-old, anyway. Even with some hefty "earth-stirring," how could the coins be this many miles from Grimm's Hollow? "Listen, Ollie. I haven't forgotten about the pennies. I told you I'd help you search for them, and I will. But first I need to find . . . well, a lot of things." *The Book of Fortunes. Mother.* "But the most pressing is my friend, Henni. She went missing just tonight. We think she traveled down this gully. Have you seen her?"

"Nope."

How can he be so certain? Does he even know what she looks like? "She wears a red kerchief and her hair in two braids."

"The woman in red didn't say anything about a red kerchief, just your cape." His gaze sweeps over me. "Looks like you found that at least."

I bite my tongue against the urge to ask him more about the woman in red. His attention span is too fleeting, and Henni is my priority. "So you didn't see any other girls tonight?"

He mulls over the question. Or I think that's what he's doing until he says, "You didn't even *try* looking for the pennies, did you?"

"Ollie, please." I reach for his shoulders to help him focus, but of course my hands grasp nothing. "I know the pennies are important to you, but—"

"What happened to your shoes?"

I don't have time to tell that story. "I lost them."

"That's too bad. It's not fun to lose things in this forest, is it? I know because I lost my pennies, *and—no—one—will—help—me—find—them.*"

My teeth grind together. If he were tangible, I would strangle him. "Ollie, for the last time—"

"Tell him I know where the lost drummer is," Axel says abruptly.

I shuffle back a step. "You've been following our conversation?"

"Enough of it. At least from your end." He unhitches himself from the gully's wall, far more composed than he was a moment ago. "The gist of it is we need Ollie's help, but he won't give it unless we give something in return, right? We don't have his pennies, but I can tell him about his lost drummer."

I face Ollie again. He's mashing his lips together, his eyes narrowed at his cousin. "Why should I care about the drummer? I can't play with him anymore. Even if I could, it wouldn't help me be at rest with Mama."

I murmur his words to Axel, who draws his shoulders back and ventures a step in the general direction of Ollie. "No," he concedes, "but if I had as fine a set of tin soldiers as you did as a boy, and I lost one of them, I wouldn't be at rest whether I was alive or . . . well, like you."

Ollie plants his legs wide and squares his shoulders, matching Axel's stance. They remind me of villagers on market day working to strike a fair bargain. "All right." Raindrops fall around him— fall through him, none landing or clinging to his body. "I'll answer one question in return for Axel's answer about the drummer."

I cross my arms. "But you have to give a solid answer—a helpful answer," I stipulate. "Saying 'I don't know' doesn't count. Promise?"

Ollie rolls his eyes. "Promise."

I look to Axel and nod. "Tell him."

Axel scratches the golden stubble on his jaw. "Does Ollie remember the boarded-up house past the barley field? My uncle—er, Ollie's father—called it the old shack?"

"I know it." Ollie leans his weight on one leg. "But I never took my tin soldiers there."

I pass along the message.

"Well, you might not have"—Axel addresses Ollie directly now—"but a jackdaw once did. They're thieves for shiny things, and I found the drummer in a nest up the chimney."

Ollie's mouth drops open. I brace myself for him to throw some kind of ghostly fit over the tragic fate of his toy. Instead he bursts into laughter. He even wheezes like Axel has a habit of doing. "Smart jackdaw."

I might laugh with him if Henni weren't in danger. But we're already stalling too long. I bend closer to Ollie. "There, you've learned what happened to your drummer. Now will you help us? We need to know if you saw Henni tonight." I describe her again. "Or any girls resembling her."

Ollie rubs his neck. "Um, you should ask something else because the answer is *no,* and I promised to be helpful."

I shake my head at Axel, my stomach twisting. "He doesn't know." *Poor Henni.* What's become of her?

Worry lines crease between Axel's brows. "What now?"

"We still have one more question."

"But only if you hurry." Ollie tosses a wary gaze around the gully. "I can't stay in one place for long."

I frown. "What happens if you do?"

"The dead people in the trees start talking to me, and I don't like the ones in this part of the forest. They're still angry about their deaths. They were gruesome." He shudders. "'Gruesome' sounds like a funny word, but it's not funny at all. The dead people said it means horrible and scary and gross all mixed together." He wraps his arms around himself. "I don't like to hear about gruesome deaths."

"I wouldn't either." I send a silent supplication to the forest, *Don't let Henni die a gruesome death. Please don't let her die* any *death.*

Axel gently prods me with his elbow. "What's your question?"

I refocus myself. "The Book of Fortunes, do you—?"

Ollie shakes his head. "Never seen it."

"The woman in red, then. How do I find her?"

"Oh, I can't tell you that." Another shudder chases through him. "You don't want to know."

"I *do* want to know. And you promised to give me a solid answer!"

"But I have to be helpful too. I also promised to do that. And telling you where that woman lives would *not* be helping you."

"Ollie!"

He winces, his eyes shifting around. "Oh no. They're starting to talk." He claps his hands over his ears. Lightning flashes through the forest canopy. "I said you had to hurry, Clara!" He backs away and starts to fade.

"No, please!" Panic grips me. He can't go without giving me something to cling to, something to help me on this impossible journey. "Last time we met, you said you thought I might be different. You talked about magic touching rare people, just like it touched this forest, and how the woman in red said I might be one of those people." I'm rambling so fast I have to pause to catch my breath. "So . . . how am I magic?"

It seems like the silliest question in the world. But foolish or not, I'm desperate to learn just about anything from Ollie right now. His transparency is thinning to near nothingness.

He pinches his eyes shut against the onslaught of voices only he can hear, the dead barraging him with their horror stories. "You were born with gifts." Thunder booms. "It's in your blood, she said."

My thoughts clatter. I blink rain from my lashes. Who told Ollie this? My mother? Is she gifted too?

I steady my trembling legs. "How is it in my blood? I can't

read fortunes in cards. I don't foresee like my grandmother. I've never caught any glimpses of the future."

Ollie is dwindling. I only see patches of him. Two eyes. Suspenders. A mop of curls. "Your gifts aren't with the future." His voice fades with his appearance. "She said you see the past."

"B-but," I stammer. That doesn't make sense. I've never seen the past. "How can I—?"

Ollie vanishes. I flounder on my feet.

"Clara?" Axel touches my arm.

"He's . . . he's gone."

Axel steps around me to see my face in the glow of his lantern. "What was all of that about?" He searches my eyes. "A woman in red? You having magic? What did Ollie tell you?"

I shake my head in a daze. I can't find the right words.

Another flash and roar seize the sky. A second later, it cracks open and unleashes a fury of rain. I pull up the hood of my cape. Axel points ahead. There's a large tree to the left of the path that inclines out of the gully. It looks like a promising shelter. "Hurry!" he shouts.

We rush forward. Climb the exiting path. Duck under the large tree. We're above the lip of the gully now, and I survey our surroundings . . . or what I can of them through the heavy rainfall.

From what I can make out, we're in a stretch of the forest that's filled with massive pine trees. Their trunks are wider than my cottage. Even if it were daytime, I doubt I could see how tall they reach. Their scraggly boughs tangle together in a dense canopy, but the rain still finds its way to us and the tree we're under. Fat drops slide down my hair and glance off my cape and spatter the skirt of my dress.

"Clara." Axel moves his mouth to my ear, his voice low and strained. His hand tenses around mine. "There are people ahead."

People? We've never come across more than one person at a time in the Forest Grimm. Perhaps it's Henni, and she's with someone.

I struggle to see clearer, and make out two figures in the darkness twelve yards ahead. I can't pin what it is about them, but a foreboding feeling slithers through my stomach. Henni can't be one of them.

"Who are you?" Axel demands loudly. I wince at his sharp tone, but I understand why he used it. We haven't met anyone on our journey who didn't seek to harm us. Ollie doesn't count; he's a ghost. And whoever these two are, they can't be ghosts if Axel can see them.

"I'm Clara Thurn, and this is Axel Furst," I offer when they don't respond. "We're from Grimm's Hollow."

Again, we're only met with silence. The rain falls even harder and starts to penetrate my cape. I shiver and wipe the wetness from my brow. "Hold up your lantern," I whisper to Axel. "Maybe they need to see us better."

"No, we should leave." He steps backward. "I don't have a good feeling."

"We can't leave. We came here to find the Lost." I don't have a good feeling either, but I won't abandon someone I know. "What if that's the Tragers or the Brauns out there?" Some villagers entered the forest as couples, not wanting to risk the chance of being separated if they never returned.

Axel lifts his lantern hesitantly. Several feet away, a man and woman flinch as if scared by the light. Their eyes are dark, their skin is pale, and their hair shines startlingly white. They're holding hands like we are, an eerie and twisted reflection of us.

On second glance, they aren't quite old enough to be adults. They're closer to our ages.

"Do you know them?" Axel murmurs.

I shake my head. And that's the most disturbing thing about the boy and girl: I'm absolutely certain I've never seen either of them before in our small village. They could be from the lower valley, but that's a two-week journey from Grimm's Hollow, and even longer from where we are now, deep in the forest. "What are your names?" I ask. "Where are you from?"

As one, the boy and girl slowly turn to look at each other, and whatever passes between them is lost on me. They don't smile or frown or so much as raise a brow before they return their gazes to us. Neither of them answers.

"Perhaps they speak a different language," I whisper to Axel, though that likelihood is even rarer. Grandmère speaks a different language, but she's from a land a month's journey from here, and that's on horseback. Languages beyond that place feel too make-believe to be real, like trolls and fairies and other strange wonders in the small collection of books back at home in my cottage. No one in Grimm's Hollow has ever heard them spoken before.

"Where is your home?" I try again, inching closer to the boy and girl. I tug Axel along with me.

Finally a look of recognition crosses their faces. "Home?" the girl repeats. Something about the way she talks is a little off, like she has an accent or a slight difficulty with speech.

"Home." The boy nods and waves us forward, his expression neither cold nor welcoming.

Axel forces a smile, but he leans toward me and asks in a thin voice, "What do we do?"

I'm torn between my urge to be helpful to anyone Lost in the forest and my sense of dread. Do I really need to help them if they aren't from Grimm's Hollow? Maybe they're not Lost or cursed. Maybe they've always lived here.

"We're looking for our friend, Henni." I raise my voice against the rainfall.

Another spark of recognition flashes across the boy's and girl's faces. They share a glance, and this time I catch a glimpse of the expression that passes between them. It's pointed. Pressing. The girl bends her head to the boy's ear and whispers something.

Licking his lips, the boy turns back to us. The rain drenches his hair into his eyes. "Henni. Yes." He beckons us to follow him again.

My instincts scream to run the other way, but I can't. What if they *do* know where Henni is? What if they're really generous and want to help, but their manners are odd because they live here alone?

The chances that they're good-hearted are slim—the forest hasn't granted us any friends yet—but I think we need to follow them for Henni's sake.

Axel's gaze traps mine. It holds a flood of emotions and unspoken words. I feel his concern and protective affection, but also his firm resolve. He's ready to follow the boy and girl too.

At least we know we'll be walking into danger this time. We'll stay on our guard. And we'll be together, eyes open and hand in hand. He'll be there for me, and I'll be there for him.

The boy and the girl turn away from us and wander deeper into the forest, a silent summoning for us to follow.

Axel and I huddle closer, shoulder to shoulder, and walk after them.

CHAPTER 27

he boy and girl lead Axel and me to one of the giant pines. Its girth is even wider than the hulking trees surrounding it, and it stands on a network of huge aboveground roots. They look like a clawed hand reaching into the earth from the arm of the trunk. Vines hang in curtains over the roots, and lush vegetation covers the ground encircling them.

That's all I can make out of this place past the torrential rain. I feel like I'm literally breathing water. I'm desperate for any kind of shelter. When the boy and girl part a section of vines for us and reveal an arched entrance under the root system of the pine, I practically race inside with Axel. Five steps in, I come to an abrupt stop, taking in everything with wide eyes.

We're standing in a bell-shaped space, round overhead with a seven-foot ceiling made of gnarled roots that branch away from the tree and enclose us in a twelve-foot circular room. The walls are also made of roots, but they're interwoven with the vines I spied outside. Now that I can see the vines more clearly, my mouth waters.

The most delectable assortment of fruits and vegetables are growing on them. Grapes, raspberries, peas, cucumbers, melons, tomatoes, and pole beans. Most aren't even in season, but they're still bright in color and ripened to perfection. They look as if with just one nudge they'll drop from their stems and fall into my waiting hands.

"I know what you're going to say." Axel's face disarms me

with a pained expression, though beneath its tightness, there's a scrap of cautious hope. "We shouldn't eat any of this . . . right?"

"I suppose not. Not after what happened with Ella's mushrooms." As if punishing me for declining, my stomach emits a growl that rivals the thunder outside.

Someone giggles from behind us, a girl whose sweet laughter I'd recognize anywhere. My heart leaps, and I spin around. Standing in this strange house beneath a tree is Henni. She's lingering just beside the arched entrance. I probably raced right past her when I burst inside.

I gasp and throw my arms around her. She must not hate me completely, because she hugs me back and laughs again. "The food isn't poisonous, I promise," she says. "I've been eating it for two hours now, and I'm perfectly fine."

I don't know what to say. I'm angry that she took such a foolish risk to eat it in the first place—and to leave us behind, for that matter—but the selfish, starving part of me is also grateful, because now I might be able to eat too. "Are you sure?"

She nods, beaming. "I'm not hallucinating, and I haven't been sick in the slightest. You were right to trust in signs of good luck. I followed them, and look where they brought us!"

"But how did you know the pebbles meant good luck?"

"It wasn't the pebbles." She grins furtively. "It was the fox that darted across the path when I first saw the pebbles."

A fox crossing is indeed a sign of good luck, but what if Henni was wrong? "Are you sure it wasn't a black cat?" It wouldn't be the first wildcat we've seen in this forest.

"Oh, Clara," she chides me in her loving way. "Stop fretting and eat the food. I haven't died yet, have I?"

The joke lands wrong and strikes a frayed nerve, but I suppose she's right about the food. The boy and girl are another matter. They snuck inside when my back was turned and are watching us with unnerving black eyes. "Very well." I glance behind me at Axel. "Let's eat."

He looks like I just gave him the prized pony from the village fair. He throws off Henni's pack, drops the lantern, and practically hurls himself at the tomatoes. I suppress a giggle as I watch him shove them down his throat. "Don't forget to chew."

He bats a dismissive hand and reaches for a cluster of grapes.

"Try the raspberries." Henni gives me a little shove. "They're sweeter than sugar."

The raspberries climb up from the ground and tangle with cucumbers that cling to slender root offshoots. I set down my pack and tentatively approach them, conscious of the heavy gazes of the boy and girl studying my every move. I didn't even think to ask them if we could start devouring their food.

"Don't worry about Hansel and Gretel," Henni says, sensing my hesitation. "They're happy to share."

I don't know how she can tell if they're happy. When I smile at them, they only stare back unblinkingly. "I'm impressed you learned their names," I murmur for only her to hear. "They don't seem overanxious to speak, do they?"

"They will if you talk in plain enough terms," Henni replies, as if she's known them for ages. "I think they're twins," she adds, like that somehow illuminates her point.

I reach for the raspberries, pluck a handful of them, and pop one in my mouth. A burst of incredible flavor lands on my tongue, and my eyes grow round. "Did raspberries always taste this wonderful?"

"Nope," Axel says. "Nothing has ever tasted this good." He's cracked open a melon and is scooping up its soft flesh with his hand. "Not lamb chops, not roast goose. Most definitely not squirrel meat."

The girl, Gretel, snaps up her head. "Meat?"

Axel nods, talking around mouthfuls of melon. "We tried to catch a squirrel in that cage there." He points a sticky finger at our ramshackle creation, which I've knotted on top of my pack. "But no luck. Not that I'm complaining. Like I said, what you have here"—he digs out more melon—"is unsurpassable."

I'm too busy inhaling raspberries to add my hearty agreement. The fruit is better than iced gingerbread and plum dumplings and peppermint sticks, all the sweet things I remember eating as a child when sugar wasn't so hard to come by.

Axel's ramblings and my gorging seem to be lost on Hansel and Gretel. She looks to her brother, who really must be her twin for how similarly they look in age and appearance. They both even have a thin streak of red hair among all their shocking white-blond locks. She repeats the word she said a moment ago: "Meat."

A wrinkle forms between Hansel's brows. He nears the squirrel cage we've brought. Gretel follows behind, traipsing lightly on her toes like she's anticipating a wonderful surprise. Hansel shakes the cage and peers inside it. He turns to Gretel. "No."

She waves an impatient finger at my pack. "Meat."

Hansel clumsily fidgets with the cinch.

"We don't have any meat." I pluck a cucumber and tear my teeth into it. "Or any food, for that matter. That's why we're so"—I choke on a large swallow of crisp perfection—"grateful."

Hansel ignores me. He finally succeeds in prying open my pack, and he dumps its contents on the ground. I should probably be upset, but all I care about is getting more food in my belly.

Gretel kneels beside Hansel. They curiously pick through my belongings: the red veil, my shoe, my tin of lures, my flint kit, my obsolete map, my last candle, and my emergency apothecary supplies. They prod things, shake things, even bite things.

They have to be the strangest people I've ever met. "We really don't have any meat."

Gretel stands and marches toward me. I shrink back, surprised at the fire in her coal-dark eyes. She grabs my hand and yanks me toward the other side of the room, where a nook breaks away from the circular chamber we're in. It's also encaged in roots, but the ground is covered with . . . "Bones." My voice croaks, though I'm not sure why I'm so disturbed. They're just tiny bones, small creatures that Hansel and Gretel must have eaten before collecting their remains.

"Meat," Gretel enunciates, and points at them, like she's the one who has to speak plainly to be understood.

I nod, but ease a step away from her. "Clearly you like meat, but I promise we don't have any. No meat." I cut my hand through the air for emphasis.

Hansel stalks toward me. I retreat another step, feeling the sick crunch of bones beneath my bandaged feet. "Axel, tell him we don't have any."

Axel finally looks up from his clean-picked melon rind. His brows slant down when he sees me being cornered. "Whoa, what's going on?" He wipes his hands on his trousers and strides toward us.

Henni scurries over too. "I'll help Hansel and Gretel understand."

"I think they already do," I say. "They understand 'no' and 'meat,' and they don't seem very happy about it."

Axel glances behind me at the bones. "We didn't catch any squirrels," he tells Hansel again. "No. Squirrels."

Gretel whirls on him. "Meat," she demands.

Henni raises her hands, trying to calm everyone. "No meat," she tells Hansel and Gretel as if talking to small children and not teenaged strangers. "But we have medicine, how about that?

Med-i-cine." She pantomimes injuring her hand and rubbing a salve on it. "Medicine is good. You like medicine?"

Gretel's nostrils flare. She speaks through clenched teeth. "Meat!"

The edge of Hansel's mouth curls in a wicked grin as his gaze rakes over Henni.

My friend's confidence shrivels, and she tucks closer to Axel for protection. "I think you were right, Clara," she hisses. "I saw a black cat."

"Don't worry." I elbow past the twins to reach her. "Now that we've found you, we can leave." I face our hosts. "Thank you for the food, but we have to be going now."

Henni doesn't wait to see how they respond. She scrambles for my pack and stuffs the red veil inside it. Axel takes my hand, and we creep backward without removing our eyes from Hansel and Gretel. As simpleminded as they may seem, their threatening looks are very real and deadly.

Axel squeezes my hand twice, some kind of signal. I don't understand it. I meet his gaze. Shake my head. Whatever subtlety he was going for is lost as he shouts, "RUN!"

We whirl and race for the archway. Henni sprints with us.

Slam.

A thick tree root stomps in front of us and blocks our exit. We backtrack, but another root lashes out and snatches Axel's knife from his belt. We dart in every direction, but the tree moves faster. More roots lurch up, snap down, and encircle us. In mere seconds, we're trapped in a woody cage in the center of the room, an inner enclosure of roots within the outer claw of Hansel and Gretel's home.

Standing outside the trap, the twins wear smug grins. Gretel reaches inside the cage and pinches Henni's upper arm. "Meat."

CHAPTER 28

he red rampion didn't protect us," Henni says mournfully.

"We knew it couldn't keep us safe forever." Axel rams his shoulder against one of the roots of our cage. Like all the other roots he's been testing, it doesn't snap or budge.

Several hours have passed. It's morning now. Grayish light seeps in the chamber beneath the pine tree, squeezing in through tiny gaps between the draping vines.

The rain let up a few minutes ago, and once it did, Hansel and Gretel stepped outside to do who knows what. Perhaps discuss in their fragmented language how they plan to devour us for breakfast.

I shudder and work faster at digging the escape hole I've been making. So far it's only a few inches deep, and at the rate I'm going, it could take days to finish. The earth is packed hard, and I worry that Hansel and Gretel don't have the patience to let us starve to death before nibbling on our flesh. If that were the plan, they probably wouldn't have let us gorge ourselves on their food to begin with.

I blow a lock of hair out of my eyes. "Maybe the red rampion is still protecting us more than we realize." I hope against all hope that it's true. "The roots aren't fighting us anymore. Perhaps the tree only attacked us in the first place because Hansel and Gretel willed it to."

Henni shifts away, turning more of her back to me. "I don't

think that's how the forest's magic works. People can't control it." Her mood dwindled soon after we became trapped. Whatever kindness and forgiveness she had granted me has vanished.

"Maybe people can't, not fully anyway," I relent. "But I wasn't wearing my cape when I first found Ella, and she told me the forest wouldn't harm me in her hollow because she had made peace with it. What if she was the one holding the forest back from hurting me?"

"Then why didn't she make it attack you when you ran away?" Henni asks.

I note how she says "you ran away" instead of "we." "Maybe that requires more magic, and hers wasn't strong enough. Fiora's magic seemed to be powerful enough," I add, "at least with the way she could control her hair."

"Fiora has been in the forest longer than Ella," Axel adds. He shifts to lie on his back and pushes against another root with his legs. "It has to have something to do with that."

"I'm sure it does." As soon as I agree, a knot forms in my stomach, and I regret the words. If Axel's logic is true, then my mother would be more powerful than any of the missing villagers, and the longer a person lives here, the more powerful—and more mad—they become.

"I don't see how any of this helps us," Henni mutters. "*We* don't have magic."

What if I do? What if Ollie spoke truthfully and I can see the past like my grandmother sees the future? But even if I could, how would that benefit us?

"You know what would help?" Axel snaps at Henni. "You lending a hand in getting us out of here instead of sulking over there and feeling sorry for yourself."

Henni flinches. Her eyes start to water, and she presses her lips in a stiff line. She crawls over to where I'm sitting and starts digging the hole with me, her gaze downcast.

The three of us fall quiet. Axel's jaw remains hard, but his neck is flushed red. He's never lost his temper with Henni. Until now, they've only bickered in a harmless brother-sister way. I'm sure he feels bad about it, but I don't blame him. If I wasn't trying so hard to make amends with her, I might have snapped too.

Henni is the first to break the silence, her voice small and trembling. "I wasn't feeling sorry for myself, Axel. I was feeling sorry for Ella." A tear slides onto the bridge of her nose and rolls down it. "It's my fault she became Lost."

He lets go of the root he's been wrestling. "What do you mean?"

She worries at her lip and picks at the dirt beneath her fingernails. "The night before you and Ella were supposed to marry last summer, Mother and Father asked me to take some of the wedding gifts to the little house you and Ella were going to live in together. You had already moved in, but when I knocked on the door, you didn't answer. So I went inside and . . ."

She breaks off, her fingers shaking. I stop digging and hold her hands to steady her.

She sucks in a deep breath. "I found a letter you had written to Ella."

Axel's brows knit together. "I burned that letter."

"You tried to. It was at the edge of your hearth, but it was only half burned. I saw Ella's name on the envelope and I . . ." She squeezes her eyes shut. ". . . I read it."

Axel goes as still as the roots encaging us. "And you showed it to her?"

She nods, her tears streaking faster. "I've never been sorrier for anything."

Axel remains motionless, struggling to absorb what she's told him.

My gaze shifts between my friends. "What was in the letter?"

Henni wipes her nose on her sleeve. "Axel confessed he didn't love Ella. He said he didn't want to go through with the wedding."

I turn back to Axel, confused. "But you told Ella the same thing for yourself that night."

"He hadn't told her yet." Henni sniffs.

"And that wasn't all the letter said." Axel kneads the back of his neck. "I wrote it as a way to work up the courage to tell her something more—something I didn't think I could admit in person. But then I decided against it and threw the letter in the fire. It would have only caused her more pain. So I never mentioned that part to her . . . though if she did read my letter, I'm not sure why she stayed silent about it."

"She didn't want to believe it could be true," Henni murmurs softly, brushing away more tears. "That's what she told me. Before I gave her the letter, I'd been helping her try on her veil. She looked so happy and beautiful and . . ." Henni hangs her head. "Maybe I resented her for that. Everything always came so effortlessly to Ella. She didn't have to try to be noticed. She was loved by everyone, my parents most of all, and I was just the quiet girl, the girl easy to forget. And when Ella became Lost, I became even more invisible."

"Oh, Henni." I hug her. "You're my best friend. You were never invisible to me."

She smiles sadly and wipes her eyes again. The dirt on her hands smears onto her cheeks. "That's why I never told you about the letter."

I pivot back to Axel. *What aren't they telling me?* "What did the letter say?"

His blue eyes hold mine, warm but also pained. "I wrote to Ella that I didn't love her . . . because I was in love with someone else."

His words fall whisper soft, but they crash through my chest and stab my heart. *I'm partly to blame for what happened to Ella?* As hard as it was to lose my mother, at least it wasn't my fault that she left Grimm's Hollow.

The cage seems to spin. I struggle to steady myself. "But you couldn't have loved . . ." I stammer, unable to say "me." "Not back then." Not back when Ella was perfect and breathtaking and didn't possess a shred of madness. Not when I was sixteen instead of seventeen and ten times more awkward and graceless.

"It wasn't your fault, Clara," Henni says. "If I hadn't shown Ella the letter, she would have fought for Axel. She would have persuaded him to follow through with the wedding."

I still can't fathom everything they're saying. How could Ella have been so threatened by me? "I never meant to . . ." I scoot backward and press the heels of my hands to my eyes.

"You didn't do anything wrong." The cadence of Axel's words treads between confidence and vulnerability. "I'm responsible for the way I've always felt about you." *Always?* "Even if it took me too long to realize it," he adds quietly.

He must be exaggerating. How could he have loved me that long when I've locked the deepest part of myself inside me? When I've set limits on my life since I was a child, back from the time Mother first gave me the acorn from the Grimm oak?

It's only been in the last few weeks that I've caught heart-wrenching glimpses of what my life could be like if I allowed myself to live within the warmth of Axel's love.

But it's a life I can never have.

"No!"

Gretel's voice startles me. I flinch as she comes through the archway of the root chamber. Henni shifts to block the hole we're digging, and I rapidly cover it with a fold of my cape.

Hansel marches inside after his sister and forges a straight path for our packs. He's left them by the archway, just out of reach of our cage. He digs inside Henni's pack and pulls out Axel's knife. He stowed it there last night.

"What is he doing?" Henni squeaks.

Without warning, Hansel wheels around and raises the knife on us. The roots of our trap draw back and widen, making room for him to enter.

"Don't even think about it!" Axel launches himself across the cage to protect Henni and me.

"No, Hansel!" Gretel stomps her foot. The roots tighten again and prevent her brother from reaching us. "They sleep." She points at us. "They die. We eat after."

He growls, but she isn't flustered. Chin lifted, she pries the knife out of his hand.

Seething, he shoots a dark look at us and storms outside.

Gretel spares us a glance that's just as withering. "Sleep," she commands, and leaves the chamber, following Hansel.

CHAPTER 29

We refuse to sleep, even as two more days pass and we remain imprisoned. Clearly we're meant to die before Hansel and Gretel eat us—hardly a comfort—and we don't know if sleeping will kill us directly. Perhaps the food we ate was poisonous after all, and we have to be in a slumber before it takes effect. Or maybe we're meant to slowly starve to death, a "sleep" we won't wake up from.

My stomach rumbles as I keep digging the hole with my friends. The raspberries and cucumbers I ate two nights ago didn't satiate my hunger, and without any water to drink, the pangs in my belly grow more brutal by the hour.

It's the middle of the night now. I can barely see Axel or Henni, but I feel their hands moving in tandem with mine as we work together.

The biggest problem with the hole we're digging is that we keep running up against underground roots. We've had to start over twice now, seeking a spot that's unencumbered.

Then there's the problem of hiding the dirt. We've been spreading it out evenly across the ground, adding it to the earth of our floor. So far Hansel and Gretel haven't noticed the gradually rising foundation of our cage. They peek in on us from time to time, occasionally grabbing fruits and vegetables to eat, their faces sour as if it pains them to swallow the food.

They never stay for long. Maybe we're too tempting to be around. When Gretel isn't clenching her jaw, she's licking her lips. And Hansel, who has taken to wearing Axel's knife tucked in the waistband of his trousers, keeps massaging its hilt with a sweaty hand.

Henni's fingers stumble around mine as she scoops out another handful of dirt. "We're going to die before we ever finish this hole. I can literally feel myself wasting away."

"We're not going to die," I assure her. I won't allow Hansel and Gretel to be my Fanged Creature. I've resigned myself to death, but not to letting two cannibalistic strangers eat the flesh off my bones after my heart stops beating. "We just need to keep digging and stay awake."

Staying awake is our most difficult task.

As we weaken with hunger and fatigue, each of us starts to nod off. My head careens onto Axel's shoulder, and he jostles me awake, only to collide with me a moment later as he dozes off. Then when Henni's hands don't return to the hole, I paw around in the dark and find her planted facedown on the ground and quietly snoring.

Over the next hour or so, in a blur of half-consciousness, I realize the three of us have piled up on each other, our bodies limp but occasionally flinching as we vainly strive to fight off sleep. I've blanketed myself over the hole while Axel's arm and one leg are draped over me, and Henni has crashed on top of him.

Who knows how long we sleep for, but when my eyes crack open again, it's light outside—our third day in the cage.

Axel's body fidgets, slightly jerking and spasming in his sleep. "Stop," he mumbles. "I don't like that."

For a moment, I worry he might be reacting to some kind of poison, but then he jolts awake and blurts, "Ouch!"

He rolls over, knocks Henni away, and looks outside our cage. Hansel is nearby. Past the roots of the cage, he has Axel's hand in his grip. He's hunched over it like a dog lapping up water. Except he isn't lapping. He's biting—gnawing on Axel's smallest finger.

"What the—?" Axel springs up and yanks his hand away. He throws his fist back at Hansel and punches him squarely in the face.

Hansel recoils, stunned. He covers his nose, where Axel's knuckles hit the hardest.

"Serves you right!" Axel spits out.

Hansel bares his teeth and snarls viciously. Axel jerks closer, grabs the bar-like roots of the cage, and growls back.

Hansel darts outside through the archway.

Axel collapses back on his haunches. Brings his bleeding finger to his chest.

"Are you all right?" I scramble closer and take his hand, examining his pinkie. The flesh is cut deep beneath the second knuckle, but his finger is intact and not broken.

"He's going to kill us." Axel rubs the space between his brows. "He won't wait for us to die. He'll stab us in our sleep." A heavy sigh rattles out of him. "I shouldn't have lost my temper."

I tear off a scrap of my chemise to wrap his finger. "I don't see how you could have restrained yourself."

"I would have punched him too," Henni adds.

Axel lets out a small chuckle. "I'd like to see that." He releases another long exhale as his expression sobers. "We need to escape before we fall asleep again."

"But the hole is only halfway dug," Henni says. "How will we stay awake?"

I think about it for a moment. "Maybe we can trick Hansel and Gretel into opening the cage. They're not the brightest people. Perhaps we can use that to our advantage."

Axel scratches his jaw, shifts closer. "Hansel already opened the cage once. It was Gretel who stopped him. If we can some-how goad her into letting him do it, we might get our chance."

I finish bandaging his finger. "If we do get the cage open, are you sure you can fight off Hansel? He'll have a knife and won't be weak like us."

Axel pulls his brows low, his eyes steely. "I can take him."

We bide our time waiting for the twins to return. Axel abandons digging the hole and yanks away thin roots from its walls instead. He braids them together and fashions a garrote. I hope he won't have to use it to strangle Hansel or Gretel. We entered this forest to save people, not kill them.

I scoop up a fresh handful of dirt and squeeze it tight for a drawn-out moment, watching Axel as he snaps the garrote taut between his hands. "I never told you what Ollie said before he vanished."

Axel's gaze jerks up. The tension in his garrote slackens.

"Who is Ollie?" Henni breaks her methodical rhythm of digging the hole.

I inhale, long and deep, and tell her about the little ghost, my two encounters with him, and how he's related to Axel.

"I can't see him or hear him like Clara," Axel adds. "But we proved he's real."

"He's been able to communicate with others, though," I say. "The dead people in the trees . . . and maybe my mother." I share what Ollie said about a woman in red, all the while feeling the weight of the acorn in my pocket. "Whoever it was, they told Ollie I was born with gifts because of my bloodline."

"You can read fortune-telling cards like your grandmother?" Henni's eyes grow round. "Why didn't you ever tell me?"

"Because I can't. I *don't*." I rub a stubborn smudge of dirt on my arm. "Ollie told me—" I cut myself off. No, it sounds too ridiculous, even in my own head.

"Ollie told you what?" Axel presses.

I lower my gaze. "He said . . . I can see the past." A self-deprecating laugh tumbles out of me. "If I *could*"—I take a measured breath—"maybe it would help us now." I eye Axel's garrote again. At the very least, maybe it would help prevent him from using *that*.

"How could it help?" Henni asks.

"Well, if my gift is like my grandmother's, I might be able to read other people's pasts like she does their futures. If I can read Hansel and Gretel's past, I might learn something that can provoke them more, give us a better shot at them opening the cage—and hopefully scare them away from attacking us when we try to escape."

Axel picks at the thready roots of his new weapon. "But have you ever seen—read—someone's past?"

My jaw stiffens. I should have known he'd react like this. "You've always been skeptical about Grandmère's abilities. Now you don't believe in the possibility of mine."

His brows dart up. "That isn't true—or fair, Clara. Give me a moment to turn everything over in my head, all right?"

I force my teeth to unclench and give a small nod. I don't know why I'm being so defensive when I'm just as doubtful about myself possessing magic. I only brought it up because I'm desperate.

He takes a calming breath. We're all half mad from starvation and exhausted to the bone. "You're right about the fortune-telling. That's always been hard for me to swallow. I don't like the idea of an unchangeable future; we should have a choice in our fate. But the past is different. It's done, written in stone." He cuts his hand through the air. "I could put faith in a gift to read the past. All I want to know is if *you've* experienced it before." He leans closer and rests his elbow on his knee. "Have you ever known something about someone else that they never told you themselves?"

I think of the steady stream of villagers that frequented my cottage over the years, people who came to learn their fortunes from Grandmère. I overheard most of those readings. Our cottage was small, and my curiosity was large. Fate has always been my obsession, whether my own or anyone else's. I put so much focus on it that I never allowed myself to dwell on the past.

Chest sinking, I shake my head. "The only time that comes to mind is something that happened recently. At the meadow ball, I saw glimpses of *your* past," I tell Axel. "But I was hallucinating on mushrooms, so it doesn't count."

"It counts if it's true and I never told you before." His eyes warm on mine. "What did you see?"

Those dreamlike moments swirl back to life in my mind. I see the vision of my mother in my cornflower-blue dress and red hooded cape. I remember the steadying touch of her hand as she turned my head toward the flashes of Axel's life as they played out on the stage of the meadow.

Some of those memories have to be my own recollections. I was there with Axel when we raced with our pails of sheep milk, when he teased me at the harvest festival, when he threw tufts of wool in my hair, and when we delivered the twin lambs.

But there were other memories too, times I wasn't by his side. Did I make them up? "I saw your uncle about to . . . to beat you as you were plowing his field."

Axel schools his features, though his jaw muscle tenses. Maybe I shouldn't have mentioned it; it can't prove any magic on my part. I never witnessed Axel's beatings firsthand, but I knew they happened. His bruises along with his uncle's temperament weren't difficult to piece together. "Anything else?" he asks, eager to move past the subject.

"You repaired the roof of the Tragers' cottage when they were sick, and you helped take care of Luka Eckhart when his mom was pregnant and his dad broke his foot."

Henni looks between us. "Did you ever tell Clara about those things?" she asks Axel.

"I'm not sure." He chews on his lip. "Did the Tragers or Eckharts ever mention them to *you*?" he asks me.

It was all so long ago. "I don't think so."

He sits back. "And was that everything you saw in your vision?"

I think through it again. "There was one more memory. You must have been fifteen because your hair was longer. You were with Fiora. She waved you over to her when you were passing by her house. She gave you a sealed envelope and whispered something in your ear. You nodded and ran off like you were going to deliver it to someone. I never saw who, though."

A look of astonishment crosses Axel's face. "I'm sure I never told you about that. Fiora wouldn't have either. She made me promise on my father's bones that I wouldn't open the letter or ever reveal who I gave it to."

Henni tilts her head. "Who *did* you—?"

"My father's bones," Axel says pointedly.

"So does this mean . . . ?" My throat closes against the words. Hope has become a fragile thing lately. "Did I really see . . . ?"

"The past?" Axel's grin banishes my lingering doubts. "Well, you've made me a believer."

I laugh, then toss a scowl at him. "Took you long enough."

Gretel strides through the archway. I suck in a tight breath. In a flash, Henni covers the hole we've been digging with her skirt. I steady myself, remembering our plan to goad Gretel into allowing Hansel to open the cage. He hasn't accompanied her, but that doesn't mean this moment is wasted. I need to study her, search for a means to exploit any weaknesses . . . perhaps find a way to work upon her pity, if she's capable of any.

Knowledge of her past would help.

I strain to channel my newfound ability as Gretel walks around the cage and tests the strength of the roots. But all I summon is the onset of a bad headache. Maybe I need hallucinogenic mushrooms to conjure up my gift.

I focus my breathing, trying to reach a meditative state on my own. I concentrate again on Gretel, paying attention to every detail that crosses my mind. The dress she wears is too tight in the chest and too short in the skirt. Its green fabric is even more tattered than my cornflower-blue dress. Come to think of it, Hansel's clothes are just as worn and ill-fitting, and he's always barefoot like his sister.

My gaze snags on the frayed edge of Gretel's skirt, where the stitches of the hem have come undone. There's a little mark there that I can't make out clearly, but something about it pricks my memory. Whether that prick is magical or just an ordinary recollection remains to be seen. "How long have you lived here?" I ask her.

Gretel's stark-blond eyebrows twitch. I haven't addressed her since my first day in this cage. She doesn't answer. I wonder if she even understands me.

"Were you born in the forest?" I try again. "What happened to your mother?"

Her dark eyes pop wide when I say "mother." That's a word she recognizes.

"Did she go missing?" I press, realizing it's possible to lose someone in the Forest Grimm even if they never lived in Grimm's Hollow. "Is she Lost?" It could explain why Hansel and Gretel's language is so stunted and why they've outgrown their clothes, especially if their mother went Lost years ago.

Gretel doesn't reply, her face wary and pensive.

Henni scoots closer, trying to assist me with communicating. "Mother gone?" she asks Gretel. "Mother bye-bye?" I cringe at her baby talk. "Mother sleeping?" Henni swallows thickly before she adds, "Mother dead?"

Gretel's posture tenses, and her lip curls with contempt. "Witch," she hisses, and rushes out of the chamber.

Axel rubs his brow. "Well, that went well."

"Did she just call me a witch?" Henni rears back, affronted.

"Maybe." I stare at the archway Gretel just passed through. "Or maybe she was trying to say that a witch killed her mother." I nibble on my lip, thinking about the mark near the hem of Gretel's skirt. Was it a spot of embroidery? I turn to Axel. "Can I see your scarf?"

"But he can't take it off," Henni says.

"It's all right." I crawl over to Axel. "Just keep hold of one end while I check something."

He does as I say while I feel along the hem of the scarf that was once the bottom edge of my cape. Moments later, my fingers press against the spot I'm searching for, a little bump tucked under the hem. I rip the stitches apart and roll back the fabric to reveal a small embroidered letter: *F*.

"What is it?" Henni peers over my shoulder.

"A signature for the person who wove this wool," I say. "Gretel's dress had the same mark: an *F* for Fiora."

Henni gasps. "Did you see a memory of Fiora too? Was she with Gretel?"

"No." I do my best to douse my flare of disappointment. Did I really think I'd harness my gift so easily? "No one's memories except my own."

Axel tips his head down to look in my eyes. "But you think Fiora is the witch who killed Hansel and Gretel's mother?"

"She's certainly capable of it," I say.

Axel's brows draw together as he considers this. "Or maybe Hansel and Gretel stole Fiora's clothes to make clothes of their own. Think about it. Fiora wasn't wearing a dress or even a chemise. She just had on those exceptionally tight underclothes." I arch a brow. "Which were very unflattering," he adds hastily.

"Or Fiora could have made the clothes for Hansel and Gretel," I say, meeting him halfway in his theory.

"Why would she do that?" Henni asks.

I stroke the little *F* on Axel's scarf. "Remember how she thought you were what she lost? Maybe she also thought the same thing about Hansel and Gretel. She could have been trying to help them for a time."

"Or she could have been keeping them prisoners with her hair." Henni rubs her throat with trembling fingers.

"Either way, I think we've found out how to strike a nerve with Gretel." I hand Axel back his scarf and sit up taller. "We keep bringing up the witch."

CHAPTER 30

ours pass. Neither Hansel nor Gretel have returned. We call their names and hear nothing. I'd fear they have abandoned us, but how could they when they're so viciously keen to eat us after we're dead?

My arms fold over my ravenous stomach. I stare at the archway of the chamber with a bleary-gazed focus. Henni has propped herself up against the side of our cage, her eyelids batting closed then flinching open again. Axel sits with his knees to his chest, rocking in place as he stares at the food growing on vines beyond our reach. He mumbles the names of every fruit and vegetable. Perhaps it's his trick to stay awake. Or maybe he's delirious.

I'm humming the song Fiora sang from her tower while she lured Henni up in the clutches of her red hair. I've forgotten all the words, except for two lines . . .

Dearest, come back to me
I'll fend off the murdering wolf.

It must be late afternoon, judging by the angle of the light threading into our chamber. Its brightness is wavering, darkening faster than the sun dips toward the horizon. A stark flash pulses, followed by a deafening clap of thunder. I jolt, unprepared. Seconds later, the sky unleashes, and the rushing sound of rainfall fills the air.

My heartbeat quickens. If Hansel and Gretel are nearby and ignoring us, like I suspect, they'll need to take shelter soon.

I hum Fiora's melody louder, singing the words I know and making up others.

The witch is coming
The spider is red.

Axel and Henni also sense the twins' impending arrival. We gather in the center of the cage and leave the partial hole we've dug exposed. If the twins see it, it will upset them. And that's exactly our intention.

The hurried slaps of barefooted running race closer. They're almost here. I sing louder. My throaty, dehydrated voice punches the words of the song that might provoke them most. "Witch. Spider. Wolf."

Hansel and Gretel burst in through the archway. They're dripping wet, eyes livid, fists clenched.

My song turns into a chant, the same three words over and over: "Witch. Spider. Wolf."

Axel and Henni join the chant with me. "Witch. Spider. Wolf."

Hansel growls.

Gretel shakes the roots of the cage. "Stop!"

"Witch!" I hit the ground with my palms.

"Spider!" Henni lurches into an arachnid crouch.

"Wolf!" Axel howls and throws his head back.

Our chanting builds faster, louder.

Hansel prowls around the outside of the cage.

"No!" Gretel yells at us. Her hands cover her ears.

I pull up the hood of my cape. Stroke the fabric like it's red hair. "Witch! Witch! Witch!" My only word now. Targeted at Gretel.

Axel's eyes latch on to Hansel's. He pounces toward him. Snarls past the roots. Flashes white teeth. "Wolf! Wolf!"

Henni torments both of the twins. She races around the cage on all fours like she has eight legs. "Spider! Spider! Spider!"

Gretel stomps and wails.

Hansel whips out Axel's knife from his waistband.

My friends and I scream our chant now, our voices ragged with hunger but sharp with desperation. The frenetic energy feeds me, pumps adrenaline through my veins. This had better work. If Hansel and Gretel don't open the cage, we'll have only killed ourselves faster. We're using every last drop of life to spur them to action.

We hiss and roar and snap our jaws at our captors. Axel stretches his garrote taut between his hands. He and I exchange a fleeting glance. I shake my head slightly, and he nods. The garrote will be his last resort. He'll do everything he can to not kill the twins.

Hansel and Gretel may not be from Grimm's Hollow, but perhaps they were also tangled up in the curse. And if that's true, then they can be saved like the rest of the village once the curse is broken.

Axel, Henni, and I thrash and shout, doing all we can to incite the twins to open the cage. But the twins continue to restrain themselves. Hansel's face purples with scalding anger. He stalks near Axel, just out of reach past the roots. His eyes stray to his sister, looking for permission. Her body shakes. Furious tears streak down her cheeks. But her stubbornness holds, fierce and unbroken. She doesn't yield to Hansel.

We have to push her past her limits so she will.

I slither across the cage to the roots separating her from me. I grab them like the prison bars they are and press my face between them. "You witch!" I seethe. "You die! You meat!"

Gretel's mouth gapes open. Her bloodless skin pales to a sicklier shade of white.

Lightning flashes from outside, illuminating her from behind.

A muscle in her jaw tics, and she draws herself taller. Pure hatred pulses off of her as her gaze shrewdly slides to her brother. In one calm and terrible breath, she speaks the word he's been waiting for: "Kill."

The entire cage dismantles. Walls fall down. The ceiling lifts. Roots retract and rejoin those of the outer chamber.

Hansel leaps for Axel, knife raised. Axel anticipates him. He rolls out of the way and springs up again before Hansel can turn around. Axel lunges with his garrote. Hansel revolves as Axel tries to strangle him. Hansel drops the knife and grabs Axel's arms, struggling to wrestle them away from his neck.

Gretel and I rush for the knife at the same time. I beat her to it. My fingers almost close around the hilt when she grabs the hood of my cape. She yanks. I'm jerked backward, gagging.

Henni snatches up the knife. Axel and Hansel grapple for control of the garrote. "Let her go!" Henni shouts at Gretel, who keeps choking me.

I can't see Gretel's face, but I imagine her smirking, threatened least of all by Henni.

"Now!" Henni demands. My vision blackens. Gretel won't stop. She's going to kill me. She's stronger than I am, not near to death with starvation.

Hansel overpowers Axel, who is also weak. He kicks him to his knees, stomps on his hand, and steals the garrote from his slackened grip. Hansel moves to wrap it around Axel's neck when Henni yells, "Hansel and Gretel, stop! Bad!" she scolds. "Very, very bad!"

Hansel tenses. Gretel eases my chokehold by a fraction.

Henni stands in front of the archway, holding the knife with both hands like it's a heavy sword. The blade rattles as she shakes. "If you don't let my friends go, I'm going to k—" Her voice gives out. She sucks in a breath. "I'm going to h-hurt you."

Hansel snickers. Gretel giggles. Her chokehold on me tightens again.

My eyes blur, but my chest swells with warmth. I'm going to die because Henni can't kill Hansel and Gretel, and yet I love her for it. I wouldn't change who she is to save me.

A howl pierces the rainfall. Henni's downcast eyes lift. "Do you hear that?" she asks the twins, and squares her shoulders. "The wolf is coming for you because you've been awfully bad."

Hansel laughs again, but his pitch is strained. "No."

"Yes," Henni replies. "The wolf eats bad people. Hansel and Gretel are bad."

"Not bad," Gretel says.

The wolf howls a second time, and the sound reverberates to my very bones. Only the Grimm wolf could make a noise that sharp with terror.

"Very bad." Henni looks between the twins like a mother who has caught her children in the midst of a pillow fight instead of strangling their guests to death. "The naughtiest."

The third howl comes, disturbingly close.

Gretel releases my cape. Hansel drops the garrote. I fall forward on my hands and knees and gasp for breath. Axel drags me to my feet. "Get the packs!" he shouts at Henni. "We have to hurry. The wolf is coming for Clara."

I have no doubt about it. Not after all my encounters with her.

Henni snatches up the packs and races outside. Axel and I follow, his arm supporting me. The rain slaps our faces. Smears our surroundings.

"This way!" Henni shouts. She's found the head of the gulch with the pebble trail.

We clamber after her. Another howl rings through the air. It ends with a rough bark. I look behind me. Hansel and Gretel have emerged from their chamber under the pine. Between them and us is the Grimm wolf.

Even with the rain lashing down on her, the wolf's hackles are raised. She stalks back and forth. Scratches the ground. Claims her territory. She faces the twins with her back to us.

I can't believe what I'm seeing. Is she . . . protecting me?

Hansel and Gretel take each other's hands. They look like they did when I first saw them, eerie reflections of one another. Behind them, roots of the pine snap up and snake toward the wolf.

But the wolf isn't intimidated. She holds her head high, ears erect, and draws up to her full stature. She releases a loud and spine-tingling growl.

Hansel and Gretel cower. The roots shrink back to their resting places.

The Grimm wolf pivots to me. Lightning flashes, illuminating her large eyes. They're unmistakably violet.

Goose bumps prickle down the back of my neck. I can't place why, but I feel a kinship with her, a connection that goes beyond stunned gratitude. The bond runs deeper than that, a memory I can't quite dredge to the surface.

"Hurry, Clara!" Axel tugs me. I nod at the wolf, acknowledging what she's done for us, and race away with my friends into the gulch.

CHAPTER 31

hen we step out of the gulch and return to our former camp by the stream, night is falling quickly. The rain let up half an hour ago, but the ground is still sodden. We kick out mulch and pine needles from beneath the trees to clear a dry plot of earth to sleep on, forgoing our soaked bedrolls that are tied on top of our packs.

As we light our lantern and settle down, I catch something silver gleaming at the bank of the stream. I drift over and find three fat trout lying side by side, freshly caught but not flapping, dead though their scales are still wet.

Beside the fish, large canine paw prints mark the ground. The Grimm wolf was here. She beat us back by another route, and by all appearances, she left us a gift.

I glance around the dark woods. I don't see her, but through some kind of sixth sense, I feel her nearby and watching. For once, the thought is a comfort.

When I show Axel and Henni the fish and paw prints, they're also untroubled by who brought us the food. They witnessed the Grimm wolf come to our defense earlier.

Henni pulls out dry pine cones from her pack and lights a fire while Axel and I gut the fish. Soon our dinner is roasting over a small campfire.

Henni sits cross-legged and warms her hands. I stand close to the flames, rotating this way and that, trying to dry my dress. Thankfully it isn't too soaked. Even if it were, I'm far too exhausted to strip it off and spend the night in only my chemise and cape.

Axel has removed his vest and loosened his scarf, but he also keeps on his remaining damp clothes. He's lying on his side by the fire and chewing the end of a long blade of grass, the same way he used to chew on straw back in Grimm's Hollow.

"Clara?" Henni asks me. I turn, intrigued by the tone of her voice. It's gentle, which is natural to her, but also steadier and stronger. Bolder instead of timid. It's as if the last three days have aged her by three years, and a girl who is eighteen has just addressed me instead of someone only fifteen. "We tried our best in this forest."

I nod, unsure if I like where this conversation is heading.

"We're lucky to have been spared our lives," she adds.

I steal a quick glance at Axel, wondering if he's been talking to Henni about this. Have they planned some kind of intervention? But he only shrugs with a little shake of his head.

Henni sits up taller and rolls her shoulders back. "I think we need to leave and go back home."

I freeze. "What are you talking about?"

"We've tested our luck here, but it's clear the forest will only allow us to save one person."

"How is it clear?"

She talks over me. "You could always return later and—"

"I'm not returning later."

"But we've found Ella."

My nostrils flare. "Ella isn't my mother," I snap.

Henni takes a long breath, like she expected my response. "We know where Ella is. We can follow the stream right back to her. It's the only sure path."

"But there's nothing sure about saving Ella. We already tried to save her, and it's impossible. Her mind is gone. She's not your sister anymore. She's Cinderella, and she won't hesitate to kill you."

Henni gives me a pointed look. "And your mother, wherever she is in this forest, won't hesitate to kill you."

Her words, though delivered calmly, hit me square in the chest and dagger sharp. "You're wrong!"

Henni sighs. I hate the way she's treating me. It's like how she treated Hansel and Gretel, as if she were *their* mother. But I only have one mother, and Henni has vastly underestimated her.

"My mother is wiser and more mature than Fiora and Ella and Hansel and Gretel put together. She won't be mad or deadly like they were." When Henni looks skeptical, I turn to Axel for support. "Tell her my mother will be different."

He pulls the grass from his mouth and gnaws at his lip. "I think that's the problem, Clara. Your mother *will* be different. Different from who she used to be."

"So you think we should just run back home too?"

"I didn't say that."

"But we need to," Henni interjects. "And we need to bring Ella with us. Luck is no longer on our side."

I glare at her and whip a hand at our roasting fish. "What is *this* if not luck? The Grimm wolf is on our side." I was wrong about the wolf being the Fanged Creature and the cause of my death. "She'll feed us, guide us. Can't you see how she's led us already?" It's all so clear now. "She chased you to us, Henni, when you first entered the forest. She helped us escape into the river after we ran away from Fiora's tower. She saved me from the sycamore when I lost my cape. She even warned us about Hansel and Gretel. None of us should have followed that pebble trail." I jut out my chin. "The Grimm wolf is going to lead me to my mother, I know it."

"And then what?" Henni throws her arms up, finally losing her temper. "Your mother will be the strongest and most vicious of the Lost. She has been in this forest the longest. How do you imagine the wolf will help you then? Will she drag your mother by the teeth over miles and miles of the journey back home?"

Axel lifts a hand to warn Henni. "Take it easy, all right?"

She presses her lips together and inhales a forced breath through her nose. "I'm sorry, Clara. I don't want the truth to cause you any pain, but you're deluding yourself about your mother and how you can save her."

My jaw locks. "I drew the Red Card."

"It's only a piece of paper." Henni's voice is unbearably gentle, like she's having to explain something difficult to a child. "It means nothing."

"I can also see the past."

"You saw it once."

"I'll learn how to do it again." I can't have been given a gift only to succumb to my fate and die without truly being able to make any use of it. "And if my mother has descended into madness, I'll see how it happened so I can help her reverse it."

"Madness isn't cured so simply."

I can't listen to her anymore. I march a few feet away and pace at the edge of the light ringing our campfire.

"Ella is the most reasonable of the Lost we've found." Henni barrels on with her newfound confidence. "She's savable. She's our only chance to do something good in this forest and leave while we still have rational minds to make decisions with. The red rampion can't protect us forev—"

"Stop!" I whirl and cut my hand through the air. She's testing the limits of my rage, speaking of abandoning someone sacred to me—someone I've prepared to give up everything for. I can't believe she'd suggest I'd save myself only to run home without her.

Henni falls quiet. *At last.* I pace around more, kicking up mud and mulch with my bandaged feet, vainly trying to calm myself.

Axel clears his throat. "The fish are ready."

He removes them from the flames, and I grab mine, eating it with my back turned to my friends. I don't even wait for the meat to cool. I let it scald my lips and burn my tongue. I swallow each bite without tasting it.

Despite my exhaustion, it takes me hours to fall asleep that night. I squeeze the acorn in my pocket until its stem bites into my flesh, and my palm comes away wet with blood.

Fresh rain awakens me the next morning, its fat drops splashing my face. My ankle is already untied from Axel's. I turn to find him under the shelter of a nearby spruce. He's crouched and faced away from me. His head hangs low, and his fingers knot into his hair.

"What's wrong?" My stomach prickles.

He scrubs his hands down his face. "It's Henni . . . she's gone. She left a letter for us, and she took the red veil."

"What?" I lurch to stand, but I stumble in the folds of my twisted skirt. The first step I take—the first step of the day—falls on my left foot instead of my right.

I flinch. No, I can't have a bad omen, not when Henni has already left us. What if it means we won't be able to find her again?

I race for the letter. It's resting at the base of the spruce, anchored by stones, and written on a torn-out page from Henni's artist's notebook.

Dearest Clara and Axel,

I wish you the very best as you continue your journey, and I hope you'll do the same for me. My obligation is to my sister and seeing her safely return home. Clara, I truly hope you find your mother and that I'm wrong about who she has become. Axel, please forgive me for not asking you to join me. I accept

where your heart belongs now. I know you could never aban-
don Clara, even if it meant saving Ella.

Affectionately,
Henni

My eyes burn. I hold myself rigid for several long seconds, rereading the letter until it's a senseless blur that only means one thing: I've failed my friends. I've failed Henni and Axel and even Ella.

I spin away and stride decisively to my pack. I sling it over my shoulder and start traveling down the path of the stream—but not toward the unknown stretches of the Forest Grimm. I go back in the direction we came from, before Hansel and Gretel diverted us. I follow the stream toward Ella's hollow.

"Clara, stop." Axel rushes after me. "Let's talk about this."

There's nothing to talk about. There's only saving the people I love in the order that I have to save them. I'll never forgive myself if Henni dies in this forest or becomes as mad as her sister. Besides, Axel will come to resent me if Ella isn't rescued. "I can't save my mother until I set everything right."

CHAPTER 32

Once lost to us, Henni isn't so easily found. Axel and I travel as quickly as we can, but we have yet to catch up with her. Aside from the stream, the woods we pass look completely different from the ones we first saw when journeying in the other direction.

Sometime between then and now, the trees have moved and scooped up great plots of earth with them. The landscape is rockier than before, and the narrow stream widens into small ponds where the earth has sunken in from the incessant rainfall. As the day waxes on, we plod through muddy grass and sludgy ground.

The uneven terrain has my back and hips throbbing again. The only benefit of being trapped in Hansel and Gretel's cage was that it provided relief from the strain of traveling, especially the toll it takes on my crooked spine. How I mourn for my lost shoe.

When night comes, I grit my teeth against the pain and refuse to stop. If I do, our chances of finding Henni might diminish altogether. Besides, there's nowhere dry to sleep anyway. Our lantern barely guides our way through the downpour, and the flickering candle inside it is burning to a nub. I only have one candle left in my pack, so I finally relent to Axel's persuasions and snuff out the flame. In the darkness, we step into the stream so we don't lose our path and slowly tread onward.

Fighting a constant surge of anxiety, I try again to access the magic of being able to see another person's past. I imagine myself as Henni. Picture her journeying alone. Try to envision where she would have stopped to make camp or pushed onward without sleep.

I see nothing.

I have no idea how to call upon my gift. Perhaps I need some kind of tool to channel my ability, like how Grandmère needs fortune-telling cards to read the future. Though I didn't require anything other than my own inebriated mind when I glimpsed visions of Axel's past.

Three times in the night I feel a tug in the center of my breastbone. The Grimm wolf is nearby, following at a close distance behind us. I can't say how I'm sure it's true except that when I stare over my shoulder into the darkness, the tugging sensation inside me pulls stronger. That pull can't be magic. It feels more familiar. It's like I'm sensing myself.

In the morning, the wolf continues to trail us, though she keeps out of sight. We trudge through the rain and the stream until it grows too narrow for our feet. A quarter of a mile later, it washes away into nothing more than flooded grassland among outcroppings of limestone.

I gasp. Turn panicked eyes on Axel. "It's gone." He picks his way around the muddy landscape, searching for the place where the stream should re-form again. But there is no place.

"I don't understand." I look behind us at the way we came. "The water isn't supposed to move, only the forest. You told me that." I stare at him, my last tether to sanity in this forest. "You said we could depend on it for navigation."

"We still should be able to." He peers around us again and scratches his head. "This doesn't make any sense."

I feel my panic rising, my breaths coming faster. The forest seems to be closing in on me, pinching me tight on all sides with no hope of escape. Because I can't escape—I can't do what I came here to do—without saving my best friend first. The clock of my life is ticking faster again, counting down the days—minutes—hours—seconds until my death. Perhaps the Fanged Creature will be my own heart giving out on me. "How will we find Henni if we've lost our path to her?"

Axel's mouth opens and closes, struggling to form words, but all that comes out is a heavy exhale. Even he can't find anything encouraging to say. I stumble against a surge of light-headedness. He *always* finds the silver lining, the way to keep our hope alive.

I clutch my burning chest, trying to force my lungs to open. I look behind me and scan the distance where the Grimm wolf must be watching. Why does she always follow when she should be leading us? "I need your h-help!" I shout with air I can't waste.

Flurries of black crowd my vision. My legs buckle. Axel catches me on the verge of passing out. "Clara, calm yourself. Breathe. We're not lost yet."

I shake my head, my cheek pressed to his shoulder. My gasps turn to sobs. "We *are* lost. We should have gone with Henni. She was right. I'm deluding myself. I've tested my luck, but there is no more luck." I'm going to die without saving anyone.

"Shh, that's not true." He strokes my arm for a moment, and then his hand goes still. "In fact, there's luck with us now. See for yourself."

He gently turns me around and points a few feet away. At the foot of a limestone boulder are clusters of red-spotted mushrooms. "I'm not saying we should eat them." He chuckles. "But they *are* a good omen."

I scrutinize the mushrooms past heavy sheets of rainfall. "There's clover growing around them too," I murmur.

I take a tentative step in the sludgy earth and then another, the hope in me a fragile spark that might fizzle to ashes if I'm not careful.

One more step. I chance a smile and look back at Axel. "I think they might be four-leaf—"

The ground falls away. I shriek and plummet.

"Clara!" Axel grabs for my arm, but the sinkhole expands. He crashes inside with me.

We tumble onto a mud-slick slope, but keep dropping, sliding downward as clods of wet earth rain around us. The slope gradually hardens, and the soil gives way to eroded limestone.

At last the limestone levels out and we barrel-roll into shallow groundwater. Dazed, I sit up and wipe a thick layer of mud off my face. My clothes are caked in filth, and my bandaged feet are half unraveled. I take a weary look around me. We've fallen into a cave beneath the sinkhole. Wonderful.

Axel pushes up from the water and groans, flinging the mud off his sleeves. He looks me over as he crawls toward me. "Anything bleeding or broken?"

"Just my pride." I reach to salvage my sodden pack from a mound of sludge, but a sharp spasm zings up my spine. I hiss, wincing.

Axel scoots closer. "How's your back?"

"If it wasn't already crooked, it is now." Sarcasm drips from my voice.

He chuckles and grabs my pack for me, then glances up at the hole we plummeted through. It's at least fifty feet above us. "Well. . . . that was an adventure."

I try to laugh, but instead I burst into tears. I'm still a mess of raw nerves. I was already past my tipping point before we nearly crashed to our deaths. "Damn the mushrooms! Damn the clover! Damn everything! There's no such thing as good luck!"

"Hey, now." Axel shifts closer. "We're alive. After a fall like that, I'd say we're more than lucky."

He moves to wrap his arm around my shoulder, but I shove him away. "It isn't luck that Henni is gone," I say, lashing out.

"It isn't luck that we keep losing our way. It isn't luck that I lost my shoe and that everyone we meet here is monstrous."

"Clara." Axel reaches for me again, but I jerk back, water splashing around me.

"It isn't luck that I can never love you!" My voice cracks. "Not the way that I want to."

His brows wrench together. "Don't believe that. We're not star-crossed. I don't care what your fortune says."

"I'm going to die!" I choke out, fully sobbing now. "I've known it since I was a little girl."

"What do you mean?" The cords in his neck stiffen. "Are you sick?"

I shake my head, roughly wiping beneath my eyes, which only smears the mud around my face worse. "It's my fate to die here. Grandmère read it in the cards for me."

"This is about more cards?" Axel's gaze fills with sympathy as well as a pinch of exasperation.

"You don't understand. There are two cards she drew over and over again during my readings, even though every time they broke her heart: the Midnight Forest and the Fanged Creature. They mean I'm going to die in this forest, Axel. I can't escape my fate."

"What about the Red Card? You told me you're the Changer of Fate."

"That doesn't undo the rest of my fortune. I'm still going to die." *Just like my father died after Grandmère foretold his fate in her cards.* I swallow a thick lump in my throat. "The only fate I can change is my mother's. I have to save her. I'm *going* to."

He searches my face. "So you're telling me you chose to go on this journey believing it would mean your sure death?"

I nod.

"And all that time you hoped to win the lottery, you were also racing toward your death in order to save your mother?"

I nod again.

"And this is why you've been keeping your heart at a distance from me—because you truly believe you're going to die in this forest?"

I force one more nod, biting my lip as my chin trembles.

He releases a pained breath and holds my gaze for a long moment. "Come with me."

I don't understand. "Come where?" We can't climb out the way we fell in here. The limestone is too slick and steep.

"There's a pool." He tosses a glance at a spot behind me. I look over my shoulder and spy a turquoise body of water several yards away. Steam rises from the surface. A hot spring.

"What about it?"

Axel grins softly and rises from the groundwater, holding out his open hand. "Come with me."

I can't deny him, not when I've spilled all the secrets I've been holding close for as long as I remember. I have no more energy left to resist the way he makes me feel, the comfort I sense him offering. I need every ounce of it . . . for as long as life lets me have it.

I give him my hand. In this moment, I'd give him anything.

He guides me into the pool. A shiver of goose bumps rushes over my skin from the steaming heat. It penetrates my bones and muscles and eases the aches and pain. Axel kneels in the shallow end of the water and removes my linen bandages, letting them float away.

We wade in deeper. The mud starts to rinse from our clothes. When I'm standing up to my waist in the water, Axel moves to untie the strings of my cape. I stiffen, but his eyes are reassuring. "You'll be fine. Hold on to the end of my scarf."

I take it in hand and allow him to remove my cape. He lets it soak with my bandages and shrugs off his vest as well.

He pulls me deeper in the water until it reaches my chest. He cups his hands in the pool and brings the water to my face, my neck, my collarbone, washing me clean of the mud. His hands are gentle and soothing, warm from the heat of the spring.

He ducks under the surface a few times, rinsing himself off as well. When he rises, he lifts me into a cradle hold. He dips my head lower, so all my hair is in the water, and he combs his fingers through every lock.

I can't look away from his eyes. The turquoise from the pool reflects in his irises, turning them the most beautiful shade of blue. Each facet glistens and dances with the ripples his movements stir in the water.

After my hair, he washes my ears, and the sensitive skin behind them, the hollow of my throat, the divot between my nose and lips. His touch is patient, adoring, healing.

Once he finishes, he draws me up from the water and sets me on my feet in the pool, but I still feel like I'm floating under Axel's fervent gaze. My hair drips warmth down my back as he takes my face in his hands. "I'm not going to let you die, do you hear me?"

"But—"

"Love is stronger than death, stronger than fate." His eyes shine. "And I love you, Clara Thurn. I'm always going to love you."

Tears spill from my eyes again. He brushes them away, kissing the places where they fall on my cheeks. With strong and steady hands, he brings me closer until our hips meet flush. He tilts up my chin and cups the back of my head. His gaze flits once to my eyes, as if asking for permission, and in answer I lift on my tiptoes to reach him. He meets me halfway, and his soft mouth presses against mine.

His kiss is warmth and color and light, every bold and beautiful thing. It's rain in the village and fire on a winter's night and wind through the lofty trees. It's dizzying but grounding, tender but uninhibited.

It's perfect.

I keep hold of his scarf as my hands slide up his chest and clutch his wet shirt to draw him even closer. He opens his mouth and kisses me in ways I didn't imagine were possible. I sigh into him, savoring every touch and feeling. He's been dear to me for as long as I've known him, a friend who could make me laugh on the darkest days, a steady force beneath his charming smile.

I fell in love with him on the night he helped me deliver the twin lambs, and I should have known he loved me in return long before we entered this forest. I should have at least realized it on the morning before he was supposed to marry Ella.

I came to the Dantzer farm to milk the cows so the family could tend to their wedding preparations. Axel wandered into the dairy stalls and drew up a stool next to mine. He told me funny stories to help me bide the time, and then after a spell of silence, I caught him looking at me in a way that wasn't funny at all. His hand lifted to my hair, and he pulled away a bit of straw that had lodged itself there. "You've been a good friend to me, Clara," he said softly. "You've been more than a good friend."

I didn't let myself hear what he was trying to tell me, but I hear it now. I feel it in the way he touches me like I'm sacred to him. I sense it in the strength of his arms around my body and the tenderness of his mouth moving over mine.

I don't know if Axel is right about love and if it's really strong enough to break the chains of my fate, but I do know I can count on him until the very end. He won't give up on me—on us—until my dying breath. There's hope enough in that to keep me fighting to believe we could have a future that outlives this forest.

We kiss in the pool for what feels like hours. Somewhere

along the way we've taken off our outer clothes, my dress and his shirt and trousers, and I'm left in only my chemise, and for him, his linen pants.

Eventually we slip out of the water, spread out our clothes to dry, and lie down on the surrounding limestone, warmed by the steam. We sleep in each other's arms, his scarf wrapped around us. We only intend to take a nap, but when I wake up again, it's nighttime.

The open roof of the cave reveals glittering stars. I languidly gaze at each brilliant spark of light. Were stars always this beautiful? They're cut gems spilled across a velvet sea, treasures that keep multiplying the longer I keep staring.

A streak of white darts across the sky. A shooting star. I sigh. Even more beautiful.

Wait, a shooting star? My heart skips a beat.

I sit up and look into the far recesses of the shadowy cave, memorizing the direction the star pointed when it fell.

I keep that spot in mind for the rest of the night, barely sleeping. When morning dawns, I nudge Axel awake. "I think I've found it."

His brow wrinkles above his bleary eyes. "Found what?"

"Falling water. Lost words found," I recite, part of the riddle that offered clues on how to find the Book of Fortunes. I kiss his lips and draw back, beaming. "*Sortes Fortunae.*"

Axel pulls up on his elbows. Glances around. "Falling water?"

"Well, we *did* fall, and into water. Plus a star shot across the sky last night. It pointed there." I nod at the entrance of a tunnel on the other side of the cave. "Care to join me?"

He smiles crookedly, feigning indifference. "What's the rush?" He tugs me back into his arms. "It's not going anywhere, is it?"

I laugh as he rolls on top of me, kissing my jaw and neck and shoulder, where the neckline of my chemise has fallen loose. "Come on," I prod. "You know you want to see it."

He grunts noncommittally. "At the moment, I find other things more tempting."

I allow him one more kiss, a lengthy, heated gnawing at my lips that threatens to undo every stitch of resolve in my body, then I push him off, rise to my feet, and throw his clothes at him. "Hurry."

His lower lip juts in a pout. "You're a cruel, cruel person, Clara Thurn."

We dress quickly and pass through the tunnel. It widens to another cavern with natural holes in the rocky ceiling, open to the sky above. On the far side is an underground waterfall that cascades in soft veils, rushing down tiers of limestone ledges.

My brows lift at the sight of it, and I smirk at Axel. "Wouldn't you say that passes muster for falling water?"

He sizes up the waterfall and nods. "It'll do."

We cross shallow groundwater to reach the falls. Red-spotted mushrooms grow in clusters along the edges. I climb the first limestone tier, then the second, searching for a spot where the Book of Fortunes must be hiding. Behind the third tier is a deep crevice. I slip my hand into it, where the stone is dry, and my fingers graze the edges of a stone box. I grin.

"Is it there?" Axel asks from below.

Adrenaline rushes through my limbs. "Yes, I just need to pry it out."

I grit my teeth and nudge the box toward me, inch by inch, a painstaking task as it's heavy, though just the right size to hold *Sortes Fortunae*.

Finally the box slips to the edge of the crevice. I would remove the lid, but there isn't enough space. I pull the box out by another handsbreadth so it balances halfway on the lip of the tier. Maybe if I can—

The book slides off the crevice shelf. I gasp, watching in horror as it crashes into the groundwater at the base of the falls. It submerges to the bottom—two feet—which wouldn't be too tragic if the lid had remained intact. But it didn't. It tumbled loose during the descent.

I curse and scramble down the limestone. "Axel, grab it!" The book shouldn't get wet. It may have been made from the mystical hands of the forest, but that doesn't mean it's indestructible. The pages are still paper. The last thing I want is for them to turn to pulp.

He springs for the box, jaw muscle bulging as he hefts it from the water. He drags it onto the gravelly dry ground. I join him just as he's reaching inside the box to dredge up the book from the silt-choked water. He frowns, paws around. "It isn't here."

"What do you mean?" I feel inside for myself, but my fingers only brush against the distinctive cold of small metal objects. I draw a few of them up and stare blankly at what's in my hand. Necklaces, pendants, ancient coins of silver, a signet ring engraved with a sword and oak leaf. Treasures, though they may as well be tree rot for how little they mean to me.

Axel rakes his fingers through his hair. "Maybe the book dropped out of the box when it landed."

He returns to the spot where it fell. Kicks around the cloudy water. I remain rooted on the gravel, my body numb, my head shaking back and forth like it's caught in broken clockwork. "This isn't right." Not with the red-spotted mushrooms, the four-leaf clover, the shooting star. Not with every fiber of my being pulsing with certainty that I'd finally found the book, that my long search was truly over.

Axel paces back and forth, rubs the nape of his neck. "What if it stuck up on the ledge?" He bolts for the limestone tiers and climbs them. I don't dissuade him, even though the book couldn't have fallen out from up there.

I let the treasures I'm holding tumble back into the box. Meaningless relics, likely from a person of importance long ago. Perhaps a captain or a general in the great battle that was said to have taken place in this forest. At some point he must have known his war was doomed, so he safeguarded his most precious belongings here.

It doesn't matter. He's long dead, absorbed by the trees, while his riches have done nothing to preserve his memory except to make me wish every foul thing upon his resting place.

I sigh, my chest caving inward. I know whoever once owned this treasure isn't to blame for my failure to claim *Sortes Fortunae* today, but I wish someone were.

Axel hops down after searching the crevice shelf. He's empty-handed, of course. He sucks in a deep breath and treads toward me, forcing a tone of reassurance when he says, "It's going to be all right. This isn't a setback. Nothing's changed. We were just mistaken."

"*I* was just mistaken, you mean." I wipe a hand beneath my nose. Am I crying again? How ridiculous. All I do lately is leak water from my eyes. "Look where my obsession over signs has brought us."

He crouches beside me. "Well, I don't think you made a sink-hole open up to a cave with an underground waterfall. Who could chide you for having a peek around here afterward?"

I muster a shrug. "I guess."

He draws me into his lap and kisses my left temple. "We keep going. Nothing has changed," he repeats. "We keep going."

I turn into him and lean my brow against his, nodding. "We keep going," I whisper.

He smooths back my hair, and I lay my head on his shoulder. My gaze drifts to the cave wall left of the waterfall. I vaguely observe vines growing there in thick, twining ropes. A small patch is in bloom with creamy white and yellow flowers. Honeysuckle.

A plant said to ward off evil, herald in prosperity . . . and bring good luck.

I tense, pulse pounding, and pull away from Axel's shoulder. "What is it?" he asks.

"I . . ." I'm not sure. I just need to see. . . .

I stand and tread over to the vines. Reach the flowers. Brush them aside. Draw a tentative breath. *Please, please, please . . .*

Behind the flowers is a natural shelf of limestone embedded into the cave wall. Resting upon it, wrapped in layers of large waxy leaves, is a rectangular object. I bite my lip. Pull it out. Axel is waiting right behind me. "Is it . . . ?"

Still speechless, I revolve and pass it to him, too scared to hold it any longer. What if I drop it, like I dropped the stone box, and dash to pieces the dream I must be having? Could I have been right about the signs after all?

Axel carries the wrapped object to a dry boulder in the cave, which he uses as a table. I stare over his shoulder as he peels away the leafy layers protecting whatever is hidden inside. The sunlight slants in on us from two large almond-shaped holes in the cavern roof. They're like all-seeing eyes with black tears made from sediment streaks of run-off water. It makes this moment feel all the more sacred, like we're standing before a shrine of a deity.

Axel peels the last layer away, and my heart lurches, legs buckle. My throat tightens with staggering relief and gratitude. "We—we found it," I croak out.

He laughs and scrubs a hand under his eye. "*You* did, Clara."

I grin, but then return my gaze to the book, studying it harder. This long-awaited triumph feels too surreal to be true. "That *is Sortes Fortunae,* isn't it?"

Although the Book of Fortunes' incredible craftsmanship is awe-inspiring—by all appearances so delicate that a sneeze could break the fine roots threading the binding, though durable enough to withstand the humidity of this cavern for three years—I still expected it to be more, well, extraordinary . . . perhaps radiating a golden glow or buzzing with mystic energy. Which is ridiculous because I've seen the book before, when Grimm's Hollow wasn't cursed. Sometime between then and now, my imagination has run wild.

Axel peers at the book from different angles, examining it for himself. "As far as I recall, this is what *Sortes Fortunae* looked like." He stands taller and shoots me a wry glance. "But I know the best way to test it."

"What?"

"Make your one wish."

CHAPTER 33

rimm's Hollow used to hold a public wish ceremony once a month. Any villager who was ready to use their one wish participated. For Axel, that was the ceremony right after he came of age at sixteen. He was the only person to make a wish that month, and he wore the traditional wreath of oak leaves on his head.

Those who gathered to watch him took turns pinching his arms, also tradition, meant to remind him he was wide awake and not dreaming and to use this once-in-a-lifetime opportunity wisely.

I was the last in line that day, and when I pinched him, he pinched me back. He winked and whispered in my ear, "For when it's your turn."

"You never told me what you wished for," I say to him now. "What the book wrote to you, I mean."

He smirks. "Knowing the depth of your curiosity, I'm surprised you weren't spying on me at my ceremony."

Villagers weren't allowed to observe the actual wishing. Curtains were drawn across the pavilion where *Sortes Fortunae* lay on its pedestal, and Axel, just as he was supposed to, would have made his wish so quietly that no one but the book could hear him.

I give his arm a little shove. "Of course I wasn't spying."

He laughs and kisses me, just a quick peck at first, but then his mouth lingers longer, moving softly, slowly, stirring up dizzying waves of pleasure inside me.

"Are you trying to evade my question?" I murmur.

"Maybe." He grins against my lips.

I draw back with a scowl. "One day I'll make you tell me."

"You can try."

I roll my eyes. "Go away so I can make my wish."

"I can't stay?"

I fist a hand on my hip. He knows very well he can't be within hearing distance.

"Fine." His arms circle around my waist. "But I know what you're going to wish for anyway." He tugs me close for one last kiss. "And you're going to do wonderfully," he whispers.

My stomach flutters. "Thank you."

I watch him leave through the tunnel that connects to the other cavern. Once he's gone, I face the book again and inhale a deep breath. I trap it in my chest for several seconds and exhale slowly.

It's time.

Each person who makes a wish on the Book of Fortunes must begin with a simple incantation. I know it by heart. Every villager does. "*Sortes Fortunae,* hear my voice," I say. "Understand my heart and its deepest desire. My name is Clara Thurn, and this is my one wish."

I shift on my feet. Shake out my hands. Elongate my spine.

I think of the last words of the riddle:

A selfless wish
The curse unbound.

That's what I'm about to do, make a selfless wish.

My mother's face surfaces to mind. I see her as she appeared at Ella's meadow ball. Older but still beautiful. Wise eyes and a kind smile.

I know I was only hallucinating then, but perhaps the forest's magic bled into the vision and it really was her trying to communicate with me.

"I wish," I begin.

Did you keep the acorn I gave you? Mother's words from the vision flood back to me.

My hand drifts inside my dress pocket, where I still carry her gift.

". . . that you forgive the people of Grimm's Hollow and . . ."

Why won't you spread your wings?

I clutch the acorn tightly and try to focus, but her words won't stop coming.

Wake up, dear heart.

". . . a-and that by doing so, you break the curse and restore our peace."

Fight. Live.

I release a shaky exhale. *I'm sorry, Mother. But I promised myself that* you *would live, not me.*

My wish is spoken, and I chose its words carefully. With one request of the book, I had to find a way to save my mother and the whole village, so I asked for the curse to break. When it does, Mother won't be Lost anymore. I'll find her and show her the path that leads out of the forest. The trees will stop moving, and the map I memorized long before I came here will be accurate again.

My wish will also save Henni and Ella and Fiora . . . perhaps even Hansel and Gretel. When the curse breaks, they should also return to their former selves and be able to find their way free of this place.

I try to smile at the thought of all of them safely back home again, but a pain rips through my chest and rises to my lips, preventing them from lifting at the corners. If only I could join everyone when they return to Grimm's Hollow. But I know that with the wish I've made and whatever actions I'll have to take to obtain it, their happiness will only come at the cost of my death. And I'm sure I've just set it in motion.

What Grandmère foretold is unfolding before me. But becoming the Changer of Fate can't undo my own fate. The rest of my fortune must be fulfilled. And I've played out all the cards she drew for me except one: the Fanged Creature. The curse won't break until I die.

I swallow against another surge of rising pain in my chest. I accept what will become of me. I accepted it before I came to this forest. My death in these woods is my destiny.

Making ready to open the book, I touch the cover: a wooden plate engraved with "*Sortes Fortunae*" and carved designs of trees framed by a thin border of tiny star flowers. Red rampion, I realize, although the wood isn't painted. Ollie's words flicker to mind: *The first to grow forever holds the seed of magic.*

The etched red rampion is at least a comfort, another sign that I was meant to draw the Red Card and come here. I've already made my wish. I just need to find out how to accomplish it.

With a steeling breath, I open the book to a random middle page, preparing to receive the book's instructions. The wish-asker must blindly select a page for the book to communicate through.

The page is blank. I wait for green ink to appear, said to be dyed from the leaves of the forest. Seven heartbeats later, it surfaces on the page and scrawls out one letter at a time, forming words as if an invisible hand is writing them.

Abandon the boy and capture the wolf.
Only then will you obtain your deepest desire.

I blink twice at the instructions. They can't be right. I scan them again to be sure, but before I finish rereading, the words disappear. The page goes blank again.

"Wait!" I stammer. "Write it one more time!"

The page remains empty.

I nudge it. "I don't think you heard my wish correctly. I'll speak it again."

A gust of wind surges into the cavern. It slams the book shut.

I flinch backward, my chest constricting. I don't understand. How can the book be asking me to leave Axel? And capture the wolf? What does that have to do with breaking the curse?

"Clara?" Axel's voice echoes in through the tunnel from the other cavern.

"Give me a few more minutes!" I call back. "I—I can't be interrupted."

Waves of hot and cold flash through my body. I need to sit down. Think. No, I can't sit. My legs are too restless. I pace back and forth. Wrench my hands together. Fidget with my sleeves. Pick at the hem of my cape.

Mother's accusing words lance through me: *Are you prepared to let your friends suffer? If it came down to it, Clara, would you save them or me?*

That was the dream version of her speaking—the ominous version, not the lovingly patient one I saw at the meadow ball. The former couldn't really have been her; it had to be my conscience speaking. But that makes it even harder to ignore.

I lean against the boulder, my head hanging as I take several long breaths. I try to summon my courage. I know what I must do. It's what I promised myself long before I entered the Forest Grimm.

"Please forgive me, Axel," I whisper. My heart squeezes, crumbling to fragments I won't be able to piece back together again. The ache inside me has grown fangs. It's almost unbearable. But I have to bear it. I *will* follow through with my fate.

I push away from the boulder and stride to the waterfall, my hands fisted, my jaw set. I climb the ledges on the cave wall that aren't dripping wet, and I drag myself out of the cavern through the open roof.

I leave the book behind. Axel will need to return it to the village. Besides, I have no more use for it. It's told me what to do, and once I do it, the curse will break. The trees will stop moving, and Axel will find a reliable path leading home. Henni and all the Lost Ones will do the same. My mother will do the same. She'll walk back to our cottage and run into Grandmère's open arms. Grimm's Hollow will flourish once more. All will be right again.

I stand in the grass and brush the sediment from the cavern off my dress and cape.

I've done half of what the curse requires. I've left Axel. Now all I have to do is capture the wolf. A near-impossible task. My only advantage is that I won't have to find her.

If there's one thing I've come to rely upon in this changeable forest, it's that the Grimm wolf will always hunt me down first.

CHAPTER 34

I dash away from the cavern and the sinkhole that opens to it. The trickle of the stream is gone, washed away now that it's no longer raining. Maybe the trickle never was the stream. Maybe Axel and I got lost in the darkness the night before last and accidentally followed a branching path of flooding water.

It doesn't matter. I wouldn't have followed the stream now anyway. Axel would find me too easily.

I hitch the skirt of my dress up to my knees and race faster. Who knows how long it will take him to realize I'm gone?

At the thought of him, a sharp pain pierces my chest, but I do my best to bottle it up and bury it deep. I have to focus on the present, not what's past. Not what I can never have.

I run and run until the hours blend and blur together. I can't tell what time it is. The sun is lost behind a shroud of thick clouds. All I know is that I feel the clock of my life ticking louder than ever. My impending death isn't far off.

It isn't until I stop running, my weakened legs about to give out, that fate confronts me in the distance. The Grimm wolf stands several yards ahead in the dense clutches of the forest, beautiful, stoic, and monument-still. She's waiting for me, like she knows what her fate is too.

Sortes Fortunae didn't say that I would succeed in capturing the wolf, so maybe I won't really have to go through with it. Perhaps it's just the attempt that's necessary. But will doing so trigger my own death? Maybe my blood is what the forest needs to break the curse.

When I reach her, I look directly into her violet eyes, and an unnerving prickle of familiarity crawls over my skin. If she were a normal-sized wolf, I would have to kneel to be level with her face, but very little about the Grimm wolf is ordinary.

My hand sinks into the fur at the back of her neck. I stroke it gently. "Is it time for our story to end?"

Her ears tilt toward me. Her tail rises slightly. I think that means *yes*. She turns and pads away, then looks back, pausing like she's waiting for me to follow.

I do. We walk side by side in companionable silence, though I find myself scanning my surroundings for some means to capture her. A willow branch or sturdy vine to bind her legs. A cliff's edge to push her off of. Would that count? Would it kill her? I was never instructed to slay the wolf—a blessing, since I doubt I could go through with it—but how am I supposed to overpower her?

We journey onward at an unhurried pace. I don't know if the wolf is leading me somewhere, or if she's just biding her time. Maybe she's going to make my job easy and tangle herself in a patch of brambles, and the Book of Fortunes will accept that I've done my part. Or perhaps the wolf is waiting for the right time to kill *me*.

My gut says to run back to Axel and forget what the book instructed. But a strange sense of calmness keeps me tethered to the wolf, to my destiny, and to the end of the curse as the Changer of Fate.

The Grimm wolf guides me out of the trees and onto a rickety bridge made of thick wooden planks. Together, they remind me of a great arched door that's fallen across a riverbed choked with moss and lichen.

This *is* a door of sorts—a drawbridge lowered across an empty moat. The drawbridge's chains are covered in ivy and thorns, and they're fastened to a stone arch that's mostly hidden in greenery like the rest of the castle's towers, ramparts, and battlements.

A thrill of awe chases through me. This is the fortress from legend, the place where the great battle raged centuries ago.

No one in Grimm's Hollow has ever been here before. It's only known from stories passed down through generations.

I look behind me, my gaze sweeping the forest. I've been so focused on the wolf that I didn't absorb how many dead faces are watching me in the spruce, pine, and larches. No tree here is faceless, and the expressions in the knots that form the eyes and mouths are horrific. I see their terror, their agony, their sheer seething rage.

My stomach sinks like I've swallowed a large stone. "Why did you bring me here?" I ask the wolf.

In response, she walks onto the drawbridge and once again waits for me to join her before advancing any farther. I do, although I know it's foolhardy—this place has a palpable history that creeps into my bones and replaces my marrow with ice—but there's nothing to hold me back from irrational courses of action now. Every strange twist of fate is exactly that—fate. And it's finally come for me.

The wolf leads me to the other side of the drawbridge and moat, but she doesn't pass through the stone arch. At the foot of the arch is a grassy area where wildflowers are growing.

She sniffs about them, halting with her hackles raised every time she hears a noise. The flapping of bird wings. The whistling of wind. She doesn't want our presence here to be noticed, I realize, which both doubles my nervousness and piques my curiosity. Why would the Grimm wolf, of all creatures, feel wary?

She continues to paw through the wildflowers. Tucked behind the tall stems of poppy and larkspur are clusters of red star flowers. My heart pounds. I haven't seen red rampion growing like this since Devotion Day when I stumbled upon them while searching for lingonberries with Henni.

The wolf wraps her jaws around a few stems and yanks, pulling up the flowers by the roots. She sets them at my feet and nudges them closer with her snout.

"Um, thank you."

She prods me again. I'm unsure what she wants me to do—my cape already gives me the rampion's protection—but I pick up the flowers anyway.

The wolf huffs and turns away. She yanks up another clutch of red rampion, then settles down into the grass and starts eating the roots.

"Oh, I see." She's providing me with food again, like she did with the fish. I kneel beside her, brush the dirt off the little parsnip-like roots, and take a bite. They taste like radishes, only milder, and my empty belly wants more. I eat those the wolf gave me, and then reach past her to pluck up another bunch.

"Just a moment, Clara. We need to talk."

I gasp. Freeze. That was Grandmère's voice, rich like my mother's, but weathered with age and colored with the accent from her native country.

I turn slowly, looking past the wolf to scan our grassy patch and the arch and drawbridge beyond. No one is there. Deep inside me, I knew no one would be.

I swallow and meet the Grimm wolf's large eyes—beautiful and strikingly violet, just like Grandmère's. "How . . . how . . . ?" My tongue is tangled. I don't even know what to say except "This is impossible. You—you're impossible."

"I'm an Anivoyante," she says calmly. "An animal seer, though we can only possess the bodies of wolves."

I brace a hand against the ground, reeling from the sight of her wolfish mouth moving while real words—human words—pour out of her. I don't fully understand what's happening, but I suspect it's the red rampion that's giving her the ability to speak. "*We?*" I stammer. "How many of you are there?" Was my mother one of them? But if she and I have gifts like Grandmère, does that mean—"Am I going to turn into a wolf?" My pulse roars in my ears.

"No, *ma chère*. I am the only Anivoyante left in our family. The rest were killed long ago. That is why I came to Grimm's Hollow. Your grandfather said the people here believed that an enchanted forest gave them a Book of Fortunes. I hoped they would also accept other kinds of magic, and above all, they wouldn't fear them—fear me."

"But you never told anyone." Hurt and frustration tighten my throat. "You never told *me*. And you never said I'm gifted with a part of our family's magic. I had to learn that from a ghost!"

If she's surprised by my supernatural encounter, she makes no sign of it. She only lowers her eyes and shakes her head, unnerving me again with how human her gestures are. "I never told your mother either. She also shares some of my gift. I planned to tell you both, but when your grandfather died and there was no one else living who knew about me, I grew afraid for you. I feared what would happen if others found out what magic lay in your blood. And I hoped you wouldn't notice your ability as a Voyante of the Bygone. You've lived seventeen years without discovering it and—"

"—you knew I would die soon anyway," I finish as the realization hits me. I sit back stiffly. "That's why you didn't tell Mother and me. We were both fated to our untimely deaths in this forest."

Grandmère bows her head again. "*Je suis désolée.* I am so sorry."

I think of the Fanged Creature fortune-telling card, painted to show a vague beast of indeterminate breed with pointed teeth. I see it crawling out of the picture, evaporating to black smoke, and absorbing into the skin of my mother and me, slipping into our veins and infecting us with a deathly plague. One way or another, whatever the Fanged Creature is, it's bound to kill us.

Unless . . .

I shift closer, wild hope surging through my chest. "Does the Fanged Creature mean something else? Could it simply mean that I carry your blood—and that I won't die?" If Grandmère didn't tell me the truth about something as important as her identity and mine, maybe she also deceived me about my fortune.

"Oh, *ma petite chérie.*" Her pointed ears turn down. "How I wish that card could mean another fate."

My shoulders wilt. I feel like I did when I was a little girl, every time I made Grandmère draw the cards for me in hopes she would read a different fortune, one where I'd live happily ever after. But it's her heart breaking now that I wish I could mend. I feel her pain like I've always felt it. "It isn't your fault."

She releases a dreary sigh. "I've tried everything possible to change your story, Clara. I even forbade you to wear the cape your mother made. I knew it would allow you to enter the forest." When she says "forest," her tone dips in pitch and volume, and I know she means something darker than the Forest Grimm. She also means the Midnight Forest, the card representing a forbidden choice that will lead to my death with the Fanged Creature.

"Why didn't you destroy the cape then?" It's not that I wish I'd never come here or that I'd made a different choice, given the chance. I'm only trying to unlock all the mysteries that have been building inside me these past few weeks. Besides, Grandmère wouldn't have needed the cape herself. Animals have always been able to cross the forest border freely.

"Because I am an Anivoyante, and a seer must respect what is foretold," she answers. "I might try to nudge you down a different path, but I could never take away your agency. If I tried to use any force on you, I wouldn't succeed. Fate is all too powerful. Only a rare individual has any hope of changing destiny, and I have never drawn the Red Card for myself. Besides, I knew you would one day enter the forest, and I would rather you be protected by the cape."

I think of the last time I saw Grandmère in our cottage. It wasn't Henni's fortune she read then, but mine. And among the cards she drew was the Red Card, though Grandmère never knew it. I knocked the cards to the floor before she'd removed her veil.

I open my mouth to tell her what truly happened that day, but different words tumble out instead, a revelation that feels more urgent: "I found *Sortes Fortunae* this morning, and I made my one wish."

I don't know how I expect Grandmère to react, but it isn't with sheer concern bordering on fear. Her wolfish eyes open wider. Her tail lowers. "Do not be deceived, *ma chère*."

"What do you mean?" My brows tug together. "The book doesn't lie."

She ducks her head closer, and I catch my distorted reflection in her pupils. "What was your deepest desire when you opened *Sortes Fortunae*? Was it saving the village, or was it something else?"

I draw back a little, even more confused. "You know I can't say what I wished for." But of course Grandmère must realize that I *did* wish to save Grimm's Hollow. Freeing the village from the curse also frees Mother and the Lost Ones, once I fulfill the book's instructions.

"But what was in your heart?" Grandmère presses.

A mournful cry rises on the air. It's coming from within the castle walls. A woman is weeping. I turn toward the sound, my heart in my throat. It's a call that's haunted me for three long years. Only this time it isn't the wind or any force of nature playing upon my imagination. This time it's real. I know that voice, that rich and beautiful tone.

I grab the red rampion flowers, spring to my feet, and bolt through the stone arch. My cape flaps wildly behind me. I rush inside the castle courtyard. "Mother!"

CHAPTER 35

Like the outer walls of the castle, the stones of the courtyard are covered in ivy and thorns. It's hard to make out where the entrances are in the towers and castle keep. Mother's voice echoes, her weeping bouncing all around me. The only thing I'm certain of is that it's coming from somewhere above.

I scrutinize the upper windows that aren't completely cloaked in greenery, but I can't see a dark-haired woman peering outside. "Mother!" I shout again.

The Grimm wolf—Grandmère—catches up to me. "You need to leave! You are not prepared to meet her."

How can she say that? This is everything I've worked for. "Then why did you bring me here?"

"For the red rampion growing outside. It's the only way I could speak with you. When I'm in the forest, I must remain a wolf, otherwise the trees will cast me out. I do not have your cape. Clara, I must warn you—"

"It's too late. I've already made my wish."

"And I hope your heart chose wisely. I'm afraid your mother is beyond saving, *ma chère.*"

"No." *I can't listen to this.* "I won't give up on her."

"She is irredeemable. The forest has her in its deepest clutches. She was the first to be Lost after the curse. Your mother has suffered the most."

"That's why I have to help her!"

"You don't understand." An impatient growl reverberates in Grandmère's chest. "Your mother has *changed* the most."

I back away from the wolf. "You've seen her, haven't you?" A deep sense of betrayal hits me like a fist to the gut. "How many times did you visit her when you didn't even attend Devotion Day with me? When you said the cape was forbidden?"

"None of that matters," she snaps. "What matters is that you hear me now. Your mother isn't Rosamund anymore. She is evil. She never had the red root to protect her."

"Then why didn't she take the cape?"

"She didn't fully understand the purpose of red rampion back then. All she knew was that *Sortes Fortunae* told her to make the cape for you, just like it told Ella to come to her to dye her wedding veil red." Her wolfish brows twitch together. "I believe your mother used her one wish to try to save your life."

My eyes sting, my love for Mother piercing deeper, even as my frustration rises. We can't both save each other. The forest would never allow that. Our shared fates are too powerful. One of us has to die here. "That's exactly why I can't abandon her! I have to save *her* life."

I stride away and scan the towers and castle keep again for any doors or windows. Grandmère stays close beside me, sometimes darting in front to block my path. I stubbornly change directions and continue searching. Mother's incessant weeping lances my nerves and heightens my urgency.

Grandmère keeps arguing, trying to convince me how hopelessly changed Mother is, that we have to leave here before it's too late. I'm barely listening in the first place, but I shut her voice out completely when my eyes clap on a lone flash of red among all the green—a rose growing from the thorns that surround a latch on an almost hidden door of the castle keep. Set into the paving stones a few feet away from it is another door—a trapdoor made from a wooden grate cloaked in ivy.

Capture the wolf.

My vision narrows, tunneling on the trapdoor. I rush to it. Yank back the ivy. Lift the door on rusted hinges. "Where do you think it leads?" I ask Grandmère. All I see inside is darkness. "Could Mother be down there?" I lean forward.

"Be careful, Clara!" Grandmère bounds toward me. "That's an oubliette, a secret dungeon. There are no stairs or ladder. If you fall inside, you won't be able to climb out."

Perfect.

The moment she reaches me, I nimbly sidestep and shove her hard from behind. She's large and strong, but she isn't prepared, and her claws can't gain traction on the paving stones. She yelps and falls through the hole.

I slam the grate closed. "Grandmère?" I call to make sure she's all right.

From several feet down, her shadowy face turns up at me. Her eyes are wide, shocked. "What have you done?"

"What the book said I needed to. I'm sorry. I'm sure Mother will release you soon."

"You can't go to her! I had you eat red rampion for more protection, but it isn't enough. Nothing is enough!"

"Have faith in me. Remember when you drew cards for Henni? That wasn't her; that was me—my hand over yours. You turned the cards you always did, but then you turned two new cards—the Changer of Fate and the Pierced Swans. Don't you see? The Red Card changes everything. Not for me, but for Mother."

"No, Clara. Stop! You can't—"

I don't stay to hear her finish. I race for the rose and the latch. I fling the door open and run up the twirling stone steps.

Mother can't be evil. I've done my part in breaking the curse. I've abandoned Axel and captured the wolf. Now all I want to do is say goodbye.

"I'm coming, Mother!"

CHAPTER 36

The twirling steps are worn and uneven. My left foot catches one, and a sharp pain flares up my lower back. I hiss and lean against the stairwell for support. The ache in my crooked spine has been a constant throb since I lost my shoe at the meadow ball, but now it rages hot, as if it's been bottling up anger all this time.

I grit my teeth and press onward, forcing myself up step after step on bandaged feet. I can't stop now. I'm so close to Mother. I can feel her presence, even though her weeping has silenced. It hushed the moment I passed through the door with the rose above the latch.

I finally reach the top of the stairs and limp down a stone-lined corridor. Thorns and ivy have made their way into the castle to frame the archway at the corridor's end. Woven among them are red roses. The largest hangs down in full bloom from the pointed center of the arch.

As I pass beneath and enter the room beyond, three crimson petals rain down on me. I barely feel their velvet touch; I'm too stunned by the blinding red before me.

Roses bloom everywhere. They snake up the walls, border the windows, and drip from the ceiling, anchored by a lattice of climbing ivy and thorny vines. Their petals even carpet the stones.

In the center of the room stands a large bed, a relic from the past with weathered posts and a moth-eaten canopy of gauzy faded fabric. Despite its deteriorated state, the bed looks hauntingly romantic with more roses, thorns, and ivy strewn in spirals around the posts as they sweep upward into the swags of the canopy.

Heart clattering, I shuffle toward the bed. I'm half tiptoeing, half limping, my breath caught deep in my chest. This is where I'll find Mother. I sense it just like I've always sensed she's remained alive in the forest.

I round one of the bedposts to where the canopy parts and look within to the literal bed of roses. If there is a mattress beneath, it's completely hidden by the pillowy scarlet blooms.

A breathtakingly beautiful woman lies atop them with her eyes closed. Her sable hair and snowy complexion form the perfect complement to the abundance of red surrounding her.

"Mother." The word falls from my lips in a sacred whisper. I didn't mean to speak aloud. She is sleeping, and I don't wish to disturb her. Her chest softly rises and falls. She looks so at peace. The wrenching sound of her weeping has gone, and the tears on her cheeks have started to dry.

Unable to help myself, I shift a little closer. As if she can sense my presence, like a sleeping baby senses its mother nearby, her emerald-green eyes slowly blink open and capture mine. Her lashes are still a little wet as she gazes harder.

I wait, breath bated, for her to say something, anything, though what I wish for the most is that she say my name. It would mean she remembers me. She remains silent. Pressure builds in my chest, and I blurt, "I didn't mean to wake you."

The ghost of a smile lifts the corner of her mouth, a mournful curve absent of any mirth. "I never sleep. I only lie here vainly hoping I might slip away into a dream again." She speaks without any recognition of me. It's more like she's talking to herself than confiding to her daughter.

My heart pricks with a stab of disappointment, but I quickly stifle the sensation. It doesn't matter that I'm not familiar to her. I will be soon enough. I've done everything *Sortes Fortunae* has required. The curse is going to lift. Perhaps it already has, but the undoing will be gradual rather than instantaneous.

"I've brought you something." I hand her my clutch of red rampion flowers.

She gently takes hold of my offering. I shudder as our fingers brush in the exchange. Despite the summer warmth in the air, her skin is ice cold.

"Not roses?" Her dark brows draw together. "I am fond of roses. That is why they call me Briar Rose."

The wound in my heart reopens, tearing an inch wider. I should have expected Mother to have a changed name like Rapunzel instead of Fiora, and Cinderella rather than Ella, but it still hurts to hear how she has forgotten she's Rosamund. "They?" I ask, stuck on the word. Has she met other Lost Ones here?

Mother's gaze lingers on mine, as if she's considering letting me in on a secret, but then the moment passes, and she raises her chin. "I will accept your gift. You chose the right color."

Before I can ask her why, she rises, red separating from red as she pulls away from the rose-flocked mattress to stand barefooted on the stones scattered with petals.

I openly stare at her dress, a wondrous concoction of crimson and scarlet and ruby red—all sourced from nature. Instead of fabric, layers of poppies, tulips, lilies, dahlias, buttercups, and wildflowers form the gown—and, above all, roses. She truly is the woman in red that Ollie told me about.

Some flowers are in season and some are not, but all are vibrantly in bloom. My mother's hold on the magic of the forest is somehow keeping them from wilting.

Strewn together over a framework of ivy around her body, the flowers don't even cover all of my mother's skin. Sections of her waist and hips are exposed, as well as a slit that runs up her left thigh, and the flowers draping her chest and right shoulder barely cover her breasts.

I admire the boldness of the dress and the power my mother exudes wearing it, but at the same time I startle to see her clad in something so sensual. She was always a confident woman, never ashamed of her body, unafraid to bathe in the copper tub we brought in the kitchen without curtains strung around her. But seeing her flaunt herself so brazenly is still strange and unsettling.

I'm reminded of how young I was when I saw her last . . . how much I may have never known about Rosamund Thurn, even then.

She tucks the red rampion I gave her into the length of her single sleeve and stands tall, gazing down on me from the four inches separating us. The crown of red roses in her hair completes the ravaging beauty of her queenly appearance.

"Do you dream?" she asks, searching my face. "Is that why you were called to me?"

"I . . ." I'm not sure how to answer. Why *am* I here? *How* am I here? I've undone the curse, or at least started its unraveling. Haven't I?

I fidget and cast my gaze out the windows, but I can't see the forest past the ivy and thorns. I suppose I don't need to. My mother should be proof that the curse has lifted. Except she isn't. She still believes she's Briar Rose.

Then there's the problem of me. If I'd truly broken the curse, wouldn't I be dead already? I assumed my life was part of an unspoken trade I agreed to when I made my one wish. My sacrifice to save Mother. The fulfillment of my fate.

I don't understand what's left for me to do, except . . .

"I think . . . I need to bring you home."

That has to be my final task, whether or not *Sortes Fortunae* spelled it out for me. Perhaps when my mother crosses the line of ashes and returns to Grimm's Hollow, the curse will fully lift and my life will end as she's ultimately saved from the forest.

"Home?" She arches a dark brow. "And what place do you believe that is if not the walls of this castle?"

"Home is beyond the forest."

"There is no beyond. There is only the forest."

"That isn't true. We have our cottage, our sheep. Your favorite lamb, Mia, is grown now. She's a mother like y—" My voice breaks, and I steady myself, blinking back my gathering tears. "She and her offspring give the softest wool."

"I have no need of wool."

"But you're cold. I felt your skin."

"Warmth is in red."

"What do you mean?"

"Red is magic. It's the answer for everything. It clothes you. It satiates hunger. It saves."

I think of what Grandmère said, that Mother never had the red rampion to protect her when she entered the forest. Maybe, since then, she has come to realize it's what she was lacking, what she needed, even if she can't remember why.

"Red does save," I concede. "It's why I wear this cape."

A petal falls from her rose-wreath crown as she tilts her head at the cape, reaching out to touch the fabric.

"Someone made this for me," I add, hoping to stir her memory. "A book told her to. She spun the wool, dyed it red with rampion, and asked Fiora Winther to weave it together. Then this someone, she cut the pattern to my size and sewed the pieces to make a cape." I catch my lower lip between my teeth as my mouth trembles and my tears spill over. "She did it because she loved me."

Mother lifts her hand toward my face. I ache to lean into her palm, but her hand never comes to rest against my cheek. Instead, she collects the moisture from my tear on her finger and examines it curiously. "Do you cry because you also do not dream?"

"I dream."

Her green eyes snap up to mine. "Then you *must* sleep."

I nod, but frown at the same time. *Doesn't everyone sleep?*

She releases a pent-up sigh, takes both of my hands, and clutches them to her chest as she draws me close. "Then it is you I have been waiting for."

An awkward beat passes. "Yes," I finally answer, because I'm sure I am that person, even if it's not for the reason she thinks. "Like I said, I've come to take you from this forest."

"I cannot leave until I've found what I have lost."

"And what is that?" Does she have any memory of Father? Mother came into the Forest Grimm looking for him. She never realized he was already dead before she set foot in these woods.

Herr Oswald, chairman of the village's governing council, was the one who brought the news. From the moment he set foot on our sheep farm, his head was bowed and his hat was in his hands. At first, I feared something had happened to Mother. She'd embarked on her journey four days previous, and in the meantime, two sightings of the Grimm wolf had occurred. But Herr Oswald instead told Grandmère and me what had happened to Father: his body washed up from Mondfluss River in Grimm's Hollow, all tangled up in his net. A fishing accident, he explained.

That image of my father, lifeless after suffering, is a torment I've buried deep. I never fully mourned him. I couldn't or I'd lose myself to grief and have no hope of saving the last parent left to me. The one I'm finally reunited with now.

"I'll remember what I've lost when I can sleep again," Mother murmurs, at last giving me an answer. "It will surface in my dreams. That is why I need your help."

"But I can't . . . We don't have time for a nap." The clock of my life will stop ticking soon, and I won't waste any moments I have left with her.

"Please." Her eyes water. "I can't endure this agony any longer. I haven't slept in three years."

Three years? She must be exaggerating. But doubt twists through my gut as I take in the dark rings beneath her striking eyes, the bloodshot edges of the whites, and the desperate, almost frenzied look she gives me. "How could I help you fall asleep?" Does she want me to sing her a song or brush her hair or—?

"I need your blood."

I shrink back a step. Pull my hands away. "My blood?"

"Just a drop," she adds hastily.

"But how can my blood help you sleep?"

"Red is magic." She echoes what she told me moments ago. "It is the answer for everything."

But it isn't the color red that's magical, only when it's red rampion. And that enchantment isn't in my blood like it is in Fiora's. Even if it were, red rampion's power is only one type of magic, just like Grandmère's magic is another. It can do many things—protect people, and even wake up the land and grant it power, according to Ollie's poem. But it isn't a remedy for every ailment. It can't cure insomnia.

I take another backward step. "I don't know."

"I'm begging you." Tears stream down her face where the skin is cracked and sore from excessive weeping. "Have pity on a stranger."

But she isn't a stranger. She's my mother. And it's because I know her and love her that I'm hesitant to give her something that won't save her in the end. Instead, it will drive her to more despair. And behind that despair—that madness—is the evil of the curse, just like it is with all the other Lost Ones. If I'm not careful, I'll stoke the fire of that evil—the evil Grandmère warned me about—and Mother will become vicious and deadly, impossible to persuade to ever leave this forest, the same way Fiora and Ella became murderous and impossible to help.

"Give me one drop," she pleads. "That's all I ask. One drop will let me sleep for one blessed night."

I waver on my feet. I hate to see her so upset. This is nothing like the joyous reunion I'd imagined.

Perhaps I *can* help her. Perhaps there is magic in this world I don't yet comprehend, magic that goes beyond the forest and red rampion and *Sortes Fortunae* and fortune-telling cards. Magic that's stronger and deeper that binds mother to daughter, and both of us to Grandmère, whose magic I've only scratched the surface of understanding.

Could that magic be healing?

I stand taller, though it makes the pain in my back flare brighter. "Do you have a knife?"

Mother's mouth slowly curves, revealing her teeth. Her incisors are longer and sharper than I remember. "No . . . but I have a spindle—the spindle of a spinning wheel."

CHAPTER 37

Mother takes my hand and leads me to the far side of the bed, where, hidden behind the rose-strewn canopy, is a spinning wheel. It's just as ancient and weathered-looking as the bed, and one of the last things I expected to see in a castle that was once a mighty fortress. This place must have sheltered more than soldiers and warriors.

The spinning wheel is old, but its design is similar to the one Mother once used in our cottage. While Grandmère read us stories by the crackling fire, I would comb fleece into soft rolls of fiber, and Mother would spin them into fine yarn.

Unlike the wheel in our cottage, this one is covered with ivy and thorns, like much of the castle. A prickly stem with a single red rose winds around the spindle, the bloom opening two inches from the spindle's pointed end. It indeed looks sharp enough to draw blood.

"Do you still spin wool?" I steal a glance at my mother's fabricless dress. I know the answer must be *no,* but I can't help wondering why she chose this object among others in this castle as her instrument for drawing blood. There must be an armory somewhere. Weren't any weapons left inside?

Mother doesn't acknowledge my question. She stands behind me and lifts my arm, guiding it with a gentle nudge. "All you have to do is touch the spindle with your finger."

Perhaps she chose the spinning wheel when she still remembered home, remembered me, and realized she should have spun more yarn dyed with red rampion for a cape of her own, not only mine. Now that recollection seems to have dwindled to only the need for red blood.

"You never asked what my name is." I know I'm just delaying the inevitable, but again I feel the silent ticking of the clock ending my life. Like the last toll of Ella's poison-formed enchantment, my own midnight is coming soon, and when the hands meet at twelve—when my finger touches that spindle—I fear the prick will be the bite of the Fanged Creature. What if I die in this room rather than when Mother crosses the line of ashes? I want her to know who I am first.

"Please." She prods me another inch toward the spinning wheel. "You can tell me your name after I sleep."

"But you don't need to dream to remember what you lost. I'll tell you." I look over my shoulder and meet her narrowed eyes.

She stiffens. "You can't know—"

"You lost your husband, a shepherd named Finn Thurn. But he isn't in this forest. We buried him beside your father in the plot at the edge of the north sheep pasture."

Confusion ripples between her brows. "No, I've lost more than a man."

"You're right. You lost a mother, my grandmère, the wolf who comes to visit you."

Mother's mouth draws into a hard line. "The wolf never shares her blood with me."

"She doesn't have to. It's in your veins. You were born of her, and I was born of you." I swallow. "I'm Clara Thurn. Your daughter. You were the one who made me this cape. You lost me, Mother. And I lost you. I *love* you. And I've come to this forest to save you."

Her jaw muscle flinches. She retreats a step. "I don't know what you're talking about!"

"Look at me!" I choke on a dry sob. "Can't you see our resemblance? I'm nearly your reflection."

She squeezes her eyes shut and rapidly shakes her head. "No, I won't hear any more of this madness! If you want to save me, give me your blood. Touch the spindle!"

My tears fall freely. I bow my head and summon my courage. I've done all I can now. I've found my mother, I've spoken to her, and I've told her who I am. I can't force her to remember me. All that's left to do is give her my blood. If it helps her sleep, I'll drag her resting body home.

I turn. I reach. Almost touch the spindle. But I can't force my finger to descend.

One drop of blood? It's too simple. It's Fiora capturing Henni because Henni "felt" like what she'd lost. It's Ella poisoning my friends and me because she wanted to grant us enlightenment. It's Hansel and Gretel allowing us to gorge ourselves on their food like welcoming hosts.

I can't give my mother my blood. She wants something more than sleep. The dread pooling in my stomach warns me that it might be my death. And although I agreed to die to save her, I never meant being murdered by her. Could a spindle's prick do that?

I slip backward by an inch. Start to retract my hand. "I think—"

Mother shoves me from behind, striking the sorest spot of my S-curve. I cry out. Lurch forward. Touch the spindle by accident.

I cringe, but the bite doesn't sting. Not until the rose stem snakes out and latches on to my finger. A sharp thorn juts out and pierces my flesh.

I jerk my hand away, stunned. "What just—?"

Dizziness seizes me. The walls tilt. The stone floor gives way. I'm reeling, falling . . .

I'm dying.

This is my clock struck twelve. My midnight.

As was promised long ago, this is the story of how I die.

And this—this is my death.

The last thing I see before I collapse to the stones is my blood glistening red on the thorn of the spinning wheel.

CHAPTER 38

I'm not dead. Not yet. Not unless the hell that traveling preachers warn about is real, and I'm stuck there, paralyzed in my body, my eyes and mouth the only things I can move, although not enough that I can focus my vision or form any words. Whatever was on that thorn has stunned me, incapacitated me. Above all, it's cast a powerful spell of fatigue over me.

I fight the desperate need to sleep. If I do, will death finally claim me? I'm not ready to die. Not like this.

Dimly, I'm aware I'm being dragged by my arms, no tenderness in my mother's manacle-like grip around my wrists. I'm taken from the rose-red room to the corridor to the winding stairs of the castle keep. There, my mother lifts me, draping my limp body over her shoulder, and carries me down the twirling flight. Her strength rivals Fiora's, and she moves with Ella's elegance and Hansel and Gretel's determination.

She doesn't exit the door I came through from the courtyard of the castle. She passes through another corridor on the main level of the keep. It opens to a separate door leading to a different location . . . some kind of garden.

I try to take in my surroundings, but I can't see much beyond more stones, thorns, and ivy. My head bounces against my mother's back. Past the floral scent of her dress comes a foul odor on the air, sickly sweet like rotting meat.

The stench grows stronger as we pass through a gauzy curtain, soft as spiderwebs. It's strung between two garden walls.

As the fabric wisps over my dangling hood and flutters back into place again, I catch a glimpse of it and gasp. It isn't a curtain; it's Ella's veil—the veil Henni stole from my pack before she left me and Axel.

An anvil's weight of dread drops inside me. What has my mother done with my best friend?

Painstakingly, I muster the strength to turn my head. Once I do, my eyes fly wide. Dead bodies are strewn about the castle garden. Lost villagers. I spy at least six of them: Alaric Starck, Ida Gunther, Emmott Martin, Leoda Wilhelm, Garron Lenhart, Hamlin Vogel. Others are so decomposed I don't recognize them.

Where their skin still remains, it's leached to morbid ashy shades. All are in various states of being slowly dragged from the garden. Emmott, Garron, and Ida have ivy snaked around their ankles and legs. Leoda and Alaric are caught in thorns, pinned to the outer ring of castle walls. Hamlin is partway absorbed into a tree just beyond the wall, his face half flesh and half bark.

Bile scalds my throat. Did my mother kill all of them? How many more villagers have also been to this castle and are now entombed in the forest?

My mother sets me down and lays me in a bed of ivy. She tucks my hood back and smooths my hair off my face. Her eyes are empty pits of hemlock green. Her touch is careful, not caring. I feel like a doll she's arranging for display, just a means to an end—and I fear what that end will be, how it will happen.

"You should sleep now," she coos, and my eyes bat heavily, resisting the temptation. "It isn't painful when you can't wake up. I'll show you."

What isn't painful?

She stands and sweeps out of view for a moment. As she does, I see another person lying a few feet away from me. Her eyes are closed, and a red kerchief is tied over her braided chestnut hair.

Henni.

Tears spring to my eyes. Is she dead like the other villagers? I scan her appearance. Pale skin and lips. Sunken-in eyes. But there—! Her chest is faintly rising and falling. Her breaths are shallow, but she's still alive.

Mother kneels on her other side, brushes Henni's hair away from her neck, and stretches her own mouth open wide. Her lips curl back from her teeth, her incisors lengthening half an inch. A terrible grin spreads across her face as her eyes rivet to mine.

I don't recognize her at all now. She isn't my mother anymore. She's cold and heartless. She might have inherited some of Grandmère's magic of being an Anivoyante, but unlike me, it's as if her portion leans toward the animalistic side. And as she's become Briar Rose, it's turned vicious and corrupt.

She bends over Henni, latches her teeth onto her neck, and starts to suck.

I gag against a swell of nausea. I can't believe what I'm seeing. Mother is drinking the blood of another human—someone she knows and loves, even though she can't remember her.

Henni's eyelids flutter, her hands tremble, but she doesn't wake up. My mother is draining her life away, and Henni can't do anything to stop it.

I strain to shout, scream, pull my heavy body up so I can do something. Shove my mother back. Strangle her.

I wince. Could I really do that? Could I kill her?

A commotion rises on the air. Voices—Grandmère's and someone else's. Someone with a deeper register that launches a thousand butterflies inside me. *Axel.* Did he track me here?

My mouth struggles to form his name. I fight to move, but I only achieve a pathetic twitch of my fingers. If I can't call to him, he won't be able to find us in time. The castle is vast, and this garden is hidden.

I pinch my eyes shut in concentration. The barest noise escapes me. "H-help!"

My mother's head yanks up from Henni's neck. Blood drips from the corners of her lips. "Impatient for your turn?" she asks. "Yes, I am too."

She rises tall, and her dress of red flowers billows around the high slit on her thigh. She stalks toward my bed of ivy. "Your blood could be the answer, the red that finally helps me remember what I've lost."

She kneels beside me like she's at an altar. Her incisors lengthen again. With a whimper, I realize at last what our shared fortunes amount to. She's the Fanged Creature in the Midnight Forest, and I'm the daughter she sacrifices.

Her icy lips meet my neck. Her teeth lance into my flesh. A cry rips out of me—the pain is stark and agonizing—but my voice is paper-thin. The chill on my throat floods into a rush of liquid heat. I feel the blood in my veins gurgle up and slosh into my mother's mouth. The woman who gave me life is taking it from me, swallow by swallow.

Whatever she gleans from the taste of my blood encourages her to bite deeper, drink harder. She's not going to snack on me like she did with Henni. She's going to empty me until my heart stops beating. Perhaps a buried part of her senses our connection, and she wants more, believing I'm her answer, her final satiation.

But I've already told her what she lost, and she didn't believe me. Will she come to herself when I die? Is that when the curse will finally break?

I shudder as a horrible chill takes hold of my body. My pulse beats a rapid staccato. Black stars fleck my vision. My head throbs in a whirl of dizziness.

My eyelids sag . . . then fully close.

This is it. I'm truly, inconceivably, and irrevocably dying.

A deep and savage growl bursts into my awareness. I crack my eyes open. Fur and claws streak past me. My mother is knocked back. She tears a chunk of my flesh away as her teeth rip from my neck. The pain is astonishing, but I'm too weak to scream.

My eyes flicker closed. I drag them open again. Axel's handsome face crowds my vision. His eyes are wide, terrified. He clamps his hand on my neck. His mouth forms the shape of my name, but my hearing is fading. It sounds like he's calling from the bottom of a well.

I only catch fragments of what he's saying.

"Don't leave . . ."

". . . can't die."

"I love . . ."

Then his lips are on mine, a prince's kiss to a sleeping princess, like in Grandmère's book of children's stories. But the kiss doesn't revive me. More blackness showers across my vision. My skin grows clammy. I'm shivering, slipping away. My eyelids are impossibly heavy. I can't keep them open any longer.

They crash shut.

Everything is darkness, emptiness . . .

. . . and then the strangest sensation takes hold of me. It's as if I'm turned inside-out, though I can't physically feel how it happened.

I'm in the air. Hovering above Axel. Looking down at him. He's shaking my lifeless body. Weeping. Calling out my name again and again. The moment is lengthy but brief all at once. Time is different now. Slippery and sludgy. Axel says my name one last time, then he hangs his head. His hand drops from my neck and lands on a book beside him. *Sortes Fortunae.* He's brought it with him, along with my pack.

As soon as he unwittingly touches the book, his shoulders

go rigid. He looks up at my mother and Grandmère. The two of them are locked in a vicious fight. Mother is holding her own, just as strong as the wolf.

"Is there a spinning wheel here?" Axel asks Grandmère, his words rushed.

Her wolfish head rises. She doesn't stop wrestling her daughter. "Yes." She quickly tells him where to find it, not wasting any breath to ask why he wants it. "But do not touch the thorns."

He races back inside the castle keep. I try to follow, but I'm stuck here, tethered to the view of my body.

I'm dead, I realize.

My body below me is limp and splayed among the ivy, my jaw slack, my skin as pallid as the other dead villagers'. A mangled gash at my throat pools crimson blood onto the stones.

I stifle my horror and turn my ghostly gaze to Mother. Why hasn't she changed, returned to her former self? She's still Briar Rose, fangs bared and wrestling with the wolf. I don't understand. My death was supposed to save her.

"I hate this place."

I startle to hear Ollie's voice and see him sitting on a garden wall.

He peeks about our surroundings and shudders at the dead villagers being absorbed by the forest, destined to become trees. He won't even look at what's become of my body. "You shouldn't have come here. I warned you about the woman in red. I said you shouldn't try to find her."

I glimpse at the ferocious person attacking Grandmère. "But she's my mother."

He shrugs like that doesn't change anything. "This is what happens when you make the wrong wish."

He heard me make it? "How was it wrong?" I sweep closer. "I was selfless."

He juts his chin out stubbornly, but then his lower lip wobbles. "You promised to help me find my pennies."

"Oh, Ollie . . ." Guilt swells inside me, but I have no breath to sigh it away on, no means to release it. "Please understand, I had more than you to save."

"But you didn't save anyone, and now you're dead."

I wince against his words, but I have no heart for them to sting. Instead, the hurt lingers intangibly, and I suffer all the worse for it. "Axel will help you. He knows about your pennies."

"Axel doesn't see me or hear me. Until you came along, only the Lost people did. But you see the past, Clara. Ghosts and memories. I was counting on you."

Ghosts? I hadn't considered that seeing the dead could be part of my gift. Ollie is the only spirit I've encountered. "I'm so sorry."

Axel runs back to the garden, panting. He's holding a thin iron rod, twelve inches long and pointed at the end. The spindle. He's broken it off the spinning wheel.

I worry about the poisonous thorns, but they're gone, and his fingers aren't bleeding. He's managed to remove the thorns and the rose without getting pricked.

He kneels over my body. I hover lower so I can see his face. His skin is flushed, and his eyes shine wet. "Axel?"

He doesn't hear me. He's blind to me, deaf to me. I've become like Ollie, a phantom lost to his awareness. The thought is crushing.

"I'm not supposed to tell you what I wished for when I was sixteen," he murmurs to the shell of me lying in a pool of blood. "But you're dead so I don't think this counts." He briefly squeezes his eyes shut when he says "dead" and takes a shaky breath. "I wished that I could bring back to life the person I loved the most." He wipes at his nose. "I meant my father, but his body was never found, so I could never try what the Book of Fortunes instructed."

I float an inch nearer, wishing I could touch him, lay a solid hand on his shoulder. I know my voice won't reach him, but I can't help asking, "What did it say?"

He strokes my dead face. "I was told to drive a red spindle into the heart of the person I loved more than anyone." Tears spill from his eyes. "Don't you see?" His voice hitches on a sob. "That's you. The book knew this would happen and where we would be when it did . . . although I never knew what the red spindle meant before. But it's all right. I think I do now."

"Red spindle?" I glance to Ollie, as if he can help enlighten me, but the boy has vanished.

The wolf yelps. My thoughts scatter. My mother is sinking her teeth into Grandmère's neck.

Axel flinches, momentarily distracted, but then he exhales and bows his head. His beautiful golden hair dangles in his eyes.

He draws my cape closed over my chest. Rises higher on his knees. Holds the spindle with both hands in the air above me.

I understand now. I place a ghostly hand on his shoulder. He's my truest love, the Pierced Swan I'm forever bound to, my Changer of Fate.

"Do it," I whisper. I choose to live. It's what my mother—my real mother—always wanted for me. Her greatest desire. Her one wish. It's why she made me the cape and gave me the acorn and taught me to be bold and fearless.

Axel takes a steeling breath, and in one deliberate and powerful movement, he stabs the spindle into my heart.

CHAPTER 39

I inhale a sharp and desperate breath and jolt upright, yanking the spindle from my chest. It clatters to the stones.

I'm in my body again. Pain flares through my crooked back and throbs in the wound at my neck, and I bless every torturous feeling that tells me I'm alive.

Axel chokes out a laugh that's almost a sob. He crushes me in his arms, kissing me again and again, my brow, my cheeks, my lips. "It was always you," he whispers, taking my face in his hands. He presses our foreheads together. "It was always you."

I'm in a daze of emotions and sensations, still getting my bearings and taking in all that's just happened—and is still happening. "Grandmère," I gasp. "We have to help her."

A few feet away, the Grimm wolf lies near Henni. A low, keening howl peals out of her while my mother continues to feed at her throat.

I glimpse the Book of Fortunes, its spine wet with my blood, and the spindle beside it. A mad idea forms in my mind.

I tear a scrap of fabric from the bottom of my cape and grab the spindle.

"What are you doing?" Axel asks.

"Saving her."

"The wolf?"

I shake my head. "My mother."

"I don't think—"

"I have to try."

I spring to my feet, momentarily wobbling from lightheadedness. "Mother!" I call.

She doesn't turn. She keeps drinking Grandmère's blood.

"Rosamund!"

Again, she doesn't acknowledge me.

I ball my hands into fists. "Briar Rose."

She looks up and slowly wipes the blood from her mouth. "You," she seethes, no recognition in her voice for her daughter, only the victim who shouldn't be living, let alone standing. "Didn't I bleed you dry?"

My jaw clenches, but I force a grim smile and grace her with a nod.

"Then why are you still troubling me?"

"I haven't given up on you."

She laughs darkly and rises to her feet, looking down her nose at me. "I've tasted you, and you gave me nothing. You can't save me, child."

"I can. Because I *am* your child. Your blood is in me. Every stubborn, unrelenting, hopelessly hopeful part of you is in my flesh and bones." I stride toward her. "It's given me the courage to overcome insurmountable odds and outrun my fate time and again. And because you're in me and will always be a part of me, I have the faith to do what I must do now."

She smirks. "And what is that?"

"Use the red spindle."

Her brow furrows. Before she can ask what I mean, I hurriedly wrap the spindle in the scrap of my red rampion–dyed cape. I grit my teeth and slam the iron point into her heart.

Her eyes fly wide. She stumbles to her knees. I kneel with her and clasp her arms. "Come back to me, Mother."

I wait for her expression to ease, her pain and shock to wash away, for clarity and peace to descend over her features. But she only shakes violently and glares at me with horrible accusation.

Her breaths suck in and out, ragged and fractured and gurgled. Blood sputters from her mouth.

I waver. Shoot a worried glance at Axel. This isn't supposed to be happening. Cold sweat flashes up my neck. "What did I do wrong?"

He digs his hands in his hair. "I don't know."

Mother slips from my arms and hits the stones hard, her head smacking with a sickening thud. She moans, and her eyes lose focus. Her gaze roves all around her like she's trying to find something to cling on to, to keep her pulse pounding.

"I-I'm sorry," I stammer. "I didn't mean to . . ."

Grandmère painstakingly pulls herself up on four legs and comes to join me on Mother's other side.

"What do I do?" I cry.

She stares down at her daughter, her violet eyes heavy. "There's nothing to be done, *ma chère,* except to say goodbye."

Tears splash down my face. "No, this can't be goodbye. This isn't how the story ends."

"It is, dear heart," she says, using Mother's term of endearment for me. "I saw it long ago."

Unbearable pain wells inside me. I don't have enough room to hold the ache of it. "Please, please, please." I lie down beside my mother and pull her close, the embrace I never received when I found her again. "You told me to fight, to live." I don't know if it was truly her in my vision at the meadow ball, but I have to believe so because I have nothing left to hold on to but that hallucination of her love. "I *did* fight. I'm here. Now I need you to do the same. Fight, Mother. Stay with me."

Her head rolls to the side so she can see my face. Her eyes are my eyes, my mirror reflection. Her trembling hand comes to touch a fold of my cape at the shoulder. She brushes it once with her fingers, then lifts her palm to my cheek. My tears slide over the back of her hand. "Clara?" Her brows lift, tugging inward. "My . . . beautiful . . . girl."

Her breathing stops. Her eyes grow vacant.

My chest collapses. I feel her loss at once, like my own soul has also departed. Sobs rack through my shoulders. I kiss her forehead and tuck my head beneath hers, enfolding my arms tighter around her. "Don't go." But she's already gone.

I want to lie there forever, keep her body warm, remember the echo of her voice when she finally said my name. She remembered me. I felt her love at last.

Memories swell inside me. I'm a little child in Mother's lap. We're in the north pasture, weaving clover blossoms into crowns. Two male lambs lope around us, their fuzzy heads butting as they practice being rams. Mother laughs. "Be wiser than boys, Clara."

Now I'm even younger, maybe four. I'm crying because I stole the sheep shears and cut my own hair, and the result is a crooked disaster of startlingly short bangs. Mother kneels in front of me, turns my head this way and that, and declares, "Quite good for your first try." She draws her long braid in front of her shoulder. "Now trim mine."

Now I'm a fussing infant, so young, I realize, that this memory must be Mother's instead of mine. She lifts me from my cradle, leaving Father asleep in bed, and carries me outside our cottage, under a beautiful starlit sky. "Come, little one. If we're going to be awake together, we may as well enjoy the wonders of the night."

Now Mother is alone. She's knotting the final stitch of the slit she cut in her mattress to hide the red cape. Once it's done, she rises, brings her candle to light the way, and drifts into my bedroom. I'm sleeping with the covers drawn over my head. She gently peels them back so she can see my face. My dark lashes flutter for a moment, but I don't awaken. "Choose courage, dear heart," she whispers, brushing a lock of hair off my brow. "Live fearlessly."

A powerful shudder runs beneath me. The memories vanish. I'm grounded back to the present, still holding Mother's body, but the stones below us quake violently.

Grandmère stiffens and looks at our surroundings. "Clara, we must leave! The castle is crumbling!"

I follow her gaze, and my mouth falls open. The ivy and thorns are shrinking back from the castle and its walls. Without them, the stones crash apart, as if they were the only mortar holding them together.

"Clara!" Axel reaches for me, and Grandmère springs for Henni.

I bolt up to sitting, but clutch my mother protectively. "I can't leave her."

A large chunk of a tower breaks away. It strikes the ground like a clap of thunder. Stones ricochet. I narrowly duck one that flies by my head.

"Go, Clara!" Grandmère shouts. "You can't have survived only to die now."

I meet Axel's eyes. Behind his desperately urgent gaze, I feel his sympathy. "Your mother would understand," he says. He secures my pack on his shoulder and tightens his grip on *Sortes Fortunae*, tucked beneath one arm. "It's time to say goodbye."

My vision blurs. More tears fall. I turn to Mother and gently close her eyes. Kiss her cheek. I pull the acorn from my pocket and press it in the curve of her palm, closing her fingers around it. "I love you," I whisper.

I take Axel's hand. We rush to Henni, who is struggling to open her eyes. We help her to her feet.

"The veil," she says breathlessly.

For once I don't argue about what rightfully belongs to her

sister. I pluck the veil down from where it's strung between the garden walls. I wrap it around Henni's shoulders.

We dodge tumbling stones and collapsing walls as we race from the castle garden. We dash through the castle keep, the courtyard, the stone arch to the drawbridge, and across the rickety planks to the safety of the forest on the other side.

Grandmère is behind us. The second she crosses the drawbridge, it crumbles apart into the empty moat, and the rest of the castle caves in with it. A great cloud of dust and ash billows upward from the massive destruction. My mother is buried beneath it all. The moment is surreal. I stare numbly, coated in silt, and expel a tremulous breath. I try to accept that this is her final resting place.

My friends stand beside me, our arms wrapped around each other. I sense them also trying to absorb the weight of everything that's happened . . . and what can possibly come next.

"What does this mean?" My voice sounds quiet and strange after the cacophony of the castle's fall. "Did the curse break?"

Axel gnaws on his lip. "Well, there's one way to find out." He cautiously removes his scarf and drops it to the ground. As soon as it hits the grass, tree roots snap up and lash toward him. He hastily grabs the scarf and ties it back on again. The roots settle. "I think we can safely say no."

But I'm not so sure.

Neither is Henni. "Maybe *part* of the curse broke," she says, tugging Ella's veil tighter around her shoulders.

Axel slips his pinkie finger around mine, then weaves our hands together. "At least it broke over your mother, Clara. She was Rosamund in the end."

"Yes, *ma chère*." Grandmère nuzzles closer, a surprisingly loving gesture for someone who never offers embraces freely. "Her soul is at peace now."

Henni stares in a daze at Grandmère. "I'm not the only one who hears the wolf speaking, am I? I thought I was dreaming back at the castle."

"The wolf is my grandmother." I smile. "She's an Anivoyante, a seer who can possess the body of a wolf."

Henni swallows hard, like this revelation did nothing to help her accept the reality of a talking animal. "Of course."

Grandmère's eyes flicker to the trees. The entombed dead surround us, their terrorized faces frozen in the bark. "You three have been in this forest long enough," she tells us. "It's time you return home while the red rampion can still protect you."

My gaze flits to Henni again. Leaving here will be the hardest for her. "If you want to go back for Ella, I'll stay with you."

"I'll do the same," Axel adds.

Henni draws a deep breath and burrows her nose in the folds of Ella's veil. "No, your grandmother is right. We don't know how to save Ella yet. Once we do, we'll return." She lifts her head and squares her shoulders. "Besides, we have *Sortes Fortunae* now, and my sixteenth birthday is coming up. I'll make my wish then. I'll find a way to—" She catches herself. "Well, I can't tell you *what* I'll wish for. But it should help."

"Just be sure it's what your heart truly desires," I say, thinking of my own experience with the Book of Fortunes.

Henni nods solemnly. "I will."

For all our hope about the future, I can't help turning my gaze back to the ruins of the castle. So many endings happened there, so many deaths. My mother killed me . . . I killed her . . . I also saved her . . . and Axel saved me. I suppose, for that reason, it's also a place of beginnings.

It's too much to process in this moment, too much to believe. It's also hard to let go of. I don't trust I ever will, and I wouldn't want to. My story will forever be linked to my mother, just like it will be linked to Axel. The Fanged Creature and the Pierced Swans will always be the cards drawn for me. I'll carry them as I live out my life, to face whatever my changed fate has in store.

The Midnight Forest will also remain a part of me. When I leave these woods, I won't leave behind the imprint they've made. This forest is in my blood. I feel that as vividly as the truth that I'm the bloodline of Grandmère and Mother, Marlène and Rosamund Thurn.

I will choose courage, I promise my mother. *I will live fearlessly.*

"There is a stream a half mile east from here." Grandmère points her snout in that direction. "Follow its current for one day until you reach Bremen River. Then follow that river against the current for several days until you reach Snow Falls. A stream branches south of there. Follow it for two days until you come to a fork, and then stop following the water. Head directly south for two miles, and you will arrive at the Twins."

I think of the two towering trees that guard the path leading from the meadow in Grimm's Hollow into the denseness of the Forest Grimm.

"You will be home," Grandmère adds, her voice growing raspy and weak.

My heart kicks as I notice terrible weariness weighing down on her and withering her once-proud posture. "Aren't you coming with us?"

"I am wounded, child. I must return a faster way. I have a better chance of healing in my human form. There are remedies and—" Her words cut short, and she whines a wolfish cry. A fresh runnel of blood purges from the gash on her throat.

"Grandmère?" I drop to my knees and press my hand to her neck. Her head is drooping. She expended the last of her strength by speaking to us.

"I must go." The corner of her mouth lifts sadly. "Take my

luck," she whispers, the Grimm's Hollow version of "good luck." "You are always in my heart, *ma petite chérie.*" She nudges her nose against my cape. *"Mon petit rouge,"* she adds, and I know enough of her native language to understand its meaning: *my little red.*

I hug her close, and when I pull away, her violet eyes shift to brown, and her facial expressions become more animalistic, less human.

She's no longer my grandmère, only a Grimm wolf.

She sniffs once, pawing at the ground, and then she springs away.

CHAPTER 40

I consider traveling back to the underground falls for the silver coins in the stone box. Would Ollie accept them instead of his pennies? Surely they would provide riches for the poor man he was meant to help, whoever that person is.

But on second thought, I leave the treasure where it lies. It may benefit the poor man, but it isn't what will help put Ollie's spirit at rest. Those are the stolen pennies, the simple wrongdoing he can't forgive himself for, the tether that binds his soul to the forest.

Following the route Grandmère laid out for us, Axel, Henni, and I start traveling home. I keep an eye out for Ollie, but I don't see him again. I can't shake the heartbroken look he gave me back in the castle garden, the defeated set of his shoulders. "I promise I'll find a way to help you," I whisper to the woods, and hope Ollie is listening.

The journey home is painstaking. Time passes both quickly and slowly. Quickly because we know where we're going and how to get there. Slowly because each step demands energy we don't possess.

The three of us are undernourished, Henni and I are still recovering from blood loss, and my crooked back is on fire. I keep tearing away more strips off my chemise to replace each set of linen bandages that frays to rags. I even wrap them thicker under my left heel to mimic the wedge-lift I lost with my shoe, but it's a poor substitute and does nothing to ease the pain.

Axel carries me when the throbbing is past endurance. He shares humorous memories about his father to distract me, though I think they're also a source of healing for him. He has never talked so much about his dad before. After his father died, Axel seemed to have locked most of those memories away, and now that he's saved me with the red spindle, the way he thought he'd save his father, it's like he's somehow free of a burden that's haunted him for years.

At the very least, he's free of the heartache.

My own heart is still mending when it comes to the loss of my mother, but with that grief also comes a sense of peace. I can breathe deeper now, enjoy the present better. I notice more beauty around me, new colors in birds' wings and pictures that unfold endlessly in the clouds. The scent of morning dew and the fragrance of night-blooming flowers are wonders I never dwelled on before, blessings I took for granted.

The supplies in my pack are dwindling quickly, but we still have my kits for tackle and flint. They help us catch fish and cook them over pine-cone fires. It's enough to survive on. The trees don't move as often anymore—perhaps an effect of the partially broken curse, if Henni's theory is correct—and when they do, they don't scatter so far.

We stop tying our ankles together at night. Instead, we sleep with linked arms and clasped hands. Sometimes when I wake in the morning, I find that I've folded myself into Axel and he's draped his arms and legs around me.

After several days have passed since we've been following Bremen River, our surroundings start to look familiar. We've caught up to the place where we journeyed between Fiora's tower and Ella's hollow. Three days after that, we reach the spot in the river where we jumped in after racing away from Fiora.

And we aren't the only ones here.

Four people are standing along the riverbank—two women gathering water into buckets, and a couple of children throwing stones into the water.

They look so peaceful and contented—so ordinary—that it takes me a moment to recognize two of them. Fiora and Ella.

Fiora stands tall, not crouched like a spider. Over her form-fitting woolen shirt and leggings, she wears a makeshift skirt that seems to be constructed from the train of Ella's wedding dress.

The most notable difference in Fiora is her red hair. She's cut it, perhaps with the knife I lost when I threw it at her, because now that knife is strapped to her waist. Her hair falls to her lower back, still long by normal standards, but no longer miles and miles of strangling lengths. It only moves now when the breeze rustles through it.

All of us stare at each other for a few uncertain moments—I, for one, am tentative about placing my trust in these two that they won't harm us again—but the tension releases when Ella's gaze finally pulls from Axel, who's confidently holding my hand, and latches on to her sister.

"Henni!" Ella breaks into a wide smile and races over to her, throwing her arms around her neck.

A beautiful flush rises to Henni's cheeks. "You remember me?"

"Clearer than ever." Ella squeezes her tight. "I'll admit, some things are still a little fuzzy. Everything that's happened over the last year is, actually. I wasn't sure if you had really come to my hollow or if that was just another one of my fantasies."

You mean the fantasies where you poison and kill people? I press my lips together against sharing the thought aloud. It isn't a fair quip when Ella no longer appears to be lethally vindictive and a deranged jilted bride.

Henni draws back and studies her sister closely—Ella's clean face and brushed hair and bright eyes—and she seems to come to the same conclusion. Ella is Ella again. "Yes, I was there." Henni's mouth curves into a radiant smile. "We all were." She tips a nod at me and Axel. "We wanted to bring you home, but . . ." Her smile falters.

Ella's brows knit together as Henni's words trail away, like she's struggling to remember what her sister is leaving out from the story. "I hope I wasn't too difficult. I don't think I was myself for some time, you see. The forest did something to my mind and—" She breaks off, lashes lowered as she turns to Fiora. "Fiora says the same thing happened to her."

Fiora shyly meets our gazes. "It's true. And for me, the forest changed more than my mind. My hair, it—" She tentatively smooths a lock and releases a pent-up sigh. "I don't know where to begin."

"It's all right. We understand," I say. "We saw your hair for ourselves."

"Oh?" She cocks her head. "Did we meet, then?" She divides a look between the three of us.

"You could say that." Henni swallows.

"It was a *high* time," Axel adds drolly, "although we did get a bit *choked* up."

I stifle a snort and elbow him.

"How did you all find each other?" Henni asks Fiora and Ella.

"We followed the water," Ella replies, her voice settling into its naturally airy pitch. "I'm not sure if you've realized this yet, but the water in the forest doesn't move like the trees. When I came to my senses again, I followed this river, and it brought me to Fiora—although her children found me first by following a stream."

I turn wide eyes on Fiora. "Wait, you have children?"

She takes a steadying breath. "Yes. Though you wouldn't have met them in Grimm's Hollow. I . . . bore them out of wedlock." Color rises to her cheeks. "I kept them a secret for as long as possible, but after they turned three years old, they became impossible to hide. They learned how to unbolt doors and open window latches. They would sneak outside, and I'd barely catch them in time before passing villagers discovered them."

Poor Fiora. She was always a recluse in Grimm's Hollow, like her father, and apprehensive of drawing any attention to herself. The pressure of trying to hide the scandal of being an unmarried woman with children must have been excruciating.

"So you brought your children to the forest to raise them after they turned three?" I ask gently.

"Yes." Fiora tucks a lock of hair behind her ear, self-conscious. "They're six now. It's hard to believe so much time has passed. Like Ella said, our memories in this forest are fuzzy."

It's probably better that way. If my mother had survived, I wouldn't want her to recall what she had become here . . . and who had suffered at her hands.

"Well, we'd love to meet them." I smile, tipping my head at the two children playing on the riverbank.

Her gaze softens. "Of course." She opens her arms to beckon the boy and girl. "Hansel, Gretel, come and say hello."

The two of them turn and eye us suspiciously. Axel tenses. I struggle to close my gaping mouth. The twins have the same starkly white-blond hair with a thin streak of red, just like the pair of older twins we met under the giant pine. They're also wearing the same clothes, which fit much better now, but—"They're . . . they're . . ."

"Little?" Ella suggests.

I nod, speechless. This Hansel and Gretel look to be around six years old, just like Fiora said, but nowhere near the teenaged years of the other Hansel and Gretel.

"Believe me, I was startled as well," Ella says. "I watched them slowly shrink as they traveled with me. But Fiora assures me they were never meant to be older—er, bigger—than they look right now."

"They must have grown like my hair grew here," Fiora adds as the children finally rush over to her and hide behind her skirts, curiously peering out at us. "Though I don't understand any of it."

I think I might. "Have you ever eaten red rampion? A little red flower with roots that taste like parsnips?"

Fiora gives me an eerie look, like I've just said something I shouldn't have known about. Her gaze cuts to the Book of Fortunes that's poking out from the top of Axel's pack. "I . . . ate it during my pregnancy when I was at risk of losing the twins."

"Really?" Henni brightens. "That's also what your mother did when she was pregnant with you!"

Fiora wraps her arms around herself and nods, clearly uncomfortable with how much we all know about her. "And you believe the rampion made my children grow faster in the forest?"

"It could have," I say, "just like it helped them grow in your belly. Maybe it's also why your hair grew so quickly here too." I lift a fold of my cape to show her. "This is dyed with red rampion. I have to wear it to be safe in the forest, but you don't have to wear anything. The rampion is in your blood just like it's in Hansel's and Gretel's."

Fiora looks down at her children and frowns. "I'm still not sure I understand."

"I don't know if I do either, not fully." I offer a small smile. "But I do know that the red rampion is protective. It should have protected you and your children for a while, but you were here too long, and you've been cursed like us and everyone else in Grimm's Hollow. The magic in your blood must have become twisted."

"But you're not cursed any longer," Henni assures her, and turning to me, adds, "Look at them, Clara. They can't be cursed anymore. The children are small now and—"

Fiora yelps and yanks her arm away from Hansel. A little set of teeth marks indents the skin at her wrist. "No more biting!" she scolds him.

Hansel juts his lower lip and hides behind her skirt again.

"You'll have to forgive him." Fiora exhales. "He and Gretel are still learning their manners. The three of us were separated for too long here, and . . . well, we lost our grip on reality. I fear they still resent me a little. When food became scarce, they didn't understand why I could no longer satiate their hunger. They were so young then. They still are." She kneads her brow, her chin quivering. "After they forgot I was their mother, they started to call me a witch."

"Witch," Gretel repeats with a giggle.

Fiora gazes down at her daughter with a mournful smile and brushes her fingers over her cheek.

The last pieces of the Hansel and Gretel puzzle finally click into place for me. Their stunted speech, their voracious and strange appetites . . . The twins were somewhere between three and four years of age when they became separated from Fiora, and left to raise themselves, they never advanced in language. Their minds had aged to six years old when we met them in the forest, but they were still younger in many ways.

"Well, I hope your kids like fish," Axel says cheerfully, always keen to lighten somber moods.

"Oh, they'll eat just about anything." Fiora smiles.

Axel pales and forces a strained chuckle.

"Do you think it's true, then?" Fiora turns her attention to me and Henni. "Are we really no longer cursed?"

I consider her, my gaze drifting to Ella and Hansel and Gretel—four people who tormented us and would have killed us if we hadn't escaped them. But nothing about them seems vicious or cunning anymore. They're common people, kind people—people who are a little scarred, no doubt, but no longer murderous . . . despite Hansel's penchant for biting.

Perhaps that *does* mean the curse is broken, at least for them. "I think so."

Was it the red rampion that saved them? Each of them had a connection to it and was protected by it for a time.

I remember what I spoke to *Sortes Fortunae*: *I wish that you forgive the people of Grimm's Hollow, and that by doing so, you break the curse and restore our peace.*

Those may have been the words I said, but the book felt what was in my heart. It knew I wanted to save my mother, but it also felt my desire to live and not sacrifice my own life.

What it instructed me to do makes sense now:

Abandon the boy and capture the wolf.
Only then will you obtain your deepest desire.

If I hadn't abandoned Axel and captured the wolf, they would have teamed up and prevented Mother from killing me.

I had to die in order to live again. I had to meet my fate before it could be broken.

But what if, when I made my wish, the Book of Fortunes also

heeded the words I spoke, even though they weren't as heartfelt as my deepest desire? Were they enough to partially break the curse—and break it fully for Fiora, Ella, and Hansel and Gretel?

I want to believe it's true, that I've done something to save at least some of the Lost Ones without having to lose them like I did my mother.

I fold my arms. "If you really want to test whether or not you're still cursed, I can show you the place."

A few days later, I bring them to the Twins, the sentinel trees in the forest near the bordering meadow of Grimm's Hollow, where Devotion Days are held.

The meadow is vacant of people. Golden light from the morning sun glistens over scattered wildflowers dotted among the dead grass. My spirits rise at those glimpses of color and life. They're another sign that some of the curse is lifting.

As we approach the line of ashes that separates the Forest Grimm from Grimm's Hollow, Fiora clutches her children's hands tightly, Henni walks arm in arm with Ella, and Axel supports me as I limp, my back and hips throbbing with sharp pain. I'm practically salivating at the thought of my soft bed and feather pillow back home in my cottage.

Fiora and Hansel and Gretel reach the line of ashes first. Fiora sucks in a tight breath as the three of them step over the line together. Once they set foot on the village side, she collapses to her knees and weeps. Hansel and Gretel run around the meadow, laughing and chasing each other.

Henni and Ella step up to the line next. Ella pauses and whispers something in Henni's ear. Henni glances back at us and nods at her sister.

Ella swallows and approaches us slowly. "I know that things are over between us, Axel, and that you care deeply for Clara. But I'm still ashamed of how long it took me to accept that." She lowers her eyes and takes a small step toward me. "I want to ask for your forgiveness."

Axel shakes his head and places a gentle hand on her arm. "You have nothing to be sorry about. It's my fault for not telling you sooner how I felt."

Something like amusement flits across her face. "Which is why I'm not asking for *your* forgiveness." She inhales deeply and meets my gaze. "I'm asking for Clara's."

I rear back slightly. "I . . . don't understand."

She bites her lower lip and slides the satchel she's been carrying off her shoulder. "I found this near my hollow. I couldn't remember why, but it felt important, so I brought it with me."

She withdraws my shoe. My breath catches. I take in the scuffed leather, the uneven eyelets, the laces still undone from when I loosened them unwittingly at the meadow ball—every small imperfection that marks it's mine.

I could cry. It's a simple shoe. A common shoe. But it's a shoe with my wedge-lift inside.

It's the most beautiful shoe in the world.

"I realized soon enough who it belonged to, but . . ." Ella trails off, her lovely doe eyes falling to the ground again. "Like I said, I'm ashamed of how long it took me to accept the two of you."

I throw my arms around her, almost weeping. "Thank you," I croak. I don't begrudge her anything. I was only in this forest for a few weeks. She was in it for a year and caught in a loop of heartbreak. "I'm just glad you didn't poison me to death."

"Don't press your luck." She laughs. "I also brought my arsenic."

As we talk, Axel opens his pack. He pulls out my right shoe. I haven't been able to part with it, even though I couldn't wear it without the other. I kick off my linen bandages and lace it on, and when I move to slip on the left shoe with the wedge-lift, Axel lowers on one knee and asks, "May I?"

Warmth rises from my chest and sweeps up to flush my cheeks. I nod shyly.

His hand is warm and tender as he lifts my foot and slides it into the shoe. I go a little weak in the knees as his river-blue eyes rise and capture mine. He really is a charming prince.

Ella looks between us and imparts a genuine smile before she returns to Henni. They cross the line of ashes together.

Alone for the moment, Axel grabs me by the sides of my cape and tugs me close. "How does it feel to be wearing not one but two bona fide shoes?"

I toss my head back and release a dreamy sigh. "It's the best happily ever after. For my feet, anyway."

"And the rest of you?"

"I'm just grateful I have an *after* to speak of, never mind *happily ever*. That can wait. For now I'm contented to be breathing."

"Not to mention deliriously enraptured with your feelings for me."

I shrug, feigning indifference. "That goes without saying."

"What if I want you to say it?" His head dips nearer.

I grin and roll my eyes. "You're deliriously enraptured with your feelings for me."

"That's not what I said." His lips graze mine.

"No?"

He shakes his head slightly, his mouth brushing back and forth across my lips.

A shower of prickles rains over me, raising goose bumps along every inch of my skin. I close my eyes and lean into his kiss.

Henni gives an exasperated sigh. "Will you two cross the line already? I want to go home and not worry about the forest eating you alive because you won't stop kissing. You shouldn't tempt fate."

Axel smiles against my lips and kisses me deeper.

I surrender myself to the moment, to him, to time I can enjoy without rushing, to a life I can live without limits, and an infinite array of possibilities.

What is fate, after all, if not to be tempted?

EPILOGUE

AFTER THE FOREST

"Tell me again, *ma chère*, the story of how I die."

The old woman lay on her bed in the cottage she shared with her granddaughter, a girl of seventeen who had just brought in fresh wildflowers to replace those wilting in the vase on the bedside table. "You're not going to die," the granddaughter insisted. "You need to stop looking at your cards."

The granddaughter removed the fortune-telling deck from the table and slid them into her apron pocket, well out of sight. This wasn't the first time in the last few days that Clara had hidden the cards, but no matter where she tucked them away, Grandmère seemed to find them again.

How Grandmère managed to sneak out of bed, Clara didn't know. The old woman could barely hold a spoon to her mouth to sip up broth. She'd been ill ever since she was injured in the forest, although the wound at her neck had finally healed.

Perhaps when Clara slept at night, Grandmère slipped into the skin of the Grimm wolf, and as an animal, she had a spark of vitality.

"Is that red rampion?" Grandmère squinted her violet eyes at the fresh flowers Clara began to arrange in the vase.

"They're poppies." Clara smiled, though her brows pinched inward. Every day Grandmère asked for red rampion, and every day Clara reminded her it was nowhere to be found. The flowers no longer grew in the spot where Clara had first discovered them, just past the border of Grimm's Hollow.

Grandmère's memory was failing her, a fact that worried Clara just as much as Grandmère's waning health.

"Such a shame." The old woman heaved a weary sigh. "I would have liked to speak to Rosamund one last time."

A sharp pang pierced Clara's heart. "Mother is gone from us, remember?" She sat on the edge of the bed and pressed a hand to Grandmère's forehead to check for a fever. "She's buried in the forest. She's at peace."

For a moment, Grandmère seemed to return to herself. The strained and faraway look left her eyes, and she focused on Clara with the lucidity she once possessed. She lifted an age-worn hand and touched her granddaughter's cheek, her fingers trembling. "I am sorry you had to kill your mother to save her, *ma chère*. I should have had the strength to do that long before you came to the forest."

Clara swallowed hard, her eyes growing hot and blurry. "We both did our best. I'm just grateful Mother got to see you from time to time. I'm glad she wasn't always alone."

As she reached beneath the covers to hold Grandmère's other hand, Clara found it wasn't empty. The old woman was already clutching something. "What's this?" she chided, pulling away two fortune-telling cards.

Grandmère didn't have the grace to look ashamed. "That is my fate, child." She clucked her tongue. "It is not for your eyes."

As stubborn as her grandmother, Clara didn't look away. She examined both cards, the first of which was a beast with pointed teeth. At the sight of it, her stomach tightened. The Fanged Creature held a meaning she was all too familiar with: an untimely death. But the second card was more mysterious: Fortune's Cup, painted as a crystal goblet. "Which way was this card turned when you drew it?"

Fortune's Cup represented an object in one's life that was either tied to prosperity or downfall. Turned up, Fortune's Cup foretold good luck. But turned down, Fortune's Cup promised tragedy.

"Never you mind." Grandmère batted a wrinkled hand, and Clara's chest sank at the dismissal. If Grandmère didn't wish to discuss Fortune's Cup, it meant she had drawn it turned down.

Struggling to compose herself, Clara sat up taller and inhaled a calming breath. "Don't worry about the cards, Grandmère."

"The cards never lie, child."

"But they don't fully tell your story. Back when you kept drawing the Fanged Creature for me, did you imagine I would live to see this day? We can't know everything. Fate always provides a loophole." Clara leaned closer and kissed Grandmère's cheek. "Besides, today is Henni's Wish Ceremony. She can't tell us what she's going to wish for, but of course she'll ask *Sortes Fortunae* to break the rest of the curse. Once we're free from it, your fate is sure to change."

Although a bit of hope had returned to Grimm's Hollow— some of the crops had started to flourish, and rain sprinkled on occasion—the curse hadn't fully lifted. The village wasn't anywhere near thriving yet, and no more of the Lost Ones had returned home. The most telling sign was how Clara still couldn't cross the forest border without her red cape. When it wasn't wrapped around her shoulders, roots sprang up and shoved her out.

Grandmère didn't reply to Clara's words of reassurance. Her eyes drifted closed, and a light snore rattled from her chest.

Three raps sounded on the front door of the cottage. Clara tucked the covers around her grandmother and went to see who had called.

When she opened the door, a beautiful boy with tousled golden hair and sparkling blue eyes grinned crookedly at her, and her heart flip-flopped, cartwheeled, and somersaulted all at once.

Axel stepped up to the threshold, kissed her mouth, and pecked her lightly on the tip of her nose. He had a lovely habit of pressing his lips to all sorts of places on her face.

"It's time to wish Henni happy birthday," he said, and held out his hand.

Clara and Axel were neither the first nor the last to arrive at the meadow with the pavilion that held the Book of Fortunes. The whole village was gathering there to celebrate the momentous occasion. Even Fiora, who scarcely left her house, had come with Hansel and Gretel.

Clara and Axel found the two children eating a lingonberry pie that Ella had made—she'd located a hidden crock of sugar in her parents' cellar—and thus far Hansel hadn't bitten anyone or anything but his rare sweet treat.

Most of the villagers were lined up to take turns pinching Henni's arms, as was tradition, to remind her that she was awake and not dreaming and to use this opportunity wisely.

Clara and Axel also took their place in the line, but since it was long and she had time to spare, she broke away and wandered over to the Tree of the Lost.

Wistfully, she gazed at the rainbow array of cloth strips and ribbons knotted to the hazel branches. Each of them fluttered in the warm breeze and reminded her of all the Lost yet to be found in the forest, many of whom had probably perished and been absorbed by the trees.

She eyed the strip she was looking for, one made of Thurn

wool and dyed rose red. She untied it from the tree and fastened it around her wrist.

A red-breasted robin lifted from one of the branches and flew away.

Clara watched it for a moment and softly smiled.

When she drifted back to the line, it was almost her turn to greet Henni. Axel had just pinched Henni's arm, probably too hard, because she yelped, giggled, and smacked his shoulder.

Clara took care to be gentler and gave Henni more than a pinch. She also wrapped her arms around her and whispered, "Take my luck."

Henni's eyes glistened. "Thank you."

Henni couldn't have looked lovelier in her white dress and the wreath of oak leaves crowning her shining chestnut hair. When she walked to the pavilion, the old ladies of Grimm's Hollow dabbed their eyes with handkerchiefs, and the young men stared like they'd never realized Henni existed before today.

Reaching the curtains that veiled the pedestal holding *Sortes Fortunae*, she inhaled deeply, smiled once more at her friends, and saved her last look for her sister, Ella, who nodded and beamed back at her.

Henni slipped behind the curtain.

Clara couldn't see what she was doing now—none of the villagers could, which was just as it should be—but everyone knew that Henni was quietly making her one wish on the Book of Fortunes.

Clara waited for her friend to emerge from the curtain with a wide smile on her face, but the minutes passed, and Henni still remained hidden.

"Something is wrong," Clara murmured to Axel. Before he could reply, she rushed over to Herr Oswald, the chairman over-seeing the event, and begged him to break custom and let her go behind the curtain to check on Henni. "I won't hear her make her wish," Clara promised. "Surely she's already spoken it or is too afraid to. Please, let me help her."

Reluctantly, Herr Oswald gave his permission, and Clara raced behind the curtain.

Henni stood before the pedestal in a daze, her arms hanging heavy at her sides, her stare bewildered as she looked down at the open Book of Fortunes.

"Is everything all right?" Clara set a hand on Henni's shoulder.

"It keeps opening to the same spot," she stammered. "But there's nothing there."

"What do you mean?"

Henni just shook her head, at a loss for more words.

Until that moment, Clara had resisted the urge to peek at the book, but now her curiosity won over. She lowered her gaze.

There in the center of the book, where the leaves met and were bound together, was a thin strip of paper with a ragged edge—the remnants of a page that had been torn out.

"What's going on back there?" Herr Oswald called.

"What do I do?" Henni whispered to Clara, her voice trembling.

"Everything's fine!" Clara answered Herr Oswald. "Just give us a moment."

She frowned at the book and tapped a finger on the pedestal. "Maybe this is the same spot where the riddle was torn out." She thought of the page *Sortes Fortunae* had left behind when it abandoned Grimm's Hollow.

"I don't think so," Henni murmured. "If that were true, the book would have replied to me on the page before or after it. But it needs the one that's missing."

Clara thought of what Axel had told her on Devotion Day,

and what Henni had also said when they'd returned to Grimm's Hollow: *You shouldn't tempt fate.*

But then she remembered how Axel had come to think differently, how he'd whispered after the meadow ball, *You're the person who tempts fate. You don't run away from it.*

According to him, that was why Grandmère had drawn the Red Card for Clara, because she was the Changer of Fate.

"Don't tell anyone what I'm about to do," Clara hissed.

Henni blanched, but nodded.

Clara closed the Book of Fortunes and drew a long breath. She spoke the incantation: "*Sortes Fortunae,* hear my voice. Understand my heart and its deepest desire. My name is Clara Thurn, and this is my second wish."

Henni stifled a gasp.

"Don't listen," Clara whispered.

Henni stuffed her fingers in her ears.

"I wish to know where your missing page is," Clara said in the quietest voice possible. "The one meant for Henni."

She turned the cover over, and the book opened to a new spot.

For several pounding heartbeats, the page remained blank. Clara began to fear that she had done something unforgivable.

Henni fidgeted beside her. "Maybe we should—"

"Wait, look!" Clara pointed to the page.

Letters of green ink scrawled across it, rapidly spelling out several words:

Only one page holds the secret to finally restoring peace.
Only one person is to blame for breaking it.
Both must be found, for one has the other,
And together they hide in the Forest Grimm.

Adrenaline flashed through Clara's veins. She scanned the words again. They felt more like a new riddle than a set of simple instructions. But one thing felt certain—her quest wasn't over yet. There was still a curse to finish breaking, and to do that, she needed to find a missing page . . . as well as the person who possessed it.

Once again, what she sought could only be found in one place, and to that place she would return. . . .

The Forest Grimm.

ACKNOWLEDGMENTS

I conceived the idea for *The Forest Grimm* several years ago while daydreaming about what I love reading most—myths and fairy tales, especially the darker, truer versions that come closest to their folklore origins, like the ones written by the Brothers Grimm. In writing this book, I wanted to go even further in exploring how these Grimms' fairy tales might have come to be, at least in my wildest imaginings. Special thanks to my literary agent, Josh Adams, for being the biggest champion of this story and giving me the courage to write it.

I'm beyond delighted that my editor, the incredible Sara Goodman, also fell in love with Clara's story. Thanks for your keen talent in helping me focus and tie together this mash-up of darkly twisted fairy tales.

Sara's team at Wednesday Books has also welcomed me with open arms and made me feel right at home. My abundant thanks go to editorial assistant Vanessa Aquirre; jacket designer Olga Grlic; mechanical designer Soleil Paz; interior designer Devan Norman; managing editor Eric Meyer; production editor Melanie Sanders; copy editor Christina MacDonald; production manager Gail Friedman; marketing specialists Rivka Holler and Brant Janeway; publicists Meghan Harrington and Alyssa Gammello; creative services specialists Britt Saghi, Kim Ludlam, Tom Thompson, and Dylan Helstien; and audio producer Ally Demeter. Additionally, I'm indebted to Colin Verdi for illustrating such a lush and gorgeous cover.

My family is everything. Thank you, Jason, Isabelle, Ethan,

Ivy, and Aidan for keeping me grounded, laughing, grateful, and humble. I love you beyond words. You are my why.

My parents, Larry and Buffie, are my role models in life. Thank you for teaching me that art and creativity are invaluable in this world, and that I can make a living doing what I love.

My endless thanks go to the ancestors on my dad's side of the family, those who share my maiden name. You inspired me to set this story in a region like the one where you came from in the Black Forest, with ties to Germany and France. I hope I did you proud.

I've made so many wonderful writing friends over the past several years. I'd like to especially thank those who carried me through writing and publishing this novel: Sara B. Larson for helping me brainstorm the perfect solution when I hit a tricky spot, Emily R. King for late-night calls with huge outpourings of love, and Stephanie Garber and Jodi Meadows for their timely publishing advice.

I'm indebted to the authors who took the time to read and provide such lovely blurbs this book, authors whose writing I also love so much. Thank you, Rebecca Ross, Charlie N. Holmberg, Tricia Levenseller, and Mara Rutherford.

Music is a tremendous source of inspiration to me, so I'd also like to pay tribute to Amelia Warner for composing the film score to *Mary Shelley*. At least 90 percent of this novel was drafted while listening to that beautiful and haunting music.

And lastly but truly firstly, my forever thanks go to God. You are my peace, my light, my breath, my clarity. Thank you for your perfect, matchless, and everlasting love.